The Day It Rained Blood

Anonymous

5

2/23

Books by Anonymous –

The Book With No Name
The Eye of the Moon
The Devil's Graveyard
The Book of Death
The Red Mohawk
Sanchez: A Christmas Carol
The Plot to Kill the Pope
The Day It Rained Blood

The author can be found on Facebook and Twitter as Bourbon Kid.

"One day, so much blood will be shed that the skies will fill with it, and rain it back down upon us."

Anonymous

Prologue

Sanchez hated karaoke machines almost as much as he hated listening to drunk people singing. He hated weddings too, but for the first time in history his bar The Tapioca was hosting a wedding reception. Sanchez had begrudgingly agreed to it because the happy couple Dante and Kacy were friends of his, and because Flake had assured him a wedding would be good for business.

The evening had been a roaring success in spite of all the shitty Lionel Richie impressions. The reason for its success lay with Flake. She had put together a decent buffet and hired the karaoke machine. Since moving in with Sanchez she had transformed the Tapioca from a place where people got beaten up and killed every night, to a place where people just got beaten up.

But typically, at midnight everything went wrong. If Sanchez had stuck to his "no weirdoes" policy it would never have happened. A creepy old man had shown up with a gift for the barmaid, Beth. It was a rubbish gift too, just some dirty old piece of cloth with the letters JD sewn into it. It transpired that the cloth was from Beth's great love, JD, or as Sanchez knew him, the Bourbon Kid, a serial killer who had wiped out The Tapioca client base on more than one occasion. As soon as Beth had the cloth in her possession she had an emotional breakdown, so Flake gave her the rest of the night off, and to rub salt in the wound, she gave herself the night off too, so that she could comfort Beth. So Sanchez was stuck serving drinks and had no way of escaping the sounds from the karaoke singers.

His nightmare finally looked like coming to an end at around four o'clock in the morning. The bride, Kacy, a beautiful brunette who had seemingly drunk twice her own body weight was passed out and slumped over a table in the corner, occasionally snoring and drooling over the table, or farting and waking herself up for a few seconds before nodding off again.

The only person still awake and drinking was the bridegroom, Dante, a handsome dark-haired young man. He was sitting on a stool at the bar, wearing a black tuxedo, which had looked so smart during the wedding, but now looked like he'd been wearing it for a week. Half the buttons were missing, the tie was undone and the jacket was soaked in beer and wine. So for once, Sanchez was the smartest person in The Tapioca. His bright yellow suit hadn't picked up any stains, so far.

Dante had a bottle of Shitting Monkey beer in front of him on the bar. He was sitting on a stool staring at it, but he'd reached a point where he was so drunk he was only licking the rim of the bottle every now and again instead of taking a swig.

'Are you drinking that, or inhaling it?' Sanchez asked.

Dante livened up at hearing Sanchez's sarcastic remark. 'Yeah, I was just thinking, you know?' he said, the words melding into one another.

'Me too,' said Sanchez. 'I was thinking it's time to call it a night.'

'Do you think the vampires will ever come back?' asked Dante.

Sanchez shrugged. 'They'd better not. I've put a sign up over the door that says "no vampires" but you never know, do you? It's possible they could see me as a target, you know, because...'

'Because you're fat?'

'No.'

'Old?'

'I'm not old,' Sanchez reeled at the accusation. 'I'm in my thirties.'

'That's old,' said Dante. 'I'm only twenty.....' he paused and stared into space. 'Five? Or is it six?'

'I don't know,' said Sanchez. 'But it's four o'clock and I think you've had enough.'

Dante didn't respond. He just stared at his reflection in the bottle of Shitting Monkey. Sanchez had seen many drunks in a similar state just before they passed out. Dante's head drooped a few times, but just when it looked like he was about to fall asleep he perked up again and looked up at Sanchez. He had a weird smile across his face, the kind that only a drunk person can have.

'Wanna hear a something stupid?' he said.

One

Baby checked her reflection in the mirror. She had never worn glasses before and was surprised by how old they made her look. She was only twenty, but the glasses made her look at least five years older. They were part of her undercover outfit. She was supposed to look like a psychiatrist in a private mental hospital. So, on the recommendation of her boyfriend, Joey (who had been a patient in a mental asylum for a chunk of his life) she was wearing a long white coat with plain blue surgical scrubs underneath. The idea was to not draw any attention to herself, so that when she showed up at the Lady Florence Mental Hospital, she would be able to complete her mission before anyone realised she was an impostor.

She wished Joey was going with her, but he'd been sent on another mission somewhere else. This was to be her first solo mission since becoming a member of The Dead Hunters. Her time in the team had mostly been spent training. She had learned to use guns and knives, but even though she had become quite adept at those things, she was still the weakest member of the group when it came to combat. What she did have, which some of the others lacked was a good way with people. And even though it could be said that her colleagues Jasmine and Elvis were also good with people, their skills largely involved seducing members of the opposite sex. What Baby possessed was the ability to empathise and understand people from all walks of life. People were drawn to her.

When she was finally happy with her appearance, she left the ladies' washroom and walked out into the bar area of what had become the headquarters of The Dead Hunters. They had taken up residence in a bar named Purgatory, situated in a private part of The Devil's Graveyard, a vast area of desert that one only came to with purpose or extremely bad luck. The private part was unreachable to anyone who had never been there before. Only those who had met Scratch, the owner of the bar and gatekeeper of the steaming-hot place beneath it, could make it past a haunted crossroads that led to Purgatory.

Scratch was standing behind the bar, waiting for Baby when she walked out of the washroom. He was a man of only two colours, red and black. His suit and shirt were bright red, but his skin and necktie were darkest black. He had a red bowler hat on his head, one of many (often ridiculous) red hats that he owned. It didn't matter how outrageous they were because they all suited The Man In Red.

Baby sat down on a stool by the bar.

'You look great,' said Scratch. 'I think you should put your hair in a ponytail though.'

Baby could have kicked herself. She had intended to tie her hair up and was annoyed that she had forgotten because she was so preoccupied with how her glasses and coat looked. It was a sign of how nervous she was.

'I did mean to do that just now,' she said tying her hair back in a ponytail with a blue band.

Scratch slid a clipboard across the bar to her. 'Use this to make notes if you think it will help,' he said.

Baby picked it up. It had a few sheets of white paper clipped to it. She pulled a biro pen from her breast pocket and pulled the lid off with her teeth.

'Any tips on how I should start questioning Salvatore Rocco?' she asked.

'Just get straight to the point,' said Scratch. 'Ask him why he was trying to break into that country mansion in Colorado.'

'Yes, but how do I introduce myself?'

'Tell him God sent you.'

'Won't that make me sound crazy?'

'It's a mental hospital. Practically everyone in there is crazy. Rocco's been there for two days already. So even if he's not insane, he probably *thinks he is* by now.'

Baby wasn't sure if that even made sense, but she nodded politely. 'Okay. Then what? What exactly do you want me to find out, because I'm a little unsure?'

Scratch smiled, displaying an unusual level of patience with her. 'According to the newspaper, Rocco claims that in a previous life he was Julius Caesar. What I want you to find out is if he was possessed by the ghost of Cain.'

'And who exactly was Cain before he was a ghost? Was he someone important?'

'Have you ever read The Old Testament?'

'Maybe once, when I was a kid.'

'So you know the story of Adam and Eve, yes?'

Baby nodded. 'More or less.'

'Okay, well, Cain was the first son of Adam and Eve. And he had a younger brother called Abel. Abel was a decent fella, but Cain was an asshole, and he was jealous of Abel. He was also a psychopath, the first one ever, in fact.'

'The first ever psychopath?'

'Yes. And he was such a psychopath he killed Abel out of jealousy.'

'You know, I do vaguely remember this,' said Baby.

'Good, because the aftermath of all this is that by killing his brother, Cain became the first person to ever commit a murder. As a result, when he died his spirit didn't go to Heaven like everyone else's. But back then, there was no Hell. God hadn't thought to invent it. Didn't think he'd need it. So Cain's spirit was cursed to roam the earth for eternity. But after a while, Cain discovered that his spirit could enter the bodies of other people, and if those people were brain dead, or in a coma, he could take over and control their minds. Over many centuries now, he has possessed the minds of hundreds of men and women, the most notable of which was Julius Caesar. In more recent times, he's been responsible for a lot of those lone wolf killers you see in the news.'

'Really, like who?'

'Don't worry about that for now, it's not important. What I'm saying is that Cain has been awake in a conscious state for so many thousands of years, he's gone completely off his cake.'

'Off his cake?'

'Nuts, mental, insane, bonkers, off his cake.'

Baby had written the words "off his cake" on her clipboard. She drew a line through them, not wanting to see the phrase again and wonder what it meant.

'Okay, I get it,' she said, looking back up at Scratch. 'But how will I know if Salvatore Rocco was possessed by Cain?'

'The first thing you need to do is check his forehead. See if he has a scar on it, shaped like the letter C.'

Baby scribbled the information down. 'And what does that signify?'

She looked up at Scratch and realised from the look on his face that she had just asked another stupid question. It was bloody obvious what the C signified. She burned red with embarrassment, which was made worse when Scratch decided to answer the question anyway.

'It's known as the mark of Cain. Anyone who has it on their forehead has probably been possessed by him at some point in their life.'

'What if Rocco is *still* possessed?'

'I don't think he is. It looks like he woke from his coma when the security guards in Colorado threatened to shoot him. Trust me, as soon as Rocco was conscious again, Cain wouldn't be able to stay in his body.'

'But isn't it possible Cain is still in there and just pretending not to be?'

Scratch shook his head. 'I doubt it. Rocco is claiming he's seen life through the eyes of Julius Caesar. Cain would never admit that. But he did possess Caesar a long time ago, and it looks like Rocco has seen the memories. Either that or Rocco really is a total fruitcake.'

Baby scribbled some more notes down and hoped Scratch couldn't see them because what she was writing seemed like gibberish. When she was finished scribbling, she asked a question that had been on her mind from the start.

'What if Rocco attacks me?'

Scratch reached across the bar and patted her on the shoulder. 'You'll kill him, Baby. You're fully trained now. If this man makes a move on you, your instincts will take over, trust me. And if by some fluke, Cain is still in there, you'll see him exit the body when you kill Rocco.'

'Kill him?' The words made Baby shake. 'People love Salvatore Rocco!'

'They did,' Scratch agreed. 'Back when he was a racing driver. He's been a vegetable for six months ever since that crash. He'll never race again.'

'Doctors said he'd never walk again,' Baby added.

'That's right, but somehow he got up and walked out of hospital without anyone noticing. I'd say that's a little bit odd.'

Baby had seen the crash on television. Joey was a big fan of motor racing and Salvatore Rocco was one of the best drivers around. But a seven-car pile-up had done for him.

'Okay, but you're absolutely sure I can handle this guy if he attacks me?' Baby checked.

'Pretty sure, yeah.' He handed her a keycard. 'This will get you into any room in the hospital. Now go on, go.'

Pretty sure! Those two words didn't exactly inspire confidence, but Baby didn't want to look weak, so she hopped off her stool and headed for the Men's toilets.

It was a curious oddity that by passing through the door to the Men's toilets in Purgatory, a person could end up in any washroom in the world. Baby was about to end up in the private bathroom in Salvatore Rocco's room in The Lady Florence Hospital. She'd used the portal twice before with mixed results. On one occasion she'd appeared in a bathroom where an old man was taking a shower with his housemaid. And on the other occasion she'd walked into a bathroom where the floor was covered in urine. She hoped the next one would be a better experience.

She waved goodbye to Scratch and walked through the door of the Men's toilets, straight into a posh bathroom in a private hospital. The door closed behind her and her way back was gone.

There was a bath, shower, toilet and bidet in this place. For a fleeting moment it reminded her of the en suite bathrooms in Silvio Mellencamp's Beaver Palace, the hideous place where she'd worked as a hooker before Joey showed up and rescued her. She quickly put thoughts of that place out of her mind. It was time to get down to business. She took a deep breath and opened the door that took her out of the bathroom and into Rocco's private suite.

Salvatore Rocco was cowering on his bed with his knees up against his chest. His rather revealing white gown was scrunched up against his torso and Baby could see more than she cared to. She barely recognised him from his time as a racing driver. He'd been a tall, handsome man with a healthy tan. The man in front of her now was a quivering, pale skinned mess with crazy, unkempt hair that covered half of his face. He almost jumped out of his skin when he saw Baby walk out of his bathroom.

'Oh God no!' he said, panicking. 'I was confused. I didn't mean to tell anyone anything. *I swear.*'

Baby put her finger to her lips to hush him. 'It's okay,' she said. 'I've been sent here to ask you about what happened to you.'

'*Nothing happened to me.* Like I told your colleagues, I imagined everything. I'm fine now.'

'It's okay, God sent me to help you.'

Salvatore backed up into the corner, tears welling up in his eyes. 'God? God sent you? What *the shit* are you talking about?'

'It's okay,' said Baby in her best soothing voice. 'I'm not here to hurt you. Everything will be fine now, I promise. You're safe.'

Salvatore closed his eyes as if he was trying to wish her away, hoping that when he reopened them, she would be gone and his nightmare would be over.

Baby sat down on the end of his bed, making sure she left him enough room so that he didn't feel threatened. 'Listen,' she said, calmly. 'I don't think you're insane. I came here to ask you if you thought you were possessed by the ghost of Cain.'

Salvatore opened his eyes. 'I *was* possessed by something, but I don't know what it was.'

'Do you have a mark on your forehead?'

'What kind of mark?'

'It's a C shaped scar that appears on the forehead of people who've been possessed by Cain.'

Salvatore lifted his floppy fringe and revealed a bright red C shaped mark on his skin, just below the hairline. 'I never had that before,' he said. 'Is that it?'

11

Baby tried not to sound excited, but couldn't help herself. 'Yes, that's it!'

'So what does it mean?'

'It means you've nothing to be ashamed of. Cain has inhabited the bodies of people in comas for centuries. You're one of the lucky one's, you survived.'

'Lucky? What? You mean I'm lucky that I snapped out of a coma before he had the chance to make me kill people? Did you hear, I woke up outside that mansion with security people pointing guns at me. That's not a nice way to come out of a coma, trust me!'

'Why were you, or rather why was *Cain* going to the mansion?'

'I don't know. I wasn't conscious through any of it. But ever since I woke from my coma I keep having flashbacks, memories of what happened while he was in my head. And other stuff, memories of his, I think. I can't get rid of them. Will they ever go?'

Baby had no idea, but she felt sorry for him so she fibbed. 'Yeah, they usually go after a few weeks.'

'Who the hell are you anyway?' said Salvatore. 'How did you come from my bathroom?'

'My name is Baby. God sent me. But don't worry about that for now. Just tell me what else you saw.'

'This is what I told the cops, and it's why they locked me up in here. It sounds stupid, but I saw life through the eyes of Julius Caesar. I saw his memories.'

'What sort of memories? And how do you know it was Caesar?'

'It's hard to explain. Mostly I saw images. Like I saw a vision of a bunch of weirdoes in togas sneaking up behind Caesar with their knives drawn.' He tugged at his hair and visibly cringed. 'Or maybe I really have gone insane? How the hell am I supposed to know what to believe?'

Baby offered a conciliatory smile. 'My boyfriend is insane,' she said. 'He seems to be coping with it quite well these days.'

CLICK!

A door opened behind Baby. She stood up and turned around. A fat, balding Chinese man in blue overalls was backing into the room with a mop and bucket. When he turned around, Baby saw the name Xang sewn onto a white label on his overalls. He looked surprised to see Baby.

'Oh, I'm very sorry,' said Xang. 'I just came to clean the floor.'

'That's fine,' said Baby, trying to control her nerves. 'I'm finished here anyway.'

'IT'S HIM!'

Salvatore grabbed his pillow and held it up like a shield, while pointing at Xang and staring at him, his eyes wide with terror, his lips moving but not making any sound.

It took Baby a little too long to realise what he meant. The janitor threw his mop at Baby and pulled a gun from his overalls. As Baby batted away the mop handle she noticed the scar on the right corner of the janitor's forehead. It was the same as the mark on Salvatore Rocco's head. The mark of Cain.

The janitor ignored Baby and aimed his gun at the cowering figure of Salvatore on the bed. He fired two shots into the pillow Rocco was using as a shield. Blood spurted out through the pillow and Rocco slumped back against the wall behind the bed.

The echo from the gunshots reverberated around the small room and made Baby's ears ring. But her training kicked in when she saw the janitor swing his arm towards her, ready to shoot her dead next. She lunged at him and grabbed his wrist, pushing his gun away from her. She followed up with a move Joey had taught her. She hooked her leg behind one of the janitor's knees and hauled him off balance. He stumbled forward and fell onto the bed. Baby pounced on his back and prised his gun from his hand while he was still stunned. There was no time to reason with him, or worry about the consequences of what she was about to do. She pressed the barrel of the gun against the back of his head and squeezed the trigger.

BLAM!

The bullet blasted through his skull, spraying blood up in the air. The recoil from the gun sent Baby sprawling back across the room, slamming her against the far wall. Xang's lifeless body crumpled and slid off the bed onto the floor.

In the middle of all the craziness, a black shadow, the size of a man, leapt out of the janitor's body. It stood in front of Baby, staring at her. It had ghostly white eyes in the centre of a dark contorted face. Baby pointed the gun at it, ready to fire off another round, but before she could, the shadow blinked once and leapt into the wall by the side of the bed, vanishing through it.

Baby stood frozen in her stance, pointing the gun at the wall where the ghostly apparition had disappeared. This was just the beginning of her troubles. A black man in a doctor's overalls burst into the room to see what all the noise was. Baby instinctively turned the gun on him, but had the good judgement not to pull the trigger when she saw he was a doctor. By the look on his face he nearly shit himself. He stared down the barrel of Baby's gun, then turned and ran, yelling for someone to call the cops.

Baby took a few deep breaths and assessed the situation. Salvatore Rocco was laid out on his bed, with a blood stained pillow on his chest. A pool of blood was forming around him on the bed. On the floor nearby was a dead janitor named Xang, who was probably not a real employee of the hospital, just some poor shmuck who Cain had found in a coma somewhere else.

As if Baby didn't have enough problems, a fire alarm rang out nearby, wailing at a level loud enough to wake the dead. Baby wished she could go back to Purgatory through the bathroom, but the portal was closed. And now she was alone in a room with two dead bodies, holding the gun that killed them both.

Two

'I am sending my son Thomas to the school in Crimson County.'

Bishop Atlee Yoder knew it was coming. He'd known it for a long time. The people of the Amish community in Oakfield had been unsettled for years. Particularly in the Fall, or as it had become known over the years, The Fall of Evil. And now for the first time in the history of their community, a woman was sending her child to the school on the other side of the island, beyond the Black Forest. The woman in question was Agnes Graber and she had showed up at Yoder's church at eight o'clock in the morning. She was in a determined mood, so he'd allowed her into his private office for a chat. He was still in his nightgown, which put him at a disadvantage from the start. He was sitting behind his desk, with her towering over him on the other side, ranting and wagging her finger at him.

'Agnes, I beg you to reconsider,' he pleaded. 'The people in Crimson County don't understand us, you know that. And if you go, others might follow.'

'That's what you're afraid of, isn't it?'

Agnes was the first of her generation to question their religion. Yoder feared she wouldn't be the last. She was thirty-seven years old, and a year earlier she had lost her husband and daughter during the Fall. Her daughter, Elsa was one of the many people, mostly children, who went missing every year during The Fall of Evil. Within a few days of Elsa's disappearance, Agnes's husband Lyle foolishly ventured into the Black Forest looking for his daughter. That was the last anyone saw of him too.

'All I'm saying,' said Yoder, 'is don't make a rash decision. The prophecy says that Christ will return after the three Northern stars fall.'

'I know,' said Agnes. 'But it's been two weeks since the Northern stars fell, so where the hell is he?'

'The gospel says nothing of how long it will take the saviour to arrive, only that it will be after the stars fall.'

'I know what the gospel says,' Agnes snapped. 'But I'm not prepared to wait another twenty years. My boy Thomas is all I've got left and I don't want to lose him. I want him to learn about things like science and evolution, so that he can make his own mind up about the world instead of sucking in all your religious nonsense.'

Religious nonsense? How bloody dare she! In normal circumstances, Yoder would have been the one wagging his finger at her and raising his voice. But these were difficult times for the church, and he had to show restraint.

15

'Agnes, I wouldn't want you to fall foul of the Lord. Be wary of your blasphemy. The gospel says we should not mingle with those who seek to destroy us.'

'Fall foul of the Lord? What's left for him to do to me? He's already taken my husband and my daughter.'

'It's all part of God's plan.'

'God's plan?' Agnes was indignant. 'According to God's plan, Christ is going to return and deliver us from evil. But every year we wait, hoping that this will be the year, and *it never is*. For all we know, Christ might not return for a thousand years, if at all! How many more of our people have to die in that forest before he shows up?'

Yoder didn't take kindly to her tone, nor her blasphemous doubts about their religion. The very foundation of their society had been built upon the Gospel of St Susan. For where most Christians were familiar with the gospels of *Matthew, Mark, Luke and John*, the people of Oakfield followed the lesser known gospel of *Susan*, which contained the same information as the other four gospels, but also included details about what Jesus was doing during his early twenties before he became a prophet. There was also a prophecy in chapter 40 of the gospel of Susan that predicted the second coming that Agnes was calling into doubt. The prophecy was very clear that a saviour would come after the fall of three Northern stars. And three Northern stars over Oakfield had fallen from the sky in early October.

'To doubt the second coming, is to doubt the word of God,' said Yoder, hoping to placate the angry woman before him.

'Father, I don't mean to doubt you, or the gospel,' Agnes replied, showing a little more graciousness than before. 'But we've lost four children already this Fall. We cannot go on like this. I certainly cannot go on like this. I'm at the end of my tether, so for the sake of my sanity and the future of my son, Thomas, I've enrolled him in the high school in Crimson County.'

'But what do you hope to achieve with this?'

Agnes pressed the palms of her hands on Yoder's desk and leaned across it. 'In case you haven't noticed, Atlee, no one from Crimson County ever goes missing during The Fall of Evil.'

'You don't know that.'

'Yes I do. Because if any of their children went missing they would come to us and ask if we had seen them, just like we always go to them when ours vanish.'

'Agnes, sit down.'

'There's no need. I'm done here. I just wanted you to hear it from me first.'

Agnes stormed out of Yoder's office and slammed the door behind her, leaving him to mull over what had happened. He feared that over the coming days and weeks, many more members of the Amish community would begin to question, or even reject their religion.

Yoder was at his wits end. These were drastic times, which traditionally called for drastic measures. He cast his mind back to a recent trip he had embarked upon. He had travelled to Rome earlier in the year for the funeral of Pope John Paul George. At the event he had met up with many Bishops and Priests from all over the world, who were joining in the celebration of the Pope's life. One Priest in particular had left an indelible mark on him. The Priest was called Vincent Papshmir, and Yoder's talks with him over a bottle of wine had stayed with him ever since. Papshmir came from a city Yoder had never heard of before, a city called *Santa Mondega*. During one particular drunken diatribe, Papshmir had claimed to know the people who assassinated the Pope. He called them *The Dead Hunters* and among other things, he claimed they hunted down and killed vampires, zombies, werewolves and all kinds of other undead monsters that were living in secret within the modern world.

Even though Papshmir drank a lot of wine during Yoder's meeting with him, and he swore an awful lot (practically every sentence included words like motherfucker, cuntbag and fuckhead), he was intriguing, unlike any other Holy man Yoder had ever met. He had all kinds of conspiracy theories, including one outlandish claim that the Government wasn't trying to catch The Dead Hunters because they were relying on them to do things that regular soldiers and assassins couldn't. Papshmir had given Yoder a piece of card with the contact details of someone who he believed knew the whereabouts of The Dead Hunters. So even though it was against Oakfield's strict laws to seek help from outsiders, Yoder took the card. And he was glad he did.

He rummaged through his desk drawers until he found the piece of card Papshmir had given him. The handwritten message on it said –

To hire The Dead Hunters, go The Tapioca bar in Santa Mondega. Ask for Sanchez.

Three

Six of the seven members of MAWF were sitting around the dining table in the Brinkman Room of the Riverdale Mansion in Colorado. It was a long oak table, gleaming and very old, a darn sight older than anyone in the room. They were surrounded by soaring windows swathed in heavy silk curtains of the deepest indigo, shot with twenty-four karat gold thread. It was a room designed for rich people who loved the sight of expensive things. That was exactly what MAWF was about, money, power, expensive things, and more money. It was common procedure for the group to meet no more than three times a year, but today was a special day. It was the first emergency meeting in six years.

The members of MAWF were all considered equal, but Arnold Rothman always sat at the head of the dining table. The M in MAWF stood for Money and Arnold Rothman had more than anyone in the world. He was the major shareholder of ninety percent of the world's banks. His motto was "your money is my money". At the age of twenty-eight, and after his father's death, he had taken control of the banking system. Aside from a few bumps in the road, he'd kept it running smoothly for thirty-two years.

The A, W and F stood for Arms, Water and Fuel, which were controlled by the other members of the group. Linda Murdoch secretly owned every water company in the Western world. She was the mastermind who made tap water taste like shit so that people would pay to buy it from bottles as well. Four of the other members of the group controlled the distribution of fuel and energy like gas, electricity and oil. That left Rupert Galloway, the seventh member of MAWF and the biggest arms dealer in the world. He was unable to attend the emergency meeting because he'd been involved in a serious car accident, which had left him in a coma. His perverse sense of humour was sorely missed.

After discussing the shocking news of Rupert's accident over breakfast and coffee, Arnold Rothman steered the conversation around to the matter that had brought them all together.

'I assume everybody is aware of the death of Salvatore Rocco?' he asked, looking around the table.

The others all nodded. The meeting had been called to discuss Rocco's attempt to break in to their country mansion. But since the meeting had been called, Rocco had been assassinated.

'Was his murder anything to do with us?' asked Linda Murdoch, the youngest member of MAWF. She was supposed to be forty-seven years old, but she looked like a twenty-five year old because she'd spent a chunk of her wealth on the best cosmetic surgery available.

All eyes turned on Rothman, as if they thought he was behind it.

'It was nothing to do with us,' he assured them. 'But I've been given the identity of the person responsible for it, and it's rather concerning.'

He lifted his briefcase from the floor and set it down on the long wooden table. He opened it up and pulled out a brown envelope he'd been given less than an hour earlier. He opened the envelope and pulled out a batch of A4 size photos.

He handed them to Linda Murdoch, who was seated on his left. 'Do you remember these people?' he asked.

Linda flicked through the photos. She recognised the people in them straight away.

'These are the people who assassinated the Pope,' she said, frowning at Rothman. 'The Dead Hunters, what's all this got to do with them?'

'One of them, the young girl, Baby, she's the assassin who killed Salvatore Rocco this morning. She waltzed right into his private room in The Lady Florence and shot him dead. Killed a janitor too.'

'Why would she do that?' asked Linda.

'Beats me,' said Rothman. 'I can only think that maybe Rocco was working with The Dead Hunters. When his attempt to break in here failed, perhaps they felt the need to eliminate him, in case he gave them up? That's the best I can come up with. But I have people working on it right now.'

'What people?' said Linda.

'General Alexis Calhoon's team is looking into it. Calhoon knows more about these Dead Hunters than anyone.'

'Is it possible they're after us?' asked Roland Navarone, a frail, seventy-nine year old man, sitting to the right of Rothman. He was the richest oil baron in the world, and was known for being paranoid, a trait that was getting worse with age.

'It's possible,' said Rothman. 'They killed the Pope, and he wasn't easy to get to. And something, or *someone* has just put Rupert Galloway in a coma, so I'd say it's a good time to beef up security. Something's definitely going on.'

Within seconds of Rothman mentioning Rupert Galloway, the double doors at the end of the room flew open and the fifty-eight year old arms dealer strolled in, looking like a man who *should be in a coma*. His skin was grey and his hair a mess. His trousers and sweater were ripped, bloodied and covered in dirt, which was very unlike him. He also had cuts and bruises on his hands and face, including a very distinct C shaped scar on his forehead.

'Rupert?' said Rothman, standing up.

The others followed suit, their chairs scraping back on the marble floor as they rose as one.

'Sit down,' said Galloway, waving them all down. 'You all need to listen. Something incredible has occurred.'

'But your accident,' said Rothman. 'What happened?'

'You're not going to believe this,' said Galloway, gesticulating like Tom Cruise in a court room scene. 'I've been to the other side.'

'The other side of what?'

Galloway pointed at the ceiling. 'I've seen life after death.'

It was understandable that his claim was met with silence and more than a little scepticism.

'I know what you're thinking,' he said, looking around at each member of the group. 'But I can prove it.'

'Prove what?'

'I had an out of body experience. After the car accident I had last night, I passed over. I was in the afterlife for half an hour or so. And I met with the Angel Gabriel.'

That claim confused everyone even more. Linda Murdoch even snorted coffee out of her nostrils.

'Rupert,' said Rothman in his most diplomatic voice. 'I think you need to go back to hospital. You've had a serious accident.'

Galloway closed his eyes and drummed his fingers against his forehead for a while, then snapped back into Tom Cruise mode. 'All right,' he said. 'This is gonna sound crazy, but bear with me. I'm going to exit my body.'

'What?'

'Just wait, watch.'

Rothman liked to think that everyone else at the table was thinking the same thing as him. Either Galloway had gone insane, or this was a terrible practical joke. But this wasn't Galloway's sense of humour, which usually involved laughter at the expense of someone other than him.

Galloway pulled out a chair at the end of the table and sat down. He placed his hands down on the table and did some kind of weird breathing exercises, while the others exchanged worried glances with each other.

'AAAAAGH.'

Galloway cried out in pain and then suddenly his whole body shook like he was having a fit. But almost as soon as the fit started, his body went limp. The life vanished from his eyes and he slouched back in the chair. His head lopped to the side and his jaw dropped open. And then Rothman saw it. Everyone saw it. A shadow, a swirling black mass floated up behind the chair that Galloway was slumped in.

The shadow had a face. The features, the eyes, mouth and nose didn't stay still, they fizzled back and forth as it looked around the table. It was a ghostly apparition all right, or at least it was exactly how Rothman expected a ghost to look.

'What's happening?'

Rothman had no idea who asked, but they were speaking on everyone's behalf.

The black shadow darted around the table, circling the group like a miniature typhoon, freaking everyone out. Nobody dared to move, hoping that it would all soon be over. The terrifying shadow dance lasted almost a minute before the shadow flew back into the flaccid body of Rupert Galloway. Almost immediately, Galloway sat up straight again and shivered like he'd just come in from the rain.

'Does anybody need to see me do that again?' he asked.

Rothman wasn't sure how to respond. He and the others were all gawping at Galloway, trying to make sense of what they had seen.

'Okay,' said Galloway. 'I understand you're a little shaken by what just happened, so let me explain what I'm here for. The car accident I was involved in, it was all part of God's plan. The Angel Gabriel told me that the world is in great danger. If we don't act now, there is a great war coming, a war which will end humanity. Only the seven of us in this room can prevent it from happening. You see, God approves of the work we've done at MAWF. The way we've restored order to the world with our globalisation project has really impressed him and shown him that the human race is worth saving.'

Even though Rothman had no fucking idea what was going on, or what Galloway was talking about, the bit about God approving of MAWF and their globalisation project did please him. It's not every day God says you're doing a good job. So with that in mind, he decided to humour Galloway and his weird black shadow thing.

'Erm, what does God want us to do exactly?' he asked.

Galloway pointed at him and answered with a wink. 'Release the angels.'

'The angels? What angels?'

Galloway stood up and pointed at the floor with both hands. 'The mummified bodies in the vault below ground, *they're angels.*'

The mummies Galloway was referring to were concealed inside sarcophaguses. There were four of them and inside each sarcophagus was a mummified body, wrapped from head to toe in a strange gold thread. They were thought to have been dead for over two thousand years. On Arnold Rothman's first day as a member of MAWF he had been taken down to see them. It was part of the ritual of becoming a member of MAWF. He remembered it like it was yesterday. He also remembered being told that the gold thread wrapped around the bodies was never to be removed.

Linda Murdoch said exactly what Rothman and the others were thinking. 'Are you saying you know who those four mummies are?'

'Yes I am,' Galloway replied. 'Like I just said, they are angels. Gabriel told me all about them. God dispatched them to earth many centuries ago when humanity was in trouble. It is in trouble again, so we have been ordered to set them free to fulfil their destiny.'

'What destiny?' said Rothman.

'You've seen it. We've *all* seen it. There are revolutions going on all across the world, right now. Sooner or later, all the good we have done for the world will be undone. So, before it's too late, we must release the angels.'

It was hard to believe what Galloway was saying because, deep down in spite of all the good that Rothman and the others had done for the world, they had still kept ninety percent of the wealth for themselves. He'd always worried that if God was real, he might not see that as a good thing.

'What would we be releasing these angels for?' he asked.

'To eliminate the men who seek to destroy the world.'

'What men?'

Galloway started walking around the room again, wagging his finger at nothing in particular.

'You've already had one warning,' he said. 'Salvatore Rocco was brainwashed. He came here to kill all of you. He's just the first. Your enemies have found ways to turn ordinary men and women like Rocco into assassins. But where he failed, the next one might not. One thing is certain, there will be more like him. If we don't set those angels free to protect us, everyone at this table will be dead within a matter of weeks. And I promise you, in spite of all the good we've done, if we don't do this, and do it now, God will see to it that when we die, we will all go to Hell.'

Four

Sanchez hated Amish people. The beards, the crap clothes, the way they held up traffic with their stupid horse drawn carriages and their refusal to accept technology, there was nothing to like about them.

The Amish man that walked into the Tapioca one Thursday afternoon looked like the worst kind, a bible carrying old bastard with a grey neck beard.

'The Amish pub is down the road,' said Sanchez, hoping to trick the man into visiting Santa Mondega's recently opened gay bar. The man ignored him and took a seat. He took off his stupid hat and placed it on the bar.

'Are you Sanchez?' he asked.

'I might be. Who are you?'

The man reached inside his jacket and pulled out a money clip. It looked like he had about five hundred bucks.

'My name is Father Yoder,' he said.

Sanchez's face lit up. 'Yoda?'

'It's spelt Y-O-D-E-R.'

'I don't care how it's spelt. It's still Yoda.'

Sanchez was disappointed that he was on his own. If Flake had been around she would have appreciated some of his hilarious Star Wars puns, or his Yoda impression.

'I'd like a glass of water please,' said Yoder.

It was at times like this Sanchez was livid about Flake throwing away the bottle of piss he used to keep behind the bar to serve up to strangers. This Amish guy with his stupid name deserved to be served a glass of Sanchez's finest. But those days were gone. Sanchez hadn't served piss to anyone for a long time. He missed those glorious days. Instead he grabbed the soft drinks dispenser and poured the man a glass of fresh water.

'That's three dollars,' he said, placing it down on the counter.

'Three dollars? For water?'

'It goes up to four dollars if you get on my nerves.'

Yoder handed over a five-dollar bill and replaced his money clip inside his jacket.

Sanchez rang up the sale in the till. 'By the way, we don't give change here,' he said.

'So you *are* Sanchez?' Yoder said, sniffing his glass of water.

'What do you want?' Sanchez asked.

'I'm looking to hire a group of people known as The Dead Hunters. And the word on the street is, you know how to get in touch with them.'

'Well I don't.'

'I'm willing to pay.'

'How much?'

'Ten dollars.'

Sanchez scoffed. 'Ten dollars! Try a hundred.'

'Done.' Yoder reached inside his jacket again and pulled out his money clip. He handed Sanchez five twenty-dollar bills. 'Can you arrange a meeting with them for me?'

Sanchez had no idea where The Dead Hunters were. He'd seen Rex and Elvis briefly at a Christmas party a couple of years ago, but apart from that, he'd only heard about them on the news like everyone else. But seeing as how this Amish preacher was paying cash, Sanchez decided to give the impression that he might know how to reach them.

'I can speak to them for you,' he lied. 'But I can't guarantee that they will help you.'

'That's all I ask,' said Yoder.

'So what do you want them for?'

'I've come a long way to see them, from the village of Oakfield on Blue Corn Island. We have a problem there, the kind of problem your friends specialise in dealing with… if you know what I mean?'

'I might,' Sanchez replied nonchalantly.

'I've heard they deal with monsters, like vampires and such. Is that correct?'

'Are you sure you want to get mixed up with these people?' Sanchez warned him. 'Because one of them is likely to kill you just for having that stupid neck beard.'

'Believe me, I have no choice,' said Yoder. 'My people have no one else to turn to.'

'Do the women have beards too?'

Yoder frowned. 'No, not usually. How is that relevant?'

'It's not. I just always wondered. So, what kind of monsters have been bothering you?'

Yoder took a very small sip of water and looked surprised that it tasted okay.

'The island that my people live on is a hundred and fifty square miles,' he said, sounding like he was about to give Sanchez his life story. 'On one side is our village, Oakfield, and on the other side, closest to the mainland there is a town called Crimson County.'

'You're boring me already.'

Father Yoder tutted. 'I'm giving you some background.'

'Don't bother. I'll only forget it. Just get to the good stuff and I'll pass that on to The Dead Hunters.'

'Well there's a dense forest in the middle of the island. It's five miles deep and at this time of year it is inhabited by something evil.'

'You mean squirrels?' said Sanchez. 'Vicious little fuckers aren't they?'

'No, not squirrels. There is a creature in the forest. It comes out at night and takes anyone foolish enough to pass through the forest.'

'Okay, so you want it killed, I get it.'

'It's not that simple. This thing is hundreds of years old. It won't die easily, I know that much because many have tried and failed. For centuries, men were foolish enough to think they could hunt it down and kill it. But no one has ever gone into the Black Forest and come out alive during the Fall of Evil.'

'The Fall of what?'

'Evil. That's what we call the period from mid October through to the end of November. That's when the monster with one eye appears and snatches away innocent people. For the rest of the year it hibernates, living off the blood of the people it snatched during the Fall. We've already lost four young children so far in October.' He paused. 'Should you be writing this down?'

Sanchez grabbed a pen and a pad of paper from under the bar and started writing, narrating out loud so that Yoder could verify the details. 'Okay, so, *Preacher... looking... for... young... children.*'

'No,' said Yoder. 'The children are already gone. It's too late for them. They won't be found. I want your friends to remove the beast that took them.'

'Okay, I've got it,' said Sanchez, writing some more. *'To ... take out... the... One Eyed Monster.'*

'That's right,' said Yoder. 'And let them know that I'm happy to pay them.'

'Uh huh. *Willing.... to pay... good money.'*

'And their discretion is of vital importance. I don't want the people of Oakfield knowing that I have used outsiders to solve this problem,' Yoder continued.

'Discretion.... important,' said Sanchez, adding a full stop at the end. 'Anything else?'

'Yes, tell them to come and find me in the church before they do anything. It's easy to find. It's the biggest building in the village, a quite magnificent erection.'

Sanchez put the pen down. 'It's okay,' he said. 'I can remember that part.'

Yoder reached into his jacket pocket and pulled out a folded piece of paper. 'This is a map containing directions for how to reach Oakfield,' he said, sliding it across the bar to Sanchez. 'How long do you think it will be before The Dead Hunters arrive? This matter is of utmost urgency.'

Sanchez unfolded the map and took a look at it. It was rubbish, and looked like it had been drawn by a child. There was a circle in the middle of the map, with a few trees drawn on it and the words "BLACK FOREST"

'This forest looks rubbish,' said Sanchez.

'Like I said, it's inhospitable, a dangerous place, not safe for people.'

'Have you ever considered renaming it? You could call it the Black Forest Ghetto.'

'Why?'

'Black Forest Ghetto. Geddit?'

'No.' Yoder looked confused. 'Can you just pass the message onto The Dead Hunters, please?'

Sanchez folded up the map. 'Fair enough.'

'So when do you think they will arrive?'

'They'll get there when they get there,' said Sanchez with a shrug. 'I don't suppose you've got a phone number they can contact you on?'

'We don't have phones,' said Yoder. 'We don't use any technology in our community. God forbids it.'

'Of course he does,' said Sanchez, cursing himself for even asking. 'I'll just tell them to follow the map until they see your magnificent erection then, shall I?'

'That would be great,' said Yoder, sounding genuinely grateful. 'Thank you so much for your help.'

'Bye then.'

Sanchez folded up the piece of paper he had written the mission details on and stuck it under the bar with the map, confident that he wasn't going to see any of The Dead Hunters any time soon. He was wrong, of course.

Five

Cain's plan was working perfectly. He couldn't believe how easy it had been to convince the members of MAWF that he was Robert Galloway and that he'd had a meeting with the Angel Gabriel. It was all bullshit of course. Anyone who was anyone knew that Gabriel didn't like meetings.

Arnold Rothman, the greedy old fart who had enough wealth to wipe out poverty all over the world, agreed to escort the man he thought was Rupert Galloway down to the vault where the mummies were kept. Except, as only Cain knew, they weren't really mummies. And they certainly weren't angels. Quite the opposite in fact.

Getting down to the vault was nigh on impossible for an outsider. It required two members of MAWF who had to pass through a series of retina scanners to operate security doors and an elevator. Cain had seen it all before, a few weeks earlier when he had scoured the entire building in his spirit form. He'd returned a short time later in the body of Salvatore Rocco, in the hope of breaking in and making his way down to the vault. A bloody disaster that had been. First he was captured by security, then to make matters worse, Rocco regained consciousness before Cain had exited his body. This time around, things would be different. Taking over the body of Rupert Galloway had got him into the building with ease.

'Do you know the names of these angels?' Rothman asked him as they stood side by side in the elevator that took them down to the vault.

'Zitrone, Yesil, Ash and Blanco.'

'It's very exciting. What else do you know about them?'

Cain could tell from Rothman's tone of voice that he was quite sceptical about what he'd been told. If he knew the truth, he'd probably be even more disbelieving.

The four mummified people in the vault beneath Riverdale Mansion were actually immortals, better known to mankind as the Four Horsemen of the Apocalypse.

Cain had first met them thousands of years earlier. The Four Horsemen had conquered the Mayan civilisation in the country now known as America. They had turned all of their enemies into ghouls, green-skinned cannibals that lived on the flesh and blood of the living. There had come a point where the human tribes on the continent were close to extinction. That was when Cain found the Horsemen and promised to show them other civilisations across the oceans, where they could conquer the rest of humanity. But their plans were scuppered in a story long forgotten by everyone, with the exception of those who followed the ancient gospel of Susan.

Susan's gospel told the story of what Jesus did during the years that never get mentioned in the Bible. The years when he and his first group of disciples sailed to the Americas and conquered the ghouls. In a final showdown with the four immortals, Jesus triumphed. But in a show of mercy, instead of killing them, he sentenced them to a lifetime of hibernation, wrapped from head to toe in a thread made from a golden fleece. When Jesus left America, his disciples led by Susan, stayed behind, guarding over the Four Horsemen and passing their story down through generations.

It was obvious to Cain that the story had fallen by the wayside because Arnold Rothman and his MAWF associates had no idea what their four prisoners were capable of.

The elevator doors opened after a descent that took almost two minutes. This wasn't just underground, this was deep, deep, deep underground. They walked out into a large hall, filled with ancient riches and artefacts from thousands of years ago. Cain breezed past everything he saw and headed to the end of the hall where the four sarcophaguses stood against the wall. Each of the stone coffins had a painting of its inhabitant on the front. The only notable difference between them was the hair colour of the person in each painting. One had white hair, one had green, another black. But the one Cain was drawn to, was the one with the yellow hair.

Arnold Rothman was struggling to keep pace with him. 'Rupert,' he wheezed. 'What's the hurry?'

'You'll see. Help me open the yellow one.'

The two of them lifted open the sarcophagus, which took a while because it was made of stone, and Arnold Rothman was not built for heavy lifting. The body of Rupert Galloway was knackered too, from the car accident that Cain had organised.

Inside the sarcophagus, was the body of Zitrone, the leader of the Four Horsemen. The gold thread wrapped around him glowed and lit up the room as it was exposed to the light.

Cain pulled a flick knife from his back pocket.

'Where on earth did you get that?' asked Rothman.

'The Angel Gabriel gave it to me,' Cain replied, inwardly sniggering to himself.

He used the blade of the knife to cut into the golden thread. It was tough, and for a while he feared he might blunt the knife, but eventually he cut through enough of the thread that he was able to start unravelling it.

'Come on, give me a hand,' he barked at Rothman.

Rothman didn't look keen. The old banker was a tad squeamish about unwrapping a dead body, which was understandable. So Cain did most of the unravelling himself. It took almost five minutes, but it became easier once the mummy's arms were free and it started moving, tearing the thread away from itself.

Cain stepped back and watched his old friend, Zitrone, the blond Horseman rip himself free from the golden fleece that had imprisoned him for millennia. He was wearing nothing other than a grey loincloth to preserve his dignity, and a scowl on his face that indicated he was mad as hell.

Arnold Rothman took a few steps back, his eyes wide with shock.

Cain reintroduced himself to his old friend. 'Zitrone,' he said, smiling.

Zitrone ignored him and stepped out of the open sarcophagus. He drank in his surroundings for a moment, no doubt wondering how he had ended up in someone's basement. But then he looked at Cain. His eyes were drawn to the C shaped scar on his forehead.

'Cain?' he said. 'What took you so long?'

Arnold Rothman interrupted their reunion with an obvious question. 'Who's Cain?'

'I am,' Cain replied. 'Zitrone, would you please feel my forehead?'

While Rothman tried to make sense of it all, Zitrone pressed his hand against Cain's forehead. One of Zitrone's many gifts was that he could read anyone's mind when he touched them. He read Cain's thoughts and understood them instantly.

What followed was a demonstration of Zitrone's power and vengeful personality. He flew at Arnold Rothman and grabbed him by the throat. Rothman's skin turned pale, ageing more than a year with each passing second. He tried to struggle, but Zitrone's infamous death touch worked like a lethal poison. He lifted Rothman off his feet and hurled him across the floor. Rothman bounced onto his back, clutching his throat with both hands, trying desperately to breathe.

'It's good to see you again,' said Cain. 'We have a lot of catching up to do.'

'Where have you been?' Zitrone demanded, anger seeping from every pore of his body.

'I've been searching for you for centuries,' said Cain. 'Not for one moment did I rest. They hid you well. And this man,' he pointed at Rothman, who was now limp and close to death. 'He and his partners have been keeping you secret down here all this time.'

'What about the man who imprisoned us? Did you kill him?'

'No, I fled. The son of God came after me with the Brutus Dagger. If I hadn't fled he would have killed me with it.'

'Where is he now?'

'He's gone. His own people nailed him to a cross, and left him for dead, so he returned to Heaven. But now that you're free, it's possible God will send him again. The gospel of Susan even predicts it.'

'What is the gospel of Susan?'

'It's a book written by one of those who helped Jesus to imprison you. She predicted that one day you would rise up again, and that he would return to do battle with you once more.'

Zitrone clenched his fists. 'This time I'll be ready for him.'

'You'll need to be a little patient, my friend. The world has changed a lot since you were last here. There is much for me to teach you.'

'So start teaching me while I free the others.'

Six

'That's three nothing to Jasmine!' said Joey, slapping Rex across the chest.

Rex didn't reply right away. He was too engrossed in the game of pool they were watching. He had money riding on it, money he didn't want to lose to the likes of Joey.

It was early afternoon, though you couldn't tell inside the dark, dingy bar Rex, Joey, Jasmine and Elvis had stopped in. They were in Texas, killing time and drinking beer. Rex and Joey had been watching Elvis and Jasmine play pool for the last fifteen minutes while sitting at a small table in the corner of the bar. Every surface in the place had a slightly sticky feel, including their table, which neither surprised nor worried Rex. He took a sip from his bottle of Shitting Monkey beer.

It was a curious game to watch. Jasmine didn't seem to have a clue what she was doing, yet she was pulling off some outrageous shots. Elvis, on the other hand, was playing poorly by his standards. Rex had seen him win at pool hundreds of times, so to see him losing three frames to nothing against a chancer like Jasmine could mean only one thing.

'He's hustling her, can't you see?' Rex replied finally, taking another sip of his beer. 'He'll win the next four frames, I guarantee it.'

'I think she's hustling him right back,' said Joey. 'She's pulling off all these impossible shots and making it look like luck.'

'Dream on. You watch, now that she's winning, Elvis will get her to double up on the bet.'

Joey laughed. 'I doubt it. You weren't here when they made the bet.'

'Why? How much was it?'

'It wasn't for money. If Elvis wins, Jasmine has to sleep with him.'

'WHAT?'

'Yeah. I bet you wish you'd thought of making that bet.'

'Shut up.'

'You like her don't you?'

Rex glowered at Joey. 'Don't start with that again.'

'But you do. It's written all over your face, at least it is when you're not staring at her ass!'

Rex picked up his beer and took another sip. He watched Jasmine bend over to take a shot. She was wearing a skin-tight purple catsuit that didn't leave much to the imagination. And she did have an amazing ass. When she wiggled it or bent over to take a shot, it was positively hypnotic.

Joey waved his hand in front of Rex's face. 'Hello? You still with me?'

Rex was mulling over the possible outcomes of the bet between Jasmine and Elvis. She was already three frames ahead, so she obviously wanted to win.

'You're right,' he said, wagging his finger at Joey. 'Jasmine *is* gonna win. She obviously doesn't want to lose and have to sleep with Elvis.'

'Do you know what the other side of the bet is?' said Joey, a wry smile breaking out on his face.

'No. I bet it's something stupid though.'

'It is,' Joey agreed. 'If Jasmine wins, Elvis has to sleep with *her!*'

Rex spat his beer out over the table. 'WHAT?'

'I'm kidding. But you definitely like her.'

'Idiot.' It was hard at times like this to remember that Joey was The Red Mohawk.

During his days as a Hell's Angel, Rex had slept with many women. His big muscular physique and reputation as a brawler and king of the bikers had made it easy to pick up girls. But since he'd been brought back from the dead to work for Scratch, he'd not had much time for women. Being a member of The Dead Hunters meant travelling the world, never staying in one place for long enough to get to really know anyone. That was fine if you were Joey, because he was in love with Baby, and she with him. That left Elvis and Rex in an unofficial battle to see who could hook up with Jasmine, even though by rights, she was too young for either of them. The only other member of their gang, the Bourbon Kid, was never around, preferring to work alone unless Scratch insisted otherwise.

Jasmine took her shot and hit a bunch of balls all at once, scattering them in all directions. The one she was following with her eyes bounced off all four sides of the table before nestling in the corner pocket. Jasmine punched the air. It looked like she was going to win again.

Rex downed the remainder of his beer and slapped Joey on the arm. 'It's your round. I'll have another Shitting Monkey.'

Joey still had half a bottle of beer left. 'Slow down lover boy,' he said. 'Give me a minute to finish this one.'

During the ten months or so that Rex had known Joey, he'd come to realise that he wasn't a big drinker. After initially hunting him down in connection with a plot to kill the Pope, Rex and Elvis had befriended him when it became clear that he was actually more like them, a vigilante. Joey's alter ego, the Red Mohawk was responsible for hundreds of murders, and most of the victims deserved what they got. Joey came as part of a package, joining The Dead Hunters at the same time as Baby and Jasmine. Ah, Jasmine. Every time her name popped into Rex's head, he got a little sweaty.

'So what *really* happens if Jasmine wins?' he asked.

Joey took a big swig from his beer and burped up some air before answering. 'Elvis has to buy her a car.'

'A car? He bet *a car* on the outcome of a game of pool?'

'I'd say Jasmine hustled him real good. He thought it was a bet worth making.'

'Yeah, I'll bet he did. Serves him right.'

Joey finished off his beer and stood up. 'You should make the same bet and challenge her to arm wrestling. Shitting Monkey, right?'

'Huh?'

'You're drinking Shitting Monkey, yeah?'

'Uh, yeah, thanks.'

Joey walked off to the bar to get the drinks, while Rex carried on watching Jasmine destroy Elvis at pool. Elvis, true to his name, was wearing a black jumpsuit with a thick gold belt. He was in decent shape for a man in his late thirties, and he still had a thick head of jet-black hair, styled in a quiff. His Elvis impersonation was topped off with a pair of gold-rimmed sunglasses. Rex needed to get a pair of sunglasses. Maybe that way Joey wouldn't keep catching him staring at Jasmine.

The Bon Jovi song, *Dead or Alive* started chiming out of a pocket on Rex's denim waistcoat. He'd set it as the ringtone on his phone because it reminded him of a time he'd seen a John Bon Jovi impersonator shit his pants. The incoming call was from General Alexis Calhoon. The General occasionally threw some work their way. It was an arrangement that worked well. She was in charge of the government's attempts to catch The Dead Hunters, but in actual fact she was an ally who tipped them off if her people were closing in on them.

'Hello General, wassup?'

Calhoon didn't greet him with a "hello" or a "how's things?" she just got straight to the point as usual. 'Are you missing a member of your group?'

'What's he done now?'

'Nothing, it's Baby. She's been arrested. I thought you should know.'

Rex let out a frustrated sigh. 'Okay, where is she?'

'She was picked up in the Lady Florence Mental Hospital. She killed Salvatore Rocco and a janitor, although she claims the janitor killed Rocco. Not that it matters of course. She's being transferred to the new top secret prison on the island of Hubal. Do you know it?'

'Hubal? Yeah. Used to be an island full of monks.'

'That's right. Someone killed all the monks a few years back, so we took over the island and turned it into a prison for folks like you.'

Rex was well aware of who was responsible for massacring the monks, but kept it to himself. 'So how do we get Baby back?'

'In the early hours of tomorrow morning a prison truck will be transporting her to the harbour of your old home town, Santa Mondega. From there she'll be put on a boat to Hubal. I suggest you hold up the truck on the main highway into Santa Mondega. The road will most likely be empty, so I was thinking you could get her back without killing any of my guys? Is that possible, please?'

'Sure thing, General. Thanks for the heads up.'

Rex hung up the phone and looked over at the bar. Joey was there, paying for the drinks. He reminded Rex of himself when he was younger. He had an impeccable physique and wore a lot of sleeveless vests. He was currently wearing a red one that matched the red leather jacket he always wore. The jacket was hanging on the back of the chair next to Rex, with a yellow skull mask poking out of its side pocket. It baffled Rex why Joey still wore the mask, but he was an odd individual, pleasant and reasonably witty most of the time, but a completely unpredictable psychopath whenever the mask was on his head.

Joey walked back to the table with four bottles of Shitting Monkey. He handed one to Rex. 'There ya go buddy,' he said. 'Is Jasmine still winning?'

There was no time for that now. Rex got straight to the point. 'Calhoon just called. Baby's been arrested.'

'Shit.'

Joey reached for his jacket, but Rex grabbed his arm. 'It's okay. We're picking her up tomorrow. She's fine. So just chill out and let's have some beers.'

'YeeeeHAAA!' Jasmine punched her fist in the air and cheered. She had just potted the black and beaten Elvis four nothing at pool. 'You owe me a car, loser!' she jeered.

Elvis tossed his pool cue onto the table. He high-fived Jasmine as a sign that he had taken the defeat in good grace. But then he saw Rex holding Joey by the arm.

'What's up with you two?' he asked.

'Baby's been arrested,' said Rex. 'But Calhoon's given me a time and place where we can go get her. We just have to promise not to kill the people guarding her.'

'Oh no,' said Jasmine. 'Is she okay?'

'She's fine. We just have to extract her from a prison truck on the highway to Santa Mondega tomorrow morning.'

Elvis peered over the top of his sunglasses. 'We're going back to Santa Mondega?'

Rex smiled. 'Yeah.'

Jasmine skipped over to the table and sat down next to Rex. 'That's your home town isn't it? I've always wanted to go there.'

Rex got a waft of Jasmine's hair. It smelled like peaches. Her long dark hair was impeccable and the creamy brown skin on her neck and face was so smooth. He took a deep inhale through his nose and hoped the others were too preoccupied to notice.

But then Elvis sat down next to Jasmine and slid his arm around her shoulder, which woke Rex up from his Jasmine trance. He glanced to his left and saw Joey was sat down next to him again, watching him.

Elvis prodded Rex in the arm. 'You know what?' he said. 'Once we get Baby back, we should go celebrate at The Tapioca. Sanchez owes us some free beers from that whole Christmas thing we did for him.'

Joey raised his bottle of beer. 'To Baby and Santa Mondega!'

The others raised their drinks and concurred, "To Baby and Santa Mondega".

'This is gonna be great,' said Elvis.

Seven

Cain and the Four Horsemen helped themselves to some antique swords from the underground treasure trove in the Riverdale Mansion and headed upstairs to the Brinkman room, where the five remaining members of MAWF were patiently waiting for the return of Arnold Rothman and Rupert Galloway.

Zitrone, the blond Horseman, was the first through the doors, with his sword drawn. He grabbed hold of Roland Navarone, who was way too old and frail to fight back. To the sound of screams from the other members of MAWF, Zitrone thrust the blade of his sword through Navarone's throat and hacked his head off. Cain hung back by the entrance and admired his friend's handiwork. Zitrone sure knew how to make an entrance.

The other three Horsemen, Ash, Yesil and Blanco followed Zitrone's lead and charged into the room. Each of them picked out one of the terrified MAWF members and set about dismembering them with great gusto. It made for quite a sight. Cain had seen some crazy shit in his time, but four scantily dressed immortals butchering a room full of pensioners was a new one.

There were five members of MAWF in the Brinkman room, but only four Horsemen, which meant that Linda Murdoch was the lucky person who got to watch the other four being ripped apart. Quite what was going through her head was anyone's guess.

Cain enjoyed the sight of her frozen in her seat, as much as he enjoyed hearing the terrified screams of her colleagues. Seeing their blood spray across the room onto the walls and onto Linda Murdoch was quite exhilarating. She seemed to be curling up into a ball, hoping to make herself invisible, which was impossible because she was wearing a bright white dress, now splattered with the blood of her colleagues.

Cain pranced around the dining table on his way to see her, a gleeful grin on his face. He was waving a short sword in his hand, taunting her with it. The best she could do to fend him off was to pick up a bunch of A4 sized photos on the table and throw them at him. They hit him in the chest, some scattering to the floor and others landing on the table in a dramatic heap. *Oh the desperate things people do when faced with death.*

'Rupert! What are you doing?' she cried.

'I'm not Rupert, you dumb bitch!'

He grabbed a handful of her hair, ready to begin slicing her head off, when one of the photos on the table caught his eye. He stopped and stared at it. He recognised the woman in the photo. He put his sword down on the table and picked up the photo.

'Who is this?' he said, holding it in front of Linda's face.

For a while it looked like she was too terrified to respond, but she saved herself from some unnecessary suffering when she eventually blurted out an answer.

'*Baby*, her name is Baby. She's part of a gang of vigilantes who killed the Pope.'

Cain looked at the photo again. This was the doctor in the Lady Florence asylum who had disarmed and shot him while he was in the body of a useless, dimwit janitor. He had passed it off as a fluke at the time, presuming that he'd just been caught out by a lady doctor who'd got lucky.

'Why was she talking to Salvatore Rocco?'

Zitrone appeared at Cain's shoulder. He had finished with Roland Navarone, so while his colleagues were still busy disembowelling their chosen targets, he hovered behind Cain and showed an interest in his discussion with Linda Murdoch.

'What's going on?' Zitrone asked. 'Why aren't you killing her?'

Cain ignored him and focussed on Linda. 'Look at me,' he said, aware that she could see Zitrone looming behind him. 'Answer my question.'

'I don't know,' said Linda, before hastily adding, 'but we thought maybe her gang were plotting to kill us, seeing as how they got to the Pope.'

'Why would they want to kill you?'

'I don't know. But earlier on you said some people were going to kill us, didn't you?'

'I was talking shit, *obviously!*' Cain mocked. 'I didn't know *these* people were trying to kill you. Who do they work for?'

'We think, I mean, we thought, they worked for the Devil.'

Zitrone moved behind Linda. He and Cain exchanged a look that spoke a thousand words. Cain gathered up the other photos that had fallen onto the floor and started flicking through them.

'I know some of these people,' he said. He grabbed a handful of Linda's dress and hauled her up from her seat. 'Are you sure these people work for Scratch?'

'Scratch?'

'The Devil. Are you sure they work for him?'

'I only know what I've read about them. It's all top secret stuff that only the people at this table and a handful of government officials know anything about. The rest of the world just thinks they're a bunch of devil worshipping vigilantes.'

Cain studied a photo of a Hell's Angel with shoulder length brown hair.

'Rodeo Rex works for the Devil?' he said, tossing the photo at Linda Murdoch. 'I don't believe that. This guy worked for God. He was on my tail for years. But then he died.' He looked at the next picture. It was of an Elvis Presley lookalike. He threw that at her too. 'And this is his buddy Elvis. He's dead too!'

'That's what we heard,' said Linda, sensing a real chance to save her neck. 'But they showed up at a charity event last year and massacred hundreds of innocent people, including the Pope. One of the survivors that day was a government spook called Alexis Calhoon. She says they work for the Devil now.'

Zitrone pointed his sword at the back of Linda's neck. She didn't look around but it was obvious she knew he was there.

'And where do these people hang out?' Cain demanded. 'Where do we find them?'

Linda looked devastated, which suggested she had no idea, but she continued to speak.

'We've been trying to catch them for some time,' she said. 'But according to Calhoon they hide out in a part of the world that can only be accessed by those close to the Devil.'

'You mean Hell?'

'I don't know...... Yes..... maybe.'

Zitrone slid his sword around the front of Linda's neck and leant down to speak in her ear. 'Are you saying that the people in these photos know the location of Hell?'

Linda gasped in fear and pain before stuttering ,'I... I... guess they do, yes.'

Cain had known for a long time that there was a gateway to Hell situated somewhere on earth, but he had never been able to find it. It was supposedly unreachable by anyone other than Scratch and the people he granted access to.

'This is interesting news,' said Zitrone. 'How do we find this entrance to Hell?'

'I... I really don't know.'

Zitrone made a noise of disgust and re-gripped the sword, ready to behead Linda.

'Zitrone, leave her a moment,' said Cain.

Zitrone halted, but kept his stance, ready to kill. The other three immortals had gathered behind Zitrone by this point.

Cain held up another photo, making sure they got a good look at it. Then he moved it back into Linda's eyeline.

'Tell my friends about this man,' he said.

Linda swallowed hard. 'That's the Bourbon Kid,' she said.

'What do you know about him?'

'He's a serial killer.'

'But what makes him different to the others?'

'It's…. It's going to sound kind of silly.'

'Not to them it won't.'

Linda wiped a tear away from her cheek. 'His father was a monk named Ishmael Taos. Taos is dead now, but he lived for hundreds of years because he drank the blood of Christ from the Holy Grail. So technically, the bloodline of Christ lives on in the Bourbon Kid. It gives him great healing powers, making him hard to kill.'

'That's right,' said Cain.

Zitrone and the other Horsemen murmured between them. The blond Horseman removed his sword from Linda's neck and prodded it in Cain's direction. 'He's a descendant of the man who imprisoned us!'

'Yes,' Cain agreed.

'I want him dead.'

'Of course you do.'

Zitrone slid his sword back across Linda's throat and spoke into her ear again. 'So where do we find him?'

'He's impossible to find,' she replied, tears streaming down her face.

Zitrone pressed the blade harder against her throat, drawing a little blood.

'Wait,' said Cain. 'Don't kill her yet. I can find this man for you. I can find *all* of these people. Think for a minute. These Dead Hunters know where the gateway to Hell is. I can follow them and find its location.'

Zitrone pulled his sword away from Linda again. 'I like it,' he said. 'We can open the gateway and unleash Hell on earth. The dead will carry out our bidding and we will have our revenge!'

'That is what I was thinking,' said Cain. 'But thanks for spelling it out.' He clicked his fingers in front of Linda's face, in order to get her attention again. '*You, Linda!* Where do we find this woman, Baby? Is she in prison now?'

Linda nodded. 'She's in custody at the moment. But tomorrow she's being transferred to a maximum security prison on the island of Hubal.'

'Good.' Cain could feel a plan formulating in his mind. 'Do you wish to stay alive Mrs Murdoch?'

'I would like that very much.'

'I thought so. Now, here's what you're going to do. My four colleagues have been imprisoned for so long that they couldn't possibly move in the outside world without drawing attention to themselves. So I'm going to give you a list of things that I want you to show them.'

'Like what?'

'Like how to use a cellphone, dumb shit like that. They have very advanced learning powers so you'll only need to explain things to them once. If in the time I am gone, you teach them everything they need to know, I will let you live.'

Ash, the dark haired Horseman, stepped forward and shoved Cain in the arm. 'Where exactly are you going?' he inquired.

'I'm going to find The Dead Hunters.'

'How do you know where to look?'

'Common sense, my friend. If Baby is being taken to a prison in Hubal, then the others will either try to rescue her, or execute her. Scratch can't have one of his crew in a prison where she might talk about him. So when the rest of The Dead Hunters show up to get her, I will be in the shadows, watching and listening. I'll find out the location of Hell, and on top of that, you can have this Bourbon Kid fellow.'

Eight

Four armed guards. It made Baby feel like a badass. Someone thought she needed four armed military officers to escort her to prison. It was a breakthrough moment. No one ends up in the back of a prison truck with four armed guards unless they're considered a threat to society. And even though the orange prison overalls she'd been forced to wear were hideous, they added to the all-around sense of accomplishment.

The four guards in the back of the truck with her hadn't said a word for the entire journey. Two of them sat opposite her, staring right through her as if she wasn't there. The other two were sitting on either side of her.

The truck had been on the road for two hours when it suddenly veered to one side, as if it had a flat tyre. The driver pulled back a metal slide hatch and yelled through to the others.

'We've got a puncture!'

A loud pop followed that statement and the truck wobbled. The driver ducked back out of sight to wrestle with the steering wheel. *Two flat tyres in the space of ten seconds!* Baby knew what that meant. All four of the armed guards knew too. The driver poked his head through the hatch and yelled again.

'We've got another fl......'

He didn't finish the sentence because a splodge of blood burst out of the side of his head and he vanished from view.

The truck slowed to a stop and all four guards sprang to life. One of them pulled the driver's slide hatch shut and then joined the others, crouching down on one knee with his assault rifle pointed at the back doors. Baby slid along the bench and rolled onto the floor behind them, in readiness for a flurry of bullets coming her way.

She had only counted to eleven in her head by the time the back doors flew open. Right on cue, all four guards blindly opened fire. Baby covered her ears and closed her eyes until the shooting stopped. As shootouts go it was very brief. If Baby had to put a number on it, she'd have guessed at five seconds, tops. After another three seconds of silence she opened her eyes and saw all four of the guards were dead. Rodeo Rex was standing in the road outside, holding his magnetic metal hand up. He had caught all of the bullets that the guards had fired. Behind him, holding two pistols was the Red Mohawk. A smile broke out on Baby's face when she saw the yellow skull mask with the red crest along the top of it.

Rex dropped a handful of bullets on to the ground at the Red Mohawk's feet. 'I told you just to wound them,' he said, angrily.

Joey took off his mask and stared at the dead bodies in the truck. 'I did wound them,' he said.

'You *killed* them. I specifically told you just to *wound* them.'

'They are wounded. Those are head wounds.'

'Yeah, *fatal* head wounds, you moron.'

'You never said anything about what type of wound it had to be.'

Baby interrupted the bickering. 'Would somebody please get these handcuffs off of me?'

Joey climbed into the back of the truck and grabbed a set of keys from one of the dead guards. He kissed Baby and unlocked the cuffs at the same time. The kiss lingered long after the cuffs came off. Baby could kiss Joey all day if there was time. When their embrace ended, she nodded at the handcuffs he was holding.

'Let's keep those,' she said, rubbing her wrists.

Joey stuck the cuffs in a pocket on his red leather jacket. 'How's your day been?' he asked.

'Not good. Look at this outfit! Orange really isn't my colour.'

Rex shouted at them. 'Would you two hurry up! We've gotta get moving.'

Joey helped Baby out of the truck and onto the highway. There was nothing but desert wasteland as far as the eye could see. Baby saw Joey's motorcycle parked at the side of the road next to Rex's chopped Harley.

'Where's everyone else?' she asked.

'I was wondering that myself,' said Rex.

Joey pointed down the highway. 'Here they come.'

Elvis and Jasmine cruised down the middle of the road in a pink Cadillac with the roof down. Elvis was behind the wheel. He slowed the car down as they approached and Jasmine hurdled over the passenger door instead of opening it.

'Hey everybody!' she said. 'You okay, Baby?'

'Yeah, I'm okay, Jas.'

Rex shook his head. 'Where the fuck have you two been?' He growled his question at Elvis, who was still in the car and making no effort to get out.

'Car trouble,' said Elvis.

The Cadillac had a busted headlight and a dent on the driver's side. Jasmine crouched down and inspected the damage.

'It's not that bad,' she said.

'You crashed?' said Rex, exasperated.

Jasmine stood up. 'Yeah, I got bored and so I thought I'd surprise Elvis with a hand-job. Turns out he can't multi-task, so we crashed into a pylon at the side of the road.'

Joey and Baby shared a wry smile. The sexual tension between Elvis and Jasmine had been obvious for some time, but so had Rex's jealousy and not-so-secret infatuation with Jasmine's ass.

'It doesn't matter,' said Joey. 'We got the job done easily enough anyway.'

'That's not the point,' said Rex. 'She shouldn't be dishing out hand-jobs on the highway. You gotta respect the roads. And it's not right, leaving us to do the dirty work.'

Jasmine winked at Rex. 'Okay honey, next time you can give Elvis a hand-job, then you'll know what dirty work is all about.'

Rex looked like his was going to respond but then Elvis poked his head up over the windscreen of the Cadillac. 'Hey, I'm sorry Rex. Look, I came as soon as I could. I mean, you know, we got here as quick as we could, after the accident.'

'Forget it,' said Rex. 'We need to get out of here right now, because Joey killed all the guys in the truck.'

'I thought you were supposed to wound them?' said Elvis.

'Head wounds,' Joey replied.

Rex rounded on Joey. 'You're not funny you know. That's five innocent men dead because your girlfriend got arrested again. This is becoming a regular thing isn't it? She's been arrested twice now, and if I'm not missing anything, she's been kidnapped twice too. And every time it happens, you use it as an excuse to kill a bunch of innocent people.'

Joey took a step towards Rex. 'You'd better watch your mouth.'

Elvis honked the horn on the Cadillac and shouted over to them. 'Hey, would you two act your age! We need to get moving.'

Baby grabbed Joey by the hand and pulled him towards his bike and more importantly, away from Rex.

'So where are we off to now?' she asked.

'A place called The Tapioca,' Joey replied. 'Elvis and Rex know the bartender pretty well, so we should be safe there.'

Nine

'Sanchez, there's some people in the bar that wanna speak to you.'

Sanchez was livid. It seemed like every time he was on the toilet, Beth would pop up from the bar downstairs and shout something through the door at him. Her timing was really off too. He was seconds away from dropping a log and now he had to try and hold it in so she didn't hear the splash, or the inevitable trumpeting noises that would accompany it.

'It's not the old woman from the Health and Hygiene Department again is it?' he shouted through the door.

'No. It's a group of weirdoes. One of them thinks he's Elvis.'

'Elvis?'

The realisation that his great buddy, Elvis might be in the bar, took Sanchez by surprise causing him to stop concentrating on clenching his butt cheeks. So his unfortunate response to Beth's revelation that Elvis was back, was a loud splash and a five second fart that sounded like an elephant yawning. The wafting odour was a sneaky bonus.

Beth shouted through the door again. 'Christ, Sanchez, what have you been eating?'

'Never you mind. Just tell Elvis I'll be down in a minute!'

'Okay.'

Sanchez finished up in the toilet and put on a brown waistcoat to cover up the splash marks on the back of his shirt. He hurried downstairs to the bar. Beth was waiting at the bottom of the stairs for him. And something about her was different. She was wearing a tight black top and skinny jeans. She even had a new haircut. Her hair was usually very plain and tied back in a ponytail, but now it was a dark Pixie style cut with a red streak through it.

'You took your time,' she said. 'Your friends are on their third round of drinks!'

'Yeah, well I ran out of wet wipes. What's with the new look?'

Beth ran her hand through her hair. 'Umm, well, it's Halloween soon, so I thought I'd update my image a bit.'

'For Halloween?'

It was times like this when Sanchez remembered why he used to call her *"Mental Beth"*. Who the hell gets a new haircut and image for Halloween? Mental people, that's who.

'You think I'm mental, don't you?' said Beth.

'No.'

'Yes you do. It's not just about Halloween. It's because, well, you know, JD might show up on Halloween night, because it's our anniversary and stuff.'

'Yeah, you're right. You are mental. Where's Elvis?'

'Over there.' Beth pointed at a table near the wall. It wasn't just Elvis sitting there. To Sanchez's great delight, Rodeo Rex was sitting next to him. There were also two women and a man he didn't recognise sitting across from Elvis and Rex.

'Who are the others?' Sanchez asked.

'I think they're the other members of The Dead Hunters. The woman in the purple catsuit is called Jasmine. She seems nice, very friendly. The other two are a couple. The guy in the red jacket is called Joey. He's weird. You should avoid him.'

'Why?'

'Because he wouldn't like you.'

'Why not?'

'Trust me, he'd find you annoying. I think he's the Red Mohawk, you know, the psychopath who escaped from an asylum a few years ago and went on a killing spree?'

'Really? How can you tell?'

'He's got a yellow skull mask in his jacket pocket, and it's got a red Mohawk on it.'

'Great. That's all we need. Another nutter who kills people for fun.'

Beth didn't reply to the diss about serial killers and pointed at the girl next to Joey. 'The girl with him, everyone calls her Baby. I don't know her real name.'

'She looks like she's just escaped from prison,' said Sanchez, referring to Baby's orange overalls. 'Maybe you should give her some of your new fashion tips.'

Beth handed him a bottle of Shitting Monkey. 'Why don't you go and join them?'

'Right, yeah. If it gets busy call Flake and get her to come down and give you a hand.'

As Sanchez tried to walk away, Beth tugged at his waistcoat. 'Sanchez,' she said in her annoying, whiny voice. 'Can I ask a favour?'

'What?'

'Can you ask them if they know where JD is?'

'Why can't you ask them?'

'I don't really know them.'

Sanchez sighed. 'Okay, fine.'

Beth kept a hold of his waistcoat. 'Oh, and one other thing.'

'What now?'

'Don't forget this message from the Amish preacher.'

Sanchez had forgotten all about the Amish bishop and his stupid neck beard. Beth offered him the map Yoder had given him and the piece of paper Sanchez had made notes on.

Sanchez snatched them away from her. 'Anything else?'

'No, that's all. But don't forget to ask about JD.'

'Of course.'

Sanchez grabbed a bowl of peanuts from the back of the bar and headed over to the table where The Dead Hunters were sitting. Elvis spotted him and raised his hand.

'Yo, Sanchez, good to see ya!'

Sanchez pulled out a chair next to Rodeo Rex and exchanged greetings with him and Elvis, and nodded politely at the other members of the group.

'So then guys?' he said. 'I hear you shot the Pope. Is that true?'

'That was Jasmine,' said Elvis.

Jasmine reached out across the table to shake hands with Sanchez, but Elvis pulled her hand back before Sanchez could grab it. Undeterred, Jasmine blew a kiss instead.

'I killed the Pope because I thought he was a zombie,' she said.

'Me too,' said Sanchez, overjoyed at finally meeting someone who shared one of his conspiracy theories. 'I've been telling people that for years!'

'I got him six times in the chest,' said Jasmine. She demonstrated it by using her fingers as an imaginary gun and firing six shots at Sanchez.

'Good work,' said Sanchez. 'Serves him right. The bastard.'

No one apart from Jasmine seemed to appreciate him referring to the dead Pope as a bastard. A change of subject was required, so he elbowed Rex.

'So what brings you guys back to Santa Mondega?'

Rex pointed at Baby. 'She got arrested. Cops were taking her to that new top secret prison on Hubal island.'

'What top secret prison?'

'Exactly. So we rescued her from a prison truck fifty miles down the road and figured we'd stop by here for some beers. The place looks a lot cleaner than it used to.'

'Yeah, some old witch from the Health and Hygiene Department keeps coming round, making me change things.'

Elvis butted in. 'You still with Flake?'

'Yeah. She's upstairs watching some program about fortune-tellers.'

Sanchez slid the bowl of peanuts into the middle of the table where everyone could get to them. 'Peanut?' he said, offering them to the group.

Jasmine was the only one who took any, but Elvis grabbed her by the wrist before she could eat them.

'I wouldn't if I were you,' he said.

'It's okay,' said Jasmine. 'I'm not eating them. There's a guy over there who's asleep. I'm gonna see if I can throw some into his mouth.'

Sanchez craned his neck to see where the sleeping customer was. Sure enough, there was a guy sitting on his own, one table over. He was wearing a scruffy grey suit and a red beanie hat, which didn't go with the suit at all. His head was back against the wall, his eyes were closed and his mouth was open. Sanchez cursed himself that he hadn't thought of throwing the peanuts first.

'Jas, don't do that,' said Rex, clearly not as impressed with the idea as Sanchez. 'The guy's asleep for God's sake!'

Jasmine didn't take any notice of Rex. She took aim with the peanut and threw it at the sleeping man. It flew through the air, looping up high, then curving downwards towards his gaping mouth. It landed perfectly on his bottom lip and rolled onto his tongue. Sanchez watched with bated breath to see if the man woke. Or choked. He did neither.

Jasmine jumped up. 'YESSSS!'

Sanchez reached out to grab some peanuts from the bowl, but Rex stopped him. 'What's that in your hand?' he asked.

In all the excitement, Sanchez had forgotten about the map and the slip of paper he'd written the Amish guy's note on. He gave them to Rex.

'It's a map and a note from an Amish preacher in Oakfield,' he said. 'He came in the other day and asked if I could pass it on to you.'

Rex opened the note and read it. 'What the fuck is this shit?' he said, looking daggers at Sanchez.

'Huh?'

'Have you seen what this says?'

'Yeah, I'm the one who wrote it.'

Rex held up the note and read it aloud. *"Priest looking for young children to take out the one eyed monster in the woods. Willing to pay good money."* Care to explain to me what it means?'

'The priest told me they've got a Cyclops in the woods in Oakfield. It keeps snatching kids. He was hoping you guys could take it out.'

'Right,' said Rex, reading the note again. 'You should work on your note taking skills.'

Sanchez didn't appreciate the lack of gratitude. 'Maybe next time I'll just give him directions to The Devil's Graveyard so he can speak to you about it in person.'

Rex grabbed a fistful of Sanchez's shirt and pulled him close. 'You'd better not!' he growled. 'Don't never tell anyone how to get to the secret part of The Devil's Graveyard.'

'I wasn't going to,' Sanchez protested, his heart racing.

Rex let go of Sanchez's shirt and calmed down a little. 'It wouldn't matter anyway,' he said. 'It's a private area. Anyone you sent there wouldn't get through the crossroads anyway.'

'SHIT!'

The cry of SHIT, came from Jasmine who had thrown another peanut at the unconscious man at the next table. It hit him in the face, but lucky for her, it didn't wake him.

'Would you stop doing that!' said Rex, clearly getting annoyed. He waved the piece of paper Sanchez had given him at Jasmine. 'Here, instead of throwing peanuts at people, why don't you come on this mission with me? We've got a Cyclops to kill in the woods near an Amish village. We can make a weekend of it.'

'What? Just you and me?' said Jasmine.

'Yeah. It'll be fun. It's only a small job. It doesn't need all of us.'

A silence swept over the table momentarily. Jasmine shook her head. 'I can't. Elvis is buying me a new car at the weekend.'

Rex scratched his head. 'I could buy you a bike. I get great discounts on brand new Harleys.'

'But Elvis is buying me a DeLorean.'

Sanchez picked up on some tension at the table and decided to switch the conversation to something less likely to cause a ruckus.

'Oh, hey, Rex, is the Bourbon Kid with you?' he asked.

'No.'

'Do you know where he is?'

'No.'

'Can you find out?'

Rex swivelled his gaze from Jasmine to Sanchez. 'Why do you care?' he asked.

'I don't but, you see the barmaid Beth, over there? That's the Bourbon Kid's girlfriend and she wanted to know where he is. I promised her I'd ask you.'

A loud cough from a nearby table distracted Rex momentarily. The man who had been the target of Jasmine's peanut throwing, had woken up. He stared across at the bar, then glanced at Sanchez, before closing his eyes again and falling back to sleep.

'What a weirdo,' Sanchez muttered.

'This place is full of weirdoes,' said Rex.

'Tell me about it,' Sanchez agreed. 'You know Beth waits at the end of the pier every year at midnight on her own, hoping the Bourbon Kid will show up. I used to call her Mental Beth.'

Rex ignored him and tossed the map and the piece of paper from the Amish preacher down the table to Joey. 'Hey, why don't you take this job?' he said. 'It's just one little monster in the woods. Maybe you two could do it without Baby getting kidnapped or arrested?'

Joey didn't take kindly to Rex's attitude. 'Just because Jasmine doesn't want to go on a road trip with you doesn't mean you have to be a dick.' He picked up the note and waved it at Rex. 'Why don't you do it, if it's so easy?'

'Because I'm going to take a week off.'

Joey scoffed. 'What just because Jasmine blew you off?'

'I haven't blown him!' Jasmine protested.

'That's not what I meant.'

Rex looked like he was about to blow. He kicked his chair back and stood up. 'I'm outta here,' he announced.

Elvis tried to placate him. 'Rex, come on, stay and have some drinks. We've all been working hard, and everyone's uptight.'

Rex shook his head. 'Nah, I've got somewhere else I gotta be.'

'Can't we all go together?' said Jasmine.

'No,' Rex replied. 'I'm going to a clinic in Canada.'

Jasmine grimaced. 'Have you got the clap again?'

'No! I'm going to get rid of this metal hand that you all make fun of.'

Sanchez was shocked. 'What? Why?'

'A few years ago, I gave some of my DNA to the people who designed my metal hand. They called me a week ago and said they've grown me a brand new hand from my DNA. So I'm gonna have it transplanted to replace the metal one.'

'Well that's great news,' said Elvis, who had been unusually quiet. 'Will the new one be magnetic?'

'No.'

'That's a damn shame. Are you sure you wanna do this? Your magnetic hand has saved all our asses a bunch of times.'

'Sure, I'll miss it,' said Rex. 'But I won't miss all the jokes and creepy looks I get.'

'Won't you miss jerking off with it though?' said Jasmine.

'I DON'T JERK OFF WITH IT!' Rex yelled, which drew some strange looks from all the customers in the bar. 'You know, you guys can be real assholes sometimes. I'll see you all in a week. And don't bother calling me because I'm switching my phone off.'

Sanchez moved so that Rex could get past him and then watched the giant Hell's Angel storm out of the Tapioca in a huff.

'Jeez,' said Sanchez. 'What's the matter with him?'

'He's just a bit uptight,' said Elvis. 'He'll get over it.'

Joey had been left holding the note about the one-eyed monster mission. 'Well, I guess me and Baby are going to this job in Oakfield,' he said.

'You want us to come with you?' said Elvis.

Baby spoke up for the first time since Sanchez had arrived at the table. 'It's okay,' she said. 'We'll do it. I want to show Rex that I'm not as useless as he thinks.'

While the four remaining members of The Dead Hunters discussed the job, Sanchez became fascinated by the man Jasmine had been throwing peanuts at. He looked like he'd been in an accident and he had a lot of scratches on his face. But he had one eye open and seemed to be watching The Dead Hunters, listening into their conversations. He spotted Sanchez looking at him and closed his eye. Before Sanchez could mention it to the others, Beth came over to collect some empty bottles.

'Hi,' she said, speaking to the whole table. 'I don't know if Sanchez mentioned, but I'm Beth. I was wondering if anyone knew where JD is?'

Sanchez introduced her. 'This is Beth, the one I was just telling you about, if you know what I mean...'

Jasmine perked up. 'Are you his girlfriend?'

'Umm, yeah. Has mentioned me?'

'Err, no, but he doesn't talk a lot,' said Jasmine. 'And none of us has seen him in months.'

Elvis nudged Jasmine in the arm. 'I think it's time we made a move. It's getting late.'

Joey followed Elvis's lead. 'Yeah, we should get going too. Come on, Baby, let's go.'

To Sanchez's dismay, The Dead Hunters got up quickly and left The Tapioca, which he decided was Beth's fault. If she hadn't come over and started asking annoying questions everything would have been fine.

Within a minute of them leaving, the creepy guy at the next table got up too. As he was walking out of the bar, he took off his beany hat and wiped his chin with it. It finally became clear to Sanchez why the man was wearing the hat. He had an ugly C shaped scar on his forehead that he was probably self-conscious about.

Ten

Baby loved riding in Joey's yellow and red Ford Mustang, but by the time they arrived at the crossroads in The Devil's Graveyard she was tired and ready for a break from the road.

At the side of the crossroads, a young black man in a musty brown pin stripe suit and a fedora hat was sitting on a wooden rocking chair, playing a blues guitar. Joey pulled up next to him and Baby wound down the window so she could speak to the guitar player.

'Hi Jacko, how's it going?' she said with a smile.

'It's going how it goes,' said Jacko.

'Uh, okay. Can you let us through, please?'

'Drive right on in. He's expecting you.'

'Thanks. See ya.'

Joey took a right turn at the junction where at first there didn't seem to be a road, but as soon as the tyres hit the dirt it transformed into an asphalt and concrete highway that led to Purgatory and Scratch.

For the rest of the journey, Baby fretted about how Scratch would react to her being arrested. Her first solo mission hadn't exactly been a success, but it hadn't been a total disaster either, depending on how you looked at it. And she never knew how Scratch was going to perceive a situation. She had never seen him angry and had no idea if he *ever* lost his cool. On the whole he was a rather cold character with no visible feelings, except for occasional bouts of smugness. He had those in abundance.

As if picking up on her nervousness, Joey sought to reassure her. 'He's not going to be pissed at you, okay.'

'I know, I just didn't want to disappoint him.'

'You killed a guy, Baby. I doubt he'll be disappointed by that. I know I'm not.'

Purgatory appeared on the roadside up ahead. It looked like any other roadside bar as one approached it. The reality was much different.

Joey parked out front and they walked up to the entrance. Lucky for Baby, Joey could read her like a book. He stopped just outside the swing doors at the entrance and grabbed her. He pulled her in close and kissed her. It was a long, passionate kiss. Baby loved those moments. Feeling his body pressed against hers made her feel safe, even when she was in the middle of a desert that was rumoured to be populated by the souls of the dead.

Joey pulled away and looked into her eyes. 'You okay now?' he asked.

She had been in a trance ever since their lips touched. She looked into his eyes. For someone who killed a lot of people without mercy, he had kind eyes. When he wasn't wearing his mask, everything about Joey was normal. He had good skin, smooth short brown hair and soft lips. Just looking at him made her fears about meeting up with Scratch melt away. Almost.

'Yeah I'm fine. Let's go do this.'

Purgatory was a clean place, yet it had a very "lived in" look about it. It reminded Baby of a saloon bar from the Old West, only with a seriously unusual red glow all around the place.

Scratch was behind the bar, sitting on a stool, watching a TV on the far wall. He pointed a remote at it and switched it off as soon as he saw Joey and Baby. He broke out into a huge smile when he saw them walk in. The noticeable thing about a smile from Scratch was that his teeth were bright yellow from some angles and bright white from others. He opened a bottle of dark rum and poured them both a shot.

'How are you both?' he asked.

'Good, thanks,' said Baby.

The two of them took seats at the bar in front of Scratch. Baby looked at the glass of rum on the bar and tried to hide her disappointment at being given a drink she couldn't stand the taste of.

'You're worried because you were arrested,' Scratch said to her. 'You needn't be. You did good.'

'Told ya,' said Joey.

Baby breathed a sigh of relief. The approval of Scratch meant a lot to her. For the longest time she had felt like an outsider in The Dead Hunters. In particular, Rodeo Rex made her feel like a liability when she joined in on missions. Joey always watched out for her, and Jasmine was like a sister to her, but even so, the way to be accepted in this group was to kill. And kill well, and often. Baby hadn't done much of that, so killing the janitor at the hospital recently had boosted her self-confidence.

Scratch moved quickly to the matter in hand. 'Did Salvatore Rocco have the mark of Cain?' he asked.

'He had a C shaped scar like you described. And so did the janitor who killed him.'

'And then you killed the janitor?'

'Yes, and as soon as I shot him, this black shadow appeared, like it came out of him.'

'What did it do?'

'Nothing, it just vanished through a wall, like a ghost.'

'That's definitely Cain,' said Scratch.

Joey had quizzed Baby about it during their car ride and it was a surprise to discover that he was quite knowledgeable about The Bible, and history in general. He pressed Scratch for more information.

'Baby said Cain once possessed Julius Caesar. Is that true?'

'It is.'

'What was he doing?'

'He was in the early stages of trying to take over the world. It's the only time God ever saw fit to intervene. He sent the angel Gabriel down to earth to pass a dagger to a man named Brutus. Its blade was made from one of God's tears, shed when Cain committed the murder of Abel. The dagger is the only thing that can kill Cain, because it can pierce the heart of a spirit. But the best chance you have of stabbing a spirit is to do it while it's inside a person. Unfortunately when Brutus snuck up behind Caesar to stab him in the back, Cain saw him coming in a mirror and exited Caesar's body before the blade pierced his skin. So Julius Caesar died, but Cain escaped.'

'What happened to the dagger?'

Scratch pulled a thick cigar from inside his jacket and sucked on it, lighting it up. He blew a smoke-ring and then answered the question.

'God blamed Brutus for fucking up what should have been a simple task. So he sent his son Jesus down to earth to sort it out.'

Baby and Joey exchanged suspicious looks. And Joey who wasn't as polite as Baby, queried what Scratch was saying.

'Hold on, you're saying God sent Jesus down to earth to kill Cain? I thought it was....'

'To save mankind?'

'Yeah.'

'It was. Cain has been trying to destroy mankind for years. Shit, when Jesus was born, who do you think it was that made King Herod order the slaughter of all the new born kids?

'Cain?' said Baby.

'Fuck yeah it was Cain. He was inside Herod the whole time, overseeing the whole bloody mess.'

'I know that story,' said Joey. 'I read that when I was locked up in Grimwald's Asylum.'

'But you won't know what happened afterwards unless you've read the gospel of Susan.'

Baby had never taken much interest in religion before, but hearing Scratch's unique inside knowledge fascinated her.

'What's different about the gospel of Susan?' she asked.

Scratch took a puff on his cigar and then picked up Baby's glass of rum and drank it to wash down the taste of the smoke.

'The gospel of Susan was written by one of Jesus's earlier disciples. It recounts the tale of the missing years when he was in his twenties. During that time, Jesus acquired the Brutus Dagger, and then with his first group of disciples he went hunting for Cain. They tracked him down in the undiscovered country, which is now known as America.'

'This sounds like you're making it up,' said Joey.

'Does it sound any dafter than Moses parting the Red Sea?'

'I suppose not.'

'Right, so shut up and listen. Jesus and his disciples found America in a state of disarray. It was ruled by four elders, who had lived long enough to master the dark arts and become immortals. They used their demonic powers to destroy the entire human population of America. It's why God doesn't let many people live past a hundred anymore. These four immortals remained eternally youthful by sucking the souls out of other people. And because they were a bunch of sick fuckers, they would bring their victims back to life as undead slaves, called ghouls. But when Jesus and his buddies showed up looking for Cain, they wiped out the ghouls and imprisoned the four immortals in a cell deep underground. Those four immortals are only briefly mentioned in the other gospels.'

'I know this,' said Joey. 'It's the Four Horsemen of the Apocalypse, isn't it?'

Scratch pointed at him. 'That's right. Which is why he didn't kill them. God thought they could prove useful at a later time.'

'And what happened to Cain?' said Baby.

'Nothing. They never found him. He totally went to ground. So God ordered Jesus back to Nazareth and, well, you know the rest.'

'So what's Cain been doing since then?' Baby asked.

Scratch picked up Joey's glass of rum, which hadn't been touched either, and polished it off. Then he took another puff on his cigar and blew out a smoke monkey.

'I guess he's been plotting something,' he said. 'It's odd that he's resurfaced again after all this time.'

'So what are you gonna do?' asked Joey.

'I'll do some digging around, see if I can find out what made him take over Salvatore Rocco's mind and go to the Riverdale Mansion.'

Baby nudged Joey and gave him a look, which she hoped he would understand. And because he was the most awesome boyfriend in the world, he knew immediately what she meant.

'There's one other thing,' said Joey. 'We've got this other job that's come our way, hunting a Cyclops or something in a forest in a town called Oakfield.'

'Oakfield?' Scratch frowned. 'Is that on Blue Corn Island?'

'Yeah, that's it,' said Joey.

Scratch took his hat off and scratched his head. 'That's weird,' he said.

'Why?'

'Oakfield is where Jesus landed when he arrived in America. It was the only place uninhabited by ghouls at that time. Nowadays it's an Amish community, bunch of crazy fruitcakes those lot are. *But,* and this is very weird, they're the only people in the world who acknowledge the existence of the gospel of Susan. They base practically their whole interpretation of faith around it.'

'That's a bit of a coincidence, isn't it?' said Baby.

Scratch shook his head. 'There are no coincidences.'

Baby didn't have a fucking clue what that meant. Scratch was acting really strange, even by his standards.

'Who gave you this job in Oakfield?' he asked.

'A fat bartender in a bar in Santa Mondega,' said Joey.

Scratch raised his eyebrows. 'Sanchez?'

'You know him?'

Scratch smiled for the first time in a while. 'I fuckin' love that guy.'

'What?' said Joey.

'Never mind, it's a long story. Where did Sanchez hear about this Oakfield job?'

Joey reached into his jacket pocket and handed Scratch the slip of paper with the mission details on it and the map Sanchez had given them. Scratch unfolded the paper and read the unhelpful details Sanchez had written on it. His smile broadened as he read it. Eventually he handed it back to Joey.

'Take the job,' he said. 'But on one condition.'

'What's that?' said Joey.

'The Brutus Dagger. It's believed Jesus hid it in America where Cain would never find it. Archaeologists used to believe it was hidden somewhere on Blue Corn Island, but no one ever found it, or even came close. So while you're there, ask this Bishop Yoder if he knows anything about it. He'll have met a few of these archaeologists in his time, so find out what he learned from them. It might be useful. And if you feel like it will help, threaten to kill him. Bishops tend to be real pussies, so he'll tell you everything he knows if he thinks you're gonna kill him.'

Eleven

When Cain arrived back at the Riverdale Mansion he had ditched the body of Rupert Galloway. Galloway's body had eventually expired, the cause of death being a peanut allergy of all things. The new body that Cain had taken control of was a healthier male specimen that would last much longer.

Riverdale was a very different place to when he'd left it. As he wandered the halls and corridors looking for the Four Horsemen, he discovered that the handful of staff that worked within the grounds of the mansion had all been turned into ghouls. Cain wasn't a big fan of ghouls. They were useful slaves for an undead army but they had no conversation skills and only ever did what the Four Horsemen told them to. Fortunately their undead instincts meant that they could see that the new human body walking among them was under Cain's control, so they left him alone.

Cain found Zitrone in a gentleman's smoking room at the rear of the building. The blond immortal was sitting on his own, in a red leather chair, watching television. He had acquired some clothes, although not the kind Cain would have liked. He'd found a yellow tunic and tied some rope around the waist as a belt. And he was wearing some brown leather boots. It was a look that Zitrone was familiar with from his time on earth before his imprisonment. Now it just looked camp. So very, very camp.

'Zitrone, I'm back,' said Cain, approaching him.

Zitrone took his eyes off the television and looked around. 'Cain! What's with the new body?'

'It's a long story, I'll explain it later.'

'Fair enough. Have you seen this television?' said Zitrone, turning away again. 'It's amazing. Moving pictures on a screen. What a creation.'

'Yes. Lots of things have changed. Clothes have changed a lot too.'

Zitrone stood up. 'Yes, we've seen. I found this yellow tunic. Yesil has a green one, Blanco a white one and Ash has a black one. They match our hair colours!'

'Yes, I can see the colour connection, thank you. Is Linda Murdoch still here?'

'Ash killed her, so Yesil turned her into a ghoul.'

'Did she teach you all the things on the list I gave her?'

'Yes, she was useful. She gave us some history books to read and then introduced us to television. This stuff is fascinating. After all those years imprisoned below ground it was refreshing to learn so many new things in such a short time.'

'Where are the others?'

'They've found something called a PlayStation. I can't get them away from it.'

Cain silently cursed the other Horsemen and the bloody PlayStation and its stupid addictive games. 'Did Murdoch teach you about new forms of travel and cellphones? That stuff is vital if you're going to blend in.'

'True dat, true dat, we learned that shit real quick. It was dope.'

'What?' Cain looked up at the television. 'What's this you're watching?'

'The Wire.'

Cain picked up a remote control from a coffee table by Zitrone's chair and switched the television off. 'All right, listen,' he said. 'Just don't talk like the people in that show.'

'But it's a good show,' said Zitrone.

'I know, but you'll sound stupid.'

'Why?'

'Because you're not black.'

Zitrone perched his butt on the arm of the red leather chair. 'Chill out, man. It's all good.'

Cain clenched his fists. 'Look, forget that for now. I've found The Dead Hunters. I followed them and listened into their conversations for a while. I found out everything we needed to know.'

'So you know where the gateway is?' Zitrone asked.

'I do.'

'And the Bourbon Kid?'

'He's not the only one you know. There's six of them.'

'I don't give a shit about the other five. I want the one with Christ's blood, and so do the others. Ash is practically tearing his own face off, he's so desperate to get this punkass motherfucker.'

'Seriously, don't talk like that. It's annoying.'

Zitrone stood up again and got right in Cain's face. 'You said we could kill the Bourbon Kid. You promised! I want God to see us tear this man apart and spread his blood all over the earth.'

'I'm not sure God's going to care. This Bourbon Kid's no angel.'

'I don't care.'

'All right, calm down. You will have him. I have arranged it.'

Zitrone's eyes lit up. 'You have?'

'Yes, what do you think I was doing all this time?' Cain said, irritation creeping into his voice. 'Now listen, tomorrow is Halloween.

In the morning I will take all four of you down to the coast where I've acquired an old wooden galley ship for you. It's not ideal, but I know your stupid ghoul people will be able to row it for you. You'll take the ship and set sail for Santa Mondega. At midnight tomorrow, a woman called Beth will show up at the end of the pier in the Santa Mondega harbour. She is the Bourbon Kid's girlfriend. She waits there for him every Halloween at midnight.'

'Does *he* show up?'

'Sometimes. And if he does, you can kill him.'

'But what if he doesn't show? The journey is a waste of time.'

'If he doesn't show, you kill his girlfriend. Because then he'll come looking for *you*.'

A smile broke out on Zitrone's face. 'It's evil,' he sneered. 'I like it.'

'Good. And while you're in Santa Mondega, there's something else you have to do.'

'Name it.'

'Go to a bar called The Tapioca. There is a fat Mexican bartender running the place. Take him prisoner.'

'What for?'

'He knows where to find Scratch. Threaten him with any sort of violence and he'll do anything you command, so make him take you to The Devil's Graveyard. There's some kind of secret entrance there that will lead us to Scratch. I'll meet up with you when you get there.'

'You're not coming with us?'

'No.'

'Why not?'

'I'm going to orchestrate the deaths of the other five Dead Hunters.'

Twelve

Elvis had been happy acting as Jasmine's chauffeur, particularly in recent times, but he recognised that she needed some independence. And she was adamant that she needed a DeLorean. After two days of searching, Elvis had found one for sale on a speciality car website. So all he had to do was drive her to it in one of his banged up old Cadillacs and work out how the hell he was going to pay for it when he had no money.

The DeLorean was owned by some oddball named Grover, who lived at the top of a privately owned mountain called Mount Dracula. On the phone, Grover had agreed to knock five hundred bucks off the price in exchange for Elvis's old Cadillac. Elvis hadn't mentioned that he'd recently crashed the Caddy into a pylon and jizzed all over the dashboard. Because let's face it, if he'd told Grover that, the deal would probably have ended right there.

The old pink Cadillac had just enough muscle left in it to make the trip. The last part of the journey involved driving round and round Mount Dracula on a long, winding road that went all the way to the top like a Helter Skelter.

When they reached the summit there were small puffs of smoke filtering out of the Cadillac's engine, but it was still going, chugging and lurching its way to their destination. And what a destination it was. Grover lived in a castle, which was the only building situated at the top of the mountain. It had a bunch of used cars parked out front. The place was in serious need of a paint job, unless you liked living in a castle that was almost entirely black, with windows that had never been cleaned.

Elvis swung the Cadillac into the driveway and parked up by the front entrance.

'This is the place,' he said. 'Creepy as fuck isn't it?'

'I like it,' said Jasmine. 'It looks like the sort of place Skeletor would live in.'

She leaned over and kissed Elvis on the cheek, then jumped out of the car. She ran up towards the castle entrance, which at first glance looked like an enormous wooden door. But as she approached it, it started coming down towards her, lowered down by chains. It was actually a drawbridge, which was weird because there was no moat or ditch surrounding the castle. When the drawbridge touched down, a man sauntered out of the castle and walked across it to greet them. He was wearing blue dungarees and a red baseball cap with tufts of grey hair poking out of the sides. A thick cigar hung out of the corner of his mouth. It was unlit and he seemed to be chewing on it.

'You must be Grover,' Jasmine said, reaching out for a handshake. 'Nice to meet you.'

Grover nodded and shook her hand. But he said nothing.

Elvis rocked up behind Jasmine. 'Hey man,' he said. 'We've come about the DeLorean.'

Grover looked him up and down. Elvis was wearing a blue suit with brown shoes and the sunglasses that he never took off.

'I'm guessing you're Elvis,' said Grover.

'That's right.'

'And this is?' he said, eyeing up Jasmine.

'I'm his daughter,' said Jasmine.

Grover took a good look at her. She was wearing blue jeans, cut off at the knee and a white sleeveless crop top. She'd promised Elvis she would bend and stretch a lot in front of Grover in an attempt to help drive down the price of the car.

'You still okay to give me five hundred bucks for my Caddy over there,' said Elvis, pointing at the Cadillac.

Grover probably wanted to take a look at the Caddy, but he couldn't take his eyes off of Jasmine. She was stretching as if she was tired from the journey, so he was fixated on her body, watching her every move, with his top lip curling up into an aggressive, predatory sneer.

Elvis took the non-response as a yes. 'So it's a deal then, five hundred for the Caddy?' he said.

Grover nodded and made some kind of grunting noise, but didn't take his eyes off Jasmine.

Jasmine wiggled her hips to some imaginary music. 'Can we see the DeLorean now, please?' she asked Grover, who seemed hypnotised by her moves.

'Uh. Yeah.'

Grover stepped off his drawbridge and led them around the side of the castle to a backyard that was full of scrap vehicles, most of which were best described as "dogshit". Elvis could see no sign of a DeLorean. But Grover pointed to a fucked up old garage with a metal shutter gate on it at the back of the parking lot.

'It's in there,' he said.

Jasmine happily skipped alongside Grover, while Elvis hung back and looked around. The cars in the parking lot all looked like they had been in accidents. None of them had a price tag on them either.

Grover unlocked the metal shutter gate at the front of the garage and it sprung up revealing what lay inside. There it was, a shiny silver

DeLorean. As soon as Jasmine saw it she went giddy and had to put her hand on Grover's shoulder to steady herself.

'Wow!' she gasped, open-mouthed. 'Does it have a flux capacitor?'

'I put one in myself,' said Grover. 'It's on the back seat. Take a look.'

Elvis stayed with Grover while Jasmine bounded over to the car to inspect it. The two men stood side by side, watching goggle-eyed as she bent down to peer through the windows at the inside of the car.

'Elvis you should take a look at this!' she yelled. 'It's awesome.'

Grover took his cigar out of his mouth and smiled a gappy smile at Elvis. 'That daughter o' yours sure does have a purdy mouth,' he said.

'Yeah,' said Elvis. 'She's got a nice ass too. But if you stare at it for too long you get a broken nose and lose consciousness.'

'Riiiiii-ght.'

Jasmine bounded over to them. 'I love it. Can we take it?'

Grover reached into his dungarees and pulled out a set of keys. He handed them to Jasmine. 'Why don't you take it for a test drive?' he said. 'Me and your dad will work out a fair price.'

Jasmine ran around to the driver's side and flicked open the door, which opened upwards and made a cool hissing sound. She hopped in, started up the engine, and reversed the DeLorean out of the workshop into the yard with all the dogshit cars.

Elvis recognised that the time had come to work out an agreement with Grover for the purchase of the DeLorean. This was going to be messy because Elvis was kinda broke.

Grover tapped some cigar ash at Elvis's feet. 'You got the fifty thousand dollars?' he asked.

'Yep. Is cash okay?'

'Cash'll do fine,' said Grover, staring out into the yard at Jasmine who was attempting to reverse the DeLorean between two cars.

'Money's in my boot,' said Elvis.

'You got fifty grand in your boot?' said Grover, scratching his head and looking down at Elvis's feet.

'Nope.'

Elvis hit Grover with an uppercut punch to the chin. There was a horrible tinny sound as the car salesman's five teeth banged together. It was a good clean punch. Elvis was pleased with it. He contemplated if a second punch was necessary but when he saw Grover go cross-eyed, he knew the job was done. The old man's cigar dropped out of his mouth, he wobbled, then started to go down. Elvis caught him before he hit the ground and gently laid him out on his back. Jasmine was still reversing the car, so while she wasn't looking, Elvis pulled a small metal pin badge from his jacket pocket. He pinned it to the front of Grover's overalls and then sifted through the unconscious man's pockets. He found fifty bucks and a pack of chewing gum.

When he looked back up, the door in the DeLorean was open and Jasmine was running towards him. 'What happened?' she asked, looking down at Grover. 'Did you hit him?'

'Of course I did.'

'But he seemed so nice.'

Elvis kicked Grover gently in the ribs. *'Nice?'* he said. 'I don't think so. This asshole was a paedophile.'

Jasmine's jaw dropped. 'How do you know that?'

'Look at the badge on his shirt.'

Jasmine looked closer at Grover and saw the metal badge pinned to the breast pocket of his dungarees. There were three words written on it in gold lettering.

BOY SCOUT LEADER

She stepped back, and covered her mouth, to stop herself from throwing up. 'Oh my God,' she gasped.

'Terrible isn't it?' said Elvis.

Jasmine kicked Grover in the ribs and spat on him. 'What a sicko!'

'Yeah.' Elvis pulled her away from Grover. 'So shall we take your new car for a spin?'

The roar of a powerful motorcycle drowned out Jasmine's response. Elvis looked around and saw Rodeo Rex cruising towards them on a new Harley Davidson. He parked it next to a row of dogshit cars and climbed off. As usual, he wasn't wearing a helmet, preferring instead to wear a black headband. He seemed to have updated his image a bit too, because his jeans were ripped at the knees, and he was wearing a bright white leather waistcoat.

'What the hell happened here?' he said, looking at the unconscious body of Grover.

Jasmine ripped the "Boy scout leader" badge from Grover's dungarees and threw it to Rex.

'Does that answer your question?' she said.

Rex looked at the badge and shook his head. 'That's disgusting.'

Elvis nodded at Rex's Harley. 'Is that a new bike?' he asked.

'Uh, yeah, you like it?' said Rex.

'I think it's cool,' said Jasmine. 'But not as cool as my new car. Look, Elvis got me the DeLorean!'

Rex walked over to the DeLorean and ran his hand over the hood. 'That's pretty fuckin' cool,' he said. 'Can I take a look at the engine?'

'Sure,' said Jasmine. She jumped back into the car and looked for a switch to flip open the hood. After turning on the headlights and windscreen wipers she eventually managed to find the correct switch. Rex lifted the hood and started poking around.

Elvis looked over Rex's shoulder at the engine. Everything seemed to be in order. It was all very clean anyway.

Rex was poking around at something low down, but couldn't quite get to it. He looked up at Elvis. 'Can you step back a bit, you're blocking out the sun,' he said.

Elvis stepped back out of the way, even though he wasn't convinced that he was casting a shadow over the engine. Jasmine climbed out of the driver's seat and came to join him.

'Is it okay?' she asked.

Rex poked around under the hood some more, pulling at things and tutting. 'You've got some loose spark plugs in here,' he said. 'And the engine needs a clean. Why don't you two make yourselves useful and see if you can find some oil for me? And a cloth. I'll have this engine looking good as new in no time.'

'Can you check to see if the flux capacitor is still working too?' Jasmine asked.

Rex frowned. 'Huh?'

Elvis tapped Rex on the shoulder. 'There's one on the back seat. It's like the one in *Back To the Future*. Jasmine's hoping that it does something cool when the car hits eighty-eight.'

'Oh, right,' said Rex, sounding like he understood. 'I'll look at it, but the only way you'll really know if it works is to hit eighty-eight miles per hour in it, like they did in the movie.'

Jasmine slapped Elvis on the arm. 'See. I bet you five bucks something happens when we hit eighty-eight.'

'We won't travel back in time,' said Elvis. 'I can guarantee that.'

'We'll see.'

Rex glared at them. 'Would you just go and get me the stuff I asked for?'

Elvis peered over his sunglasses at Jasmine. He could tell she was thinking the same thing as him. Rex was in a mood again, which meant it was best to leave him be.

'Come on,' said Elvis. 'Let's go find some oil. With any luck this paedo might have a stash of money in his garage.'

Grover's garage was full of junk. But Elvis did find an old biscuit tin with two hundred bucks in it. Jasmine found a rag and an old can of oil. And a photo of a young boy, which Elvis convinced her was further confirmation that Grover was a pervert.

When they returned to the car, Rex had finished giving it a quick health check. He slammed the hood down and wiped his sweaty hands on his jeans.

'It's all good,' he said. 'I won't need that oil after all. And I think that Flux Capacitor is in full working order too.'

Jasmine ran over to him and planted a kiss on his cheek. 'Thanks Rex, you're a star!'

Rex slid his hands around her waist and was just about to squeeze her ass, when she pulled away. She took two steps back.

'Holy fuck!' she announced. 'You've got normal hands!'

Elvis couldn't believe he hadn't noticed it before, but Rex was no longer wearing a glove on his right hand. And the reason was plain to see. His magnetic metal hand was gone, replaced by a fully functional human hand.

Rex held his hands up. 'Yeah. I had my transplant done. Look, it works perfectly.'

'That's great, man,' said Elvis. He walked over to Rex and took a hold of his new human hand. It felt perfectly normal. 'Wow, I can't believe how real that feels. When did you get it done?'

'Yesterday, while I was in Canada.'

'That was quick! And it works okay?'

'You better believe it,' said Rex. 'It's flesh and bone, just like yours.'

Jasmine clapped her hands. 'Have you jerked off with it yet?'

'What? No. Why would you ask that?'

'I bet you can't wait to feel a woman with it!'

'Eh? Er, yeah, I... I guess so.'

Elvis felt the need to intervene because Rex didn't seem to be getting Jasmine's sense of humour. 'Why don't we all go for some food and beers to celebrate?'

'Sounds good,' said Rex. 'I'll tell you what, I'll race you down the mountain. Bike versus DeLorean. Loser buys the first round of drinks!'

'Oh, you're on!' said Jasmine.

Elvis looked across at the horizon. They were a mile high at the top of a mountain with dangerous winding roads. 'I'm not sure that's a good idea,' he said.

Rex and Jasmine took no notice of him. Rex hot-footed it over to his bike, while Jasmine slid over the hood of the DeLorean to get to the driver's side quicker.

'See you at the bottom,' said Rex, revving the engine on his bike.

Before Elvis could say, *'Hold on a minute, this is a fucking shit idea!'* Jasmine was buckled into the driver's seat in her new DeLorean.

The door on the passenger side fizzed and then opened upwards, so with great reluctance, Elvis climbed in and pulled it shut.

'Buckle yourself in,' said Jasmine. 'We're going *back to the future!*'

Elvis buckled up immediately. 'Just drive careful, Jas, these mountain roads are dangerous.'

'Don't be such a wimp,' she replied, revving the engine.

Rex pulled up alongside them on his Harley and shouted over the roar of the engines. 'There's a diner at the bottom of the mountain. I'll wait for you there!'

Jasmine wound her window down and shouted back. 'What did you say?'

'I said, there's a…..'

VROOOM!

Jasmine floored the accelerator and the DeLorean sped off, flicking a wave of dirt into Rex's face as they left him behind.

'This is gonna be awesome!' she grinned.

'Don't go too fast yet,' said Elvis. 'The bends on this road are dangerous, and the drop is big.'

His words fell on deaf ears. Jasmine sped out onto the road, hitting fifty miles per hour by the time they reached the first bend.

Thirteen

The echo of the Mustang's engine whine seemed out of place in the silent, serene surroundings of Oakfield's Amish community. Baby and Joey were approaching the church, their car bouncing over the bumpy dirt track. Baby noticed an older gentleman dressed all in black with grey, unkempt hair and a fluffy grey neck beard standing outside the church entrance. It had to be Bishop Yoder, because he looked exactly how she imagined.

She saw him look up at them at the sound of the car. He visibly stiffened before rushing towards them, his eyes darting back and forth across the street. He directed them round to the back of the church where they parked up out of sight of the road. Baby got the feeling that the Bishop didn't want the villagers to see them.

They followed Bishop Yoder through a back door and into his private office. It was a small room with most of the wall space taken up by bookshelves. In the centre was a small desk with a couple of rather functional wooden chairs in front of it. Yoder poured them each a cup of warm water from a flask before sitting down and gesturing for them to sit on the wooden chairs.

Baby took one sip of the water. It tasted like it had come from a puddle. She saw Joey turn his nose up at it after he took a sip too. They exchanged a knowing look and put their cups back down on Yoder's desk.

'That taste's like shit,' said Joey.

'Oh, umm, sorry,' said Yoder. 'It's probably a little warm for your taste.'

Baby and Joey didn't respond. An awkward silence fell.

Bishop Yoder cleared his throat. 'So, you are The Dead Hunters?'

Joey nodded, visibly relaxing now that they could get down to business. 'You've got something you want us to kill, correct?'

'Yes. You must have seen the Black Forest on your way here.'

'Was it that big area of land with loads of trees?' said Joey.

Baby elbowed him in the ribs. 'We did see it,' she confirmed.

Yoder looked confused, but carried on regardless. 'That's where the monster resides. It comes every year in October. Usually we don't see it, but we hear loud roars from time to time. It sounds like a bear, a really big one.'

'Can you do an impression of it?' asked Joey.

'What?'

'Don't worry,' said Baby, who was considering elbowing Joey in the ribs again. 'I know what a bear sounds like.'

Yoder rubbed his forehead and took a sip of water before continuing. 'Well, you see, every year we lose a number of our brothers and sisters to that monster. It seems that no matter how much we warn people not to go into that forest, every year someone does. And when it's a child that goes missing, there is the inevitability of the parents going looking for it. And so far, no one has ever gone into that forest during the Fall and come out alive.'

'What about the rest of the year?' Baby asked.

'No one particularly goes in then either. The forest is haunted by the ghosts of the brothers and sisters we've lost to it. Some go back hundreds of years.'

There was an obvious question to be asked, so Baby asked it. 'Has no one ever informed the police about this?'

Yoder winced and closed his eyes. He rubbed his head with both hands and without realising it he flicked a heck of a lot of dandruff over his desk. Eventually he opened his eyes again and clasped his hands together.

'There's a police force in Crimson County on the other side of the island,' he said, frustration creeping into his voice. 'We always report missing persons to them, but they won't go into the forest either. I suspect they also have lost many of their brothers and sisters. And even though we do report the missing people to the police, our religion forbids us from seeking the help of outsiders.'

'We're outsiders,' Joey reminded him.

'Yes you are,' Yoder agreed. 'But right now, this isn't the village you're speaking to. This is just me. And I'm at the end of my tether.'

Yoder reached into a drawer on his desk and pulled out a red hardback book. He showed it to them. The title of the book was, *"The Gospel according to Susan"*.

'I've read this book from cover to cover, more than a thousand times,' he said. 'In chapter forty, Susan writes about a prophecy. The prophecy predicts that on one day during the Fall, three northern stars will fall from the sky, and it will signal the start of the second coming of Christ. When Christ returns he will slay the evil that blights us, and so much blood will be spilled that the clouds will fill with it, and rain it back down upon us.'

Yoder stopped talking and looked at Baby and Joey, like he was expecting them to say they knew what he was talking about.

'That's a nice story,' said Joey.

'You've not heard it before?' said Yoder.

'Nope.'

'We have heard of the gospel of Susan though,' Baby added.

Yoder looked disappointed. 'Well, during our St Michael's Day celebrations earlier this month, three stars fell from the sky. The whole village was excited, expecting something dramatic to happen. But the only thing that's happened in the time since is that four children from our village have gone missing. No chosen one, no Messiah, no saviour has showed up. The people are angry and are beginning to doubt the gospel of Susan. So out of desperation, I came to find you. I don't want the people of the village to know why you're here. I just want you to kill that Cyclops and leave its corpse where the people will see it, so that I can convince them that Christ showed up and saved them, just like the prophecy predicts.'

Baby felt sympathy for Yoder's plight. She reached over and stroked Joey's arm. 'I think we can help here,' she said. 'I like what the Bishop is trying to do. I think it's noble.'

'Okay,' said Joey. 'We'll take the job. How much are you gonna pay us?'

Yoder grimaced. 'We don't really use money,' he said. 'I have about five hundred dollars. But I was thinking we could give you two horses and a cow if you get the job done.'

'Two horses and a cow?'

Baby almost laughed out loud. She knew Joey wouldn't be impressed by the Bishop's offer, so she moved the conversation on before Joey called him a name beginning with 'c'.

'There's actually something else we'd take instead of money,' she said. 'Do you know about the Brutus Dagger?'

Yoder looked surprised. 'The Brutus Dagger?'

'Yes, it's the dagger that Brutus....'

'I know what it is,' Yoder interrupted. 'It's the dagger that killed Julius Caesar.'

'We were told it might be on this island.'

Yoder seemed to hesitate before responding. 'It might be,' he said. He reached into his desk drawer again and pulled out a small brown leather-cased book. 'This is a journal that my father gave to me. It contains a series of what are believed to be clues that lead to the location of the Brutus Dagger.'

'Your father wrote it?' Baby queried.

'No. It was given to him by my grandfather, who retrieved it from an archaeologist he met almost a hundred years ago.' Yoder held the book up. 'I will happily give you this, if you eliminate the evil in the forest.'

Before Joey could make a crack about anything being better than horses and cows, Baby said, 'Yes, that would be fine. What sort of clues are in it?'

Yoder looked relieved and smiled at Baby before opening the book at the front page. 'I think this book has been in the wars a little,' he said. 'Many of the pages are indecipherable because the book has obviously gotten wet a few times. From what I can tell the author's name was Diana Jones, although you'll see here there's a lot of smudging just before her first name, but I think it's just supposed to say I'm Diana Jones.'

Baby looked at the author's name. It was smudged and Diana wasn't spelled with a capital D.

'So who was she?' she asked.

'She was a very impressive archaeologist. Her journal contains maps and clues for a number of other religious artefacts.' He skipped to half way through the book until he found the page he was looking for. 'Here it is,' he said, running his finger down the page. 'According to Diana Jones, the location of the Brutus Dagger lies with the Roman that followed Jason.'

'Who's the Roman that followed Jason?' Baby asked.

'No one knows,' said Yoder with a shrug of his shoulders. 'The obvious guess would be someone like Julius Caesar, or Augustus.'

'All right,' said Joey. 'Who's Jason then?'

Yoder held his hands up. 'Your guess is as good as mine. But if you can get rid of that Cyclops for me, this book is all yours.'

'You've got yourself a deal,' said Joey. 'We'll take care of your one eyed monster in the forest and when we get back, you can give us the book.' He stood up and opened his jacket, revealing a pair of semi automatic pistols he had strapped to him. 'You know, if your people used guns instead of prayer, this problem would have been sorted years ago.'

'Oh, bless you,' said Yoder. 'Will you be able to do it today? Because it is the last day of October according to the Julian calendar and I believe it is considered to be the most evil day of the year.'

'You mean Halloween,' said Baby.

'That's right, yes.'

'What the fuck is the Julian calendar?' said Joey.

Baby knew the answer to that one and piped up before Yoder could. 'It's the twelve month calendar created by Julius Caesar.'

'That's correct,' said Yoder. 'And the month of July was named after him.'

'Well that's rubbish,' said Joey. 'His name was Julius not July, or Julian for that matter.'

Baby got up from her seat and tugged at Joey's jacket collar. 'Let's get some rest before we go and kill the Cyclops. I think you're getting tired.'

'That's a good idea,' said Yoder. 'I'd prefer it if you did this job tonight when no one is around, because I don't want the villagers to see you go up to the forest. I plan to tell them you were travelling sales people.'

'That suits us,' said Joey. 'It'll be easier to hunt this thing at night anyway. You never know, if we're lucky it'll be asleep.'

Fourteen

'Fucking Hell Jasmine, slow down!'

Elvis liked driving fast, but only when *he* was the driver. As a passenger, high speed driving didn't appeal to him nearly as much. He'd never seen Jasmine drive a car before and it hadn't previously occurred to him to ask her if she even knew how.

'Don't be such a pussy!' Jasmine whooped.

She swung the car round another bend in the road. Mount Dracula was suddenly as scary as it sounded. There were hardly any stretches of straight road, just one long bend that never seemed to end. The only thing between them and a half-mile drop was a flimsy metal railing that ran around the roadside. It was low enough that a toddler could step over it, and the only thing supporting it was a bunch of rickety wooden posts.

The digital readout on the dashboard showed that they were travelling at 82 miles per hour. Elvis had both hands pressed hard against the dashboard, turning his knuckles white. Every time the number on the readout went up, so did Elvis's blood pressure.

'Can you see Rex anywhere?' Jasmine asked.

'Seriously Jaz, fuckin' slow down!'

'I just want to see what happens when we hit eighty-eight!'

'We won't travel back in time, I can tell you that.'

'I want to see what the Flux Capacitor does.'

'It won't do anything. At best it will light up or make a noise. Can't you just wait until we're on a fucking straight bit of highway in the desert? Or anywhere other than on a fucking mountain?'

'How fast are we going now?' Jasmine asked, fighting with the steering wheel as they zipped around another blind corner.

'Eighty-five, *Christ!*'

'Any sign of Rex?'

'Are you nuts? He'll be miles back.'

'Whaaa-hooo!'

Elvis had died once before in his life. But at least that time he'd already made a deal with the Devil to bring him back. If Jasmine got them both killed with her reckless driving it would be the end of them both. He was starting to wish he'd either kept his busted up old Cadillac, or hitched a ride on the back of Rex's Harley.

'Are there airbags in this thing?' he asked.

'Airbags?' Jasmine mocked. 'We don't need airbags where *we're going!*'

'And where *are* we going? *Over the cliff?*'

A brown station wagon came around the bend towards them. An old man behind the wheel probably came close to shitting himself. Elvis certainly did. His life flashed before his eyes. Fortunately, Jasmine had great reactions, so she swerved around the station wagon, missing it by inches. Elvis made the sign of the cross over his chest, not that he expected it to help much, but it took his mind off the horrors of Jasmine's driving for a few seconds, if nothing else.

'Have we hit eighty-eight yet?' Jasmine hollered.

The digital readout on the dashboard was switching between eighty-five and eighty-six miles per hour. Elvis's eyes were drawn to a different readout, which contained the dates for time travel. The "current date" and "destination date" were both the same.

'Jaz, the destination date is the same as today's date. So even if you do hit *eighty-eight*, we're not going to travel through time. So slow down, let's do this later!'

Telling her *that* was one of the dumbest things Elvis could have done. Jasmine took her eyes off the road and pressed a few buttons on the readout to change the destination date.

'JAZ! LOOK OUT!'

They were perilously close to the roadside and more importantly the cliff edge. Jasmine looked up and swerved just in the nick of time, but in doing so she overcorrected and the car skidded out of control.

She screamed, 'FUCK!!!'

'SLOW DOWN!'

'I CAN'T, THE BRAKES AREN'T WORKING!!!'

Jasmine was kicking down hard on the brake pedal but nothing was happening.

'They worked when you test drove it, didn't they?' Elvis inquired, panic flooding into his voice as the car swerved wildly around the road.

'They did. But they're fucked now!'

Elvis tried to think of a way to stop the car without brakes. The only thing that came to mind was trying to scrape the car along the mountain side of the road. But at the speed they were travelling even that was a dumb idea. Jasmine was struggling to even control the steering wheel. They needed a miracle.

On the plus side, they did hit 88 mph. But by that time they were on the wrong side of the road. Jasmine kept slamming her foot down on the brake like it was a foot pump. But no matter how many times she hit it, the car didn't slow down.

The steering wheel spun around in her hands and the DeLorean hurtled towards the cliff edge. The front of the car smashed into the metal railing at the side of the road. And from that moment on it wasn't possible to know exactly what happened. The back end of the car rose up into the air and overtook the front end as the car turned upside down in mid air.

Elvis saw flashes of the sky and the road which was becoming further away each second.

And then the road was gone. The DeLorean disappeared over the edge of the cliff, turning somersaults as it went. Jasmine grabbed Elvis's hand and squeezed it tight. He squeezed back. And down they went.

Fifteen

The time was edging closer to midnight on Halloween, and the only light was coming from the half moon in the sky above the Black Forest.

Baby and Joey reached the top of the hill in Oakfield and stopped in front of the first row of trees at the forest's edge. The air was still and barely a leaf flickered. Joey slipped his yellow skull mask over his head. Baby watched him adjust it so that he could see clearly through the eyeholes. Both he and Baby were dressed entirely in black, in order to stay concealed in the dark. Baby had used boot polish to blacken up her face, which made her feel like a badass. The only thing giving them away was Joey's mask, the yellow face and red stipe of hair on the top stood out, but as he'd pointed out to her, even a Cyclops would shit itself when it saw a mask like that in the dead of night.

'Stay close to me,' Joey said, putting his arm around her shoulder. 'This isn't a low budget horror movie, so there's absolutely no excuse for us to split up. Whatever is in here, we're better off together.'

'Don't worry, the last thing I'll be doing is wandering off.'

'Good. You ready?'

Baby was almost ready, but not quite. 'Are you listening to any music under that mask?' she asked.

'No, too dangerous. We'll need our ears as well as our eyes in here.'

Baby was surprised because normally Joey listened to music when he killed people. If there was no music playing nearby he would wear headphones underneath his mask and listen to something murderous. It reminded him of his childhood and the horrible moment when he'd witnessed his parents being murdered. He'd been hiding in a closet, sheltered away from the violence, listening to *Silent Night* through a pair of headphones. The music was meant to keep him calm to help him get through the event as unscathed as possible. It hadn't worked.

Baby had a gun strapped on one thigh, a pair of ammo clips on another and a smoke grenade and a hunting knife on her belt. Joey was similarly strapped up with weapons, and he probably had a lot more hidden beneath his jacket. The two of them were as safe, and as prepared, as they could possibly be.

'You okay?' Joey asked. He could always tell when Baby was worried. It was one of the things she loved about him.

'I was just thinking about what Father Yoder said.'

'About no one ever coming out of here alive?'

'Yeah.'

'You can go back if you want. I can take care of this without you. It's okay.'

Baby shoved him in the back. 'You mean split up? After what you just said about low budget horror movies? No way!'

'Good. So let's go. Let's be the first people to go in, and come back out alive.'

Joey led the way, past the first row of trees and into the forest. The air became noticeably thicker, sticking to Baby's throat and making her nose itch. The forest was every bit as creepy as she expected. Every black expanse between the trees looked like it was moving. They weren't far in when the moon vanished from sight, concealed behind a stand of trees that stretched higher than she'd ever seen.

She felt a twig snap beneath her feet. It sounded deafening to Baby's ears in the unnatural muffled silence of the forest. Joey somehow moved silently like a cat, never treading on anything that made a noise. Nothing seemed to surprise him either, not even when Baby snapped another twig right behind him. He had told her before that it came down to experience. In time, she too would be able to zone out the irrelevant noises and focus only on the sounds that didn't belong in the environment.

Joey unsheathed a knife that had been tucked inside his jacket.

'What is it?' Baby whispered, every sense heightened.

'Nothing.'

He carried on into the forest, occasionally stopping and looking around. Baby followed, always hanging back a yard or two, checking out what was on either side of them. While she was safe in the knowledge that Joey would deal with anything that attacked them head on, she had never felt so alert or anxious. Every once in a while she would look back at where they had come from. Each time she did, the entrance to the forest became harder to see, until eventually the time came when it was no longer there.

The deeper into the forest they ventured, the more frequently Joey stopped and looked around or crouched down and felt around for something on the ground. It made Baby nervous, but she understood why he did it. He was being cautious. It was what made him such an efficient and ruthless hunter.

They were maybe a quarter of a mile into the forest when something made him stop suddenly. He stayed still for much longer than usual.

Baby crept forward and whispered in his ear. 'What is it?'

He held up his hand, which she took as a gesture to shut the fuck up. He lifted his head and stared up at the trees, then back down at the ground, as if he was measuring the distance. But with his mask on it was impossible for Baby to read his face and get an idea of whether he was worried or not.

He crouched down and moved his head one way and then the other, like he was watching a slow motion tennis match. Baby desperately wanted to ask him what he'd seen, heard or smelt. Instead she crouched down and copied him, staring into the darkness hoping to see what it was that was bothering him, hoping it was nothing. It certainly *looked like nothing* because there wasn't anything to see, other than trees and bushes. She had a small torch on her belt and she really wanted to switch it on.

'Do you want my torch?' she whispered.

Joey stayed in a crouching position but took a step back towards her, almost treading on her toes, because she was so close. He turned his head slowly and looked at her through the eyes on his mask. And he said something that sent a chill down her spine.

'They're everywhere. *We've been set up.*'

Sixteen

Over the years, Halloween had been a night full of incident for Beth Lansbury. The piece of cloth she pulled from the top drawer on her bedroom dresser was a reminder of Halloweens from her past. And a reminder of JD, whose initials were sewn into the cloth.

As a teenager on a dark and rainy night, she had been laughed out of the school Halloween disco for dressing as Dorothy from *The Wizard of Oz*. But on her way out she'd met up with a boy dressed as the scarecrow from the same film. To call it fate would be an understatement. The boy was called JD and he became the great love of her life.

On that same night, after an altercation with a vampire at the end of the pier, they shared their first kiss. *Beth's first kiss with anyone.* At that moment it had seemed like the world was a wonderful place where dreams really did come true. But after parting from JD at midnight, she had returned home and walked into an ambush. Her stepmother and a bunch of psychotic Devil worshippers had lined her up to be their ritualistic Halloween sacrifice. In the struggle that followed Beth accidentally stabbed her stepmother in the throat, killing her.

And so her next ten Halloweens were spent in jail because one of the Devil worshippers had been a high-ranking police officer who ensured that she was found guilty of murder. After her release from prison she had ventured back to the pier at midnight on Halloween every year in the dreamy hope of seeing JD again. When word spread about it someone in town tagged her with the name *Mental Beth*, and it had stuck with her ever since. But, she thought she'd had the last laugh three years ago, when JD did return to the pier at midnight on one particularly stormy Halloween night. It had been the best night of her life. But then the next day she'd found out that JD was in fact, the Bourbon Kid, the mass murderer wanted all over the world for a string of brutal killings. She came to terms with that news and accepted it. Over time, she even grew to love him more *because* he was the Bourbon Kid, the baddest man alive.

But just like everything good in Beth's life, it didn't last. After a confrontation with a power-crazed Mummy who planned to take over the world, JD vanished again, leaving her with nothing but the piece of cloth with his initials on, a symbol that he would one day return. So as another Halloween night came around, Beth was back where she started, preparing to head to the end of the pier at midnight, hoping he would come back to her again.

She considered taking the piece of cloth with her to the pier, but it crossed her mind that if JD did show up, the piece of cloth could be her excuse for inviting him back to her room above The Tapioca, so she replaced it in the drawer and checked her reflection in the mirror above the dresser.

On previous Halloweens she had worn the Dorothy outfit for sentimental reasons, or as Sanchez had once suggested, *"Mental reasons"*. But times had changed. Beth had changed. She was more confident. She was no longer the teenage girl in the *Wizard of Oz* outfit waiting for her crush to come and kiss her on the pier. She was the grown up version and she dressed accordingly, in clothes she felt comfortable in. Skinny black jeans, dark blue t-shirt, ankle boots with high heels and a tight fitting black leather jacket. Her hair was cropped with a red streak though it and one side hung down at the front. If JD came back again, she had to make sure he didn't leave this time.

At 11.35 she made her way downstairs to the bar area. Living in a guest room above The Tapioca had its benefits, not least of all being close to work. But more importantly at times like this, it meant she could get an honest opinion about how she looked from her best friend, Flake.

Sanchez had closed the bar early to prepare for a late night visit from a health inspector who was determined to shut the place down. So he was off somewhere trying to buy cheap fire extinguishers and public warning signs. Flake was in the bar, cleaning and tidying things up. She was a slender build with a very pretty face, which made it all the more baffling how she had ended up with Sanchez. Any number of hot guys would be happy to go out with her. She could pack a punch too and had done on many occasions in The Tapioca when people had threatened Sanchez. So it was no surprise to see her doing the hard manual labour in the bar while he was out shopping.

Beth noticed that Flake was wearing her policewoman's costume again.

'Is Sanchez wearing his cop outfit too?' she asked.

'He's grown out of his,' Flake replied. 'But it has been three years. It must have shrunk in the wash.'

Flake and Sanchez had hooked up three years earlier on November 1st during a very brief stint where they became temporary cops after the Bourbon Kid massacred ninety percent of the local force. They'd kept the costumes as a reminder of how they'd met.

Beth was equally concerned about her own outfit. 'How do I look?' she asked.

Flake was still working hard at getting the crust off of the table, but she looked at Beth and smiled. 'You look like the Bourbon Kid's girlfriend,' she said.

Beth tried to contain the urge to grin like a baboon. 'I've got a good feeling about tonight,' she said. 'After seeing all JD's friends here the other day, I can't help it, I think he'll come back, even if it's just for tonight.'

'You planning on leaving with him?'

Beth shrugged. 'If he asked me to, I would. But I'm trying not to think that far ahead. I mean, he might not even show up.'

'Just a thought, but why don't I go with you?' Flake suggested.

Beth shook her head. 'If I've got someone with me he might not show his face. I have to be on my own.'

With her table finally clean, Flake picked up a chair and placed it upside down on it. 'Look, Beth, I don't mean to be rude, but are you hoping to get attacked or something? Y'know, so that he comes and rescues you?'

'No.'

'Really? Because going to the pier on your own at midnight is kind of asking for trouble. There might not be vampires here anymore but there's still a lot of assholes.'

Beth reached into her jacket pocket and pulled out a small plastic bottle. 'Sanchez gave me this bottle of pepper spray. Anyone comes near me, they get this in their eyes.'

'Wouldn't you rather have a gun?'

'I don't fancy going back to prison.'

'A baseball bat then?'

'You know me, I'll have it snatched off me before I can do any damage with it.'

'What about a knife?'

'Definitely not.'

Flake stopped wiping down tables and walked up to Beth. She smiled at her and then kissed her on the cheek. 'Okay, but be careful. You've got your phone with you, haven't you?'

'Yep.'

'Call me if you get into any trouble. In fact, call me whatever happens. If I haven't heard from you by half past midnight I'm coming to look for you.'

Beth hugged her. Flake was a true friend and the bravest woman she knew.

'Don't worry so much,' she said. 'If JD doesn't show up I'll be home before you need to call me.'

Beth checked the time on her watch for like the hundredth time in the last hour. It was 11.40 p.m. *Twenty until midnight.* Her heart was fluttering. Twenty minutes.

'I gotta go. I'll see you later, or not!'

As Beth left The Tapioca, Flake shouted one last thing to her.

'Be careful out there, Beth.'

Seventeen

'They're everywhere. We've been set up.'

'What do you mean?' Baby whispered.

There was nothing visible in the darkness of the forest, not that Baby could see anyway. But Joey didn't reply to her question, and because she couldn't see his face she couldn't tell just how serious their predicament was. He turned his head ever-so-slightly towards her and whispered again.

'They're here.'

'Who are?' Baby was conscious of how loud their whispering suddenly seemed.

'In the trees.'

The words floated around in Baby's mind. *In the trees.* What had he seen? She was afraid to ask. Truth be told, she didn't want to know. She wanted to go home.

'What are we going to do?' she whispered so quietly that she feared she may have to repeat it.

Joey twisted around on his haunches until he was facing her. He whispered softly. 'Start backing away slowly, without looking like you are. And when you hear me shout *"run"* you start running like there's no tomorrow. Go back the way we came. Don't look back and *don't stop* for anything.'

'What are you going to do?'

'I'll be right behind you. If anything jumps out at you, don't worry. I'll take care of it.'

'Are we going to be okay?'

'Of course we are. Now go, start backing away. I'll wait here to buy you some time before they realise what you're doing.'

Baby didn't like the idea of leaving him behind. But she knew from previous experience in these kinds of life and death situations, she needed to do exactly what he said. When she followed his instructions to the letter they always made it out alive, no matter how dangerous their predicament might be. She stretched her left leg back and felt it touch the ground. It made more noise than she would have liked. She twisted her body around as she continued her cautious retreat. The urge to start running was immense, but instead she stayed low and took long, slow strides.

'BABY, RUN!'

That was the starter pistol she had been waiting for. She took off like a greyhound, sprinting through the trees, waiting for the moment she would see the moonlight at the edge of the woods again.

The plan to tread lightly and make no noise was over. Baby was breathing heavily and her boots were crunching on sticks and stones every time they hit the ground. There didn't seem to be anything chasing her. She couldn't even hear Joey behind her.

After what felt like an age, she saw a sliver of blue moonlight up ahead through a gap in the trees. The edge of the forest was close. It felt like she was going to make it out in one piece.

Maybe it was the flickering moonlight between the trees, or maybe she just hadn't been paying attention before, but she suddenly became aware of the things in the trees that had troubled Joey. A moving shape appeared alongside her, running at high speed, effortlessly keeping pace with her. In the dark of the night it looked like a three-dimensional shadow. It had thin red slits for eyes that were focussed on Baby.

Another lifelike shadow appeared on her other side. This one was close enough to reach out and touch her. It could have done so at any time. Baby glanced across at it. Again it had those reddish eyes, and this one had a chain wrapped tightly around its neck. The chain was made of teeth and shrunken skulls, evidence of previous kills. A reminder of all the fools before Baby and Joey who had entered the forest.

The two shadow creatures ran alongside her for far longer than they needed to, as if they were getting a kick out of scaring the shit out of her, toying with her, knowing that she was terrified. Just when Baby was beginning to think they weren't going to make a move, the one further away angled its run towards her, moving swiftly through the trees. The closer one reached out to try and grab her with its black hand.

Stupid though it was, Baby winced and almost closed her eyes, as if that would have helped. But she never slowed down, she kept on running, waiting for the inevitable impact as the two shadows took her down. But it never came. She opened her eyes again and they were gone.

It had almost escaped her. Two sounds had pierced the airwaves. Two gunshots. She glanced over her shoulder and saw one of the shadow creatures on its knees, toppling forward. She saw the black body, the red eyes, and the red trickle of blood, dribbling down its head. At the precise moment it had made its move on her, Joey had fired a bullet through the back of its head. Baby faced forward again just in time to duck underneath a tree branch that would have taken her down if she hadn't seen it. Although she had only seen one dying shadow creature behind her, she felt sure Joey had dispatched the other one too, because it was nowhere to be seen.

She stumbled over a tangled tree root and took another look back as she regained her balance. She saw the red stripe of hair on the top of Joey's mask, maybe six trees further back. He was running too and he had a gun in each hand. Flashes of light burst from the end of the pistols. Even though Baby couldn't hear the shots, she could see he was gunning down anything that got too close.

Baby had never run so fast for so long. Her adrenaline had given her a boost, making her oblivious to how tired she was. She felt like she was going to make it out of the forest alive. But then she had one of those moments. The kind of moment where your mind registers a flashing image of something you've seen, but your brain initially discarded as background imagery. Behind Joey, chasing close at his heels were hundreds of the shadow creatures. She knew Joey was a master at killing when the odds were stacked against him, but he was outnumbered by a hundred or more, maybe a thousand or more. And these things were fast. No wonder he had decided their best bet was to flee the forest. This mission bordered on suicidal.

Another shadow jumped out in front of Baby, swooping down on her from the treetops. But before it even landed on the ground, a bullet ploughed into its face, spraying blood everywhere and knocking it back. It crashed into a tree trunk and bounced onto the floor in front of Baby. She hurdled it and carried on running. The edge of the forest was so close she could almost smell the fresh air and the grass in the field beyond the trees. She remembered what Bishop Yoder had said about the Cyclops not leaving the sanctity of the forest. She hoped to God he'd been telling the truth about that, because he'd lied about there being only *one* monster.

Another shadow raced across in front of her. It was moving fast, *too fast*. Her training kicked in and she switched direction, dodging it and ducking around a tree without losing any ground. But yet another shadow jumped out in front of her. It left her no option but to stop or run into it.

BANG!

It fell backwards as if hit by an invisible train. *Joey still had her covered.* She started running again, but she was almost out of gas.

When she reached the last row of trees, her lungs and heart were at breaking point. Panic and fear had carried her through to the end of the forest but wouldn't take her much further. She burst out into the open grassy field and staggered a few more steps. If the shadow creatures did leave the sanctity of their wood, then she was done for. She half expected one of them to jump on her back and throw her to the ground, so she braced herself for the inevitability of it. But it never came.

She stopped and bent over, clutching her stomach and trying desperately to catch her breath. An acidic taste flooded into her mouth and it was impossible to take in a big gulp of air. Every time she inhaled some oxygen it just came straight back out. She put her hands on her hips and straightened up, turning around, expecting to see Joey behind her.

He wasn't there.

At first it looked like *nothing* was there. But upon close inspection, at the edge of the forest, in a line behind the first row of trees was an army of the shadow people, their thin red eyes staring at her. She had never seen anything like them before. They were like a cross between humans and panthers, with necklaces made of shrunken skulls and teeth. They weren't leaving the sanctity of their forest, as if some invisible force-field was holding them back.

But where was Joey? Where was the Red Mohawk, her sweetheart, who had made it possible for her to escape in one piece? She waited to hear his voice. With every second that he didn't appear she began to panic.

The shadow people began chanting in a language she didn't understand. She looked from one end of their line to another for a sign of Joey. Where the hell was he? She considered the possibility he had taken refuge in the trees and bushes. He had that ability to hide in amongst his enemies without them seeing him.

Baby took a few more deep breaths and tried to compose herself. Something about having a close brush with death, made life suddenly feel so real.

'JOEY!' she cried out, the words floating away with the night.

The shadow people that were standing directly in front of her parted to allow another of their group to come to the forest edge. That was when Baby saw the Cyclops. It was a huge savage, much bigger than the other shadow people, standing over eight feet tall. It wasn't black like the others either. It had brown scaly skin and one giant yellow eyeball the size of an apple. It stopped between two thick oak trees at the front of the forest and stared down at Baby. Then it opened its mouth. It had huge sharp fangs and Baby got a good look at them as it leaned its head back and roared like a jungle beast. In its left hand it held aloft the Red Mohawk mask.

Baby swallowed hard. The forest people had somehow acquired Joey's mask, but where was he? She looked back and forth down the line of trees again for any sight of him.

Nothing.

But then the giant Cyclops stepped forward and tossed the Mohawk mask towards Baby. It landed at her feet.

And Joey's head rolled out.

Eighteen

Everyone Beth passed on her way to the harbour was dressed for Halloween. There were zombies and witches and ogres and vampires everywhere she looked. In spite of the evil costumes though, everybody was in good spirits. Santa Mondega was a very different place since the Bourbon Kid had eliminated all of the undead creatures. People, nice regular people, had begun socialising at night. Even on Halloween.

The night air was cold and damp, and the closer Beth came to the harbour, the less people she saw. The party people stayed in the town centre. The harbour was generally for drunks and people who were lost.

She stepped onto the pier, completely alone. It hadn't changed much over the years. It was in dire need of some restorative work. It was a rickety wooden death trap that would have been closed down in any normal town, and that was just the parts you could see above the water. The foundations beneath the water didn't bear thinking about. But Beth wouldn't have cared if it was as soft as cheese, because to her, this was the best place in the world to be at midnight on Halloween.

The unsteady wooden panels creaked underfoot as she walked over them. When she made it to the end she stood with her hands on the wooden railings, staring out to sea. Her annual gaze over the gentle sea waves was a very bittersweet experience. Not all of her memories of Halloween were good, but the ones that were good outweighed the bad by some distance. She lost herself in the memories of the two Halloween nights she had spent with JD. If anything was to interrupt her she hoped it would be him sneaking up behind her and sliding his arms around her.

There was a thick fog over the sea all the way to the horizon. For ten minutes, Beth was lost to the world, dreaming of the Bourbon Kid. That's what everyone else called him. To her he was JD, short for Jack Daniels. It gave her a warm, fuzzy feeling when she thought of the two of them back when they were innocent teenagers. The visions were so clear, the voices and the words were etched in her mind, as fresh as the day they were spoken. She even remembered the Mystic Lady inviting them into her shabby trailer for a warm drink.

Beth thought of the Eye of the Moon, a magical blue stone she'd thrown into the sea three years ago. JD had killed a mummy in order to get the Eye for her, because she'd been bitten by a vampire and was close to death. The magical healing powers of the Eye had saved her and brought her back to full health. But then JD had vanished again. And she'd been upset, so she'd thrown it as far out to sea as she could, from the exact spot she was now standing. The Eye, while beautiful and very valuable had brought nothing but misery and death to everyone who had owned it. Beth had done the world a favour by throwing it where it would never be found.

She did love the name though, *The Eye of the Moon*. She looked up at the sky and considered wishing upon the moon. But it was only a half moon and a barely visible one at that.

Her maudlin thoughts were interrupted, not by JD sneaking up behind her, but by the sight of a large vessel on the sea moving through the fog towards the harbour. In all her years living in Santa Mondega she had never seen a ship dock there. A few sailboats had rocked up from time to time, but never a vessel big enough to hold more than ten people.

The ship that emerged from the fog was made of wood and had billowing white sails. Beth had only ever seen ships like it in *The Pirates of the Caribbean* movies. As it came closer, she saw rows of oars sticking out of the sides, moving back and forth through the water, driving the ship forward. It crossed her mind that it might be something to do with Halloween. Otherwise why else would the crew be rowing? Thinking about it took her mind off why she was there. She checked her watch. It was five past midnight.

When the ship was no longer partially hidden by the fog, she saw some of the crew. Four people on horses were standing on deck, not moving, just staring at the shore. A number of others were on foot, moving erratically, like chimps. It was a bizarre sight, but bizarre sights were supposed to be what Halloween was about.

A huge metal anchor was thrown over the side of the ship, making a loud splash as it hit the seawater. Its thick metal chain rattled as it unravelled and followed the anchor down to the seabed. Beth was quite fascinated by it, even more so when a crewmember suddenly took a running jump off the port side of the ship and dived into the sea. The people on horses stayed on board, but a bunch of others started abandoning ship, diving overboard into the sea and swimming for shore.

Beth was the only person left in the harbour. And even though she wanted to stay a while longer, the thought of being on the pier when a hundred randy sailors climbed out of the water didn't appeal to her. Quite a few of the swimmers were heading straight for the shore, but a handful were aiming for the end of the pier, where Beth was standing.

She took a few steps back and almost stumbled when the heel of her boot caught in a gap between the wooden panels underfoot. Two of the people in the water were almost at the pier, so she turned around and walked briskly back to the promenade, trying to look casual, like she wasn't hurrying, even though she was.

Just as she was about to set foot on the promenade, she heard a thud behind her, which signalled one of the swimmers trying to climb up onto the pier. She looked back to see how he was doing. Even though it was dark, the moon offered just enough light. Beth saw a creature with pale green skin trying to haul itself out of the sea. It was thin and bony. And most definitely not human.

Nineteen

Baby staggered out onto the main road through Blue Corn Island. Earlier in the day she had ridden through it on the back of Joey's bike. Back then she didn't have a care in the world. She'd rarely been happier. But in the last ten minutes her world had fallen apart. Joey was dead. Those three words bounced around in her head, on a continuous loop, tormenting her.

The Black Forest was still too close. She could hear the mad cackling of the shadow creatures that had chased them and killed Joey, and the roars of the Cyclops that had ripped his head off his shoulders. The image of the giant beast holding aloft the mask containing Joey's head wouldn't go away. Nor would the moment his severed head rolled out of the mask onto the grass. All Baby wanted was to stop sobbing and go home. Or go back in time. Neither was possible because Baby had no home, and only Jasmine believed time travel was possible.

She started walking along the highway from Oakfield to Crimson County and tried to think, to take stock of her situation. She was in shock, she recognised that. One thing that had been drummed into her by the other members of The Dead Hunters was how to deal with the inevitable shock that followed the death of a colleague. She had been warned a hundred times, maybe more, that one day, she would have to deal with this. At the time, she thought that being prepared for it meant she wouldn't experience it. Now she realised that all she'd learned was how to deal with the shock, not the loss.

Breathe.

Evaluate your situation.

Don't panic.

She looked up to the heavens and took a few deep breaths. It didn't really help. Evaluating her situation just meant reliving the unpleasant images of Joey's decapitation. She tried to block out those images and concentrate on her surroundings. It took a while, but eventually she was able to stop sobbing and calm herself just enough to think clearly. She asked herself, *what was the logical thing to do?*

Call Jasmine.

She pulled out her cellphone and dialled the number. Jasmine would know what to do. Jasmine never panicked, and she would understand exactly how Baby felt too, because she'd lost her former lover, Jack Munson, in a gruesome incident too. His killer had cut off his face and worn it as a mask while he attacked Jasmine. So if anyone knew how Baby felt, it was her.

"The number you are calling is unavailable. The user may have switched their phone off."

FUCK. Jasmine never switched her phone off. Never, not in the entire history of the world. Of all the stupid times to do it!

Baby talked herself into breathing some more and evaluating the situation. Her next option was obvious. Call Elvis. He was probably with Jasmine anyway.

"The number you are calling is unavailable. The user may have switched their phone off."

Deep breaths, *deep breaths.* Okay, keep cool. Rodeo Rex. He's reliable. He'll answer his phone and he'll definitely know what to do.

"The number you are calling is unavailable. The user may have switched their phone off."

God hates me!

Baby couldn't believe her bad luck. What the hell was going on?

As soon as she asked herself the question *"What the hell was going on?"*, she figured out the answer. Jasmine, Elvis and Rex were probably in Purgatory. Cellphones didn't work in Purgatory because there was no phone signal.

That left only one option. *The Bourbon Kid.* Baby hadn't seen him in months. He worked alone because other people got on his nerves. So by the rule of logic, if the others were all in Purgatory, it was reasonable to assume the Kid would be somewhere else. She didn't know how he would react to her calling him. He probably wouldn't be sympathetic, but he would tell her what to do. And deep down she hoped he would come and get her, take her away from Blue Corn Island and the horror of what had happened.

She dialled his number.

EUREKA! A dialling tone. It rang four times before she heard a gravelly, "What?" at the other end of the line.

Because Baby was worried the Bourbon Kid might hang up when he realised it was her, she got straight to the point. 'Joey's dead! …..It's Baby….. Joey's been killed….. On Blue Corn Island….. I can't get hold of anyone….. You're my last hope. *He's dead.* I don't know what to….'

"Leave a message after the tone."

Baby could have cried. She certainly wanted to, *really, really* wanted to. She hadn't been speaking to the Bourbon Kid at all, just babbling at a pre-recorded message on his voicemail.

BEEP.

At least this time she could leave a message. She composed herself and took a second stab at explaining to him what had happened.

'Hi, it's Baby, Joey's been killed and I can't get hold of any of the others. I'm in Oakfield on Blue Corn Island. Please call me back. I don't know what to do.'

She took a moment to make sure she had given him enough information. The last thing she wanted to do was call him again with some details she had forgotten. She cast her mind back to the journey she and Joey had taken to Oakfield, and picked out a landmark to direct the Kid to.

'Okay,' she said, speaking even slower. 'There's a pub called The Fork In Hell on the main highway through Crimson County. I'm going to head there. When you get this message please call me back. Or just meet me at The Fork In Hell. I'll wait for you there. Thanks. Please hurry. I'm scared. I'm really scared.'

Having made the call, she felt slightly better. The stuff she'd been taught in her training was filtering back into her mind. Act now, grieve later. That was one of the bullet points for how to cope with the death of a friend, even though Joey was much more than just a friend. She needed to get as far away from Oakfield as possible. There was only one sensible way to do that. Walk down the highway to The Fork In Hell. It would be a long hike. She couldn't remember how many miles it was. And unfortunately it meant walking alongside the Black Forest for the entire journey.

She gathered herself together and started the long trek to Crimson County. The sounds of the shadow creatures and the Cyclops faded away into silence. Silence wasn't great either though, so after a few minutes of walking she made calls to Jasmine, Elvis and Rex again. They were all still unavailable. She was lonely, scared and cold. Normally at times like that Joey would calm her down. Just the sound of his voice usually did the trick. It gave Baby an idea. She called Joey's phone. It rang a few times and then went to voicemail.

'Hi, you're through to Joey. I'm not here right now, so leave a message after the tone.'

The sound of his voice nearly broke her in two. She closed her eyes and waited for the beep.

BEEP.

'I miss you. I'm so sorry.' Her voice began to wobble. She shouldn't have called him. But she missed him so much.

She was on the verge of falling to her knees and crying her heart out, but the night-time silence was suddenly interrupted by a vehicle approaching from Crimson County. It crossed her mind that by calling Joey, even though he was dead, he had sent someone to protect her, to take her away from this nightmare she was stuck in.

A Harley Davidson motorcycle appeared up ahead, cruising down the middle of the highway. She recognised the rider from his outline, which was drawn against the backlight of the moon. It was Rodeo Rex.

At last, the nightmare was over. She dropped to her knees in the middle of the road and waited for him to reach her. Deep down in her heart, she knew that Joey, her guardian angel, had answered her call for help and sent Rex to take her home.

She still had her phone up against her ear. Even though it seemed crazy and overly sentimental, she spoke to Joey's voicemail one last time.

'Thank you Joey. Rex is here now. Sleep tight. *I love you.*'

Thankfully, Rex had seen her. He slowed up his bike and pulled over by the edge of the Black Forest.

'Baby? Are you okay?' he asked as he climbed off his bike.

Baby pressed her cellphone against her chest, lay down on her back and stared up at the stars. As tears streamed down her face she took comfort in knowing that Joey was up there somewhere, watching out for her.

Twenty

Health & Hygiene checks were one of Sanchez's least favourite things. Over the years, hundreds of people had died in The Tapioca, most of them shot or stabbed, so making sure there were no traces of piss in the complimentary peanuts, wasn't exactly going to make a great deal of difference.

The newly appointed Health & Hygiene Officer for Santa Mondega was a lady called Nora Bone, a fifty-something do-gooder, with a face like a wrinkled scrotum. Sanchez hated her the minute he met her. Her personality was as dull as her dress sense. This woman dressed for wet weather even when it was baking hot outside.

Sanchez had left her to get on with her inspection and headed upstairs to change into the special new anniversary outfit Flake had bought for him. Flake was wearing her cop outfit to commemorate their exploits together on the Police Force. Unfortunately Sanchez no longer fitted into his Highway Patrolman outfit from those days. It must have shrunk in the wash or something because he'd ripped the ass out of it the last time he'd tried to put it on. So Flake had treated him to what she claimed was the coolest outfit ever. An outfit so unique, no one even recognised it. It consisted of blue jeans, a baggy black V-neck sweater and a pair of mirrored sunglasses. They all fitted Sanchez perfectly, particularly the sunglasses.

'You look so hot!' said Flake, as Sanchez admired himself in their bedroom mirror.

She was right, Sanchez agreed. She had dressed him up to look like her favourite eighties movie character, Marion Cobretti from the film *Cobra*. Cobretti had been played by a young, muscle-bound, Sylvester Stallone back in the day. Sanchez was the spitting image, only shorter, fatter, older and without the muscles. Or the toothpick.

'You forgot the toothpick,' Sanchez complained.

'Shit. I've got some somewhere,' said Flake. 'Give me a minute and I'll find them.'

Sanchez checked his watch. 'It's past midnight. I'd better go down and check on that Hygiene woman.'

Flake gave him a peck on the cheek. 'See if you can get rid of her while I go find you a toothpick. When she's gone, we can play those games we talked about.'

Sanchez was excited about playing some "games" with Flake. For the first time in ages they had the place to themselves because Beth was out. He left the bedroom and bounded down the narrow staircase that came out behind the bar.

Nora was already waiting for him. She had finished her inspection and was sitting at a table in the bar area. She had a clipboard in her hand and was flicking through a few pages of notes that she had made.

Sanchez walked out from behind the bar and sat down at the table with her.

'Are you done?' he asked.

'The toilets in here are disgusting,' Nora replied, peering over her spectacles at him.

'Can't argue with that,' said Sanchez. 'I recommend using the Disabled toilets. I always do if I haven't got time to rush upstairs. You certainly wouldn't want to take a dump in the Men's toilets here, *trust me.*'

Nora's pupils enlarged, which was quite a sight because they already looked huge, due to the thick prescription glasses she wore.

'You use the Disabled toilets?' she vented, her voice full of disgust.

'Only if I'm taking a dump.'

'You should *never* use the Disabled toilets.'

'But they're my toilets. This is my bar.'

'I don't care. Those toilets are for disabled people only. Using them when you're not disabled is a hate crime.'

'A hate crime?' said Sanchez. 'I don't hate disabled people, besides the only one we get in here is Oscar the Cripple and I'm pretty sure he craps in his shorts. You should see him, he really stinks.'

'You can't call Disabled people *cripples!*'

'Why not?'

'It's offensive.'

'Oscar doesn't mind.'

'That doesn't matter. It's still offensive.'

Sanchez didn't want to get on the wrong side of Nora so he tried to placate her. 'Fair enough,' he said. 'We'll come up with a new nickname for him. How about Oscar the Gimp?'

'He shouldn't have a nickname,' Nora snapped. 'He should be treated the same as everyone else.'

'But everyone has a nickname in this place,' said Sanchez. 'We've got Fat Debbie, Ugly Pedro, Mick the Wanker....'

'Wanker?'

'He's British.'

'I don't care. And I don't care much for all the offensive nicknames you have for people either.'

Sanchez was glad he hadn't mentioned any of the cruder nicknames. Or told her what name he called her when she wasn't around. 'Okay, well I'll keep all that in mind,' he said, diplomatically. 'Was there anything else, apart from the stinky toilets that you wanted to discuss?'

'Yes, that sign above the door that says NO VAMPIRES, that'll have to be taken down.'

'Why?'

'Because it's racist.'

'Against vampires?'

'Yes.'

'But vampires kill people and drink their blood. I'm not having them in here.'

Nora tutted and wrote something down on her clipboard. 'Vampires have rights like everyone else,' she said. 'Just because some of them are killers, doesn't mean they all are.'

Sanchez scoffed. 'I dunno, I've met a fair few and they were all bad. One of the worst ones used to live upstairs.'

'Really?' said Nora, softening a little.

'Yeah her name was Jessica.' Sanchez paused as he remembered how for years he had been infatuated with Jessica, before finding out she was a bloodsucker. 'She was sexy as Hell,' he said, gazing up at the ceiling.

'Sexy?'

'Yeah, she had an amazing body. Every guy in here wanted a piece of her.'

Nora shook her head. 'Objectifying women. I'll add that to the list,' she said, scribbling on her clipboard some more.

'Oh no, it's not like that,' Sanchez protested. 'She was a total bitch, really.'

Nora gasped. 'Misogynist!'

'What?'

'You really are a disgusting little man.'

Sanchez checked his watch. Flake would be down any minute. 'Look, it's getting late,' he said. 'Can we wrap this up?'

'Wrap it up?' Nora sneered. 'I've got a whole list of things here.'

'Like what?'

Nora tapped her clipboard with her pen. 'Hygiene rules state that if I find more than three issues deemed to be of a serious nature, I can shut this place down.'

'And how many have you got there?'

'Seventeen.'

'Seventeen?' Sanchez was shocked. He had imagined it would be far worse. Seventeen wasn't bad. 'So how much do you want?' he asked.

'What do you mean?'

'A hundred bucks? The last Hygiene officer, Stinky Dave, used to take a hundred bucks to overlook all the issues he found.'

'Stinky Dave, *as you call him*, was fired for taking bribes,' said Nora. 'I, on the other hand cannot be bought. As of tomorrow when I submit my findings to the Department of Health and Hygiene, this bar will be closed down.'

Sanchez hadn't expected Nora to be quite such a cow. 'Can I offer you a drink?' he asked.

'Not a chance. I'm done here. The thought of spending another minute listening to a hateful idiot like you turns my stomach.'

'Hateful?' said Sanchez, surprised by her ferocity.

'Yes, a hateful idiot,' said Nora, reiterating her point.

Sanchez couldn't recall ever hating anything, apart from strangers, bus rides, going to church, snow, karaoke, being woken in the middle of a dream, Amish people, rap music and, of course, Nora Bone.

Nora gathered her things together and headed over to a coat stand by the door where her grey raincoat was hanging. In a moment of classic timing, Flake came bounding down the stairs behind the bar, in her cop outfit, carrying a baseball bat. She didn't see Nora putting her coat on, so she shouted out to Sanchez.

'What did the old cow say?'

Nora finished putting her coat on and reappeared. 'I'm closing you down,' she sneered. 'Good night.'

Flake glared at Sanchez. 'Did you give her the hundred bucks?'

'She wouldn't take it. She's shutting us down tomorrow.'

Nora was in the process of letting herself out of the front door, so Flake hurdled over the bar with her baseball bat, primed and ready for use.

'Sanchez, hold her down while I smash her head in!'

Sanchez didn't move, but he heard Nora Bone slam the front door shut behind her in a mad rush to leave before her brains were smashed in. Flake bounded up to Sanchez and gave him a high five.

'She won't come back.'

'I'm not so sure,' said Sanchez. 'I think she was serious.'

Flake took Sanchez's sunglasses off and kissed him on the lips. 'Let's worry about her tomorrow,' she said. 'We've got better things to be doing right now.'

Twenty One

Rex crouched down on one knee and placed his hand on Baby's shoulder.

'What's happened?' he asked. 'Why are you crying?'

As soon as Baby opened her mouth with the intention of saying, *"Joey's dead"* she started sobbing. She was sick of crying. Her throat was sore and her face was sticky from all the tears that had streamed down her cheeks since Joey's death.

'Where's Joey?' Rex asked, looking around as if he expected Joey to show up.

Baby wiped away some tears and tried to compose herself. 'He's dead,' she said. Saying it out loud on the phone had been hard, but saying it to Rex's face was agonising.

'Joey's dead?' Rex sounded surprised.

She nodded.

'How?'

She pointed to the forest. 'In there.'

Rex looked into the forest as if he expected to see something. There was nothing to see so he looked back at Baby. 'What happened in there?'

'I don't know. There were these things, like shadows. There were hundreds of them. They…. they cut his head off.'

She barely got the words out. She began to cry hysterically again. She wanted to be strong, to act like a true Dead Hunter and vow revenge, but Joey was gone and so was any fight she had left in her. She'd never felt more alone in the world, and that was saying something because Baby had been alone for most of her life.

Rex looked her in the eye. 'Have you told any of the others?'

She shook her head. 'I can't get hold of anyone. No one is answering their phones. Yours is switched off.'

'Yeah, I lost it somewhere. Did you try the Bourbon Kid?'

Baby nodded. 'He didn't answer.'

'Do you know where he is?'

'I haven't seen JD in ages.'

'JD?' Rex sounded puzzled.

'Yeah, I left him a voicemail.'

'Would *he* know where the Bourbon Kid is?'

Baby stopped sobbing. Something wasn't quite right. Rex didn't seem to understand that when she said "JD" she was referring to the Bourbon Kid.

But then something occurred to her, something she should have noticed sooner. His right hand, which was on her shoulder, normally he wore a glove on that hand. She should have realised when he touched her with it. It was made of flesh and bone. Not metal.

'Your hand,' she said, staring at it.

Rex looked at it. 'Oh yeah,' he said. 'I had a transplant. Got rid of that goddamn metal thing. But don't worry about that now. Try calling the Bourbon Kid again.'

Baby wiped some more tears from her eyes so that she could get a better look at Rex's face. He was wearing a headband around his forehead. Poking out underneath it was a small red mark. Because Baby was still in a state of shock, she thought nothing of reaching out and pushing the headband up an inch to get a better look at the red mark. She pulled her hand away again when she saw that it was in fact a scar, a C shaped scar.

She tried to remain calm. This wasn't Rex. It was his body, it was even his voice speaking to her, but the words were coming from Cain. Baby's mind was a mess. Nothing made sense and she was too distraught by recent events to process what was going on.

Rex pulled the headband back down to cover the scar. 'I took a blow to the head earlier,' he said. 'It's messed with my memory a bit. I can't remember simple stuff. We should go back to base. I'll take you there but you'll have to give me directions because I can't remember the way.'

That confirmed it. This was definitely Cain, but how on earth had he taken over Rex's mind and body? She remembered what Scratch had told her about Cain, how he could only control the minds of unconscious people. The clue lay in the new hand. If Rex had been put under sedation for his transplant, Cain could have slipped inside his body with ease and taken over his mind.

Baby's thoughts turned to the others. And how none of them had answered their phones.

'What have you done with Jasmine and Elvis?' she said.

'What?'

'I know who you are.'

'I'm Rex, what are you talking about? I think maybe you're in shock.'

'I know I'm in shock, but I also know what that scar on your forehead means!'

'Oh.'

Where once Baby had looked into Rex's eyes and seen an honourable man who could be trusted, now she saw only evil and deceit.

The man pretending to be Rex stroked her hair, tugging at it a little harder than she would have liked.

'Jasmine and Elvis are dead,' he said, smirking. 'Someone tampered with the brakes on her new car.' He made a whistling sound and pretended his left hand was a car flying over an imaginary cliff and plummeting downwards. 'Right off a cliff,' he gloated.

'You killed them.' Baby said the words out loud. She didn't even have any tears left. Jasmine, her best friend and Elvis, an all-round great guy were dead too. There really was nothing left for her to live for.

'Your friends are all gone,' he said. 'But you, you're not a threat like the others. I'm willing to let you live. All you have to do is take me to Purgatory.'

'Why are you doing this? What do you want?'

'I want to see Scratch. Show me where to find him and I'll let you live.'

Baby knew he was lying. If he wanted Scratch, then he wanted a way into Hell, or a way of opening the gateway that kept it shut and stopped all the evil spirits from being unleashed back on earth.

'Fuck you.'

Cain tightened his grip on her hair. 'I hoped you'd see sense,' he said, the fake smile on his face evaporating. 'If you do as I ask, I promise Scratch will never know it was you. It'll be our secret, I swear.'

'*Never.* If you're asking me where Purgatory is, then it means none of the others told you, so *go spit.*'

'I admire your bravery,' said Cain. 'I really do. But you know, I was there in The Tapioca the other night, sitting right behind you, listening in on your conversations. Your stupid friend Jasmine threw some peanuts at me, remember?'

'That was you?'

'Uh huh, you know, you Dead Hunters talk too freely. I found out lots of things, like where you were all going to be, where the Bourbon Kid's girlfriend goes at midnight on Halloween, and of course, where Rex was going for his hand transplant.' He held up the new right hand and waved at her with it. 'But the most important thing I learned was that the bartender in The Tapioca knows the way into The Devil's Graveyard. So you see, I don't really need *you* at all.'

He let go of her hair and slid his hand down onto her neck. He pressed his thumb against her throat and pushed her down onto her back. Her head touched the white line in the middle of the road.

'Last chance. Take me to Purgatory, or die.'

'Never.'

Cain wrapped both hands around her neck and squeezed until she couldn't breathe. Baby panicked and grabbed his wrists, trying desperately to pull them away, but he was far too strong for her. Her vision began to blur and her body trembled. But when she was close to losing consciousness, Cain loosened his grip and allowed her to suck in some air.

'Last chance,' he said.

It should have been a tough decision. Take Cain to Purgatory or die. But the decision was actually much easier than that. If Baby gave him what he wanted, he would kill her anyway. She was smart enough to know that. And the revelation that Jasmine and Elvis were dead meant that she had nothing left. Her world had ended the minute Joey died. The loss of the others just confirmed what she already knew. *She wanted to die.* Her only chance of survival was if the Bourbon Kid had heard her voicemail message and somehow showed up in the next twenty seconds.

'You'll get what's coming to you,' she promised Cain.

Cain leant down and licked some tears from her face. His tongue was cold and coarse. He licked his lips, savouring the taste of her tears. 'Have it your way,' he said.

With both hands he squeezed her throat again, leering at her as he choked the life out of her. Even though Baby had nothing to live for and was ready to die, she still fought for her life. She writhed around on the ground, kicking at him as the life drained out of her. Eventually, when she had no fight left, she relented. Her body became heavy and limp, she lay spread-eagled in the middle of the road, with Cain sitting astride her, drooling over her, marvelling at what he was doing to her.

Baby's last thoughts were of Joey. She knew he would be proud of her. In the face of certain death she had chosen not to give up the location of Purgatory.

Her breathing stopped, her heart stopped, and she joined Joey in the next life.

Twenty Two

In recent months Beth had played a few video games. Flake was a big gamer and had recruited her for a few multiplayer shoot-em-up's. And Flake's favourite games were usually ones that involved chopping up monsters. During their team efforts, Beth had learned the difference between zombies, ghouls, vampires, necromorphs and a bunch of other undead creatures. So when the green-skinned creature climbed out of the sea onto the pier, she recognised right away that it was a ghoul. It was a scrawny male whose tattered clothes were soaked and clinging to its skin. Its eyes glowed fluorescent green in the moonlight.

Beth glanced back again and saw the ghoul staggering along the pier towards the promenade. As she hurried along the promenade to get away from it, she was still in two minds about whether or not it was a Halloween stunt. She didn't want to be the idiot caught on film running away from a bizarre Halloween themed triathlon. But then again, she didn't want to be the idiot caught on film being massacred by a hungry ghoul either. Besides, her gut instinct was telling her to get the hell out of there. The old ship, the swarm of green weirdoes swimming to shore, the glowing eyes, it all suggested something terrible. So she started walking as fast as she could, while trying to look nonchalant, as if she always walked that way.

She glanced back again and saw several more of the ghouls were climbing out of the sea onto the pier. A great deal more of them hadn't bothered with the pier and were swimming straight for the promenade instead. Some of them were about to come ashore ahead of the exit Beth needed to reach in order to escape the sea front. If she didn't pick up her pace, she would soon be sandwiched in between them and the others coming from the pier.

She broke into a light skip, whilst trying to maintain the illusion that she wasn't fleeing. But she soon wished she had sprinted from the get go. One of the swimmers reached the shore and launched itself out of the water onto the promenade alongside her. She glanced to her right and noticed that this one was bigger and uglier than most of the others. And unlike the first few she had seen, this one was naked. A horrible dangly, flaccid green penis was wobbling around between its legs, bouncing back and forth like a perverted yo-yo. That green cock was the final straw. This was no triathlon, no Halloween prank. These were undead creatures, no doubt about it, and they were hunting for human flesh.

She broke into a sprint. But the naked ghoul already had her in his sights. He set off in pursuit of her, hissing like a wild cat. His run was ungainly, like he needed a hip replacement, but he was no slouch. Beth had enough of a head start that she felt confident she could outpace him for a while, but over a long distance if he didn't tire, she'd be in trouble.

As it turned out, she had bigger problems. Further along the promenade, there were more ghouls climbing, and sometimes leaping, out of the water. Her escape route was blocked off. Three of them now stood between her and the exit route back to town. The one in the middle had a knife in its hand. A knife big enough to be classed as a short sword. He had seen Beth, *they all had*. And their intentions were clear. They wanted blood.

Beth couldn't slow down because she had the big naked ghoul hot on her heels, so as the three in front staggered towards her she used an old move that had served her well in prison during her younger days. She dropped her shoulder and fainted to go one way, but then planted her foot and darted to the other side of them. It almost worked perfectly, but at the last second, the ghoul closest to her stuck out its foot and caught her ankle with it. Beth stumbled headlong towards the sea, but avoided falling in by dancing along the edge of the promenade until she regained her balance.

She veered back across to the other side of the promenade, heading for the turning that led back into town. But the giant, naked ghoul who had been chasing her from the start leapt through the air and tackled her at shoulder height, knocking her to the ground. They both rolled along the ground and the ghoul lost his grip on her. Beth ended up on her back, dazed and staring up at the sky. But it wasn't long before the next ghoul, a skinny female, caught up and loomed over her.

Beth reached inside her jacket and pulled out the can of pepper spray Sanchez had given her, hoping it really was pepper spray, and not a novelty can of his piss. The female ghoul dived onto Beth with its teeth bared. Its soulless green eyes zooming in on her neck. Beth grabbed it around the throat to keep it from biting her, and aimed the spray can at its eyes.

She didn't get a chance to spray anything, pepper or piss, because another green hand, belonging to the naked male who had tackled her, appeared from behind her and knocked the can from her grasp. Then it grabbed her hair and yanked her head down to the ground.

In spite of their ungainly movements and animal-like hissing, the ghouls were smarter than they looked, and they knew how to work as a team. The big male held her head against the floor, his hairless scrotum inches above her head, while the female sat on her legs, pinning her to the ground so that she couldn't wriggle free. But although the female's jaws were gaping, and its eyes were staring at her neck, it made no attempt to bite her. These ghouls had other plans.

The one with the short sword sprinted up behind the female and leapt over her with its sword aloft. Beth reached out with her hands in the hope of pushing it away before it plunged the sword into her face or neck. But she flailed around and grabbed nothing.

WHOOSH!

Everything turned black. And cold.

A gust of wind blew Beth's hair into her eyes. Something flapped against her head. Dirt, blood and grit sprayed across her face. She blinked a few times. Thoughts raced through her head. *Am I alive? Am I in one piece? Is this the afterlife? What the hell is happening?*

A ghoul's head bounced on the ground next to her, its green eyes dimmed and dead. Another bounced between her legs and onto her stomach. She slapped it away, its blood sticking to her hand like glue.

And then she saw him. JD, the Bourbon Kid. His long black coat, with the hood pulled over his head, marked him out unmistakably.

SPLAT!

Body parts were bouncing on the ground all around her. JD had taken control of the sword the ghoul had tried to kill her with. He was slicing heads, arms and legs off of anything that got in his way.

Beth scrambled up into a sitting position and watched on, aghast, but also in awe as JD slammed the blade of the sword into the head of an onrushing ghoul. The ghoul fell sideways with the blade embedded in the top of its head. Only the handle of the sword was visible, poking out of the top of its skull as it hit the ground, blood oozing out everywhere.

JD reached inside his coat and pulled out an Uzi pistol. He sprayed bullets into the sea at the incoming ghouls and across the promenade at any others that had climbed ashore. The rat-a-tat of gunfire was deafening. Beth covered her ears and watched the symphony of ghoulish blood spurting in all directions.

Empty shells were scattered all around, mixed in with green corpses and black sticky blood that seeped from them. When JD's pistol ran out of ammo he tossed it to the floor. There were still more ghouls in the sea, swimming to shore, undeterred by the gunfire. But only one remained alive on the promenade. It had come from the pier and it was the biggest one Beth had seen.

With a blood-curdling roar it sprinted down the promenade towards JD, a silver axe in its right hand.

'LOOK OUT!' Beth screamed.

The ghoul launched itself ten feet into the air and swooped down on JD, swinging the axe down at his head. JD reached inside his coat and whipped out another weapon, a handgun with an enormous barrel.

BOOM!

As the ghoul dived down on JD, the blast from his handgun took its whole head off at the neck. A spray of red mist blew away in the distance and the headless green body landed at JD's feet with a loud thud.

Beth was still trying to catch her breath when JD finally turned around. He lowered the hood on his coat and looked into her eyes. All her fears melted away as she looked on his face for the first time in almost three years. He had three-day-old stubble, speckled with some blood from the dead ghouls. His piercing brown eyes stared right into her soul.

He held out his hand and she placed hers in it. He hauled her up from the ground, pulling her in close to him in one seamless move. And he said two words in his instantly recognisable, gravelly voice.

'Happy anniversary.'

Beth couldn't keep the smile off her face. 'You came back.'

'Yeah. Now let's get the fuck out of here.'

Twenty Three

Sanchez and Flake were sitting across from each other at one of the tables in The Tapioca, playing a late night game of Connect Four while they waited for Beth to return from her trip to the pier. For the first time in the history of playing the game, it looked like Sanchez was going to win. But then typically some asshole started banging on the front doors of the Tapioca.

'I'd better answer that,' said Flake.

'Hang on, just finish your move.'

'No time.'

Flake picked up her baseball bat and went to see who was outside. She peered through a peephole in the door and shouted back to Sanchez. 'It's Beth, and she's got the Bourbon Kid with her!'

Those words were enough to bring Sanchez out in a cold sweat. He shuddered and accidentally knocked the Connect Four game over, scattering the pieces everywhere. The bloody Bourbon Kid, not only did he routinely massacre Sanchez's clientele, now he had ruined what would have been a historic Connect Four victory. Sanchez cursed and grumbled on his way over to the front entrance.

Flake unbolted the doors and Beth barged in with the Bourbon Kid right behind her. Flake threw her arms around Beth and hugged her, then to Sanchez's disgust, she embraced the Bourbon Kid too. Traitor.

Beth's cheeks were red and her hair was a bit messy. She grabbed Sanchez's arm and shook it, which annoyed him. 'There's a load of ghouls heading this way!' she said. 'And four men on horses. JD thinks they're the Four Horsemen of the Apocalypse.'

'Have you been drinking again?' Sanchez inquired, removing her hand from his sleeve.

'No, this is serious.'

Flake finished hugging the Bourbon Kid and set about bolting the doors shut again. The Bourbon Kid walked up to Sanchez, his aura as menacing as ever. Sanchez resisted the urge to step back, even though his butt cheeks tightened considerably.

'Beth's telling the truth,' the Kid said. 'The things coming this way are called ghouls. They eat human flesh, and they love fat people, so do yourself a favour and get out of town before they show up here.'

'What the hell is a ghoul?' Sanchez asked.

Flake finished bolting the doors shut and re-joined them. 'Where would we go?' she asked.

'Come with us,' said Beth.

'We're going to The Devil's Graveyard,' said the Bourbon Kid. 'It's the safest place to be.'

Sanchez was struggling to take it all in, and he was still livid that his precious victory at Connect Four had been snatched away from him. 'Why would ghouls come here?' he asked, indignantly.

The Bourbon Kid replied. 'The ghouls are here because their masters brought them. The Four Horsemen create ghouls wherever they go, simply by killing people and then bringing them back from the dead.'

'So why are the Horsemen here?' Sanchez countered.

'End of the world shit, I would imagine,' the Kid replied.

'They arrived on a big ship,' said Beth. 'You really should leave town with us, because once those Four Horsemen come ashore, they'll turn more and more people into those ghoul things.'

The Bourbon Kid took Beth by the arm. 'Come on, let's go get your things. We're running out of time.'

Beth pleaded with Flake. 'Seriously you should come with us.'

Sanchez looked out of the windows. The streets outside were empty. Almost all of the Halloween revellers had gone home. And there was no sign of any nutcases on horses calling for the end of the world.

He heard the sound of boots pounding on the stairs behind the bar and when he looked back around, Beth and the Bourbon Kid had already vanished upstairs to collect Beth's things.

Flake looked troubled. 'They're going to leave,' she said. 'What do you think we should do?'

'Well, we're going to have to find a new barmaid,' said Sanchez, picking up some Connect Four counters from the floor. 'I mean, how selfish is that? She's just quitting without even a day's notice!'

Flake walked over to the window and looked out into the street. 'I think we should leave with the Bourbon Kid,' she said. 'Let's face it, as of tomorrow Nora Bone is shutting us down anyway. What have we got to lose?'

'I dunno,' said Sanchez, joining her, looking out of the window.

'We can always come back in a few days?' Flake suggested. 'In fact, Nora can't even close us down if we're not here.'

Sanchez liked Flake's thinking. 'I'll go and grab some money from the safe,' he said 'You keep an eye out here. Shout if you see anything.'

He headed behind the bar and bent down to where he kept his money safe hidden behind some crates of beer. Before he even had the chance to move some of them aside, he heard the sound of a window shattering in the bar area.

'SANCHEZ! THEY'RE HERE!'

Flake sounded scared, which was very rare. Sanchez grabbed hold of a beer pump and hauled himself back up so he could see what was happening. There was broken glass all over the floor and the furniture. And there were two ghastly, semi-naked, green creatures in the bar area with Flake. They had hurled themselves through the front window of The Tapioca. A blast of cold air followed them in.

Flake dealt with the intruders the same way she always did, with quick thinking and her baseball bat. She smashed one of the ghouls in the face with the bat, knocking it off its feet, sending it clattering into a table and chairs.

'Nice hit!' Sanchez shouted, offering her encouragement, so that she would feel good about dealing with the other ghoul, which was closing in on her.

Flake swung around and clattered the second ghoul around the head with the bat. It made a delightful clunking sound and spun the ghoul round a full 360 degrees. As soon as it was facing her again, she smashed the bat down on the top of its skull, which invoked a loud crunch and finished the ghoul off for good.

It was at times like this that Sanchez really did appreciate that he had the best girlfriend in the world. Flake was such a badass. He slept easy at night knowing that she was around.

She shouted over to him. 'Get me my shotgun from under the bar! I can hear more of them coming!'

'Right.'

Sanchez dropped down under the bar again. Flake kept a sawn off shotgun down there behind a crate of soft drinks. He moved the crate aside and grabbed the gun. The handle was a bit sticky, probably because all the mice that lived down there kept pissing on it all the time. Sanchez tried to get up in a hurry and banged his head on a beer pump.

'Ouch!' He rubbed his head and straightened up rather gingerly.

'Sanchez! Help!'

Flake never asked for help in a fight, so this had to be bad. Sanchez stopped rubbing his head and saw what the problem was. During the short time he'd been under the bar, at least ten more ghouls had leapt in through the broken windows. Some were semi-naked, others were completely naked, but all of them were looking for human flesh to feast on, and Flake was right in the middle of them, completely surrounded. She swung her bat and caught one of them on the shoulder. But these ghouls were instinctively good at working as a team. Unlike henchmen in movies, these fuckers didn't take turns to attack her, they all pounced on her at the same time, from every angle.

Sanchez aimed the shotgun at one of the ghouls and fired.

CLICK.

The shotgun wasn't loaded.

He looked behind him, hoping to see the Bourbon Kid running down the stairs to help out. But there was no sign of him. This was a nightmare. Flake was in big trouble at the bottom of a pile of ghouls. Sanchez had to rescue her, because no one else could. He had to think fast.

There was a fire alarm attached to the wall behind him with a warning written across it in big white letters.

"IN CASE OF EMERGENCY, BREAK GLASS"

Well this was most definitely an emergency. Sanchez rammed the barrel of his shotgun into the glass and smashed it.

Twenty Four

Beth opened the top drawer of her dresser and took out the piece of cloth with JD's initials on it. She handed it to him and immediately saw in his face that it still meant something to him.

It had been in her possession ever since Dante and Kacy's wedding, when a strange man delivered it to her on JD's behalf. It was meant as a symbol of JD's intent to return to her one day. So now that he had, it seemed only right to let him have it back because it meant even more to him than it did to her. JD's younger brother Casper had made it for him many years earlier, and it was the only thing left in the world to show that Casper ever existed. While he stared at the cloth, reflecting on what it meant to him, Beth packed a rucksack full of clothes.

'Do you still have the Eye of the Moon?' he asked.

'No. I threw it into the sea.'

'You did what?'

'That *thing* brought nothing but bad luck with it. I thought it was best to get rid of it.'

'That thing,' said JD, 'would have kept you alive. I slept better these last few years, thinking you were wearing it around your neck.'

'Yeah, but everyone who ever wore it got hunted down by vampires and stuff!'

Before he could counter her argument their conversation was interrupted by a ruckus downstairs. The sound of breaking glass and people screaming floated up the stairs.

'They've found us,' said JD.

'The ghouls? How could they?'

'I don't know. But they coulda gone anywhere, and instead they've come straight here.' JD reached inside his jacket for a weapon. He pulled out the Headblaster gun he had used to blow a ghoul's head clean off its shoulders earlier.

The screaming downstairs sounded mostly like ghouls, but Beth was certain she heard Flake yelling for help in amongst all the ghoulish cries. 'We've got to help Flake,' she said. 'And Sanchez.'

JD tucked his piece of cloth into a pocket on his pants and pointed the gun at the staircase outside the door. 'I think it's too late, and I'm low on ammo. Is there another way out?'

Beth pleaded with him. 'Flake would risk her life to help us if she could.'

She knew he could see in her eyes how much it meant to her.

'Okay,' he said. 'Wait here.'

He left her bedroom and walked onto the landing above the stairs. He poked his head over the bannister and looked down.

'Can you see anything?' Beth asked.

JD didn't reply. The screaming on the ground floor stopped suddenly too, and was replaced by a low hiss. A sudden gust of hot air blew up the staircase and along the landing into Beth's room.

JD started making his way downstairs to the bar, with his gun cocked and ready to fire. Beth cared too much about Flake to just wait in her bedroom doing nothing, so she walked softly over to the stairs and followed JD down. He reached the bottom when she was only halfway down. He vanished around the door frame and she heard him speak to someone.

'What the fuck happened here?' he said.

No one answered.

Beth didn't know who he was talking to, but she hoped it would be Flake, or Sanchez. She tiptoed down the rest of the stairs and when she reached the bottom she stepped into the serving area behind the bar.

The first person she saw was Sanchez. He was standing on her left, next to the beer pumps, where he so often stood, but he was holding an open umbrella over his head, which was a weird thing to do, even by his standards.

In the middle of the drinking area, the tables and chairs were overturned and some windows had been smashed. It looked like someone had turned on a disco smoke machine too. There was a white fog floating up from the floor to the ceiling. Flake was sitting on the floor in the middle of it soaked in blood and breathing erratically. JD was behind her looking out into the street through a gaping hole where a window used to be.

Beth sniffed the air. The stench was horrendous. It smelt like an unholy mix of burning human flesh and the Disabled toilets. And it was hot like a sauna, a really rotten, stinky sauna. And something was making Beth's eyes sting.

She shouted over to Flake. 'Flake, are you okay?'

Flake pressed her hand on the floor and pushed herself up to her feet. She wiped some red gloop from her face and flicked it onto the floor. Her cop outfit was soaking wet and stuck to her, as was her hair. She took a moment to compose herself before answering Beth.

'A whole load of those ghouls burst in here,' she said, her voice shaking. 'But Sanchez killed them all.'

Sanchez closed his umbrella and shook it dry. Much of the moisture from it landed on Beth's jeans and boots.

'What did you do?' she asked him.

Sanchez handed his soaking wet umbrella to her as if he expected her to do something with it. She took it from him and waited for him to answer her. But for once, Sanchez seemed reluctant to brag about his heroics, which was very unlike him. Flake eventually answered on his behalf.

'He set off the sprinkler system and it destroyed all of the ghouls. As soon as the water hit them they went crazy, screaming and dancing around like lunatics, and then *just like that*, they all burst into flames and melted. This weird foggy shit is all that's left of them.'

'I don't get it,' said Beth, looking to Sanchez for answers.

Sanchez grabbed a beer towel and started wiping his forehead with it. 'I had Father Papshmir pop over a while back,' he said. 'I got him to bless the water in the emergency tank that works the sprinkler system, so it made the water *holy*. I thought it would be a good idea in case any vampires ever came in again. All I had to do was give Papshmir a bottle of whisky in return.'

There was a moment of stunned silence from the others as they took on board Sanchez's unexpected stroke of clever forward planning.

'Don't worry,' he said, reassuring them all. 'I didn't give him *real* whisky.'

Flake was sniffing her fingers and her sopping wet clothes. 'This holy water smells funny,' she said, frowning.

Beth sniffed the umbrella that Sanchez had handed her. The water on it smelled distinctly like urine. She stared down at her jeans and shoes, which were covered in specks of the liquid that Sanchez had shaken over her. This wasn't water, *it was piss*. The whole room smelt of it. It took her a moment to figure out why, but then she glared at Sanchez.

'What?' said Sanchez. 'What's the matter now?'

'This isn't water is it? It's piss! Why is there piss in the sprinkler system? How is that even possible?'

Sanchez didn't answer, he just waved his hand like he was swatting a fly at her.

Beth tossed the tarnished umbrella to the floor. 'Why would you piss in the water tank?'

'Have you not heard of recycling?' said Sanchez. 'I was keeping our water bills down by filling the tank with recycled water.'

Beth looked at Flake, who she assumed would be disgusted by Sanchez's behaviour, particularly as she was drenched in his piss. To her surprise, Flake had a beaming smile across her face and was gazing at Sanchez like a love-struck teenager.

'You are so clever!' she said, rushing over to the bar to give him a kiss.

Beth liked Flake because she was clever, funny and hard-working, but one thing had always baffled her. What on earth did she see in Sanchez? Why did she always see the good in him? It was odd how a smart businesswoman like Flake, who took no shit from anyone, could be so smitten with a devious weasel like Sanchez, who somehow managed to be disgusting even when he was saving lives.

Flake leaned over the bar to try and give Sanchez a kiss. She didn't have much luck though, because he fought her off with a mop, claiming he was trying to dry her off. So Beth left them and walked over to join JD who was by the window, looking out into the street.

'Are there any more of them?' she asked.

'Can you hear that?'

Beth listened. It took a few seconds before she recognised the sound. *'Horses!'*

'Yeah, we gotta go.'

Beth pointed at Sanchez and Flake, who looked like they were fighting over a mop. 'We have to take them with us,' she said.

'Flake's covered in piss,' JD reminded her.

'She's my best friend.'

'My car is a two seater.'

'These things are following us,' said Beth. 'They know your car because they saw us drive off in it. But Sanchez has an ambulance parked out back. We can *all* get in that. And then the ghouls might not follow us.'

She was pleased with the argument she had come up with. JD's car was parked across the street. The sound of horses and more ghouls was getting closer. Beth sensed that JD saw the benefits of her ambulance suggestion.

'Okay,' he agreed. 'But why have they got an ambulance?'

'Sanchez uses it to beat the rush hour traffic when he's late for his dinner.'

'I don't know why I asked.'

Beth tugged at his sleeve. 'Come on, let's go.'

Twenty Five

Beth never imagined that her evening would end with her racing through town in the passenger seat of an ambulance. She was sandwiched between Flake and JD. Flake was driving, because no one in the city of Santa Mondega could get from 0-60 in an ambulance quicker than her. Flake had no respect for road signs or stoplights, which was exactly what was required in the current situation. JD and Beth were on the double seat on the passenger side. He was by the window, constantly checking the wing mirror for any ghouls or Horsemen that might show up behind them. He was holding a semi automatic pistol that he'd taken from the trunk of his car. Sanchez was hiding out in the back of the ambulance, his presence only noticeable whenever Flake swung the vehicle violently around a corner, and he bounced off the sides.

'What exactly is this place we're going to?' Beth asked.

'The Devil's Graveyard,' JD replied. 'I need to tell Scratch what's going on here, if he doesn't know already.'

'Who's Scratch?'

Sanchez poked his head through a pair of curtains behind the front seats. 'Do we *all* have to go to The Devil's Graveyard?'

JD replied. 'You don't have to. We can stop and let you out here if you like?'

'No, it's okay,' said Sanchez. 'It's just that I was thinking you could kill all these ghoulish things, like you normally do, then we could go home. Or to Hawaii, or anywhere where we won't bump into the Devil.'

JD stopped checking the wing mirror and looked over his shoulder at Sanchez. 'Do you know where those ghouls come from?'

'Detroit?'

'No, idiot. The Four Horsemen create those ghouls everywhere they go. They're like a plague. If one of those Horsemen touches you, you die. If they touch you again, you're reborn as a ghoul and become one of their henchmen. So if we stay here, chances are, you're gonna get fingered by a Horseman and turned into a ghoul, unless the ghouls get to you first and eat you alive.'

Sanchez shoved the back of Flake's seat. 'Flake, you heard him, put your foot down!'

Flake swung the ambulance around a corner. The ferocity of the turn made Beth fall against JD, which was no bad thing. Sanchez vanished from between the curtains and Beth heard him cursing in the back as he crashed into something.

For a while things were looking good. They made it to the northern bridge without seeing any ghouls or psychos on horses. The only noises they heard came from the back of the ambulance whenever Flake took a sharp turn. Sanchez still had some of the old ambulance equipment back there and it was all bouncing around with him.

They were less than a quarter of the way across the half-mile long bridge when Beth noticed something. The petrol gauge was almost on EMPTY.

'Look, we're almost out of gas!' she cried, pointing at it.

Flake didn't take any notice. She was checking her wing mirror. 'I think I see some ghouls on our tail,' she warned.

JD checked his mirror and confirmed it. 'Don't worry,' he said, 'I'll deal with them. Just keep driving straight.'

He opened the passenger side door and leaned out. Beth felt a huge gust of icy wind blow in, and lots of empty candy wrappers wafted up from the floor. Quite a few of them blew past Beth and hit Flake in the face, which didn't help matters.

JD steadied himself, holding onto the doorframe with one hand while he took aim at whatever was pursuing them. Beth put her fingers in her ears just in time. The rat-a-tat of gunfire from JD's gun was ear-splitting and even made Flake wince. It had to be hard driving an ambulance at sixty miles-per-hour with a door open, Sanchez's used candy wrappers flying everywhere and someone firing a gun all at the same time. Flake was doing it though, and it was all the more impressive because her clothes were soaked through with piss. And it wasn't even her own.

Another sound above them joined in the cacophony of noise.

'THERE'S ONE ON THE ROOF!' yelled Flake. She yanked the steering wheel wildly and zigzagged along the road to try and throw it off. The plan failed miserably and only succeeded in making JD lose his grip on the doorframe. Beth reached out to try and grab him but was too late. He fell from the ambulance and rolled away as he hit the ground, narrowly avoiding falling beneath the back wheels.

'We have to go back for him!' she wailed at Flake.

Flake looked across at Beth. 'Can you see him?' she asked.

'Just stop the car!' Beth cried, forgetting for a moment that it was an ambulance.

But Flake had bigger problems. The ghoul that had jumped onto the roof reached down from above and punched its fist through the window on Flake's door. Its gnarly, clawed hand reached in and grabbed a handful of her hair. Flake tried to fight it off while still swerving the ambulance around.

JD had left his Headblaster gun on the seat next to Beth. She picked it up with both hands and realised straight away it was much heavier than it looked. She swung it round and turned it on the ghoul that was fighting with Flake. The only way to be sure of not hitting Flake was to lean right across her. So she planted one foot on the floor and stuck the gun in front of Flake's face.

BOOM!

The ghoul's head vanished in a spray of red mist and its body fell under the wheels of the ambulance. But the ghoul wasn't the only one to suffer. The recoil from the gun lifted Beth up off the seat and hurled her back towards the open door on the passenger side. The Headblaster gun flew out of her hand and clattered against the dashboard. She flailed around, trying desperately to grab onto anything that would prevent her falling out of the ambulance.

The road rushed up towards Beth's face. She braced herself for the impact. She was inches from obliteration when she felt a hand grab her ankle. Flake had reached over and caught hold of her just in the nick of time. Beth watched the road race by as Flake struggled with the steering wheel in one hand and her ankle in the other. As the vehicle slowed down, Beth was able to grab hold of the door, which was swinging back and forth in the wind. She hauled herself up until she was able to grasp hold of the headrest on the passenger seat. Flake slowed the ambulance to a stop and Beth climbed back onto the seat, gasping for air.

'You okay?' Flake asked.

Beth nodded and rubbed her throat. 'Yeah, thanks.'

'Can you see JD back there?'

Beth was about to jump out and look for JD when she spotted another ghoul at Flake's window. It had snuck up from nowhere.

'LOOK OUT!'

Flake didn't get a chance to react. The green skinned monster reached in through the window frame and lunged at her with a knife. This particular ghoul knew exactly what it was doing too. It plunged the blade of the knife deep into Flake's neck.

Twenty Six

Scratch was sitting on a stool behind the bar in Purgatory watching his favourite show *"Butt Naked News"* on the television hanging on the wall. The evening's "butt naked" newsreader Linda Bratwurst was on one side of a split screen, interviewing a fully clothed weirdo called Hans Kapono on the other side. Kapono was ranting about an alien invasion, which he claimed had already taken place. He was convinced that the aliens were secretly running the world.

Scratch hadn't been paying much attention to Kapono's crackpot theories to begin with, preferring to study Linda Bratwurst's naked body for any sign that she was once a man. But then he heard Hans Kapono say the name *Salvatore Rocco*.

'I believe Rocco was possessed by an alien when he tried to break into the Riverdale Mansion,' Kapono claimed.

Scratch was an expert lie detector. He studied Kapono's face to look for any obvious signs of dishonesty. In doing so, he missed Linda Bratwurst crossing her legs on the other side of the screen. But after studying all of Kapono's body language, Scratch deduced that the conspiracy theorist was telling the truth, or certainly believed he was.

Scratch picked up the remote control so he could rewind the TV back to the moment when Linda crossed her legs. He was a millisecond away from pressing the rewind button when the show cut to some amateur video footage Kapono had recorded on his cellphone. A caption at the bottom of the screen read –

RIVERDALE MANSION YESTERDAY

Scratch's finger hovered over the rewind button as he watched the grainy video footage of the grounds outside the Riverdale Mansion from the previous night. The shaky camera footage was taken from high up in a tree and was focussed on the main entrance of the mansion. A tall figure walked out of the entrance onto the porch, at which point the film was paused and Hans Kapono said something about the figure in the video being one of the aliens. Scratch nearly dropped his remote. The person in the footage had bright green hair. Scratch recognised the face straight away.

'Yesil!'

Yesil was one of the Four Horsemen of the Apocalypse, all of whom had been missing for centuries.

Scratch grabbed a bright red telephone from below the bar. It was an old fashioned phone with a dial, which wasn't connected to any phone networks, but had a direct line to Hell. He dialled the number 666. The receptionist in Hell, a former talent show host called Nigel Powell, answered the call promptly.

'Yes sir, how can I help you?'

'Send up Annabel de Frugyn right away.'

'Yes sir, erm..... may I come up too?'

'Fuck off.'

Scratch slammed the receiver down and carried on watching the news. Linda Bratwurst made some sarcastic remarks about the footage from Riverdale Mansion. She then ended her interview with Hans Kapono and switched to a political piece about rumours of the Australian Prime Minister being half man, half goat.

Scratch started rewinding the show back to the moment when Linda Bratwurst crossed her legs. He was just about to press pause when he sensed someone behind him. He looked around and saw Annabel de Frugyn, the Mystic Lady, approaching the bar. She was a crusty old hag with long white hair who always wore a musty cardigan over several layers of other musty garments. Today's cardigan was blue, which was in sharp contrast to the bright red handbag hanging over her shoulder. Scratch had given her the handbag as a reward for predicting the deaths of a bunch of celebrities a few years earlier. He would never admit it out loud, but he liked Annabel. She was entertaining and she could predict the future, more or less.

'You called for me?' she said in a croaky voice.

'Have you brought your crystal ball?'

She reached into her handbag and pulled out a spherical object with white misty liquid swirling around inside it.

'Grab yourself a stool and sit down,' said Scratch.

'This will have to be done over in the corner,' said Annabel. 'It's darker over there. I need the shadows.'

Scratch grabbed a bottle of red wine and two glasses from behind the bar and followed her to the corner table. While she positioned her crystal ball in the centre of the table and waved her hands over it, Scratch poured wine into the two glasses. He filled them each halfway and set the bottle down on the table.

'I assume red wine is okay with you?' he said, sliding her glass across to her.

'Yes, thank you,' said Annabel. She picked up the bottle of red wine and took a swig from it.

'This is good stuff,' she said.

Scratch resisted the temptation to smash her across the face with the back of his hand. He knew how cantankerous she could be when he was short with her, so he bit his tongue and got down to business.

'I need you to look into your ball for any signs of an impending apocalypse,' he said.

'*I knew* you were going to say that.'

'No you didn't.'

'Oh, didn't I?'

'Would you just look in the fucking ball and tell me what you see?'

Annabel fidgeted in her chair and murmured under her breath for a while, which Scratch knew was all for effect. She closed her eyes and pretended to meditate. Scratch took a deep breath. The fake meditating drove him fucking crazy, and Annabel knew it. When she decided she was ready, and Scratch was clearly on the verge of throttling her, she reopened her eyes and began waving her hands over her crystal ball. The mist in the middle of it began moving, making strange shapes. She stared into it and made some odd facial expressions for a while, before finally announcing what she had seen.

'It was a man,' she said.

'What was?'

'Linda Bratwurst.'

'You fucking idiot. Not that. I want to know about the Riverdale Mansion!'

'Hang on.'

Annabel went all through her repertoire of fake and extremely annoying rituals again before finally giving him some relevant information.

'It was Cain,' she said.

'Cain was with Yesil?'

'Who's Yesil?'

'The person with the green hair I just saw on the news, standing outside the Riverdale Mansion.'

'Aah, the Riverdale Mansion.'

'Yes, the Riverdale Mansion.'

Annabel nodded. 'Yesil was outside the Riverdale Mansion.'

Scratch balled his fists beneath the table. '*I know that*, but I need to know why? And who with?'

'Yesil is with three others. All of them accomplished riders.'

'Zitrone, Blanco and Ash!'

'Bingo,' said Annabel, pointing at him like she was a cheesy game-show host. 'I see a blond one, a dark-haired one, a white-haired one and the green-haired one. They're working with Cain.'

'But what were they doing in the Riverdale?'

'They were imprisoned below ground.'

Scratch started piecing things together in his mind. 'I don't believe it.'

'It's true,' said Annabel.

'No, I mean, I knew Jesus imprisoned the Four Horsemen, but I never knew it was here on earth.'

Annabel took another swig of wine. 'Why didn't he just kill them?' she asked. 'That would have been a lot simpler, wouldn't it?'

'Damn right it would,' Scratch agreed. 'But God decreed that the Four Horsemen should be imprisoned, so that if mankind ever turned into a bunch of arseholes....'

'Arseholes?'

'His word, not mine,' Scratch continued. 'God speaks with a Scottish accent, y'know. Anyway, he decreed that if humans became arseholes, the Four Horsemen could be set free to finish what they started.'

'Destroying mankind?'

'Exactly. And now that Cain has set them free, that's exactly what they'll try to do.'

For once Annabel seemed to realise the seriousness of what Scratch was saying. 'Can you stop them?' she asked.

'It depends. Where are they now?'

Annabel looked back into her crystal ball. Scratch noticed a distinct lack of theatrics this time. 'They're no longer at the Riverdale Mansion,' she said, looking back up.

'So where are they?'

'They're in Santa Mondega.'

'Santa Mondega? What the fuck are they doing there?'

'They're building an army of ghouls. Then they're coming here.'

'Coming here? Are you sure?'

'Yes, their intention is to open up the gateway to Hell.'

Scratch kicked his chair back and stood up. 'We're going to have to get The Dead Hunters back here as soon as possible.' he said, picking up his glass of wine. 'Can you find them for me?'

Annabel stared into the ball again and waved her hands over it. The mist within the ball swirled around again. But then Annabel's jaw dropped. 'Uh oh.'

'What do you mean, *uh oh?*'

'The Red Mohawk has been beheaded.'

Scratch spat a mouthful of wine out onto the floor. 'He's what?'

'He's dead. Beheaded by something in a forest. I can't see what though. It's kind of hazy.'

Annabel had been known to be wrong about things from time to time. It had been one of the things Scratch liked about her, because it spiced things up sometimes. But right now, he needed her to be correct about everything.

'What about Baby?' he asked. 'She was with him.'

Annabel put her hand over her mouth and shook her head. 'She's dead too. Strangled by Rex!'

'Rex? You've got that wrong. Rex would never hurt Baby.'

'He didn't.'

'You just said he did.'

'He was possessed by the ghost of Cain.'

Scratch roared as only a demon from Hell who was really, really fucked off could. 'How the Hell did Cain possess Rex? Was Rex in a coma?' Scratch seized Annabel's bottle of wine and took a violent swig to keep himself from turning the whole bar into the Inferno.

Annabel waited for him to hand back the bottle of red wine before she replied. 'Rex was put under sedation to have a hand transplant,' she explained. 'So Cain sneaked in and took over his body.'

Scratch visualised the scenario in his head. 'So has Rex woken up yet?'

'No. Cain is keeping him in a coma by injecting the body with sedatives every hour or so. Rex is powerless.'

'*Shit the bed,* this is bad. What about the others?' he asked. 'Do they know about this?'

Annabel stared into her ball again, before announcing, 'It's not good.'

'What's happened?'

'Cain cut the brakes on Jasmine's car. She and Elvis went over a cliff and crashed.'

'Are they dead?'

Annabel took a swig from the bottle of red wine before replying. 'Yeah, they're dead.'

Scratch was panicked. 'What about the Bourbon Kid? If you tell me he's dead I'll burn all your cardigans.'

'He's alive at the moment. But the Horsemen set a trap for him in Santa Mondega.'

Scratch started pacing back and forth, processing the news and working out what it meant. Then something hit him. Something big.

'Woah, woah, woah. Hold on a minute!' he said. 'Backup a second. If Joey, Baby, Jasmine and Elvis are all dead, then how come they're not downstairs? Huh? Explain that?'

Annabel peered into her crystal ball once more. 'You're not gonna like this.'

'Tell me anyway.'

'All of them did such a good job for you, you know, they saved thousands of lives.'

'Yeah, so?'

'So God allowed them into Heaven.'

Scratch squeezed his wine glass so hard it cracked in his hand, spraying glass and wine everywhere.

'Did you just say God allowed them into Heaven?' Scratch whispered. Normally this whisper would make the strongest man quake in his boots.

'Yes,' said Annabel taking a sip from the bottle of wine, not remotely bothered.

'So he knows.'

'Knows what?'

'That the Four Horsemen are on the loose. This is bad.'

'It is?'

'Yes,' said Scratch, rubbing his forehead in frustration. 'The last time the Four Horsemen were loose, God sent Jesus to destroy them and save mankind.'

Annabel perked up. 'Ooh, do you think he'll send him again? I'd love to meet him.'

Scratch gritted his teeth. 'If God was going to send anyone to prevent this apocalypse he'd have done it already. The fact he's sent *no one* means he's had enough of mankind. He *wants* the world to end!'

Twenty Seven

The ghoul yanked its knife out of Flake's neck and made a move to stab her again. But before he could, Flake's arms fell down by her side and her head slumped forward, thudding onto the steering wheel and sounding off the horn. The ambulance was still moving and Flake's foot fell heavily onto the gas pedal. They deviated sharply across the road and collided with a motorbike in the oncoming lane. The bike hurtled through the air, separating from its rider, who bounced onto the hood of the ambulance and flew off to the side of the road. The back wheel of the bike smashed into the face of the ghoul at Flake's window and sent it sprawling away from the ambulance.

Beth reached over and seized hold of the steering wheel. She yanked it towards her to try and steady it but only caused it to veer wildly out of control. It swerved across the bridge until it eventually hit the solid metal railings at the side, slamming the passenger door shut. There was a horrible screech as it scraped along the railings for a few metres before it came to a standstill, the engine still revving loudly.

Beth didn't even get time to take stock of the situation. The ghoul that had stabbed Flake reappeared at the driver's window, and this time it had its eyes on Beth.

Beth had nowhere to go. The passenger door was shut and smashed against the railings. She pressed her back up against it and hoped to kick out at the ghoul. It climbed over Flake, who was no longer moving and had blood gushing from the wound in her neck. The ghoul's bright green eyes were fixed on Beth as it moved towards her. She readied herself to kick out at it when it was close enough. The ghoul hissed through its rotting yellow teeth, and then surprised her by leaping onto her legs before she could kick out. She screamed and struggled to free her legs, but the ghoul was stronger than her. It crawled onto her upper body, its foul breath wafting over her. It held her down with one hand and lifted its knife. The blade was already covered in Flake's blood. As it swung down towards Beth's face, she turned away.

What followed was a lot of screaming and a weird buzzing sound, followed by the smell of burning flesh. But nothing touched Beth. No blade, no ghoulish fingers, nothing.

Beth looked back. The ghoul was still there, but it had dropped the knife. It was shaking violently and smoke was pouring out of its mouth. And most curiously of all, it had a pair of electric paddles pressed against either side of its head. The hands holding the paddles belonged to Sanchez. He had charged up a defibrillator in the back of the ambulance and was leaning over the seats, melting the ghoul's head with the paddles.

The ghoul was dead for probably four or five seconds before Sanchez released it. It flopped forward onto Beth's lap, smoke pouring from its mouth, nose and ears.

Beth pushed it off her and crawled across to where Flake was slumped on the steering wheel. She pulled Flake's head back and saw blood gushing from her neck.

'Sanchez, help her! She's been stabbed!'

Sanchez dropped the electric paddles and grabbed Flake. He slipped his hands underneath her armpits and hauled her towards him. Her clothes were covered in blood from the knife wound, which was mixing in with all the piss from Sanchez's sprinkler system. She mumbled something but Beth couldn't hear it because the engine was still revving loudly.

Beth reached across to the ignition key and switched the engine off while Sanchez lifted Flake over the seats into the back. It didn't look like it was helping Flake at all.

Beth turned on him. 'I'm not sure you should be moving her!'

'I've got first aid equipment and stuff back here. Start driving. Get us out of here!'

It bothered Beth that Sanchez seemed to have a better grip on the situation than she did. That had never happened before. Ever. She crawled across to the driver's side. Flake's blood was all over the seat and the steering wheel. And the smell of the electrocuted ghoul was stinking out the ambulance too. Beth wanted the dead ghoul out, but right now there wasn't time. She poked her head out of the window to look for any sign of JD.

She saw him a long way back down the bridge standing in the middle of a cloud of smoke. There were dead ghouls lying on the ground all around him. He had taken a sword from one of them and used it to chop them all up. Only one ghoul was left standing and that wasn't for long. JD cut it in two with one swing that went from its crotch to its head. It fell apart and landed on the ground on either side of him.

For just one brief peaceful moment in amidst all the carnage, Beth's face broke into a half smile. She snapped back to reality when she heard Flake scream out in pain. She twisted round and poked her head through the curtain to see how Sanchez was doing. He was in the process of wrapping a thick medical dressing around Flake's neck. But no matter how many times he wrapped it round, blood kept soaking through it. When Beth saw the state of Flake, her face pale and lifeless, she realised that the scream she'd heard had come not from Flake, but from Sanchez.

She had never seen him so frantic. If Flake was to survive she would need professional medical help. And soon. Beth couldn't leave it up to Sanchez, so she climbed over the seats into the back to see if she could help.

'Is she gonna be okay?' she asked.

'I don't know.'

Sanchez had laid Flake down on a stretcher bed and was sitting astride her, with his hand on her neck, trying to keep pressure on the wound.

'Oh my God, what the hell is that swelling?' Beth screeched, referring to a lump beneath the dressing on Flake's neck. 'You should have let me do this. That doesn't look right.'

'It's okay,' said Sanchez. 'I've put a medical pressure plug over the wound. It helps to stem the bleeding.'

'What the hell is a pressure plug?'

'It's a medical thing. I only found out about it when I bought the ambulance. There was one in the back with the defibrillators.'

Odd though it seemed, Sanchez sounded like he knew what he was talking about. But Beth desperately wanted to help, even if it only meant offering encouragement. 'Make sure you keep talking to her. You've got to keep her conscious.'

The back doors swung open, startling Beth and Sanchez. Beth looked up and saw JD standing outside. His face and hands were covered in ghoul blood and entrails. His eyes were drawn to Flake.

'She okay?' he asked.

'No,' Sanchez shouted back. 'We need to get her to a hospital.'

'You can't,' said JD. 'You've got to go to The Devil's Graveyard.'

Beth felt a cold chill run through her. 'You're still coming with us, aren't you?'

'No, I'm going to buy you some time so you can get there in one piece.'

Beth bit her lip and nodded, which was completely the opposite of what she wanted to do.

JD tossed his phone to her as he continued to scan the road for more ghouls or any sign of the Horsemen. 'Put your number in there for me.'

This wasn't exactly the situation Beth had envisioned when she dreamed about getting his number. But after all these years it was a big step in their relationship.

'Hurry up!' Sanchez yelled at her.

The display on JD's phone showed that he had a voicemail from someone named Baby. For one fleeting moment, Beth wondered what it meant. She quickly suppressed the thought and typed in her number, before tossing the phone back to JD.

'By the way,' she said, 'you've got a voice mail from Baby!'

'From Baby?' JD frowned. He put the phone to his ear and played the message. He seemed surprised, but as he listened to the short message, his expression became grave.

'Is it bad news?' Beth asked.

'She's in trouble.'

'Oh.'

JD started to say something, but Sanchez ended the moment by tugging at Beth's jacket. 'We need to go! Start driving!'

'Sanchez knows where The Devil's Graveyard is,' said JD. He barked an order at Sanchez. 'When you get to the crossroads, tell Jacko I sent you. He'll remember you and open the road to Purgatory for you.'

'Jacko?' said Sanchez. 'The blues singer?'

'Yeah.'

'I don't think he likes me.'

'Nobody likes you! But when you get to the crossroads in The Devil's Graveyard, Jacko will let you into Purgatory.'

Flake let out a dull groan, which distracted Sanchez momentarily, reminding him of the urgency of their predicament. 'All right,' he said. 'But we need to stop for gas. We're already on empty.'

'So get going,' JD said, losing his patience. 'I'll meet you at Purgatory!'

Beth climbed out of the ambulance and ran to the driver's door with JD escorting her. 'What are you going to do?' she asked as she reached the door.

JD pointed at a motorbike lying on the road a few car lengths back from the ambulance. 'I'm going to take that motorbike and lead those Four Horsemen off in a different direction. When I've lost them I'm going to find Baby.'

'What happened to the bike rider?' Beth asked. 'We hit him with the ambulance.'

'He's dead.'

Beth felt bad for the innocent young man who had been riding the bike. This really was a horrible day for lots of reasons.

But then JD leaned in and kissed her. She placed her hands on his shoulders and kissed him back with the passion she had been saving up since they'd last been together.

JD pulled away and smiled. 'Get outta here. I'll see you in Purgatory.'

Beth smiled back at him, then opened the door and climbed in. There wasn't time to remove the dead ghoul from the passenger seat, or clean up all the blood. As she closed the door, she checked the wing mirror for one last look at JD. What she saw was a bunch of dead ghouls halfway down the bridge, and then further back two men on horses riding onto the bridge. JD walked out into the middle of the road to face them. Beth whispered a *"good luck, I love you"* to him that she knew he wouldn't hear. Then she stuck the ambulance in reverse and backed it out of the railings it had crashed into.

She floored the gas pedal and headed for The Devil's Graveyard, while a red gas light on the dashboard reminded her that they were still in danger.

Twenty Eight

Ash and Zitrone rode their horses onto the bridge and surveyed the carnage that had taken place halfway across it. The ambulance they were in pursuit of was almost out of sight, and they were almost out of ghouls. Every single one of the undead henchmen that had chased the ambulance onto the bridge had been slain. All that remained of them was a huge wall of thick smoke rising up from their corpses. In the midst of the smoke was the outline of a hooded man dressed all in black, wielding a sword taken from one of the henchmen.

'He killed them all,' said Ash, stating the obvious.

'He's the one,' Zitrone replied. 'The one with the blood of God in his veins. He is as dangerous as Cain predicted.'

'He's waiting for us. Come on, let's go kill him.'

Zitrone held out his hand, gesturing for Ash to stay where he was. 'This is the Bourbon Kid,' he warned. 'I've read all about him. If we are to kill this man, we must either have the element of surprise on our side, or we must do it as a group. Surprise is no longer on our side. So let's wait here for Yesil and Blanco.'

'But he could flee before they arrive. This is our chance!'

'No it's not. This is *his* chance to kill us. We must attack as a four, not repeat the mistakes of the past.'

Zitrone sensed that Ash was desperate to storm the bridge. Two thousand years of imprisonment can make a man rather impatient. And extremely vengeful.

Ash looked over his shoulder. 'Where the fuck are they?'

'They're creating more ghouls.'

'We don't need more ghouls.'

Zitrone ignored Ash. Something else had caught his eye. An old lady on a moped rode up to the bridge. She ignored the two men on horses, and carried on towards the smoke and the orgy of dead ghouls further down the bridge.

'See!' Ash raged. 'Even that little old woman isn't afraid. We look like fools waiting here!'

'No we don't.'

'Fuck this!'

Ash unsheathed his sword and dug his heels into his horse. The horse reared up and let out a loud screech, then it charged down the bridge towards the Bourbon Kid, with Ash holding his sword aloft, pointing it ahead like a joust.

Zitrone didn't move. He knew Ash well enough to have foreseen what was happening. What he didn't know, but he was keen to know, was just how fearsome an opponent the Bourbon Kid would turn out to be.

Ash's horse galloped past the old woman on the moped and charged towards the Bourbon Kid. The Kid's silhouette flickered in and out of view within the plumes of smoke. The horse hurdled a few dead ghouls and then leapt into the cloud, vanishing from sight along with the Bourbon Kid. The old woman on the moped breezed on through after him, seemingly oblivious to what lay in store.

Zitrone turned his head to the side, hoping to hear what went on behind the wall of fog on the bridge. The old lady's moped drowned out most of what went on, and then the sound of hooves pounding on the ground behind him killed any hope he had of hearing swords clanging on the bridge.

Yesil and Blanco trotted onto the bridge and joined Zitrone. They had a group of almost twenty freshly acquired ghouls with them.

Blanco pulled up next to Zitrone. 'Where is Ash?' he inquired.

'Behind that cloud of smoke.'

'Doing what?'

'He couldn't wait. He's gone to kill the Bourbon Kid.'

'Then what are we waiting for?' said Blanco. 'Let's go. We can cut this Bourbon Kid's heart out and feed it to him!'

Zitrone let out a deep sigh. 'No,' he said. 'Send the ghouls.'

Yesil rode around Blanco and shouted at Zitrone in a high-pitched voice. 'Why are we sending the ghouls?'

'Because that's what I said to do.'

'Okay, fine.'

Yesil turned away and screamed at the ghouls, waving them onto the bridge. They swarmed across it, screeching and yelling like wild animals.

'So what are *we* supposed to do?' Blanco asked.

'You two are to return to the ship. Sail along the coast and board every other vessel you see. Kill the people you find and turn them into ghouls. Then wait for my call.'

'Where are you going?'

'I'm going after the fat man, Sanchez Garcia. If I'm correct, he'll lead me straight to The Devil's Graveyard.'

Blanco and Yesil exchanged looks. Blanco voiced their concern. 'But what about Ash?'

Zitrone stared ahead at the white cloud of smoke on the bridge. The mix of sounds he had heard within it earlier had been silenced, drowned out by the howls of the ghouls rushing towards it.

Blanco repeated his question. 'Zitrone, what about Ash?'

Halfway down the bridge, behind the cloud of smoke, a motorbike engine roared into life. Zitrone knew what it meant. He turned to Yesil and Blanco.

'Ash is already dead.'

Twenty Nine

Beth swung the ambulance off the road and onto the gas station forecourt. She parked up next to one of the gas pumps, killed the engine and jumped out. There was nothing following them, but even so, there was no time for dawdling around. She raced around to the back of the ambulance and pulled one of the doors open. Sanchez was sitting beside Flake, mopping her brow with a damp cloth.

'How is she?' Beth asked.

'Still breathing,' he replied. 'But she's drifting in and out of consciousness.'

'Okay, look, I'm going to fill the ambulance up with gas. To save time, you're going to have to go in and pay. I'll keep an eye on Flake while you're in there.'

'Pay?' said Sanchez. 'We haven't got time to pay. We can just drive off.'

'How far is The Devil's Graveyard?'

'It's at least three hundred miles.'

'So we're gonna need some drinks. Go and get some bottles of water from the store while I'm filling up.'

Sanchez could see the sense in Beth's thinking, so he rummaged around in Flake's pockets until he found her credit card, then he hurried into the store on the forecourt.

The store had a musty, stale smell to it and it was crammed from top to bottom with typical convenience store food. Sanchez grabbed two bottles of water from a shelf and took them up to the counter. The attendant was a young man with long greasy hair who looked like a stoner. And according to his name badge he was called Keith. Sanchez took an immediate dislike to him.

'Are you with the ambulance?' Keith asked.

'Yeah.'

'You're friend is still filling it up.'

Sanchez looked out of the window and saw Beth was still filling the ambulance with gas. There was no sign of any ghouls or Horsemen though, so there was no need to panic just yet.

'There's a free hot dog for every customer spending over fifty dollars today.'

Sanchez heard the words "free hot dog" and forgot about all the ghouls and the Horsemen in an instant. 'What?'

'Hot dog,' said Keith. 'Would you like a free hot dog?'

'Hell yeah.'

Sanchez couldn't believe he hadn't noticed it before, but behind the counter there was a glass cabinet filled with hot dogs. Keith, who had suddenly gone up in Sanchez's estimation, turned his back and opened the cabinet to get a hot dog. There was a basket on the counter, filled with complimentary red and brown ketchup sachets. So while Keith wasn't looking, Sanchez grabbed as many as he could and filled his pockets.

By the time Keith handed Sanchez his hot dog, Beth had finished filling up the tank. Keith rang up the sale.

'That's eighty-five bucks.'

Sanchez settled the bill with Flake's credit card and waited while Keith took an age to pack the water bottles into a brown paper bag. When he walked back out to the forecourt, Beth had already started up the engine and was ready to get back on the road. Sanchez headed towards the back of ambulance and was just about to take a bite of his hot dog when Beth honked the horn. He looked up and saw she was waving frantically at him. Then he heard the howling. It came from down the road. Ghouls were heading their way.

Shit!

He ran over to the ambulance. The back door was still open, so he threw the bag with the water bottles into the back and climbed in after them. Beth didn't exactly give him much time. She started pulling away before he'd even managed to close the door. The door swung hard and hit his hand, knocking his hot dog loose. It slipped out of his hand and fell onto the forecourt. He watched in dismay as it got smaller and smaller, as they sped away.

As soon as they were back on the road, he saw the ghouls that had been making all the noise. They were five or six car lengths back, chasing an old lady riding a moped down the middle of the street.

Beth shouted back through the curtain to him. 'Sanchez, there's a woman behind us on a moped. They'll kill her. You've gotta do something!'

Sanchez was trying to reach out for the back door, which was flapping open in the wind. He could see the woman on the moped very clearly. It was Nora Bone, the old witch from the Health and Hygiene Department who was intending to shut down The Tapioca. She was panicking and checking over her shoulder every few seconds to see if the ghouls were gaining on her.

'Can you see them?' Beth yelled.

'Yeah. They're gonna catch her any second now!'

CLUNK.

A large handgun landed at Sanchez's feet.

'Use that!' Beth shouted. 'It's JD's gun. It's really powerful. One shot will blow the head off one of those things! Fire a few shots and see if you can scare them away!'

Sanchez picked up the gun. It was fucking heavy. He crept closer to the open door. Nora Bone was riding along the white lines in the middle of the street, about thirty metres behind the ambulance. She was wearing a red helmet and a pair of goggles, and a grey coat that was blowing around in the wind. It crossed Sanchez's mind that she looked rather like a giant shuttlecock. One that was about to be eaten alive by some nasty green creatures.

The wind was blowing the back door around, so Sanchez used one hand to keep it open and pointed the gun at the ghouls who were chasing after Nora. He could hear her screaming for help over the sound of her moped and the howling monsters. Even though he didn't like her, he had to try and help, especially as it might make her reconsider shutting down The Tapioca.

Now Sanchez wasn't good with guns. The last time he'd fired one he'd missed his target and hit himself in the face with the gun, knocking himself out. So this was his chance to prove he could shoot like a man. He closed one eye and lined up the biggest ghoul in his sights.

BANG!

Sanchez's shooting arm snapped back, almost dislocating his shoulder. That was the least of his problems though. His aim hadn't improved at all since the last time he'd fired a gun. He hadn't hit any of the ghouls. The blast from the gun had blown the front wheel clean off Nora Bone's moped. The moped buckled and the back wheel flew up in the air, ejecting Nora like she'd been fired out of a cannon. She somersaulted through the air towards the ambulance. But, with Sanchez no longer holding the door open, a gust of wind blew it shut as Nora reached out to try and grab it.

THUD!

Nora's face ploughed into the back window of the door. Sanchez made eye contact with her for just long enough to see that she was cursing him. A moment later she was gone. She slid off the back of the ambulance and down onto the road. Within seconds the ghouls swarmed all over her. Sanchez had to look away as the bloodthirsty monsters ripped Nora to pieces, gorging on her flesh. On a positive note though, they did stop chasing after the ambulance. And as Sanchez watched two of the ghouls chewing on Nora's legs, it occurred to him that The Tapioca wouldn't get shut down, not until the next Hygiene inspection anyway. So it wasn't a total disaster.

Beth yelled back through the curtain. 'What happened? Did she get away?'

'Erm…. Well… they're not chasing her anymore,' Sanchez replied.

'Oh, that's good. Well done! Where are they now?'

Sanchez took one last look out of the back window. Nora Bone and the ghouls had vanished in the distance. 'I scared 'em off,' he said. 'They're all gone.'

'Great! Now you can take over the driving.'

'I'm not driving.'

'You're the only one who knows the way to The Devil's Graveyard.'

'Just keep going straight ahead. I think I'm gonna take a nap. All this stuff has been exhausting.'

Suddenly, without warning, Beth slammed on the brakes, which sent Sanchez sprawling. He slid across the floor until his head poked through the curtains at the front, and he found himself staring into the eyes of a dead ghoul on the passenger seat.

'I'll make you a deal,' said Beth. 'If I throw out that dead ghoul, will you drive?'

Sanchez weighed up his options. The dead ghoul was leaking blood and puss everywhere. Driving was probably the less messy option.

The two of them quickly swapped places and Beth successfully shoved the dead ghoul out into the road. When they set off again, Beth hopped into the back to take care of Flake. And Sanchez drove through the night to The Devil's Graveyard, blissfully unaware that a blond man on a horse was following them.

Thirty

Cain dragged Baby's dead body off the road and concealed it behind a bush on the edge of the forest. He rummaged through her pockets and found her cellphone. To his enormous frustration he discovered it was locked. He cursed himself for not getting the passcode from her before he'd killed her. He took the phone anyway and then ran his hands over her body looking for any other items of value.

She had nothing else that he wanted, so he left her hidden behind the bush and walked back to his bike. Everything he had planned had worked so far. He'd done his part of the job. It was time to make a call to Zitrone to see if the Four Horsemen had done their part. But then Baby's phone rang. He fumbled around in his pocket for it and almost dropped it when he saw who was calling.

BOURBON KID

He answered the call and pressed the phone to his ear. Risky though it was, he whispered in a high-pitched voice. 'Hello?'

A gravelly voice replied. 'Baby? You okay?'

'Yes.' Cain sniffed a little for added effect, which also meant he didn't have to say much. Baby was a crier, and the Bourbon Kid would know that.

'I'm on my way, okay.'

'Okay.'

'I'll be with you in a few hours. Sit tight.'

The line went dead. Cain squeezed Baby's phone in frustration. The Bourbon Kid had hung up before mentioning where he was going to meet Baby. He looked around and considered his options. Should he wait with Baby's corpse, or find somewhere sheltered and hope the Kid was tracking her phone?

He hadn't made his mind up when another call came in. This time on his own phone. It was Zitrone.

He answered it bluntly. 'What do you want?'

There was a lot of background noise coming from Zitrone's end. It sounded like he was riding his horse on concrete. The clipperty-clopping of hooves almost drowned out his reply.

'Ash is dead.'

'What did you say?'

'Ash is dead.'

'How?'

'The Bourbon Kid beheaded him.'

'What the fuck?'

'He was stupid,' said Zitrone. 'It was his own fault. He disobeyed my orders.'

'Where did this happen?'

'Santa Mondega. We found the Bourbon Kid and his girlfriend at the end of the pier, just like you said. He wiped out our entire army of ghouls.'

'I told you he was a fucker.'

'Yes, well he got away, but his girlfriend is with the fat man.'

'Sanchez?'

'Yes. They're in an ambulance. I'm following them but keeping my distance so they don't see me.'

'You think they're going to The Devil's Graveyard?'

'They're going in the right direction.'

'Are Blanco and Yesil with you?'

'I sent them back to the ship. They're going to replenish our army of ghouls.'

'You might want to send them to Blue Corn Island.'

'What for?'

'I just took a call from the Bourbon Kid. He's coming here now.'

The other end of the line went quiet. Cain assumed that Zitrone was trying to make sense of what he'd said. Eventually Zitrone responded. 'How did you talk to the Bourbon Kid?'

Cain was itching for the opportunity to gloat. 'I did what I said I'd do. I used Rodeo Rex's body to get close to the others. They're all dead. The only one left now is the Bourbon Kid. And he called Baby's phone just now. I answered it and pretended to be her.'

'And he fell for it?'

'Yeah, I let him do all the talking. I just sobbed. So, Zitrone, the good news is, he's coming here now. Shall I keep him alive for you?'

'No. Kill him.'

Thirty One

The Bourbon Kid revved the bike again, accelerating. He had to find Baby, and Blue Corn Island was still a long way away. As he'd travelled through the night, he'd thought about the bridge, the poor dead kid who'd been the previous owner of the bike, killing the ghouls, and killing Ash, the dark Horseman. Feeling that sword slice through Ash's neck, dismembering his head so cleanly, hearing it bounce on the ground, it felt good. And then there was Beth. There was Beth's smile. He shook his head. Because there was also Baby. He'd phoned her while he was on the way to Blue Corn and she'd barely been able to speak. He had to be on alert. Whatever had gotten the better of the Red Mohawk wasn't something to be taken lightly.

He'd tried calling Elvis and Jasmine too, but they weren't answering their phones. He'd even tried calling Rex. *No one was taking calls.* With the arrival of the Four Horsemen and their army of ghouls, the lack of communication from the others was a bad sign.

It was five o'clock in the morning when he found the bar Baby had mentioned in her voicemail message. The Fork In Hell was the last building on the main road through Crimson County, just before a deep stretch of forest. From the outside the place looked closed, which was hardly surprising given the time of day. He parked the bike off to the side and hopped off.

It didn't look like a dangerous place, but given the events of earlier in the evening, the Bourbon Kid approached with caution. His guns were all out of ammo and he'd ditched the sword he killed Ash with because riding a motorbike with an unsheathed sword was dumber than running with scissors. So he walked up to The Fork In Hell armed only with his fists.

Like all great bars, The Fork was open twenty-four hours. He pushed open the windowless door at the front and walked in. There were only three people inside and one of those was the bartender. There was no sign of Baby.

Two fat guys were playing pool in an open area with tables dotted around it. The fatter of the two, a dark haired loser wearing a red and black checked shirt was lining up a shot. He paused and glanced up as the Kid walked in. When he saw the new customer was a man, he turned his attention back to his shot.

The Kid walked up to the bar and sat on a stool. The bartender, a rather average looking fellow with short dark hair and a thick black moustache nodded at him, but didn't speak. This place was ideal for drinking, but it didn't look like it was going to be a good place for asking questions about a missing girl. So the Kid did what came naturally.

'Bartender, get me a bourbon.'

The bartender reached under the bar for a whisky glass and placed it on the bar. He grabbed a bottle of Sam Cougar and poured a shot into the glass.

'You want ice?' he said.

'No. Fill the glass.'

The bartender hesitated. 'We don't run tabs for strangers,' he said. 'That'll cost you twenty bucks.'

The Kid took a soft pack of cigarettes from his jacket and pulled one out with his teeth. As soon as he sucked on it, it lit up on its own. After taking a drag he reached into his pocket, pulled out a crumpled twenty-dollar bill and dropped it on the bar.

The bartender acknowledged the payment and poured some more Sam Cougar until the glass was full. When he reached for the twenty-dollar bill, the Kid grabbed his hand and squeezed it.

'You seen a young woman in here on her own tonight?' he asked.

The bartender winced. 'What's she look like?'

'Have you seen her?'

'No.'

He let go of the bartender's hand and took a drag on his cigarette. While the bartender rang up the sale, the Kid took another look around the bar. It was a bland place with nothing worth looking at. And nothing suggested it would be a dangerous place for Baby to hang out. Even though she was fairly new to the killing business, she could easily have taken down all of the useless assholes in this place. It was possible she hadn't even come to The Fork In Hell. But if she had, then either the bartender hadn't seen her, *or he had seen her and was lying about it.*

In situations like this it was usually safe to assume the worst about people, so the Kid decided to go with the assumption that the bartender was a lying bastard. He stared into his glass of bourbon and thought about what to do. But then out of the corner of his eye he saw the bartender nod at someone behind him. In the reflection of his whisky glass he saw two large men had entered the bar. One of them closed the door and slid a large deadbolt across it. They did it quietly in the hope that the bar's newest customer wouldn't hear them. But the Kid had seen what they were up to. And he was ready to fuck them up.

He picked up his glass of bourbon and drank the contents in one go, slamming the glass down on the bar. He stood up and turned to face the two men who had just bolted the door shut.

The two men had blurry faces. Their bodies swivelled one way and then the other, like they were reflections in a creepy house of mirrors. They approached him with caution, ready for a fight. The larger of the two made a move to grab the Kid, so he had to be taken down first. The Kid threw a punch at his midriff to knock the wind out of him. But something strange happened. His fist hit nothing but thin air. It had been a long time since he'd failed to connect with a punch. But it confirmed what he'd known for a while.

The drink the bartender had given him. It wasn't real bourbon.

It was poison.

Thirty Two

Sanchez had surprised himself by staying awake all through the night while he drove the ambulance across country to The Devil's Graveyard. Beth stayed in the back, promising Sanchez that she would keep a close eye on Flake. But the last time he'd poked his head through the curtain to check on things, both of them were asleep.

He knew he was close to his destination because the radio in the ambulance cut off midway through the song *Melody Cool* by Mavis Staples, the first song all night that he knew the words to. Typical. But a lack of radio signal was a sure sign they were on the right road. Radio signals, and phone signals for that matter, all vanished when you were close to The Devil's Graveyard.

The sun was rising in the distance, which made driving a little less taxing. Sanchez checked his mirrors and saw no sign of any weird undead bastards following them. If his memory served him well, he was sure there would be a sign at the side of the road soon, welcoming them to The Devil's Graveyard. Most important of all though, now that there was no one around, and Beth and Flake were asleep, Sanchez would finally be able to try something he'd seen Jim Carrey do in the movie *Dumb and Dumber*.

He was desperately in need of a piss. And he had an empty water bottle on the passenger seat. So with one hand on the steering wheel he pulled his jeans and underpants down to his knees. He grabbed the water bottle and held it between his legs. While keeping one eye on the road ahead and driving steadily, he started peeing into the bottle. It wasn't as easy as it looked in *Dumb and Dumber*. As well as the risks of spillage, Sanchez had to contend with the added pressure of knowing that Beth might wake up and poke her head through the curtains to see what the noise was.

After a few false starts, Sanchez eventually relaxed and found that the task wasn't so hard after all. He was experienced at peeing into bottles anyway, so his aim was already good, and now he could add *"peeing into a bottle, while driving"* to his extensive list of urine-based achievements.

As was often the case in such situations though, just as Sanchez thought everything was going smoothly, it went wrong. Beth poked her head through the curtains to have a word with him.

'We're being followed,' she said. 'The blond Horseman is on our tail.'

She was about to say something else, but then she caught sight of what he was doing. She got a real good look too.

'Oh my God, what is wrong with you?' she said, shaking her head.

'I thought you were asleep!' Sanchez scowled at her.

Beth stopped staring and slapped him on the shoulder, which didn't help his balance at all.

'Do you mind?' he complained. 'Where's this Horseman that's following us? I can't see him.'

'I think he must have been following us the whole time,' said Beth, fretting. 'And now he's catching up with us. Can you go any faster?'

'I can't force it. I have to let it flow or it'll splash.'

'Not that!' said Beth, glancing down at the bottle again and probably wishing she hadn't. 'I mean drive faster!'

'Hang on, I'm almost done.'

Sanchez squeezed out the last few drops of urine into the bottle, which was very close to overflowing. It was hard to shake the last few drops away though, partly because he was sitting down, and partly because Beth was watching, which added unnecessary pressure to what was normally a fun procedure.

'Do you mind?' he said, giving her a disapproving look.

'Would you just throw that out the window?'

Sanchez wiggled around in his seat to shake the last few drops into the bottle.

'That's it. I'm done,' he said.

Beth pointed up ahead. 'Look! The Devil's Graveyard!'

Sanchez took his eye off the bottle and looked up. The big signpost that said, "WELCOME TO THE DEVIL'S GRAVEYARD", was coming up in the distance. He checked his wing mirror to look for the Horseman Beth had warned him about. But there was no sign of him.

'Where's the guy on the horse then?' he asked.

'He's back there somewhere!' said Beth. 'For *Chrissake* Sanchez! Pull your pants up and put your foot down!'

Beth disappeared back behind the curtain. Sanchez checked both wing mirrors. There was still no sign of any psychos on horses. He was beginning to suspect Beth had made the whole thing up just so she could watch him pee into the bottle. He cast his mind back to several other incidents in the last year or so where Beth had walked in on him when he had his pants down. On one occasion she'd seen him applying some cream for his piles. And another time she'd found him painting an elephant's eyes and ears above his dick as a surprise for Flake. There had been other incidents too, more embarrassing ones that he was trying to forget. It occurred to him that maybe all these incidents weren't just coincidence. Maybe Beth was a pervert?

While reminiscing about past incidents, he forgot that he was supposed to be driving fast. He also forgot that the bottle he was holding was full of piss and not water. He was about to take a sip from it, but the smell brought him to his senses in the nick of time. He wound down the window and hurled the bottle out into the desert.

*

Beth was trying to erase the image of Sanchez peeing into the bottle. What the hell was wrong with him? Every time she opened a door without knocking, or poked her head through a set of curtains, he seemed to have his pants down and was doing "something" to himself, or *with* himself.

She steadied herself against the side of the ambulance and made her way to the back doors so she could look out through the windows. The Horseman had clearly been on their tail the whole time. But he had kept out of sight until they reached The Devil's Graveyard. Now he was chasing them like he meant business.

His horse didn't look remotely tired, despite following them all night. It had green eyes that looked like dots from a laser pen. Beth saw the rider strike his horse on the rear with his sword, urging it on. The horse galloped faster and gained on the ambulance with incredible ease. As it drew closer, Beth got a really good look at the rider. He had thick blond hair and thin skin. His deep blue eyes sought her out and stared deep into her soul. She backed away from the doors as he rode up right behind the ambulance. The rider reached out a long bony hand towards the back door and grasped at it. He couldn't get close enough to the handle, so he steered his horse over to the side of the ambulance to get a better angle. Beth watched his skeletal hand reach across for the door. But then.....

BLAM!

The Blond Horseman got hit in the face by a bottle of piss. The look of evil that was normally etched into his face was replaced by one of shock and disgust. There was no lid on the bottle of piss so the contents splashed into his eyes and mouth, blinding him and probably making him feel sick too. He dropped the reins of his horse and it veered off the highway onto the gravel and sand at the side of the road. The Horseman let out a bloodcurdling shout, which seemed to be directed at his horse. Or maybe he was in pain because his eyes were stinging? Either way, he was seriously angry. The reason for his shout soon became clear.

THUD!

Beth almost cheered. The horse ran beneath the large "WELCOME TO THE DEVIL'S GRAVEYARD" signpost at the side of the road. The Horseman's face smashed into the sign. It knocked him off the horse and he landed in a pile of rocks and sand, while his horse carried on running into the desert.

From up front Sanchez shouted back to her.

'We just passed the signpost. We're in The Devil's Graveyard.'

'I know!'

'Can you see that Horseman anywhere?'

'It's okay, he's gone now!'

*

Sanchez pulled his pants up with one hand, while steering with the other and keeping his eye on the road ahead. It wasn't an easy thing to do, and it took quite a while before his pants were back in a position that was comfortable. He'd just got settled again when he saw a junction coming up. He checked his mirrors again and still saw no sign of the Horseman, which confirmed his suspicion that Beth had made the whole thing up just so she could spy on him taking a piss.

The junction they were approaching was supposed to be a crossroads. But where once there had been options to go left, right or straight ahead, now there was only left and straight ahead. The right turn had vanished. Fucking typical. The right turn was the one he needed.

He slowed the ambulance up and pulled over at the side of the road.

The signpost by the roadside was a tatty old wooden piece of crap. The writing on it was sketchy and impossible to read from a distance. Sanchez left the engine running, but climbed out of the ambulance so he could get a better look at it. He heard Beth slam the back doors and a moment later she came bounding over to join him.

'What have you stopped for?' she asked.

'There's a turn missing on this junction.'

Another voice called out from nearby.

'Where are you headed?'

Sanchez recognised the voice. He'd heard it many years before on his last visit to The Devil's Graveyard. It was Jacko, a young black man who never aged. He had appeared out of thin air and was standing next to Sanchez. He was in his early twenties and wearing a suit that looked ten times older than him. It was a muddy brown colour with a matching fedora hat. The last time they met, Sanchez had accidentally knocked Jacko into huge crevasse caused by an earthquake, which sent him plummeting into the pits of Hell, or something. Anyway, it looked like the experience hadn't done Jacko much harm because he didn't seem hostile, so Sanchez thought it best not to mention it.

'Oh, hey Jacko,' he said. 'Can you help us? We're looking for a guy called Scratch.'

Jacko ignored him and walked up to Beth. He took off his hat and bowed before her like she was the Queen, or someone else that Sanchez didn't like. Sanchez walked up to Jacko and prodded him in the arm.

'So which way do we go? There was a fourth turning on this crossroads last time I came here. Where's it gone?'

'It's still there,' said Jacko pointing to the junction.

To Sanchez's great annoyance the fourth turning had appeared out of thin air.

'That wasn't there just now!' he argued.

'But you wanted it. Now it's there. So hurry up and drive down it before it disappears again.'

'Wow,' said Beth. 'How did you do that?'

'Not how,' said Jacko. 'But *why*.'

Sanchez frowned. *'Not how, but why?* That doesn't even make sense. Who do you think you are? Morpheus?'

'Just drive down that road until you come to a bar named Purgatory. That's where you'll find the man you're looking for.'

'See,' said Sanchez. 'That wasn't so hard was it?'

Jacko ignored him and walked around the side of the ambulance, staring back at the road they had just come from.

'You led him here, didn't you?' he said.

'Who?'

'Zitrone, he's the leader of the Four Horsemen of the Apocalypse.'

In the distance, with dust flying up all around him was the Horseman, galloping towards the crossroads.

Jacko shoved Sanchez. 'Get moving you dumb fuck!' he snapped. 'What are you waiting for?'

Sanchez didn't appreciate being shoved, so he kicked some dirt over Jacko's shoes and ran back to the ambulance before Jacko could retaliate. Beth raced around to the back and jumped back in. Sanchez hit the gas as soon as he heard her shut the door. The ambulance went into a wheel-spin, flicking dirt and gravel up behind it.

Beth yelled out from the back. 'Sanchez, *drive!*'

Sanchez finally remembered to release the parking brake, and the ambulance roared away, flicking more dirt and sand over Jacko. With Zitrone gaining on them, Sanchez swung the ambulance onto the right turn at the junction and headed towards Purgatory.

Thirty Three

Five o'clock in the morning. The phone was ringing at five o'clock in the fucking morning. Jebediah reached over to his bedside table, quietly cursing whichever asshole thought it was okay to call at such an ungodly hour. He answered the phone and lay back on his pillow with the receiver against his ear.

'Yeah.'

'Chief, it's Pat. We've got a live one.'

'Amish?'

'No, just a stranger who came into town for a drink.'

'At five in the morning?'

'Yeah, he came in like ten minutes ago.'

'At five in the morning?'

'You said that already.'

'That's because it's five in the morning. Who goes drinking at five in the morning?'

'Err, well, this guy,' said Pat. 'He came in asking about some girl. Then he ordered a glass of bourbon, and I gave him a glass of the *knockout stuff.*'

Jebediah sat up. His wife Lucinda was fast asleep beside him. Nothing woke her up. She could sleep through thunder. And her own snoring.

It was still dark outside, but Jebediah knew that the sun would show its face soon, so time was in short supply.

'Give me five minutes to get dressed and I'll be on my way.'

'Okay, chief.'

Jebediah was a millisecond away from ending the call when he realised Pat was still talking, so he put the phone back to his ear.

'What's that you said?' he asked.

'I said there's something else.'

'Yeah, go on.'

'This guy we caught, he killed Elias and Ray.'

Jebediah let the information sink into his brain. 'What?'

'He killed Elias and Ray.'

'What do you mean he killed them?'

'They're dead.'

'I thought you said you poisoned this guy?'

'I did. I gave him a glass filled to the top with poison. He downed it all in one go. That's way more than anyone has ever drunk before. It should probably have killed him. But it didn't even knock him out like it does everyone else. It just made him drowsy. Elias and Ray set about

144

him, but he broke Elias's neck and then killed Ray with one punch to his face. I had to smash him over the head with a bat to finish him off. Look, you need to get here quick before this fucker wakes up again.'

'Christ! I'm on my way. Just don't panic. Don't do anything stupid.'

Jebediah hung up the phone. He really wasn't in the mood for this shit. And much of his day was now going to be spent concocting some bullshit story for the relatives of Elias and Ray, to explain how they were killed. He rolled out of bed and put his slippers on, then walked over to the closet. He opened the door and then reached into a secret compartment at the back, where he kept a long red silk robe and a gold mask. He threw the robe over his head and slid his arms into the long baggy sleeves. The robe unfurled all the way down to his ankles, covering his pyjama bottoms. He grabbed the facemask and headed downstairs. As he crept out of the front door he grabbed the keys for his blue and white squad car.

The drive to the Black Forest took less than five minutes. The meeting place was always the same. Down by the edge of the forest, just out of sight of the main road. He steered his car off road and drove across a dirt track until he saw the other members of the Crimson Coven. He was the last one to arrive. The other eight were already there, all dressed in long white robes and gold face masks, shivering their nuts off in the cold morning frost.

Jebediah parked up next to two other squad cars and switched off the engine. He pulled the hood on his robe up over his head and covered his face with the gold painted plastic mask. Then he climbed out of the car and hurried over to join the others, wishing he'd worn shoes instead of slippers.

'You took your time, chief,' said one of the others as he approached.

'Yeah, I didn't even have time to put my shoes on.'

The group separated as he approached. Behind them, tied down on a wooden cart was the man they had captured. The cart was ten feet long by six feet wide and made of solid oak wood. It had four metal wheels beneath it that were connected to a rail track. The old rail track had been laid over a hundred years ago. It started thirty metres outside the forest and ended about a quarter of a kilometre deep into the forest, where no one could see it. No train had ever ridden down this track. It hadn't been built for that purpose.

An old mill wheel was secured in the ground at the end of the track, built into a patch of concrete behind the cart. It had been modified and had a huge length of chain wrapped around it like cotton on a spool.

The chain was attached to the back of the cart, so whenever the cart was stuck in the forest it could be reeled back in.

Two of the Coven members were beating the unconscious victim, hitting him in the ribs with batons and verbally abusing him. Jebediah had explained to them many times before that abusing unconscious people was a waste of breath, but it never seemed to deter them.

He took a look at the man they were about to offer as a sacrifice to the Forest Gods. He was unshaven and his clothes were tattered and torn. His face was bloodied and bruised. But it was something else that really caught Jebediah's attention.

'Why the hell have you nailed him to the cart?' he asked.

One of his masked comrades spoke up. 'He killed Elias and Ray.'

'Yes, I heard. And you nailed him to the cart *as punishment?*'

'No, we nailed him to the cart because it's the only way to make sure he doesn't break free. This asshole is stronger than any man I've ever seen. And he's a fucking psycho. He caved in Ray's face with one punch!'

Jebediah didn't like the idea of nailing the victim to the cart. It was a break from normal procedure and the Gods might not like it. But time wasn't on their side. The sun was already peeking over the horizon, so the sacrifice ritual had to be done. And it had to be done now.

'Okay, let's get on with it then,' he said.

The nine members of the Crimson Coven took up their positions. Four of them stood on either side of the cart and began chanting an ancient sacrificial song.

Jebediah stood directly behind the cart, looking down on the man they had nailed to it. 'Are you sure this guy was on his own?' he asked.

The man on his left answered. 'Pat swears it. No one's gonna miss this guy.'

'Did he have any possessions?'

'A motorbike, a cellphone, a gun that wasn't loaded, fifty bucks, two packs of cigarettes and a kinder egg. We divided them up amongst us.'

It seemed rather convenient that there were exactly eight items, one for each of the group. Jebediah suspected there had been more and that he'd been fiddled out of his share, but there wasn't time to make an issue of it.

'Put the cellphone back,' he ordered. 'I don't want it being traced back to us.'

One of the others grumbled something under his breath and reluctantly tossed the cellphone onto the cart.

'All right then,' said Jebediah. 'Let's do this.'

A thin ray of sunlight trickled over the cart. Jebediah saw some dried blood stains on the wood. He cast his mind back to the young Amish boy they had sacrificed last time. He'd been no more than ten years old. The dried blood was probably his. Jebediah sighed. Sacrificing people to the Gods was a nasty business. But if they didn't keep the Forest Gods happy, everyone would suffer. Twelve sacrifices a year, balanced against the greater good of the people was hard to argue with.

The tradition of the twelve sacrifices during the Fall went back as far as anyone in Crimson County could remember. Jebediah's father had taught him the history behind the ritual when he introduced him to the Coven. The ritual was certainly working too because no one from Crimson County had been snatched by the forest creatures for as long as anyone could remember.

Jebediah joined the group in the sacrificial chant. When the chant was finished everyone stepped clear of the cart, except for Jebediah. He looked down at the stranger they were sacrificing for the last time, the man who had killed Elias and Ray. He felt no remorse. He yanked down a large metal lever on the back of the cart.

The cart started moving towards the forest, picking up speed as it rolled along the rails. By the time it passed the first row of trees it was almost up to its maximum speed of twenty miles per hour. If the Forest Gods were true to form, their new offering would be dead within a matter of minutes.

Thirty Four

What day is it? What's happened to me? Where am I? The questions were coming thick and fast. It was dark and hard to see. Trees. There were definitely a lot of trees in the surrounding area. Something was moving too. More than one thing in fact. Wake up. Wake up. *Wake the fuck up.* You're in trouble. You have blood in your eyes. Your head is swollen. You're in pain. Something is digging into your back. Who are you? Can you remember anything?

Yes.

All of these thoughts were racing through her mind. It took a while to recall how she had ended up here. The first thing she remembered was her name. *"I'm Jasmine."*

She opened her eyes. It made her head hurt even more. Images flashed though her mind. Driving over the edge of a cliff. The car bouncing off the cliffside and turning end over end as it hurtled towards the ground. But then, trees. Huge trees. The car ploughed into a tree. A branch ripped through the windscreen and slowed their descent. The car wobbled and shook, but then came to a stop, hanging in the tree maybe twenty metres above the ground. That must have been the moment she lost consciousness. A swelling on her forehead served as a constant reminder that she had banged it against something.

And Elvis. *Where the fuck was Elvis?*

He wasn't in the car. Jasmine took stock of her position. Her face was pressed against the floor. No wait, *the ceiling.* The car was upside down. It wasn't stuck in the tree anymore. It was on the ground. Upside down. There was dirt everywhere and the windows of the DeLorean had no glass in them.

Jasmine's legs were up above her head and her crop-top had ridden up around her neck. Of greater concern was the fact that the barrel of the gun she kept tucked in the back of her jeans was wedged firmly between her butt cheeks. She'd been in worse positions. In fact, there wasn't a position Jasmine couldn't get out of. She was very limber and knew her own body well. She took some time to wiggle every part of her body. Everything hurt, but it was all still working, all still intact.

In her minds eye she saw something that had already happened. Her ears reminded her of a sound she'd heard while she was unconscious. A branch had snapped, causing the car to fall out of the tree onto the ground below. That's what had woken her up. But where the fuck was Elvis?

He had been in the passenger seat when they'd flown over the cliff edge. But the passenger seat was empty. And the passenger side door was open. Those crazy DeLorean doors that opened upwards. The passenger door was open and it was pressed against the ground, which reminded her that everything right now was upside down.

'Elvis?' she cried out. But her voice deserted her and it came out sounding like a hammy actor in a dodgy movie, choking out his last words before dying.

She rolled her legs over her head until she was laid out on her stomach, ready to crawl out through the open door. The pistol nestling between her ass cheeks loosened a little too, so she reached back and pulled it so the handle was poking out over the top of her jeans again.

She became aware of a flashing red light coming from the dashboard. Through her blurred vision she saw the time and date on the digital readout. Most of the digits were broken, so only the YEAR was flashing. Was it really 2657? Or were her eyes playing tricks on her?

She pulled her cellphone from her pocket. The screen was cracked and nothing was showing on the display. She pressed a few buttons but it was clear that the battery was dead. It made her wonder, how long had she been unconscious? And again, *where the fuck was Elvis?*

She grabbed the frame of the windscreen on the passenger side of the car and tried to pull herself out. It was difficult because both she and the car were mangled out of shape. Her vision continued to swim in and out of focus and her hearing was intermittent. It was these factors that prevented her from noticing that someone was nearby. A pair of hands grabbed her beneath her armpits and dragged her out of the wreckage. She looked up to see who her rescuer was but the morning sun blinded her, wrapping itself around the face of the person above her, turning it into a shadow.

The figure turned away from her and shouted something to someone else nearby. Jasmine couldn't make out the words. She shielded her eyes from the sun and saw a pair of black boots on the person who had dragged her from the car. The rescuer walked away from her towards a group of other people. Jasmine rolled onto her side and kept blinking, hoping her eyesight would clear.

And that's when she saw the reality, the horror of where she was. And Elvis. He was on the ground, surrounded by three of them. One of them was behind him, trying to lift him up by his armpits. These people who had rescued her from the car weren't rescuers at all. They weren't even *people*. The image of the digital readout in the DeLorean flashed into her mind again. The year 2657. Holy shit!

Jasmine had never been in a car accident before but she'd heard stories about how accident victims went into shock and couldn't react to what was happening around them. How they became confused and disorientated. Well she didn't have time to be confused or disorientated. This was serious. She had been pulled from the wreckage by a gorilla wearing human clothes. Three others were standing over Elvis. All of them were wearing black boots, purple pants and vests with black waistcoats. And they all had rifles hanging from their shoulders. Further along in the woods, two more apes carrying semi-automatic weapons were running through the trees towards them. Elvis had told Jasmine many times, "Don't dither when your life is in danger, make a decision quickly and stick to it!".

At present, Elvis was in no state to defend himself. His sunglasses had snapped and were hanging off one ear. He was covered in blood too and was quite possibly unconscious.

'What shall we do with him?' one of the gorillas asked.

'Put him down.'

Jasmine knew what *"Put him down"* meant. There was no way she was going to let a gang of psychotic, talking apes put Elvis to sleep. The gorilla holding Elvis up by his armpits lowered him to the floor. Jasmine had to act, and now was her chance. She reached back and pulled the soiled pistol from the back of her jeans. She aimed it at the ape that had just dropped Elvis.

BANG!

In spite of her injuries, her blurred vision and the feeling of dizziness and nausea, not to mention the awkwardness of lying on her side, Jasmine was still a crack shot. The bullet hit the gorilla in the face and a fountain of red blood blew out through the back of his head. The others were stunned and before they had a chance to react, she fired a second shot.

BANG!

Another monkey-man hit the deck.

The others turned and ran, screaming and shouting like the cowardly bastards they were. Jasmine took aim at the fleeing apes and shot two more of them in the back. Both of them dropped to their knees and then slumped face-first into the ground. Jasmine shifted into a kneeling position and got a better view of her surroundings. She was in a forest. And there were apes dressed like people, running in all directions, fleeing for their lives.

She crawled over to Elvis and knelt down beside him. His face was covered in dirt and blood, his blue suit was bloodied and torn, and his eyes were closed. She placed her hand on his chest. He was still breathing. Thank God. She removed his broken sunglasses and stroked a few straggling hairs out of his eyes.

'Elvis, wake up. We've got to get out of here,' she said, her voice still scratchy and unclear.

He didn't reply. Jasmine tried to think. Without Elvis she wouldn't survive long, because if the monkey people didn't kill her, loneliness certainly would.

She slapped him round the face. 'Wake up for God's sake!'

Elvis opened his eyes and looked up at her. He was in a bad way. But Jasmine was just glad he was alive. She leant down and kissed him. It was a dirty kiss. Both of them had dry lips, caked in sand, dirt and blood. As kisses go it was painful too, because both of them had suffered some serious bruising and soreness. But Jasmine was a hell of a good kisser and she could tell Elvis was grateful for the affection.

She pulled away and stroked his face. 'Get up soldier,' she said with a grade of authority. 'We've got to get moving.'

Elvis forced half a smile. 'You killed those actors didn't you?' he said.

'What actors?'

'The guys in the ape costumes.'

Jasmine looked around at the fallen bodies of the four apes she had executed. They definitely looked like apes, albeit in human clothes. Dodgy human clothes, they clearly had no fashion sense.

'What makes you think they're actors?'

Elvis forced himself up onto his elbows. He pointed in the direction of the fleeing gorillas. 'See that camera and the microphone and stuff?'

Jasmine had been aware of some equipment belonging to the apes but she hadn't really focussed on it before. But there was a camera on a stand and some other filming equipment strewn around on the ground.

'Why are apes filming stuff? Do you think we were going to be part of a monkey snuff movie?'

'No. My guess is they're filming the new Planet of the Apes TV series.'

Jasmine looked at the dead ape-men again. 'Oh dear,' she muttered. 'Were they proper actors?'

'What difference does it make?'

'Well if they were CGI apes, it won't be so bad.'

'CGI apes?'

'Yeah, you know computer generated ones. I'm sure that's what they use in the movies now.'

Elvis sat up straight and winced. He looked confused and stared at her for a while, as if thought she was stupid or something. Eventually he seemed to realise what she meant.

'Yeah, actually, you know what? I think they were CGI apes.'

Jasmine breathed a sigh of relief. 'Whew, what a lucky break!'

'Yeah, but even so,' said Elvis steadying himself with his hand on the ground as he tried to get up. 'I think we should get the fuck out of here as soon as possible.'

'Well d'uh,' said Jasmine. 'That's what I've been trying to tell you!'

Thirty Five

The Mystic Lady's visions were coming through thick and fast. And they were troubling to say the least. Scratch was standing over her at a round table in front of the large television screen. The television was muted while Annabel crouched over her crystal ball looking for answers to Scratch's questions. *And he had a lot of questions.*

'The ambulance is on its way,' she said. 'And Zitrone followed it here.'

Scratch clenched his fists. 'Goddammit! Did he get through the crossroads?'

'You're casting a shadow over the ball, I can't see.'

Scratch moved away and positioned himself on the other side of the table, facing her. Annabel peered into her ball again, moving her head from side to side, looking for an answer within the white mist. Eventually, when Scratch was ready to punch her, she looked up.

'No,' she said. 'The south fork of the crossroads closed before he even saw it. He has no idea how to get here.'

'So what's he doing now?'

'He's at the crossroads trying to figure out where the ambulance went.'

'He'll work it out eventually,' said Scratch, pulling a large cigar from inside his jacket. 'What about Cain and the other three Horsemen?'

'One of the Horsemen is dead. The Bourbon Kid took care of him.'

'Which one?'

'The stupid one.'

'Ash?'

'The dark haired one.'

'Yeah, that's Ash,' said Scratch. 'He's an asshole.'

Ash's demise was the one piece of good news in a day full of shitty news. Scratch lit his cigar by sucking on it a few times, and then blew a smoke ring up above Annabel's head.

'Have you worked out where the Bourbon Kid is yet?' he asked.

The Mystic Lady waved away some of the smoke from Scratch's cigar. 'He's not on my radar at all,' she said.

'Why not?'

'I've told you a thousand times, I can't see people when they're unconscious or asleep.'

'What makes you think he's unconscious?'

'The last I saw of him, he was in a bar. He ordered a drink, and then it went hazy.'

'You're useless, you know that!'

Annabel waved some more of his cigar smoke away. Then something caught her eye within the crystal ball. 'Wait,' she said. 'I've got something.'

Scratch took his cigar out of his mouth and held it down by his side to keep the smoke away from her. 'What is it?'

'Oh dear.'

'What? *For fuckssake, what?*'

'He's in trouble.'

'Where?'

'In the same place we lost the Red Mohawk. It's a dark forest and it's got some kind of magical force field around it. I can't see what goes on in there.'

'Magic force field? What the fuck are you talking about?'

Annabel sat back and rubbed her forehead. 'This is exhausting.'

Scratch chewed on his cigar and spat some of it on the floor. 'No, this is a coup,' he decided. 'All of The Dead Hunters have been taken out in a matter of hours. Cain must be behind all of it. This is a well-planned job, and I'll bet it ends with them coming here and breaking all the evil spirits out of Hell.'

'I think you're being paranoid,' said Annabel.

'Paranoid?' Scratch baulked at the suggestion. 'Do you know what happens if they get through the crossroads now? We've got no one to stop them. The gateway to Hell is unprotected!'

Scratch was aware that he was panicking. Annabel would never have seen him troubled like this before. But desperate times in Purgatory were rare, and they usually involved a lot of panicking and a distinct lack of good leadership.

'So what do we do?' said Annabel, wiping some sweat from her brow. 'There must be someone you can send? What about all those evil bastards in Hell?'

Scratch turned on his heels and walked over to the bar. He reached over the bar top and grabbed a bottle of dark rum and a whisky glass. He poured himself a double measure and stood there, leaning against the bar, swilling the glass around in his hand while he contemplated what to do.

'No one in Hell can help us,' he said. 'Only the people who sign contracts with me *before* they die can be released from Hell without God's permission. And right now, the only people here with official contracts are *you* and *Nigel Powell*. And no offence, but both of you are fucking useless when it comes to fighting.'

'Are you sure God won't get involved?' Annabel inquired. 'Surely he could send someone?'

Scratch took a sip of his rum and tried to figure out a way around the contract business. But there wasn't a way around it. A miracle was required.

'We need to kill Cain and the three remaining Horsemen,' he said, wagging his finger at Annabel while he spoke, as if that somehow helped matters. 'To kill Cain we need the Brutus Dagger. And to kill the Horsemen we need someone who can get close enough to them to behead them without being touched. Which means we need someone who cannot be killed by the undead.'

'Know you of such a man?'

Scratch put his glass of rum back down on the bar and chewed on his cigar as he pondered his options. 'All of my resources are gone,' he said. 'If God wants the world to continue, it's up to him to send someone. But after what happened to Jesus back in the day, I'm not sure he'll *want* to send anyone. But if he does, it'll need to be someone *like* Jesus, someone who in times of great danger throughout history has stepped up and prevented the undead from destroying mankind.'

'Well if he's going to send someone,' said Annabel, 'he'd better do it soon!'

As if by chance, a voice called out from the front entrance to the bar. 'Hello? Is anyone home?'

Scratch and Annabel stared at each other. Just when they had given up hope, it seemed that the Lord had answered their call and sent someone after all. Someone who throughout history had faced down the undead and survived every single time, often triumphing against all odds.

Sanchez walked in through the swing doors at the entrance. He saw them and put his hands on his hips. 'You know this place was a bastard to find,' he said. 'You should get some more sign posts put up.'

Thirty Six

Zitrone couldn't work out how he had lost sight of the ambulance he was chasing. One minute it was there and then in a cloud of dirt and smoke it turned right at the crossroads and disappeared. But when Zitrone rode up to the junction he saw that no right turn existed. The only thing other than desert and road was a black man in a rocking chair playing the harmonica at the side of the road.

Zitrone called out to him. 'Hey you! Where did the ambulance go?'

'What ambulance?'

Zitrone didn't have time to waste arguing with someone who might be deliberately trying to slow him down. He needed to find Purgatory, and he also wanted revenge on whoever threw the bottle of piss at him earlier. He geed his horse up and galloped into the desert in the same direction the ambulance had vanished.

There was nothing in sight up ahead, and it seemed barely believable that an ambulance could have driven through such barren wasteland, but his gut instinct told him to keep going. *Gut instinct was his undoing.* He travelled less than a quarter of a mile before his horse slowed up. At first Zitrone dug his heels into the horse's side, demanding it continue. But then he realised it wasn't so much that the horse was refusing to carry on. It couldn't. It was sinking.

Quicksand.

He pulled at the reins to direct the horse away from the perilous wet sand but it was no use. The horse was stuck, and it was sinking fast. The more it struggled the faster it sank. If Zitrone wasn't careful he would be dragged down with it. He pulled his feet free from the stirrups and leapt clear of the horse and the quicksand, landing awkwardly on his side six feet away. By the time he looked back the horse was up to its neck in quicksand. And two seconds later it vanished, gone forever along with Zitrone's saddle bag containing his cellphone.

If anything, this confirmed to Zitrone that he was on the right track. The quicksand was clearly a trap, aimed at stopping anyone from finding Purgatory. All he needed were some directions from someone who knew the area. The bluesman at the crossroads was the only person who knew where the ambulance had gone. And Zitrone intended to make him talk.

He made the short walk back to the crossroads and stopped in front of the bluesman in the rocking chair.

'Hey you,' he said, clicking his fingers in the bluesman's face. 'I asked you a question before. Where did that ambulance go?'

The bluesman stopped playing his harmonica and looked up at him. 'I'm Jacko, if you don't mind,' he said.

'Well Jacko, if you want to stay alive, tell me where that ambulance went.'

'Okay,' said Jacko, slipping his harmonica into the breast pocket on his jacket. 'First of all, I'm already dead, so do your worst. Second of all, I didn't see no ambulance.'

Zitrone reached out and grabbed Jacko by his shirt collar. He hauled him up off his rocking chair and pulled him in close enough that they could feel each other's breath. 'The ambulance vanished,' he growled. 'I saw it and *I know you saw it*. So tell me, where the fuck did the ambulance go?'

'What ambulance?'

'I'm starting to not like you.'

'You know, that happens a lot,' said Jacko, 'which is odd really, because I'm a laid back kinda guy.'

'Listen you clay-brained fool, you can either tell me, or I can read your mind.'

Jacko raised his eyebrows. 'If you can read my mind then why are you even asking?'

Zitrone flicked Jacko's hat off and placed his left hand on his forehead. He began to read the harmonica player's mind, collecting memories from throughout Jacko's life, *and death*.

'Your real name is Robert Johnson,' he said. 'You died a long time ago, but not before you made a deal with the Devil.'

Jacko shrugged. 'I'm sorry, I didn't get your name?'

'My name is Zitrone.'

'Is that French?'

'No.'

'It sounds French.'

'It is not French.'

'European though, right?'

'Shut up! I'm trying to read your mind.'

Memories from Jacko's life were rushing into Zitrone's brain. Images raced around at lightning speed, only slowing when Zitrone saw something of interest. Eventually, after a bizarre episode involving a singing contest at a hotel where Jacko met both Sanchez and the Bourbon Kid, the images came up to date. The missing Southern turning on the crossroads hid the way to Purgatory. Zitrone discovered the truth about the secret entrance. Jacko could only open it for people who had been authorised by Scratch. He pushed the bluesman back down into his rocking chair.

'You've been very helpful,' he said.

'Really?' said Jacko. 'Because I don't feel like I was helpful.'

Zitrone looked around, surveying his surroundings. He was stranded in the middle of nowhere with an irritating dickhead. And no horse.

But then in a delicious moment his luck changed. He heard a vehicle approaching. Jacko rocked forward in his chair, like he was about to get up, but Zitrone pushed him back down.

A red Corvette appeared on the horizon, racing towards the crossroads from the same direction Zitrone had come. The roof of the Corvette was down and there were two people inside it. Jasmine was driving and Elvis was in the passenger side. As they reached the junction and zoomed past Zitrone, Jasmine pulled a handbrake turn. A mass of dirt and dust sprayed everywhere. Zitrone got covered in it and found that a lot of it stuck like glue to the parts of his face and clothes that had recently been doused in Sanchez's piss.

As he dusted himself off, the car sped away at high speed towards the South. The dust died down and Zitrone saw the invisible road for the first time. It appeared on the South fork as the Corvette drove along it. He wiped some dirt from his eyes and sprinted after the Corvette. He was inches away from stepping onto the highway when it vanished again. The Corvette disappeared too.

Zitrone looked back at Jacko. 'You were right,' he said. 'I can't get in without an invitation.'

Jacko smiled. 'You may as well go home, because you'll never set foot on that road while I'm here. And I'm always here.'

Zitrone started walking back down the highway in the direction he had come from. 'Don't worry,' he said as he walked past Jacko. 'I'll be back.'

Thirty Seven

Scratch had been far more accommodating than Sanchez expected. He helped Sanchez and Beth carry Flake into the bar on a stretcher. Then he arranged for Flake to lie down on a long sofa at the back of the bar, and even provided a blanket and pillow for her. He then handed Beth a wet sponge and a bowl of warm water and ordered her to take care of Flake, while he made a sandwich for Sanchez. It was rapidly becoming clear to Sanchez that Scratch had been dealt a shitty hand by the people who wrote The Bible.

At least, that's how it looked initially. Once Sanchez had finished eating his Brontosaurus sandwich, Scratch got down to business. He'd been sitting opposite Sanchez at a small round table, watching him eat the sandwich, which was a little weird, but Sanchez didn't make an issue of it, what with Scratch being The Devil and all that.

'I want you to do something for me now,' said Scratch.

'I'm happy to work behind the bar for a few hours,' Sanchez offered.

'I'm sure you are. But that's not what I want from you. I want you to go to a place called Blue Corn Island.'

'I'd love to,' said Sanchez. 'But you know I've been driving all night and I really need some sleep.' He stretched his arms and yawned to emphasise his point.

'I understand that,' said Scratch. 'But this is a matter of urgency. An evil spirit named Cain has freed the Four Horsemen of the Apocalypse. I believe you've encountered them already?'

'I have seen some people on horses recently.'

'Good. So you'll go to Blue Corn then?'

'I'd rather not. Can't someone else do it?'

'No. Someone else can't do it! Everyone that could is either dead, or otherwise engaged.'

'Oh. Right.'

'I need you to go there and find something called the Brutus Dagger. It's the only weapon in the world that can kill Cain. The Bourbon Kid is already there but he's gone missing. If you can find him, then you can look for the dagger together.'

'And what if I can't find the Bourbon Kid?'

'If you can't find him, you'll search for it on your own.'

Sanchez didn't like the sound of any of this. It sounded like a stupid plan. 'How am I going to find a dagger on an island? That's like looking for a drop of water in bowl of custard!'

'No it isn't. It's nothing like that. Could you just listen for a minute and stop asking stupid questions? The dagger we're looking for is probably hidden somewhere on the Amish side of the island. I suggest you start by asking your friend Bishop Yoder where to find it. And tell him that I'm very displeased with him because of what happened to Baby and the Red Mohawk.'

There seemed to be an awful lot to remember. Sanchez couldn't usually remember drink orders if there were more than two drinks. And he wasn't keen on meeting Bishop Yoder again. Just the thought of his neck beard made Sanchez's stomach churn.

'Are you listening?' said Scratch.

'Huh? Yeah. What happened to the Red Mohawk and Baby?'

'That mission that Yoder gave to you, they went on it, *and now they're dead.*'

Sanchez swallowed hard. 'Hang on a minute. Baby and the Red Mohawk were killed on Blue Corn Island,' he said, reiterating the facts. 'The Bourbon Kid has gone missing there, and now you want *me to go there?*'

'Yes,' said Scratch. 'You understand perfectly.'

'No way.'

'What?'

'No way. I'm not going.'

Scratch reached across the table and grabbed Sanchez's hand. 'Do you know what else we've seen in Annabel's crystal ball today?' he asked.

'The result of the Giants, Cowboys game?'

'No, the demise of Nora Bone. Do you remember her? The woman who was going to close down The Tapioca? She begged for your help earlier this morning when she was being chased by ghouls on her moped.'

'Oh yes, Nora, lovely lady.'

'She's dead because you deliberately shot her front tyre, enabling the ghouls to catch her and eat her alive.'

'Keep your voice down,' Sanchez whispered. 'I didn't do it on purpose. I'm just a lousy shot. I was aiming for the ghoulies.'

'Ghouls,' Scratch said, correcting him. 'And of course you were. But can you see how it might look to God when your judgement day comes and he has to decide whether you go to Heaven or Hell. I know God, and he doesn't believe in coincidences.'

'Neither do I,' said Sanchez, folding his arms. 'And that in itself *is a coincidence.* So that's proved God wrong straight away.'

Scratch gritted his teeth. 'Shut up,' he growled. 'What I'm saying is, if God were to find you guilty, or even just a little annoying, you'll end up down here. And I was thinking you could share a room in Hell with a Santa Claus impersonator, specifically the one you burned alive in front of a group of girl scouts a few years back.'

Sanchez remembered the incident well. Those girl scouts were vicious. And Santa was an alcoholic, child-molesting vampire with bad breath. Sharing a room in Hell with him for all eternity didn't sound great.

'But then again,' Scratch went on. 'Hell won't even exist if Cain and the Horsemen get their way. The minute they find this place they're going to open the gateway to Hell and unleash all of the evil spirits back into the world. That's what's commonly known as *The Apocalypse*.'

Sanchez could see that neither option was going to work out well for him. 'Okay,' he said reluctantly. 'What have I got to do?'

'I'm going to send you to a bar on Blue Corn Island. It's called The Fork In Hell and it's where the Bourbon Kid was last seen.'

'The Fork In Hell? You should have called *this* place that,' said Sanchez. 'It's a much better name than Purgatory.'

Scratch let go of Sanchez's hand and clenched his fists as if something was annoying him. 'Would you just concentrate on the important details for once?' he said through gritted teeth.

Sanchez looked around the bar. 'Where exactly is this gateway that they want to open?'

Scratch pointed at the far end of the bar. 'Its behind the door to the Disabled toilets,' he said.

'Why would you put it there?'

'Because we don't have disabled people in Purgatory,' Scratch replied. 'Generally, disabled people go straight to Heaven, unless they shoot their girlfriend while she's on the toilet.'

'But what happens if someone goes into your Disabled toilets to take a dump?'

'Well then that person would go straight to Hell, because it's an offence for healthy people to shit in the Disabled toilets. And let me tell you, it's a long way down.'

Sanchez couldn't help thinking he'd had a lucky escape. He'd been planning to use the Disabled toilets to take a dump. And judging from the way Scratch and the Mystic Lady were looking at him, he sensed that they knew it. Mind-reading bastards.

Annabel called over from the next table. 'He needs to go *right now!*'

'It's all right,' said Sanchez. 'I can hold it for a few hours. It's definitely brewing though.'

Scratch closed his eyes and gritted his teeth again. 'She means you need to go to Blue Corn Island now!'

'Oh, right. Have you got a map or some directions?'

'You won't need them,' said Scratch. 'I can transport you from here. Just walk through the door of the Men's toilets and you'll be transported directly into The Fork In Hell.'

It sounded like bullshit, but Scratch looked deadly serious.

'Will I need a gun?' Sanchez asked.

'Not if you find the Bourbon Kid. Ask the bartender in the Fork if he's seen him. If he says no, just head to the Amish part of the island and find Bishop Yoder. Tell him that if he doesn't show you where the Brutus Dagger is, the world is going to end.'

'Can I just say for the record, I think this is a shit plan?'

'Men's toilets,' said Scratch. 'NOW!'

Sanchez stood up. His chair scraped along the ground making a high-pitched screech, which seemed to irritate Scratch even more. But when Sanchez turned to leave, Beth was standing behind him. She had been listening into the conversation.

'Please find JD,' she said, her face earnest and searching. 'I'll take care of Flake.'

Beth had an annoying knack of making Sanchez feel bad. She looked sad. He could tell she was worried about the Bourbon Kid as much as he was worried about Flake. He pulled his mirrored sunglasses out of his jacket pocket and put them on so that Beth could see her face in them, and realise how annoying she looked. There was the added bonus of course, that when he had the mirrored sunglasses on, he looked cool as fuck.

'Don't you worry,' he said. 'Evil is a disease, and I'm the cure.'

'NOW!' Scratch shouted again.

Sanchez gave him a thumbs-up, and headed for the Men's toilets. Before pushing the door, he asked Scratch one last question.

'How do I get back?'

'NOW!'

It wasn't the answer he was looking for, but there was smoke blowing out of Scratch's ears, so he decided not to push his luck. Instead he pushed the door to the washroom open and walked through it. There was a loud whooshing sound as the door closed behind him. All that was inside was a public toilet. A set of urinals and washbasins on one wall and two stalls on the other. Sanchez looked back and saw that the door he had come through had vanished. That was a neat trick.

The only way out was a red door on the opposite wall. So after a twenty-minute pit-stop in trap two, which lightened his load considerably, Sanchez left the washroom via the red door. On the other side of the door was another bar, a rather dingy place like The Tapioca, with a dirty, unclean bartender serving drinks and a big sweaty guy sitting by the bar. The washroom door made a loud creaking noise, alerting the big sweaty guy to Sanchez's arrival.

'You okay there, buddy?' the big sweaty guy asked.

Sanchez didn't like the look of this guy. He had long, greasy black hair and a black T-shirt with the word "BOUNCER" written on it in white letters. He was probably wondering where Sanchez had come from. Sanchez was wondering that too.

'Is this The Fork In Hell?' Sanchez asked.

'Yes it is. Where did you come from?'

'Trap two,' Sanchez replied.

'I never saw you go in there.'

'It was a long time ago, if you know what I mean,' said Sanchez, waving his hand in front of his nose.

The bartender leaned over the bar. He looked even more miserable than the bouncer. 'Are you gonna order a drink?' he growled. 'Because house rules state that you can't take a dump in my toilets without buying a drink!'

Sanchez approached the bar. 'I'm looking for a friend actually.'

The bouncer got up from his stool. 'You buy a drink, or you fuck off,' he said in a tone Sanchez disapproved of. But seeing as how Sanchez didn't want to get beaten up, he decided to order a drink.

'All right then,' he said, hopping up onto a stool at the bar. 'Give me a shot of bourbon.'

The bartender exchanged a brief look with the bouncer. Then he grabbed a bottle of Sam Cougar from behind the bar and a whisky glass. He filled the glass halfway up and placed it on the bar in front of Sanchez.

Sanchez reached down to his pockets and suddenly remembered he hadn't brought Flake's credit card or any cash with him. He had no way of paying for the drink.

'Erm, actually I'm all out of cash,' he said. 'My wallet fell down the toilet.'

The bartender smiled. 'No problem. Have this one on the house.'

'Well that's very kind of you,' said Sanchez, raising his glass. 'Here's to your good health!'

Thirty Eight

Scratch had grown tired of Annabel and her crystal ball. She was beginning to get on his nerves because she wasn't seeing anything of interest, so he made his way over to the other side of the bar to get better acquainted with Beth.

'You, *Beth,*' he shouted cheerfully as he approached. 'How's your friend?'

Beth stopped patting Flake's head and looked up. 'She's lost a lot of blood but I think she's going to be okay.'

Flake looked pale and barely alive. The bandage wrapped around her neck was drenched in blood. And there was a big lump underneath the dressing.

'How serious was the injury?' Scratch asked.

'I'm not sure, but it wasn't good,' Beth replied. 'I saw it, the knife went in really deep.'

'Really deep, huh? She's lucky to be alive.'

'I know. Fortunately Sanchez had this bandage dressing in his ambulance. And he had a medical pressure plug to press against the wound.'

Their conversation was interrupted when Annabel shouted out suddenly. 'I see something!'

Scratch forgot all about making idle chit chat with Beth and rushed back across the bar to Annabel's table. 'What is it?' he asked, peering this way and that into the crystal ball.

'Elvis and Jasmine.'

'You see them? Where are they?'

The Mystic Lady pointed out of the window. 'They've just pulled up outside in a red Corvette.'

Scratch's head jerked towards the window. Annabel was correct. Jasmine and Elvis had parked the Corvette out front. Jasmine was changing her clothes for some reason. So Scratch got a good look at her naked body, not for the first time either. Jasmine seemed to get naked a lot, often for no reason.

Once she'd squeezed into a purple catsuit, she helped Elvis out of the car and they headed for the entrance to Purgatory. Elvis was badly hurt and walking on one leg with his arm around Jasmine's shoulder for support. Jasmine's face was bruised and one side of it was caked in dried blood.

Scratch clipped Annabel around the back of the head. 'You said they were dead.'

'I said they'd gone over a cliff.'

'You unreliable old goat.'

Jasmine and Elvis stumbled through the front doors. Scratch clipped Annabel around the head again and then walked over to greet them. 'What *the shit* happened to you two?'

'We went over a cliff,' said Elvis.

'I already know that.'

'Then why are you asking?'

Jasmine helped Elvis over to a table close to the entrance and lowered him down onto a chair. 'He's fucked his ankle up,' she said to Scratch. 'And his balls are sore.'

'What made you drive over a cliff?'

'Can we get a couple of drinks?' Jasmine requested.

'In a minute. First, tell me what happened.'

Beth left Flake's side for the first time and walked over to them. 'I'll get the drinks,' she said. 'What do you want?'

'Two lime and sodas please,' said Jasmine, looking surprised to see her.

'Coming right up.'

Beth headed behind Scratch's bar to fix the drinks. Scratch could see Jasmine was puzzled by Beth and Flake's presence, and he knew she would ask him about it. So he saved her the trouble.

'A lot of shit's been going down,' he explained. 'But before we get into that, I want to know what happened to you two.'

Elvis was in no state to offer an explanation. He had a black eye and a swollen face, as well as some nasty grazes.

Jasmine walked up to the bar to wait for Beth to give her the two lime and sodas. She leaned against the bar top and checked out her reflection in the mirror behind the bar.

'Shit, one side of my face is all fucked up,' she moaned.

'*For Chrissakes!* What happened?' said Scratch, losing his patience.

'Elvis bought me a DeLorean, but when I hit eighty-eight miles per hour in it, we discovered the brakes didn't work. And we were driving round a mountain at the time, so we ended up going over the edge and plummeting down to the bottom. You know like on *Snakes and Ladders* when you get near the top but that big snake gets you and you drop all the way....'

'Yes I know *Snakes and Ladders*,' Scratch interrupted. 'What I don't know is why anyone would be driving at eighty-eight miles an hour around a fucking mountain!'

'We had a bet to see if the car would travel through time.'

Scratch looked to Elvis for some sense.

'She ain't lying,' said Elvis.

Beth finished pouring the two lime and sodas and handed them to Jasmine. Jasmine carried them over to where Elvis was sitting and handed him one. She sat down next to him and carried on her tale, oblivious to Scratch's rising blood pressure.

'So, anyway, the brakes failed, we went over the cliff and crashed. Next thing you know, I wake up and Elvis is being dragged away by a gang of CGI gorillas.'

'Excuse me?'

'But, I shot most of them and the others ran away. I think their new series is gonna get cancelled though.'

Scratch glared at Elvis. 'What is she talking about?'

'She's actually telling the truth.'

'Yeah, so anyway,' Jasmine carried on. 'I stole this red Corvette from a couple of La-de-das.'

'La-de-das?'

'Yeah, you know, *La-de-das.*'

Scratch realised he didn't care what a *La-de-da* was, so he gestured for her to carry on.

'Then we came straight here,' she said. 'Did you hear from Rex? He was with us right before the crash.'

Scratch knew they weren't going to like the answer. They weren't going to like much of anything, which was annoying, because he needed them focused on what was coming. Things were far worse than they realised. He took a deep breath and let it out slowly.

'Did it occur to either of you that maybe Rex cut the brake lines on your car?'

Elvis perked up. 'What?'

'If Annabel's visions are correct, Rex has been possessed by the ghost of Cain.'

'Cain?' said Elvis. 'That's who Baby was looking for in the asylum the other day, isn't it?'

'You are correct.'

'But I thought Cain could only possess the bodies of people in a coma, or brain-dead.'

'Once again, Elvis, you are correct,' said Scratch, with a heavy dose of sarcasm.

Jasmine's jaw dropped. 'I knew it. I always said Rex was brain-dead.'

'No,' said Scratch. 'Not brain-dead, as in *stupid*, I mean *clinically* brain-dead, like someone who's been in a serious accident and can no longer communicate.'

Elvis looked troubled. 'You're saying Cain did something to Rex to put him in a coma, then took over his body?'

'Annabel thinks Cain entered Rex's body while he was under sedation for his hand transplant.'

Jasmine frowned. 'How does Cain enter the body? Is it through the butt?'

'What? No! Why would you even ask that? Listen, Rex being taken over by Cain isn't even the half of it. Something *really bad* has happened.'

'Like what?'

Scratch sighed. 'Look, there's no easy way to say this, so I'm just gonna say it. *Joey and Baby are dead.*'

Jasmine let out a sound that was somewhere between a laugh and a cry, which stopped as abruptly as it started. Scratch watched her look over to Beth first and then to Annabel. He saw the pain in her eyes as the reality sunk in. Baby was Jasmine's best friend. Jasmine let out a choked sob before looking down at the table. Elvis reached across and stroked her hair.

'What happened?' he asked Scratch.

'Rex killed Baby,' said Scratch. 'Well actually Cain killed Baby, but he was able to do it because Baby thought he was Rex.'

'How?' asked Jasmine, her voice cracking. 'What did he do to her?'

'He strangled her.'

Elvis butted in. 'And Joey? Where was he?'

'He was already dead.'

Annabel took over the story. 'Joey and Baby were tricked into entering the Black Forest on Blue Corn Island. Baby got out, but Joey was---'

'Joey was what?' said Elvis.

'There's something odd about the Black Forest. It has a force-field around it that my psychic visions can't penetrate.'

'Then how do you know Joey's dead?' Elvis demanded.

'I looked into my crystal ball and saw Joey's head come out of the forest, but the rest of him didn't.'

Jasmine stood up, her chair tipping over and falling to the ground in the process. 'It's bullshit,' she shouted. 'You're lying. You're making it up!'

Scratch tried to calm her. 'Trust me, Annabel's telling the truth.'

'She can't be!'

'I promise you she is. I always know when she's lying, because she looks away and then stares up at the ceiling.'

'I do not!' said Annabel, before looking away and then staring up at the ceiling.

'See,' said Scratch.

Jasmine barged past Scratch and headed outside for some fresh air. Beth hurried out from behind the bar and ran after her.

Scratch waited until they were gone and then carried on explaining things to Elvis. 'We think Baby tried calling all of you for help. Rex was the first to show up. And he killed her.'

Elvis shook his head. 'Fuck, I feel terrible.'

Scratch walked back to the bar, leaned over it and grabbed a bottle of scotch and a glass. 'We've also lost the Bourbon Kid,' he said, pouring some scotch into the glass. 'He went looking for Baby, but something bad may have happened to him in a bar called The Fork In Hell.'

'Something? Like what?'

'We're not exactly sure,' said Scratch trying to supress his exasperation. 'Just know that I've taken care of things. I sent someone to go find him.'

'Someone? Who's someone?'

Scratch looked away and mumbled his reply under his breath. 'Sanchez.'

'Sanchez?' Elvis had better hearing than Scratch realised. *'Sanchez Garcia?'*

'Yes.'

'Have you lost your fucking mind?'

'I know how it looks,' said Scratch. 'But I asked God for help and Sanchez showed up, like five seconds later.'

'So?' Elvis sneered. 'I asked for a cheeseburger once and was given a chicken nugget. You know what I did? I sent the nugget back and waited for the cheeseburger!'

Scratch didn't appreciate Elvis's tone. 'I was out of options. I thought all of you were dead.'

'And where is Sanchez now? And more to the point, where is Cain?'

'Annabel?'

The Mystic Lady waved her hands over her crystal ball and stared into it again. After about ten seconds she looked up at Scratch. 'I've got something!' she said.

'What is it?'

Annabel grimaced and chewed on her lip. 'Did you tell Sanchez about Cain?' she asked.

'Of course I did. You were here when I explained everything to him!'

'Yes, but did you tell him that Cain is in Rodeo Rex's body?'

Scratch cast his mind back to his conversation with Sanchez. He replayed it word for word in his head. 'Fuck! No I didn't. It won't matter though, will it? I mean he's not going to bump into Cain, *is he?*'

Annabel didn't even check her crystal ball. 'You've got to do something quick. Sanchez is in trouble!'

Thirty Nine

Sanchez took a look at the glass of bourbon. He'd been given a generous measure. And it looked like quality stuff, better than the cheap shit he served up in The Tapioca. But before drinking it, he figured he ought to do some interrogating. After all, he'd come to Blue Corn Island on a mission and he suspected Scratch wouldn't appreciate him getting drunk before he'd done any detective work. He put the glass back down on the bar, which seemed to offend the bartender, who glared at him through shuttered eyes.

'I'm looking for a friend of mine,' Sanchez said. 'He drinks bourbon. If you've met him it's kinda hard to forget him.'

The bartender and the bouncer exchanged another look. Sanchez was certain they knew who he was talking about.

'Haven't sold any bourbon in weeks,' the bartender replied. 'You're the first to order any.'

Sanchez sensed that they were lying, but he had no idea how to accuse them of dishonesty without getting himself beaten up. So he decided he'd drink the glass of bourbon and offer a compliment about how good it tasted, in the hope of getting chummy with the bartender. But just as the glass touched his bottom lip, another customer entered The Fork In Hell. Rodeo Rex marched in through the front entrance and walked up to the bar, stopping next to Sanchez. He leaned on the bar surface and addressed the bartender in a deep southern drawl.

'Bartender, I'm looking for a guy called the Bourbon Kid,' he said. 'You seen him?'

The bartender shook his head.

Sanchez was surprised that Rex hadn't noticed him. So he took his sunglasses off, stuck them in his top pocket and cleared his throat to draw attention to himself. Rex didn't even look at him. A less subtle approach was required.

'Yo Rex, good to see you,' he said cheerfully.

It seemed to take Rex a while to recognise him. When he finally registered that it was Sanchez, he looked confused. 'Sanchez, the bartender?' he said. 'What are you doing here?'

'Same thing as you I expect,' said Sanchez. 'Your timing is perfect. This asshole,' he pointed at the bartender, 'won't tell me where the Bourbon Kid is.'

'You're looking for the Bourbon Kid too?'

Sanchez nodded. 'Uh huh.'

'What do *you* want with him? Who sent you?'

Rex seemed very uptight. And not particularly friendly, or pleased to see Sanchez. Sanchez figured he probably just needed a drink to unwind, so he held out his glass of bourbon. 'Pull up a stool, drink this and I'll tell you all about it.'

Rex made no attempt to sit down but he happily accepted the drink Sanchez was offering him. He took the glass of bourbon and poured the entire drink down his throat. Then he slammed the glass down on the bar and stared at Sanchez. His nostrils flared like he was angry about something.

'Just tell me where…..' Rex didn't manage to finish the sentence. He started retching and struggling to breathe. He grabbed his throat with both hands and staggered backwards. And he kept blinking like really drunk people do when they're trying to stand still.

'Are you okay?' Sanchez asked.

Rex glared at him and choked up two words. 'You cunt!'

Sanchez didn't approve of the language, which he felt was rather harsh. But he could see there was something wrong with Rex. The giant Hell's Angel fell back onto a wooden table, smashing it in two. He ended up on the floor in a starfish pose, gazing up at the ceiling with his mouth agape.

Sanchez was beginning to regret acting tough and calling the bartender an asshole, because now that Rex was out of action, he was on his own again. The bartender looked pissed too. And Rex smashing one of his tables in half wouldn't have helped. A joke was required to lighten the mood.

'Jeez,' said Sanchez, smiling at the bartender. 'Is that guy a lightweight, or what?'

The bartender didn't laugh. Sanchez noticed he had the name Pat sewn into his shirt pocket.

'So, Pat,' he said, maintaining his phoney grin. 'I think I'll be on my way.'

Pat reached beneath the bar and grabbed a wooden club. Before Sanchez could jump off his stool and make a run for it, the big, sturdy bouncer positioned himself behind him and grabbed him by his shoulders. He had a strong grip.

'Why don't you tell us who you are, and who sent you?' said the bouncer.

Sanchez swallowed hard. 'I'd love to,' he said, thinking on his feet. 'But I need to get to the doctors. I've got a highly contagious skin disease.'

The bouncer was undeterred. He seized a hold of Sanchez's right wrist and stretched his arm out across the bar surface, pinning it down.

Pat, the bartender raised his club above his head, ready to smash it down on Sanchez's fingers.

Forty

Thomas Graber had only ever been into Crimson County on a handful of occasions. But now, at the grand old age of fourteen, his mother Agnes had enrolled him in the Crimson County high school because she had grown tired of the education system in Oakfield.

The day had started well enough. But when lunchtime came, Thomas was at a complete loss. He hadn't yet made any friends and he had no idea where he was supposed to go to eat his packed lunch. He felt out of place too. His Amish clothes had been the source of a great deal of teasing already. Particularly his straw hat, and the braces holding up his pants. His mother, Agnes had told him many times, he would one day grow into his clothes. That day seemed like a long way off though. Thomas was skinny and particularly small for a boy his age.

He was standing in a corridor, trying to read a map of the school, not knowing which way to turn, when he met his first friend.

'You're the new kid, right?'

Thomas looked up and saw a blond guy in a red and white jacket. He was big and looked like a fully-grown man. Thomas had a good idea who he was before he even introduced himself. It was either Archie O'Banyan, the captain of the high school football team, or Dick O'Banyan, his identical twin brother. The twins were well known, even in Oakfield, because of their footballing exploits. They should have left school and gone to college a couple of years back. But they had stayed on at school, partly because they were morons who couldn't graduate, and partly because the whole town wanted them in the High School football team, regardless of their age.

'I'm Archie O'Banyan,' the man-child said.

'I'm Thomas.'

Archie shook Thomas's hand. 'Nice to meet you. You having trouble with your map?'

'Yeah, I don't even know which way up it should be.'

'Give it here. I'll figure it out for you.'

Thomas handed him the map. 'I'm just looking for somewhere I can sit and eat lunch.'

'Lunch? That's an easy one. You can come with me. As captain of the football team, it's my responsibility to make sure new kids have a friend on the first day, so if it's okay with you, you can eat lunch with me.'

'That would be great, thanks.'

'Come on, this way.'

Archie walked briskly along the corridor, and Thomas tried his best to keep up. Because no matter where they went, other students got out of Archie's way, but not so much out of Thomas's way.

'I'm from Oakfield,' said Thomas.

'Yeah, I kinda guessed that from the Amish clothes.'

There wasn't any more conversation after that. Not until Archie stopped outside the boys locker room.

'I don't suppose anyone showed you the locker room yet?' he said, pushing the door open.

'Err, no. I don't even remember this corridor.'

Archie ushered him inside. But as soon as the door closed behind them, things went downhill.

'You took your time,' said a voice.

Another young man in a football jacket appeared from behind a row of lockers. He looked exactly like Archie.

'This is my brother, Dick,' said Archie. 'We're going to give you your Crimson High, first day initiation.'

Archie grabbed Thomas's hat and lifted it off his head. He threw it like a Frisbee over to Dick, who caught it and then dropped it onto the floor by his feet.

'That was my father's hat,' said Thomas.

The hat was special. It had belonged to his father who had died a year earlier, along with his older sister, Elsa, both lost to the evils of the Black Forest during the Fall.

Archie put his arm around Thomas's shoulder, squeezing him in tight. 'Every kid has to go through this on his first day,' he said. 'Don't worry.'

Thomas's heart sank when he realised what was about to happen. Dick O'Banyan grinned at him as he unzipped his pants and pulled his dick out. Then he took aim and started pissing into the hat. As soon as the first drop of urine splashed onto the hat, it was ruined forever.

Thomas wanted to tell them to stop, but he was afraid. If having his hat pissed on was the worst that happened, he supposed he could live with it. And he feared that if he showed any anger at what they were doing, things might get worse.

Things did get worse.

When Dick finished pissing into the hat, he zipped up his fly and nodded at his brother. Archie pulled some kind of lightning fast judo move on Thomas and slammed him onto the floor on his back. Dick grabbed Thomas's feet and the two brothers carried him over to a bench, while he struggled in vain. They set him down in a seated position with his back up against a row of lockers. Then Dick retrieved the soiled hat and held it over Thomas's head.

'I crown you, King of the Amish!' he said, with a broad smirk. Then he turned the hat over and pressed it down on Thomas's head. Urine rained down on him, soaking his hair and dribbling down his face and onto his clothes.

'I think he's gonna cry!' Archie jeered, high-fiving his twin brother.

Thomas did want to cry. He tried his best to fight back the tears, but it wasn't entirely successful. If this was what being at Crimson County School was all about, then he didn't want any part of it. But his ordeal was far from over. Archie grabbed him by his ankles, pulled him painfully off of the bench and dragged him across the locker room into the showers. Dick walked alongside, kicking Thomas in the ribs every once in a while.

'You need a shower, boy!' Archie jeered as he switched on one of the showers.

They pushed him underneath the shower spray and kept him underneath it until his clothes were soaked through. Eventually, Archie switched off the shower and reached down, grabbing Thomas by his face. Archie had big hands so he could squeeze the younger boy's cheeks hard.

'You listen to me Amish boy,' he said. 'You're not welcome in this school. If you tell anyone about this, or if you show up in my school again tomorrow, or any other day, I promise you next time you'll get a lot worse. You understand?'

Thomas nodded. He couldn't really speak, because he was sobbing and his nose was blocked up with snot. So Archie gave him one last parting shot, a punch to the face that would surely result in a black eye and some bruising.

With the Crimson High initiation ritual complete, the two brothers walked away laughing. Thomas stayed in the locker room, crying and wondering how he was going to clean himself up and get home.

Forty One

Sanchez had always been rather fond of his right hand, particularly the fingers, so the thought of having them smashed by a crazy bartender with a wooden club wasn't appealing. He tried to wriggle free but the bouncer who was pinning his arm down on the bar had a firm grip.

SMASH!

The door of the Men's toilets burst open and a female voice spoke out loud and clear.

'Step away from the fat guy!'

The bouncer let go of Sanchez's arm and turned around to confront the new arrival. Sanchez yanked his arm out of harms way and looked to see who had come to his rescue. He recognised her straight away. It was Jasmine. She was wearing a purple catsuit that showed off every inch of her athletic frame and looked gorgeous against her dark skin. The gun holstered across her hips bordered on obscene, it was so suggestive.

The bouncer took a step towards her. 'I don't know who the fuck you are, lady,' he said. 'Or where the fuck you came from. But this ain't none of your business, so do yourself a favour and fuck off.'

Sanchez saw an opportunity to make a few bucks, so he reached across the bar and tapped Pat on the arm. 'Five bucks says she fucks him up.'

Pat ignored him and shouted to the bouncer. 'Kick her ass, Tinker.'

Sanchez wasn't sure he heard the name correctly. 'Did you just call him Stinker?'

'*Tinker,*' Pat hissed.

Sanchez watched eagerly as Tinker moved menacingly towards Jasmine. It wasn't a clever thing to do and he obviously didn't realise who he was messing with. Jasmine whipped out her pistol.

BANG!

Tinker howled in pain and grabbed his left leg with both hands. Blood was gushing out of his knee. He lifted his foot off the floor, but in doing so, he lost his balance and fell onto his back next to the unconscious body of Rodeo Rex. He writhed around on the floor, crying like a child. While Sanchez had a degree of sympathy for him, Jasmine did not. She took a short run up and then kicked him hard, right between the legs. Tinker hurled up a mouthful of vomit, which splattered all over his face and up his nose.

Sanchez was about to applaud, but Pat the bartender lunged over the bar at him. He covered Sanchez eyes with one hand and pressed a gun against his head with the other. Then he barked an order at Jasmine.

'Drop the gun, bitch!'

Sanchez couldn't see anything but he heard the sound of Jasmine's gun hitting the floor. Then Pat issued another order.

'Right, now step away from Tinker.'

It was hard to tell if Jasmine was doing what Pat said or not, because Tinker was crying hysterically on the floor, drowning out any other noises, *the inconsiderate bastard.*

'You got any other weapons?' Pat asked.

'No,' Jasmine replied.

'Bullshit, you've got something.'

'So come and frisk me.'

Pat deliberated the offer, before wisely declining. 'Uh uh,' he said, shaking his head. 'Take off that catsuit.'

'I'm not wearing any underwear.'

'Take it off.'

Sanchez tried to wriggle free of Pat's grip, or at least get a look at what was going on. But the more he wriggled, the harder Pat pressed his gun against his head. He could hear Jasmine unzipping things. He just couldn't see what.

'That's right,' yelled Pat. 'Throw the boots over there by the door.'

Sanchez heard Jasmine tossing her boots across the floor. He cleared his throat to get Pat's attention. 'Hey, buddy, I can't see.'

Pat ignored him.

'And the catsuit,' said Pat. 'Take it off and throw it over here to me.'

Sanchez heard Jasmine slipping out of her catsuit. Then he heard Pat whisper two words. *'Holy Fuck!'*

A slight gap appeared between Pat's fingers, offering Sanchez a very blurry view of proceedings. He could see Jasmine's purple catsuit. She was holding it out in front of her.

'That's right,' said Pat. 'Throw it over here!'

Jasmine tossed her catsuit towards the bar. A part of it landed on Sanchez's head. It made a slapping sound, suggesting a chunk of it had hit Pat too. Sanchez still couldn't see what was going on, but he heard a series of low thudding sounds. Suddenly he saw a sliver of light between Pat's fingers. Jasmine was gone. It took him a moment to realise what had happened. She had performed some kind of somersault over the bar, and ended up behind Pat. The bartender let go of Sanchez and yelped in pain.

Sanchez backed away and spun around to see what was going on. Jasmine had relieved Pat of his gun and grabbed a fistful of his hair. While he was still dazed she smashed his head down onto the bar.

CRUNCH!

Jasmine yanked Pat's head back up and pressed the gun against his temple, just like he had done to Sanchez.

'Okay, pervert,' she whispered in his ear. 'What's going on here? Why are you drugging people, and what did you do to my friend the Bourbon Kid?'

'Get fucked, you fucking bitch,' said Pat, blood dripping from his nose and onto his lips as he spoke.

Jasmine nodded at Sanchez. 'Grab his wrists,' she said.

Sanchez didn't particularly want to get involved, but he had no intention of disobeying Jasmine, so he grabbed Pat's wrists as instructed.

'Okay, I've got 'em,' he said.

'Pull him down over the bar until his hands are touching the floor.'

Sanchez wasn't sure where Jasmine was going with this, but he did as he was told, hauling Pat's upper body over the bar until he was in a handstand position. His legs were still on the bar and Jasmine was holding onto them, as if they were about to take part in a wheelbarrow race.

'Don't let him fall,' she said. "I need you to hold him steady while I do this.'

'Okaaaaaaayyyyyy.'

Jasmine yanked Pat's pants and shorts down until they were round his ankles. She positioned herself between his legs, staring down at his hairy ass.

'What the fuck are you doing?' Pat cried.

Jasmine picked up the wooden club that Pat had been threatening to break Sanchez's fingers with. She leaned over the bar so Sanchez could see her face. It was an odd sight that made it look like her head was growing out of Pat's ass.

'Tell him I'm going to beat his dick and balls with this club until he tells me what I want to know,' she said.

Sanchez shouted into the left ear on Pat's upside down face. 'She said....'

'I heard what she said, but I don't know what she's talking about!'

THUD!

Sanchez didn't see what Jasmine did, but it made Pat scream really loud. Then he started crying. Sanchez looked away, preferring not to watch.

The bar room floor was quite a sight. The bouncer, Tinker was still writhing around on the ground nearby, although it looked like he was barely conscious. Not far from him was Rodeo Rex, splayed out across the floor with a broken table around him. Then there was Jasmine's catsuit and boots too. The sight of them made Sanchez's mind wander momentarily.

THUD!

Pat yelled out in pain again, screaming into Sanchez's ear. 'Don't you get it?' he wailed. *'They'll kill me.'*

BANG!

For a moment Sanchez thought Jasmine had shot Pat in the ass. But in actual fact she had leaned over the bar and shot Tinker in the face. Blood squirted out of his forehead and spilled onto the floor.

'See that?' she yelled. 'Your buddy Tinker is dead. If you want to live, if you want to ever feel your balls again, you'd better start talking.'

Pat sobbed a bit more. 'You fucking bitch,' he whimpered.

Sanchez shouted up to Jasmine. 'He called you a fucking bitch again.'

Another thud followed, and this one sounded more vicious that the other ones.

'OWWWW!'

Sanchez was curious to see what Jasmine was actually doing to Pat, but he was conscious that if he stood up and took a peek, it might appear as if he was trying to get a sneaky look at Jasmine's nakedness. And, well, Sanchez didn't fancy the idea of ending up like Pat, hanging over a bar, with his pants down, while Jasmine bashed his dick and balls with a club. Or maybe the club was going up Pat's ass? Who knew? Jasmine, that's who. And Sanchez was happy to keep it that way.

'Okay, I'll make you a deal,' said Jasmine. 'Tell me what happened to the Bourbon Kid. If I think you're lying, I'll hit you with this club again. If you tell the truth, I'll massage your dick and balls to make them feel better.'

Sanchez relayed the rather odd message to Pat. 'She's offering you a deal.....'

'Okay, okay!' Pat interrupted. 'They took your friend to the Black Forest!'

'That's the spirit,' said Jasmine. 'Keep talking.'

In a matter of seconds, the expression on Pat's face changed from terrified to slightly bewildered. Then he started taking short breaths like someone who'd burned their fingers. Sanchez glanced up to see what was going on. It looked weird.

'Come on, keep talking,' said Jasmine.

'Erm, I... I served him a glass of poison,' said Pat, the pitch of his voice getting higher with each word. 'Normally it knocks people out, but your friend, the Bourbon Kid, he was immune to it.'

Sanchez looked over at the corpse of Rodeo Rex lying on the floor next to Tinker. Rex had drunk the poison too. And now it seemed that, in exchange for information, Jasmine was jerking off the asshole who served up the poison.

'Is the Bourbon Kid still alive?' she asked him.

'How the hell should I know?' Pat replied.

THUD!

'OWWW FUUUUUCKK!'

Sanchez winced and even felt a degree of sympathy for Pat. Jasmine sure knew how to fuck a guy up. Massage his dick and make it bigger, then smash it with a club. Ouch.

Pat was wailing like a new-born baby. Blood, sweat, drool, tears and snot were all sliding off his face, making a messy cocktail on the floor.

Sanchez flicked Pat on the nose. 'Bourbon Kid,' he said. 'Where is he?'

'Okay, okay!' Pat sobbed. 'Last I heard, they nailed him to a wooden cart and rolled it into the forest.' He winced and waited to see how Jasmine felt about his answer. She liked it enough not to hit him again.

'Why would they roll him into the forest?' Sanchez asked.

'There are monsters in there at this time of year,' said Pat. 'Anyone that goes in there disappears.'

'What monsters?' asked Jasmine.

'No one's ever seen them.'

THUD!

'OWWWWW!'

Sanchez grimaced. 'I think he was telling the truth that time.'

'Oh, okay,' said Jasmine. 'Sorry, carry on.'

Pat had his eyes closed tight. Through gritted teeth he continued. 'Every year around this time, we sacrifice one person a day to the Forest Gods. In exchange, they show us mercy and leave us alone. Your friend was a stranger, travelling on his own, so I poisoned him and handed him over to the Crimson Coven. They took him to the forest to be sacrificed to the Gods. It's a tradition, it's been going on for centuries.'

Jasmine seemed to like the answer so far (if Pat's expression was anything to go by). 'Where do we find this cart you nailed him to?' she asked.

'It's about a mile from here. Drive down the road towards Oakfield. Just before the edge of the forest there's a dirt track off the road. Follow that until you come to a rail track that leads into the forest.

There's a chain wrapped around a large wooden wheel. Turn the wheel and the cart will come out. He'll be gone though. No one ever survives.'

Jasmine raised the club high above her head. 'Tell me more about this Crimson Coven?'

'Oh God,' Pat winced, fearing the worst. 'Look, they're cops. The police department, they run everything. How else do you think they get away with it?'

THUD!

'YEEEEEEEOOOOOOOOOW!'

'I ask the questions,' said Jasmine. 'Not you.'

Pat looked like he was about to lose consciousness. Sanchez almost felt bad for him. After all, the guy's dick and balls were probably flat by now.

'Anything else you wanna tell us?' said Jasmine.

Pat didn't answer. He'd gone cross-eyed and was dribbling all over himself.

'Sanchez, come here,' said Jasmine.

Sanchez stepped away from Pat and stood up straight. There was a strange smell in the air. Jasmine was naked, Pat's dick and balls were squashed all over the bar top, and no matter where Sanchez looked, Pat's asshole was in his eye line. So he stared up at the ceiling, pretending like he'd seen something up there.

'What do you want me to do?' he asked.

'I want you to grab something,' said Jasmine.

'Excuse me?'

'Grab that,' she said, glancing downwards.

Sanchez looked down. He wasn't sure what he was supposed to be grabbing. There was Pat's ass. No way. Not in a million years. Pat's dick and balls, or at least, some stuff that could only *be* Pat's dick and balls. Again, there was no way Sanchez was going to grab them. Then there was Jasmine's naked body. His eyes lingered on her breasts for a little longer than was polite.

'Would you just grab it!' said Jasmine.

Sanchez tried to read what her eyes were pointing at. It didn't make much sense but it looked like she was trying to get him to grab her left nipple. He reached out tentatively for it.

'The bottle, dickhead!' she shouted.

Sanchez hadn't noticed the bottle of bourbon on the bar, the one laced with poison. He redirected his hand and picked it up. 'Oh, yeah, that,' he said. 'What do you want me to do with it?'

'Pour it.'

'Pour it? Where?'

Jasmine nodded at Pat's ass. Sanchez closed his eyes. This was getting far too weird. But he didn't want to disobey Jasmine, so he unscrewed the lid on the bottle and held it over Pat's ass crack.

'Fill him up,' said Jasmine.

Sanchez held his breath, fearing the possibility of some unpleasant chemical reaction. He counted to three in his head, then pushed the neck of the bottle into Pat's butthole. The contents started glugging out. It made some interesting sounds. A mixture of gurgling, popping and some "ooh-ing and aah-ing, which probably came from Pat's mouth. When the bottle was empty, and Pat's asshole was bubbling and making all kinds of strange noises, Jasmine slid her hands up to his ankles and pushed his legs away from the bar. He toppled over onto his back in the middle of the floor. A pool of the poisoned bourbon started seeping out of his ass onto the floor and into Tinker's face.

Sanchez looked back at Jasmine before immediately returning his gaze to the ceiling. 'We did good, huh?'

'Can you get me my boots?'

'Uh, yeah.'

'Did you know Rex was possessed?' Jasmine asked as Sanchez was walking over to retrieve her boots.

'What do you mean?'

Sanchez hadn't given Rex much thought, what with all the cock bashing and drink pouring that had been going on. He stepped over the Hell's Angel's body on his way to retrieve Jasmine's boots. When he picked them up and turned around, Jasmine was no longer behind the bar. His eyes scoured the room for her and eventually settled on her ass. She was back on his side of the bar, bending over to pick up her catsuit, which was on the floor.

When she straightened up and turned around Sanchez looked up at the ceiling again, and spotted a propeller fan up there that warranted his attention.

'That's a nice ceiling fan, isn't it?' he said, holding the boots out for Jasmine to take, while keeping his gaze fixed on the fan.

'It is,' said Jasmine. 'Do you often get a boner when you look at ceiling fans?'

Sanchez's pants had gotten a little tighter. He hadn't realised it was noticeable. 'Just take your bloody boots would you,' he said.

'Bring them over here. And seriously, stop looking at the ceiling, it's creepy.'

Sanchez walked over and placed Jasmine's boots down on the floor at her feet. 'What did you mean when you said Rex was possessed?' he asked.

Jasmine started pulling on her catsuit while Sanchez watched and tried to think about baseball.

'Yeah, he was possessed by the ghost of someone called Cain,' she said. 'He tried to kill me and Elvis yesterday. He was going to kill you too, but lucky for you, you poisoned him.'

'Rex was going to kill me?'

'Yeah. You knew that though, right? That's why you gave him the poisoned drink?'

'Of course,' said Sanchez, his eyes following Jasmine's hand as she zipped herself up. 'I had the whole thing under control. I knew it wasn't really Rex.'

'You've got good instincts,' said Jasmine. 'You're gonna need them too, because we're going to the Black Forest.'

'Umm, Scratch told me to go to Bishop Yoder's place and look for something called the Brutus Dagger.'

Jasmine started pulling on her boots. 'You're coming with me whether you like it or not.' She grabbed a set of keys that were lying on the floor next to Tinker. 'Come on, let's take this guy's ride,' she said.

'What about Rex?'

'He's dead. What do you wanna do, say a prayer for him or something?'

'Not really.'

'Fine, then let's go.'

Sanchez reluctantly followed her out, leaving behind the dead bodies of Pat and Tinker. And the body of Rex, which looked dead, but was actually in a coma.

Forty Two

Rodeo Rex arrived at Cyber Limbs Prosthetics Corporation in fairly high spirits. After years of living with a metal hand he was finally having a real human hand fitted. He'd waited six years for this. It was hard to believe it had been that long since he'd heard about a new transplanting procedure and given samples of his DNA to Dr Elizabeth Dalton, the surgeon who had fitted his metal hand. Ever since that day, she and her team had been working on building him a new hand.

He waited in the reception area of the surgery and flicked through the shitty selection of magazines they had on offer. There was no one else in the waiting room, apart from the receptionist, Elaine, and she was the quiet type. Even so, Rex had a crack at striking up some conversation.

'Keeping busy here these days?' he asked.

She looked up from her desk and shook her head.

In her defence, Rex knew that the receptionists weren't supposed to chat with clients. Some of the stuff that went on in Cyber Limbs was borderline illegal. The rest of it was definitely illegal. So the staff had to keep quiet because anyone they spoke to was a potential undercover snoop.

It took less than fifteen minutes for Rex to flick through every single magazine in the waiting room. Celebrity gossip wasn't really his thing and he didn't give a shit about horoscopes, so there wasn't much to read. He considered switching his phone back on, even though he had enjoyed the last few days without it. But he did miss checking Jasmine's Instagram account. He was considering taking one sneaky look at it, seeing as he had nothing better to do, but then Dr Elizabeth Dalton finally showed up.

Dr Dalton was the perfect advert for the company. Her skin was youthful, smooth and unblemished. She was in her mid forties, but she looked twenty years younger. Whatever it was they did at Cyber Limbs, it was working for her. She had long blonde hair tied into a ponytail and an athletic figure that rivalled any Olympian. Rex wondered if the body she was born with had been entirely replaced with parts she created herself in the laboratory.

She greeted Rex with a beaming white smile. 'How's my most handsome client?' she asked.

Rex stood up. 'I bet you say that to all the guys.'

'Yes I do. And they all believe it.'

He laughed politely, but then got straight to business. 'I'm looking forward to seeing my new hand.' He held up his metal hand and wiggled the fingers. 'This thing's saved my life a bunch of times, but I gotta tell you, I'll be glad to be rid of it.'

Dr Dalton's smile faded. 'Yes, umm, I think you should come with me,' she said. 'There's something you need to see.'

She led Rex out of the reception hall and into a long corridor.

'Is something wrong?' Rex asked.

'In here,' said Dr Dalton. She opened a door marked "SECURITY" and showed Rex into a room filled with monitors and a fat guy watching Sesame Street, while eating donuts. He jumped up at the sight of Elizabeth Dalton and turned off the monitor that had Bert and Ernie on it.

'Hello Treager,' said Dr Dalton. 'Could you leave us for a moment, please?'

'Yes ma'am.'

Treager picked up a donut and squeezed around Rex on his way out, looking like he was worried about something.

'I have very mixed news for you,' said Dr Dalton. 'Please take a seat.'

Rex sat down in Treager's seat, which was unpleasantly warm. There was a stench of body odour all around too. Mixed in with coffee and donuts.

Dr Dalton perched on the desk, her long golden legs poking out from under her white coat.

'Why are we in here?' Rex asked.

'The good news is your hand is fixed, just like my colleague Dr Chamberlain told you on the phone the other day. Those DNA samples we took from you and the blood cells you donated, worked perfectly and we did rebuild your old hand exactly as it was.'

'And the bad news?'

'It's not here any more.'

'Where is it?'

'It walked out.'

Rex took his Stetson hat off and sat it down on top of one of the monitors. 'What do you mean it walked out?'

Dr Dalton picked up a remote control and pointed it at the monitor with Rex's hat on it. 'Take a look at this and maybe you'll understand what I'm talking about.'

She flicked through a few menus on the screen until she brought up some footage from a CCTV camera. It showed a corridor with a steel door at the end of it. The video was paused so nothing much was happening.

'The vault where we stored your hand is behind that door,' she said. 'But a couple of nights ago, it left the building.'

'And you've got it on video?'

'Yes, take a look at this.'

She pressed PLAY and the video resumed. For about ten seconds nothing happened. But then the door at the end of the corridor opened and a naked man walked out of the vault. Dr Dalton paused the video again.

'See what I mean?' she said.

Rex stared open mouthed at the computer screen. The man on the screen was his identical twin, which was really odd because Rex didn't have a twin, let alone an identical one. The only noticeable difference was that the clone had shorter hair.

'What the fuck?'

'That's what I thought when I saw it,' said Dr Dalton.

'Well who *the fuck* is that?'

'That is what we created with your DNA. We've done this procedure a hundred times. But never in all that time has any of the bodies we created come to life. It's not a living creature. It has no brain, it's just a body made of real living tissue.'

'Are you fucking shitting me?'

'Our process is quite revolutionary. It involves growing a clone of the patient and amputating limbs from the clone to transplant onto the patient.'

'Okay, so first of all, it's completely mental that you've done that. So congratulations.'

'Thanks.'

'But second, what the fuck happened? How has it come to life?'

'Well, that's the thing. Technically it was always alive, but it had no soul and it was brain-dead, like all the other clones we have.'

'So where the hell is it now?'

'We don't know. There was no one here when it walked out, because it was the middle of the night. We were hoping it would come back or we'd find it somewhere before you came for your hand transplant.'

'Rewind that footage,' Rex demanded. 'I want to see that again.'

Dr Dalton rewound the footage and they watched the naked version of Rex moonwalk back inside the vault and close the door. Dr Dalton pressed PLAY again.

'No wait, rewind it some more,' said Rex.

'Why?'

'I want to see if anyone went in there.'

'Only myself and Dr Chamberlain have access to that room. No one else can get in. It's retina activated.'

'Rewind it anyway.'

Dr Dalton indulged him and rewound the video some more. The screen flickered as it rewound the footage of the corridor, but other than that there was no movement.

'See, I told you,' said Dr Dalton. 'No one went in.'

'There!' said Rex pointing at the screen. 'I saw it!'

'Saw what?'

'Gimme that remote.'

Rex didn't wait for her to give him the remote. He snatched it from her and pressed PLAY. After about ten seconds he hit the PAUSE button. 'There, see it?' he said, pointing at the screen.

'See what?'

'Look at the ceiling.'

Dr Dalton covered her mouth with her hand. 'Oh my God. What is it?'

'It's a shadow demon, or a ghost, I think.'

The footage on the video showed the shadow of a man on the ceiling above the door of the vault. Rex moved the clip along one frame at a time and they saw the shadow vanish through the door. Rex skipped forward to the moment his clone came back through the door. He paused it and zoomed in on the face. There was a C shaped scar on the clone's forehead.

'Fuck!'

Forty Three

Jasmine was pleasantly surprised to find that the keys she took from Tinker belonged to a motorbike parked at the back of The Fork In Hell. And as luck would have it, the bike had a sidecar, so while Jasmine raced along the highway towards the Black Forest, Sanchez was able to sit next to her in the sidecar, though it was a snug fit, she noticed.

After a short drive along the highway, Jasmine saw the turning off the road that Pat had mentioned. She drove along the dirt track, which was quite bumpy, so not particularly comfortable for Sanchez. But they soon found the large wooden wheel at the end of the rail track that ran into the forest. Jasmine parked up by the wheel and climbed off the bike.

'This is definitely it,' she said.

'I'm wedged in here,' Sanchez replied. 'Can you help me out?'

Jasmine ignored him and walked up to the mill wheel and tried to turn a large wooden handle on it. A length of heavy chain from the wheel was pulled tight, a metre off the ground, stretching into the forest.

'Give me a hand, would ya?' she shouted.

She looked back and saw Sanchez roll out of the sidecar. He landed on some grass, stood up, and dusted himself down.

'What are we trying to do?' he asked.

'Help me turn this wheel.'

Sanchez didn't look enthusiastic, but nonetheless he joined Jasmine at the mill wheel and the two of them started turning the handles on either side. Once they got it going, the wheel moved quite freely and the chain attached to it began wrapping around it, pulling the heavy cart back from the forest.

When the cart eventually appeared, Jasmine left the turning wheel and rushed over to it. Sanchez wasn't strong enough to turn the wheel on his own, so it started to roll back into the forest. Jasmine grabbed a brake lever on the back of the cart and yanked it to the side. The cart stopped moving and she took a closer look at it. It was covered in blood, some of which had dried and had probably been on there for a long time. But there was also some fresh blood in patches around two bent nails that were hammered in near the front of the cart.

'We have to go in,' Jasmine said, looking back at Sanchez. He was doubled over, trying to catch his breath after turning the wheel. He looked at her incredulously.

'Go into the forest?' he wheezed.

'Yeah.'

'I'll wait here and keep watch then.'

'Good thinking!' said Jasmine. 'I'll follow the rail track. You wait here and shout if you see anything unusual.'

Sanchez sat down on the cart and took his jacket off. His black sweatshirt was glued to him from all the sweat he'd worked up while turning the wheel.

Jasmine stood at the edge of the forest and looked into it. It was really dark in there, making it hard to see more than a few metres in.

'Sanchez, do you believe in fate?' she asked.

'No,' he replied.

'Neither do I. Don't you think that's weird?'

'No.'

'I do. I think it's a sign.'

'A sign of what?'

'A sign that we think alike. My gut is telling me I'm going to find the Bourbon Kid in there. What's your gut telling you?'

'It's telling me I shouldn't have eaten the sandwich Scratch gave me earlier.'

Sanchez stood up and waved his hand behind his backside. Jasmine caught a waft of rotten eggs floating through the air. It was definitely a good time to head into the forest, she decided.

'If I'm not back in ten minutes, come looking for me,' she said.

'Ten minutes, okay.'

She stepped onto the rail track and walked along it, into the forest. Even though it was only mid afternoon, the forest was as black as its name suggested. The branches on the trees seemed to reach out as if they were trying to grab her. With the rail track underfoot, it reminded her of a haunted house ride she had been on once. Everything was dark but there was a sense that something would jump out in front of her at any second.

She had only passed six or seven rows of tress when she heard a low buzzing sound. She looked around for the source of it and saw a small light flashing on the ground not far away from where she was. It was a cellphone receiving an incoming call. She stepped off the rail track and hurried over to it, careful not to trip on any of the hidden tree roots. She snatched the phone up from the ground and answered it.

'Hello?' she said.

A man's voice replied. 'Jasmine?'

'Rex?'

'Yeah. What are you doing on the Bourbon Kid's phone?'

This was weird. The last time she'd seen Rex he was on the floor in The Fork In Hell. 'I just found it. Where are you?'

'I'm at the Cyber Limbs centre where they're going to fit my new hand. Where are you?'

'Rex, did you kill Baby?'

The line went quiet for a moment before Rex spoke, much more softly this time. 'Oh no,' he said. 'Is Baby dead?'

'Yeah, and Joey too. The Mystic Lady says you've been taken over by Cain. Is that true?'

'Technically, yeah. That's what I'm calling about. The Cyber Limbs people created a clone of me. I was supposed to have its hand to replace my metal one. But Cain took over the clone.'

Rex's story sounded kind of plausible. And Jasmine wanted to believe it.

'Okay, hold on, before I tell you where I am, you're going to have to prove to me that you're the real Rex.'

'How?'

'I'm going to ask you a question, and if you give me the wrong answer, I'm hanging up on you.'

'Fair enough. Go on.'

'Do you masturbate with your metal hand?'

'Oh *for Chrissakes*, Jasmine! How many times have I told you to stop asking me that!'

Jasmine breathed a sigh of relief. 'Okay, Rex, that's the answer I was looking for. I'm in the Black Forest on Blue Corn Island. That's where I found the Bourbon Kid's phone. It was on the ground.'

'The Black Forest?'

'Yeah, I'm with your friend, Sanchez from the Tapioca, we're looking for the Bourbon Kid, and something called the Brutus Dagger.'

'In the Black Forest?'

'Yeah. This is where Joey was killed, apparently.'

'Get out of there.'

Jasmine heard a twig snap somewhere nearby. 'Hold on,' she said. 'I think there's someone here.'

'GET OUT OF THERE!'

It was hard to see anything in the dark. She heard another voice call her name. This time it was Sanchez. He was echoing what Rex was saying.

'JASMINE, LOOK OUT!'

She put the phone back to her ear. 'Rex, I'm gonna have to call you back.'

'Jasmine. Get out of the forest and go to Bishop Yoder's church in Oakfield. I'll meet you there.'

'Yeah, yeah okay. I'm just going to check out what this noise is. I think it might be the Bourbon Kid.'

'GET OUT OF THE FOREST FOR FUCKS.....'

The battery on the cellphone died before Rex could finish the sentence. Jasmine tried shaking it to see if it might come back to life. But then she heard Sanchez shouting from the edge of the forest again.

'JASMINE! MOVE!'

And then something in the forest roared. Something that sounded like a lion, or maybe a bear. Whatever it was, it sounded big and it was heading towards Jasmine. The ground shook beneath her feet. And then she saw it. A giant monster charging towards her through the trees, followed by a swarm of smaller creatures with red eyes.

Sanchez shouted again. 'JASMINE!'

She returned to the rail track and as soon as she set foot on its wooden boards she ran as fast as she could towards the sound of Sanchez's voice. It sounded like a hundred forest creatures were charging after her. She glanced over her shoulder and saw the biggest one bearing down on her. It was less than ten metres back, taking giant leaps towards her. It had one enormous yellow eye in its forehead. There was no way she could outrun it.

But then suddenly she had another problem, coming from the other direction. The motorised cart was storming along the rail track towards her, gathering pace. She barely had time to think. As the cart reached her, she leapt up in the air, hurdling over the front of it. Her left foot landed on the cart and she used it to push off and leap further away from the pursuing monsters.

BLAM!

The one eyed monster chasing her didn't have such great reactions. The wooden cart crashed into its legs. Jasmine heard it growl in pain. The cart knocked it off balance, and out of the corner of her eye she saw its face smash into a tree branch nearby. It spun over and landed inches behind her. A bunch of its red-eyed companions came rushing up from behind and tripped over it, creating an almighty pile up, which bought Jasmine just enough time to get to the edge of the woods and out into the daylight once more.

Sanchez was sitting on the grass by the rail track, holding his stomach. 'Sorry about that,' he said.

Jasmine caught her breath and looked around. The creatures in the forest were nowhere to be seen. She looked back at Sanchez. He was rubbing his stomach like he was in pain.

'What are you sorry about?' she said. 'You saved my ass! Why are you apologising?'

Sanchez looked confused. 'I was feeling a bit sick, and I accidentally leaned on the lever on the back of the cart,' he said. 'I think it was the brake, because it set off the cart, and it ran away into the forest after you. Didn't you hear me calling you?'

'I thought you were warning me about the monsters in the woods?'

'What monsters?'

'The one's you hit with the cart! Come on get your fat ass up, we need to get out of here!'

A loud roar from the forest reminded her of the urgency of their situation. Sanchez heard it too. He stopped rubbing his stomach and got up.

'What the hell was that?'

Jasmine ignored him and sprinted over to the motorbike. Sanchez followed, jumping into the sidecar without moaning about it for a change. Jasmine started the engine and the bike raced away before Sanchez could even close the door of the sidecar.

'Where are we going now?' he asked, staring past her into the forest as they rode alongside it.

'I just spoke to Rex on the phone,' said Jasmine. 'We've got to go to Bishop Yoder's place and wait for him there.'

'Rex?' said Sanchez.

'It's a long story. I'll explain it on the way.'

All along the forest edge, black shadowy creatures with red eyes were appearing between the trees, watching them race away on the bike.

'What the hell are those things?' Sanchez asked.

'I don't know, but let's not hang around to find out.'

Forty Four

Thomas spent the rest of the school day hiding away in a toilet stall, embarrassed to leave in case anyone saw the state he was in. His clothes and hair were drenched in urine and his face was bruised and swollen, not only from being beaten up, but from crying about it most of the day as well. For several painfully long hours he shivered and sobbed in the toilet stall, while other boys came in and used the washroom. Talk of his humiliation at the hands of Archie and Dick O'Banyan had spread around the school, so he overheard many of the other boys laughing about it.

His biggest fear was that the O'Banyans would find him and beat him up again. But as far as he could tell from the conversations he'd overheard, everyone seemed to think he'd fled the school and gone home. He certainly wished he had, but he'd made the decision to wait and ride home with his mother at the end of the school day.

The final bell rang out at 3.45 p.m. Thomas heard the other students making lots of noise as they left the building. When the noise eventually died down shortly after four o'clock he gathered himself together, took a few deep breaths and walked out of the stall.

His mother was waiting for him at the school gates. Seeing the look on her face when she saw how distressed he was, only made things worse. The tears came flooding back.

'Thomas, what on earth has happened to you?'

'Can we just go?' he mumbled, his voice cracking.

'But you're bruised. What's happened?'

'Please, can we just go!'

Agnes was a smart lady and she knew her son better than anyone, so she understood from his shaking voice that he needed to get out of there.

'Okay, come on. You can tell me about it on the way home.'

Unfortunately while Agnes had been waiting at the school gates, someone had sprayed graffiti on her horse and wagon. The words *"Amish Scum"* had been spelled out in red paint on the side of the wagon. And there was a splodge of red paint all over one side of Fanny the horse too.

To avoid any further abuse, they took the longer route back home to Oakfield, travelling down to the lower side of the island. The lower side was unsuitable for cars, because the road was a bumpy dirt track. It was slightly more scenic though. On one side they had the gentle sound of waves washing up on the shore of the island. On the other was a cliff-side, a hundred feet high. At the top of the cliff was the Black Forest.

Thomas knew his mother was deeply upset about the state she had found him in, and probably felt guilty for sending him to Crimson's High School against his wishes. Seeing her fighting back the tears only made him feel worse for not being stronger and standing up to the bullies.

They were almost halfway home before Agnes brought up the subject of what had happened to him.

'Tomorrow I'll go and see the headmaster,' she announced.

'Please don't, mother.'

'Tell me then, who did this to you?'

Thomas wanted to tell her, but he was fearful of what could happen if he "snitched". The O'Banyan brothers were well respected in Crimson County because of their status as football heroes, among other things. So in the best interests of not getting beaten up again, he lied.

'I don't know,' he said. 'I didn't get a good look at them.'

'How many of them were there?'

'Two.'

'What did they do?'

Thomas closed his eyes. The memory of what the twins did to him was painful to remember. 'They beat me up in the toilets,' he said, fighting back some tears. 'And they peed in my hat and poured it over me.'

He saw his mother heave, like she was about to be sick. She pulled the reins and slowed the horse to a stop. Then she grabbed Thomas and hugged him. The two of them sobbed together for a few minutes, Agnes repeatedly apologising to him for sending him to the school, and vowing to get justice for what the bullies had done to him.

He was in the middle of pleading with her not to take matters further, when she suddenly pulled away and stared at something behind him.

'What is it? What's the matter?' he asked.

Agnes didn't reply. She climbed down from the wagon and started running towards the cliff-side. Thomas looked around to see what she was running to. At first he was somewhat perplexed, but then he saw what she had seen. There was a man lying next to some bushes at the foot of the cliff. Thomas forgot about all of his own problems for a moment and jumped out of the wagon to join his mother.

The man on the ground was shirtless and had deep cuts across his chest, shoulders and arms, like he'd been savaged by a pack of wild animals. His hair was messy and matted with blood. And his face was more bruised and cut than Thomas's. His right eye was swollen to the size of a tennis ball. His only clothing was a pair of ripped black pants.

'Is he alive?' Thomas asked.

'Yes, but only just,' said Agnes. 'We're going to have to take him back to Crimson County, to the hospital, otherwise he'll die.'

The injured man breathed out one word. 'No.'

Thomas jumped back, startled. He had assumed the man was unconscious. Agnes dealt with the situation much better, stroking the man's bloodied hair.

'You need to go to hospital,' she said.

'No,' the man repeated, his eyes still closed.

Agnes looked up at Thomas. 'We should contact the police.'

The man coughed up some blood. It dribbled onto his chin and he spluttered out a few more words. 'No, no police. You've gotta hide me.'

Thomas looked at the injured man's left hand and saw something that he hadn't noticed before. He grabbed the man's wrist and lifted it up to show to his mother what he had seen.

'Mother, look!'

It took Agnes a few seconds to realise what he was referring to. She took a sharp intake of breath and then grabbed the man's other hand to see if it was the same. She held it up to show Thomas. They looked at each other, disbelieving of what they were seeing. This man that they had found in the dirt at the bottom of the cliff, had holes in the palms of both of his hands.

Agnes stroked some hair out of the man's eyes. 'Who are you?' she asked.

The man managed to open his left eye a little. He looked at Agnes, then at Thomas. His body went limp and he let out a deep sigh, before uttering two barely audible words.

'Oh Christ.'

Thomas looked at his mother. She was thinking the same thing as him, he felt certain of it. The three falling stars on St Michael's day had been more than just a coincidence. Thomas's heart was racing. The horrors of what had happened to him earlier in the day were clearly just part of God's master plan, testing his faith.

Agnes reached out and squeezed Thomas's hand. 'Did you hear that?' she asked.

Thomas nodded. 'He said he was *Christ,* didn't he?'

Agnes looked up to the Heavens and rejoiced, *'Praise the Lord!'*

Forty Five

When Cain drank the glass of bourbon that Sanchez handed to him, he knew straight away that something was wrong. His host body began shutting down internally. Possession of a dead body was impossible which meant that unless he wanted everyone to see him violently expelled from what was about to be a corpse, he needed a fast exit in his spirit form. He quickly vanished through the floor and moved into a concealed position within the shadows. From there he watched in shock at the events that unfolded.

Jasmine appeared from the Men's toilets and killed Tinker the bouncer. Then she stripped naked, which was bewildering and awesome at the same time. But then things turned weird and Sanchez poured poison into the bartender's ass.

As soon as Sanchez and Jasmine left The Fork In Hell, Cain slid over to the body of Rodeo Rex. He was relieved to find that it was still a hospitable host, because in spite of his fears that it was about to die, it had withstood the poison enough to stay alive. It remained in a coma, which suited him just fine. He re-entered the body and took control of it again. The first thing he did was check the Men's toilets to see where Jasmine had come from. All he found was a horrifically soiled toilet in one of the stalls.

He walked back into the bar area and used his cellphone to make a call to Zitrone. But Zitrone's phone was dead. So he called Yesil. The green-haired Horseman answered within three rings.

'Hello Cain,' Yesil said in a soft, high-pitched voice.

'Where are you?'

'I'm with Blanco. We're at sea. Zitrone sent us here to amass a new army of ghouls. Our last lot were wiped out by the Bourbon Kid.'

'Yeah, I know. Zitrone told me already.'

'You've spoken to Zitrone?'

'A while ago yeah. I can't get hold of him now though, which is why I rang you.'

'We can't get hold of him either. He was following the fat man.'

Cain looked at the dead body of Pat the bartender. 'Well he's not following the fat man anymore,' he said. 'Because the fat man is here on Blue Corn Island.'

'The fat man outwitted Zitrone?'

'He had help.'

'What do you mean? Is Zitrone dead?'

'I don't know. Maybe he just lost his phone. Listen, get to Blue Corn Island now. The fat man is here with one of the other Dead

Hunters. It turns out the girl, Jasmine who I thought I'd killed, is still alive.'

Yesil sounded confused. 'Why are they on Blue Corn Island? Shouldn't they be at The Devil's Graveyard?'

'They've come here looking for the Brutus Dagger.'

Yesil gasped. 'The Brutus Dagger is on Blue Corn Island?'

'Yes, but they won't find it. It's hidden in a place full of death traps and stupid puzzles. And they'll never get past the creature that guards it.'

'What creature?'

'It doesn't matter. Look, I'll deal with them after I've looked for the Bourbon Kid. He's here somewhere and by the sound of it, he's probably dead, but if.....'

'HE KILLED ASH!' Yesil screamed. 'I want him dead!'

'I know.'

Cain heard Yesil relaying the information to Blanco. They gossiped about it like a pair of old women at a Bingo night. Eventually Yesil returned to the call.

'We're setting a course for Blue Corn Island now. And we're bringing an army of ghouls.'

'Okay, but just try and be discreet,' said Cain. 'I've got everything under control.'

Yesil disagreed. 'The time for discretion has passed. We're coming ashore and we're going to kill every person on that island until we find him.'

Forty Six

The night was drawing in when Sanchez and Jasmine arrived at the church in Oakfield. Jasmine parked the motorbike at the side of the church and marched up to the doors at the front of the building. She banged her fist against the door.

'Open up!' she hollered.

'Are you gonna kick the Bishop's head in?' Sanchez asked.

'Only if I have to.'

Sanchez had never seen a preacher get beaten up before and he was eager to see how it played out. So when no one answered the church door by the time he'd counted to two, he nudged Jasmine aside and banged on the door again to hurry things up. He counted to two again and there was still no answer.

'Can you bust open the doors?' he asked Jasmine. 'You know, with your kung-fu shit?'

A man's voice called out through the doors. 'Who's there?'

'Oooh, oooh, that's him,' said Sanchez, nudging Jasmine excitedly. 'That's Yoder, I recognise his voice.'

'Would you quit nudging me?' Jasmine hissed. 'Let me handle this.' She shouted through the door to Bishop Yoder. 'We've come to speak to you about my friends, Joey and Baby. I believe you saw them yesterday.'

'I'm sorry,' Yoder called back. 'It's late. The church is closed. You'll have to come back in the morning.'

'It's important. Open up!'

'I'm sorry, goodnight. May God be with you.'

'Don't make me kick the doors in!'

Sanchez tapped her on the arm, taking care to make sure it didn't seem like another nudge. 'You're going about this all wrong,' he said. 'Let me try.'

'What are you gonna do?'

'I'll appeal to his basic instincts as a man of the church.'

Jasmine frowned, but stepped aside anyway, so that Sanchez could get closer to the door. He shouted through it.

'Bishop Yoder, it's Sanchez from The Tapioca. Remember me?'

'I said you'll have to come back tomorrow,' Yoder replied, his voice becoming distant as if he was walking away from the doors.

'You've got to open up,' Sanchez yelled. 'We've got a young boy out here. He's badly hurt. And he's completely naked.'

There was a short delay followed by the sound of Bishop Yoder frantically unlocking the doors. Sanchez stepped back out of the way to give Jasmine some room. The door opened an inch and Yoder peered through the gap, looking for the boy Sanchez had spoken of. Before he had a chance to close the door again Jasmine kicked it hard. It hit Yoder in the face and he staggered back, allowing them to breeze in through the open door.

Sanchez sniffed the air. It was musty and stale. Bishop Yoder was standing in the main aisle, holding his nose, which had taken the brunt of the impact from the door. He was wearing a long white nightgown, even though it was only six o'clock. He looked shaken and was probably worried about what Jasmine might do to him.

'There is no injured child, is there?' he said.

'He's gone home,' said Sanchez, looking around at the inside of the church. It was as big as the church in Santa Mondega but not nearly as impressive. There were no rows of pews, just a whole bunch of wooden chairs set out in rows on either side of the aisle. The walls were covered in paintings that would have made Michelangelo turn in his grave. Where the Sistine Chapel was a work of magnificence, the Church of St Susan was a work of a blind painter, in Sanchez's opinion at least.

He walked down one side of the church, sniggering to himself at the poor standard of the paintings. Each one was six feet high and represented a month of the year. The January painting was of the Amish village covered in snow.

'This is shit,' said Sanchez, pointing at it. 'It's all out of proportion. Look, the snowflakes are bigger than the houses. It looks more like Polar bears falling from the sky.'

'It's beauty is in the eye of the beholder,' Yoder replied.

Sanchez ignored him and moved along to the February painting. Someone with even less talent than the January artist had attempted to paint a goat. Again it was all out of proportion. Sanchez turned around with the intention of making some jokes about the goat, only to see Jasmine kick Yoder between the legs. The toe of her boot scythed through his nightgown and smacked into his nut sack. The lower half of his gown almost vanished up his ass. The Bishop fell down onto his back and grabbed the injured area with both hands. He groaned in pain and his eyes started watering.

'Have I got your undivided attention?' said Jasmine, standing over him, looking like she was ready to give him another sack whack.

Bishop Yoder managed to groan a reply. 'What do you want?'

Sanchez forgot about making fun of the paintings and sat down on one of the wooden chairs so that he could watch Jasmine carry out her interrogation on the Bishop.

Jasmine grabbed the front of Yoder's nightgown and hauled him up off the floor. 'I want to know what happened to my friends, Baby and Joey,' she demanded.

'They went into the Black Forest last night,' said Yoder. 'I haven't seen them since.'

'Do you know what's in the forest?' Jasmine asked, getting right in the Bishop's face.

'I once saw a creature with one eye, moving in the shadows of the trees. It was huge. Others have claimed to have seen it too.'

Jasmine nodded. 'I saw it, about an hour ago, while I was in the forest.'

Yoder looked surprised. 'You went into the forest and came out alive?'

'No, *I came out dead.* Of course I came out alive! What are you blind? I'm right here.'

'But no one has ever come out of there alive before.'

'I didn't go that far in,' Jasmine said, softening her tone slightly.

'Well your friends did,' said Yoder. 'And I haven't seen them since. I'm sorry. I was hoping that your whole team of Dead Hunters would come. I didn't think two of you was enough.'

'What will have happened to them? Is there any chance they're alive?'

Yoder shook his head. 'There will be nothing left of them. Those creatures in there, they're cannibals. It's believed they drain their victims of blood and then feast on their remains. The blood sustains them during the other eleven months of the year when they hibernate.'

Sanchez grimaced. 'Thanks for all that extra unnecessary detail.'

'I'm sorry,' said Yoder. 'I just didn't want you getting your hopes up. Your friends are gone, and even if you could search that forest, you wouldn't find any traces of them.'

Jasmine grabbed a fistful of the Bishop's gown again. 'A third member of the team came here last night,' she said calmly. 'A nasty looking dude who drinks bourbon and kills people. Have you seen him?'

Yoder shook his head. 'No, I swear, I've not seen him.'

Jasmine clearly didn't like the answer. She pulled off a quick kung-fu trip and slammed Yoder back onto the floor. Then she whipped his nightgown up over his head, which gave Sanchez an unpleasant eyeful of what was underneath. He sympathised with the Bishop's plight but carried on watching anyway, hoping to God that Jasmine wasn't planning on carrying out any more dick torture. Fortunately she started by wrapping Yoder's gown tightly around his head, suffocating him.

'You'd better start telling me the truth,' she threatened. 'Did you set us up? Who are you working for?'

The bishop squealed an incoherent reply through his nightgown. He kicked and writhed around too, which made for some rather unpleasant viewing for Sanchez who'd seen enough testicles for one day.

Eventually, Jasmine pulled Yoder's gown back down over his head. His face was bright red and half of his neck beard seemed to have ended up in his mouth too. He gasped a few deep breaths of air.

'Get up and start talking,' said Jasmine, 'otherwise I'm going to get my buddy over there to kick you in the nuts over and over until you tell me what I want to know.'

Bishop Yoder dragged himself up onto the edge of one of the wooden chairs, looking like he might throw up. Jasmine lifted her right leg and set her foot down on the chair next to him. She loomed over him to intimidate him.

'Okay, so tell me everything you think I need to know,' she said. 'Start at the beginning and don't miss anything out, because if you do, the heel of my boot will go so far up your asshole you'll feel it on the back of your teeth.'

Yoder wiped some sweat from his forehead and nodded. 'It began a few weeks ago. Three shooting stars fell from the sky simultaneously on St Michael's Day. According to the Gospel of Susan that is the sign of the second coming.'

'The Gospel of Susan?' Sanchez interrupted. 'What's that?'

'It's the gospel that the rest of the world erased from existence. But on Blue Corn Island it is the foundation of our branch of the Amish faith. We don't acknowledge the gospels of Matthew, Mark, Luke and John because they don't contain the information about the second coming.'

'Get to the point,' said Jasmine.

Yoder eyed her boot, which was close enough to stomp on his balls. He swallowed hard and then carried on.

'After the three falling stars everyone waited for a sign of the Messiah, but nothing happened. The people became restless.'

'Restless?' Jasmine said scornfully. 'What exactly were they expecting, Jesus to show up with a rocket launcher?'

'Yes they were,' said Yoder. 'Because you see, every year we lose people to the Black Forest during the Fall. From the middle of October until some time early in November, the forest creatures steal our people from us. This year we've lost four children already, plus your two friends. So everyone was hoping that Christ would return and end the curse of the forest. That's what we believe the gospel says.'

'You should have called us sooner,' said Jasmine.

Yoder held Jasmine's gaze, though his eyes flicked down every few seconds. It was hard to tell whether he was snatching a glance at Jasmine's boot or her boobs. 'You killed the Pope, didn't you?' he said.

'That's right,' said Jasmine. 'I shot him six times in the chest. What of it?'

'I went to his funeral. While I was there I met Father Papshmir of Santa Mondega.'

'I know him,' said Sanchez. 'He blessed my piss.'

Yoder frowned and looked confused by what Sanchez had said. But he quickly shrugged it off and carried on. 'Papshmir told me about The Dead Hunters and said that you could kill the monsters in the forest. I was hoping that you would all come here, kill the forest monsters and then the people of my village would believe that Christ did it, but just didn't reveal himself to us. I hoped they would never find out that I hired you.'

Sanchez tutted. 'What a shit plan.'

Jasmine was a little more sympathetic. 'Can I see this prophecy? Is it written down?'

'Yes,' said Yoder. 'It's in The Gospel of Susan. I'll get you a copy if you like?'

'Hang on a minute,' said Sanchez, suddenly remembering that he was there for a reason. 'I'm supposed to ask you if you know the location of the Brutus Dagger.'

Bishop Yoder looked surprised. 'You know of the Brutus Dagger?'

'It's what I was sent here to find. Do you know where it is?'

'I'm afraid I don't,' said Yoder. 'But in Diana Jones's journal there are clues to its whereabouts.'

'Diana who?' said Sanchez.

'Diana Jones, she was an archaeologist who devoted a large part of her life to the search for the Brutus Dagger. She believed it was on this island and that it rested with the Roman that followed Jason.'

'What Roman?'

'I have no idea.'

'Well who was Jason?'

'I don't know that either. But I can show you Diana Jones's journal if you like?'

'The Roman that followed Jason,' said Jasmine, repeating it aloud. 'That sounds like a riddle.'

'I've often thought that myself,' Yoder agreed.

'Cool,' said Jasmine, a broad smile breaking our across her face. 'I love riddles.'

Forty Seven

While Jasmine was reading Diana Jones's journal and trying to piece together the meaning of the Roman that followed Jason, Sanchez carried on his review of the paintings on the wall. He could tell that his derisory remarks about the paintings were getting on Bishop Yoder's nerves, which made it even more fun.

'This one's dog shit,' he said, pointing at the November painting, which was the last one on the wall on the right side of the church. The left side had contained all the paintings for January through to May. Sanchez had already given his opinion on those and now he had only one left to critique. But where was it?

'Where's December then?' he asked.

Father Yoder pointed down the aisle. 'It's on the wall behind the altar because it's a bigger painting than the others. See it? It's Mary and the baby Jesus.'

The December painting was visible from anywhere in the church. It was at least six feet wide and almost twice as tall. It showed Mary cradling the baby Jesus in some dirty blankets. There was a donkey with them too, with eyes looking in different directions.

'That's the worst one of the lot,' said Sanchez. 'Did Jesus really have a massive head?'

Jasmine stopped reading and called out to him. 'Hey Sanchez, do you know anything about Jason and the Argonauts?'

'Dodgy special effects,' Sanchez replied. 'Although the skeletons with the swords were quite good.'

'What is he talking about?' asked Yoder.

'The film,' Jasmine replied. She called over to Sanchez again. 'Was there anything in the film about a Roman who followed Jason?'

'I don't think so. Have you seen this donkey?'

Jasmine put the book down and stood up. She looked at the paintings Sanchez had been providing a running commentary about, specifically the ones from July to November. Her eyes darted back and forth, looking at the pictures.

'September's my favourite,' said Sanchez.

September's painting was of a giant snake with three eyes. Its tongue was ridiculously long and it looked like it was trying to lick its knee. If indeed Snake's have knees. Sanchez wasn't sure.

'Do snakes have knees?' he asked. 'Or nipples?'

Jasmine ignored him. Something had caught her attention. She headed down the centre aisle towards the painting of Mary and Jesus and the donkey. Yoder stood up and followed her, walking gingerly, rubbing his groin, which was still sore from Jasmine's boot. Not wanting to be left out, Sanchez followed on behind them.

Jasmine stopped in front of the painting and stared at it for a while. Eventually she asked Yoder a question. 'Why are all of these paintings named after a month of the year?'

'I don't know,' said Yoder. 'They've been here for centuries. Only the person who came up with the idea would know for sure.'

Her eyes moved down to a calendar hanging on the wall below the painting. It had a picture of a choirboy on it.

'When were calendars invented?' she asked.

'Thousands of years ago,' said Yoder.

'By who? I mean who invented the months of the year, like January, February and stuff?'

'The calendar used universally around the world these days is the Julian calendar,' said Yoder. 'Created by Julius Caesar.'

Jasmine stopped looking at the calendar and started looking around the wall for something else. 'Where is December on this wall?' she asked.

'It's right there in front of you,' said Yoder. 'Mary and the baby Jesus.'

'And the donkey,' Sanchez added.

Jasmine turned around to face them both. 'I can see that,' she said. 'But look around the hall.' She pointed at the other paintings. 'Look, January, February and the others all have the name of the month written above the picture in gold letters.' She turned back to the December painting. 'But December's not here.'

'Oh, I see,' said Yoder. 'It's beneath it, look, behind the calendar.'

Jasmine unhooked the *Choir Boy* calendar from the wall and set it down on the floor. Behind it, painted in gold letters was the word "DECEMBER".

She ran her finger along the gold letters. 'I think I've worked it out,' she said.

'Worked what out?' said Yoder.

She pointed at the wall containing the paintings from July to November. 'Look at the dates above the paintings,' she said excitedly.

'What about them?' asked Sanchez.

'Look at the first letter of each month! See, J for July, A for August, S for September, O for October, N for November. J-A-S-O-N. The first letter of each month spells out the name Jason.'

'Oh yes,' said Yoder. 'That's interesting. What a coincidence.'

'It's not a coincidence,' said Jasmine. 'Look, D for December. D is the Roman that follows Jason.'

Sanchez looked at Yoder.

Yoder looked at Sanchez.

They both looked at Jasmine.

And then they both said, 'Huh?'

'Ever counted in Roman numerals?' Jasmine asked them.

Sanchez had counted to *three* in Roman numerals a few times, but he'd never gotten any further. 'Nobody counts in Roman numerals,' he reminded her. 'It's stupid. They're not proper numbers.'

Jasmine flicked him on the forehead and turned to Yoder instead. 'What's five hundred in Roman numerals?'

He pondered for a moment before replying. 'It's D.'

'I was just going to say that,' said Sanchez.

'Exactly,' said Jasmine. 'So the letter D is a Roman number. And in the calendar created by Julius Caesar, D follows Jason.'

'I'm confused,' said Sanchez.

Jasmine knelt down next to the word DECEMBER. 'Watch this,' she said.

She reached out and pressed the letter D with her index finger. 'I'm sure this is loose,' she said. She used three fingers and pressed harder

That did the trick.

The letter D moved backwards an inch and a loud grating sound reverberated around the church. The floor beneath Jasmine's feet started moving. She stepped back and almost lost her balance as the floor began sinking. Sanchez retreated too, fearing he might fall into something from an *Indiana Jones* movie, like a booby-trapped pit of spikes or snakes. Or a stupid room full of hibernating aliens.

A circular area of floor by the wall rotated downwards into the ground, accompanied by a chorus of loud grating sounds. Sanchez watched on in awe as the floor unravelled and transformed into a spiral staircase that led down into the ground beneath the church.

'This is it,' said Jasmine. 'The book says that the Roman that followed Jason would lead us to the Brutus Dagger. So it must be down here.'

Although Sanchez was impressed and more than a little baffled as to how Jasmine had solved the riddle, Yoder looked crestfallen.

'I don't believe it,' said the Bishop. 'We've been trying to unravel the mystery of the Roman that followed Jason for centuries. You did it in five minutes.'

'I told you I was good at riddles. Come on Sanchez, let's go down there and find the dagger.'

Sanchez looked down the staircase that led into the underground. It wasn't an appetising prospect. It was dark and probably full of spiders and dead stuff.

'Why don't you go look for it,' he said. 'I'll stay here and make sure no one closes the entrance and traps you down there.' He pretended to wipe his nose, but subtly pointed his finger at Yoder while he was doing it. Yoder saw it and looked appalled at the insinuation that he might close the secret entrance. But Jasmine was in agreement with Sanchez.

'Good idea,' she said.

'You'll need some light down there,' said Yoder. 'Let me grab you a torch.'

He scurried off to his private chambers to find a torch, while Sanchez and Jasmine waited by the mysterious staircase.

'That's really impressive how you solved that riddle,' said Sanchez. 'I must admit, I thought you were a moron when I first met you. Maybe you're a bit like Rain Man?'

Jasmine looked hurt. 'Are you saying I look like Dustin Hoffman?'

'Oh no, I was just saying I thought you were a moron.'

She breathed a sigh of relief. 'That's okay then.'

Bishop Yoder returned from his private quarters with a plastic battery torch and gave it to Jasmine.

'Hey, Bish, while you're here, can you take a look at something for me?' Jasmine asked.

'Of course.'

She held up Diana Jones's journal for him and showed him a picture she had come across in it. 'What's this picture of?' she asked.

'That's a map of the labyrinth where the dagger is supposed to be hidden,' said Yoder. 'I suspect it's at the bottom of that staircase you just discovered.'

Sanchez looked over Yoder's shoulder at the journal. The picture that had Jasmine confused was called *The Labyrinth*. It was a hand drawn picture of a maze with a dagger in the centre of it. There was a handwritten message beneath the picture. Written in Italics it read –

Those who look for the dagger will see only their demise.
For in the land of the dark, the blind man is King.

'What the fuck does that mean?' Sanchez asked.

'I'm not sure,' Yoder replied. 'But in Greek mythology, Labyrinths were created to hold monsters, so be careful down there.'

'What kind of monsters?' Sanchez asked.

Yoder pressed his hands together, as if in prayer. 'I believe the very first Labyrinth was built to hold a Minotaur,' he said.

'Talking bulls!' said Jasmine.

'No, I think he's being serious,' Sanchez replied.

Jasmine slapped Sanchez across the chest. 'Minotaurs are half man, half bull,' she snapped. 'I think they can talk.'

'I don't know if they talk,' said Yoder. 'But you are correct, they are half man and half bull. I seriously doubt there's one in this Labyrinth though.'

'I can handle a talking bull,' said Jasmine, closing the book.

She had a gun strapped to her thigh, so if there were any stupid talking animals down there, Sanchez felt sure she'd be okay.

She stepped onto the staircase and started her descent into the unknown.

'Good luck down there,' said Yoder. 'I hope you find what you're looking for.'

'So do I,' she replied.

'You'll be fine,' said Sanchez, offering some encouragement. 'Just keep an eye out for snakes and spiders and talking bulls.'

Forty Eight

Agnes and Thomas had successfully ridden home with the injured man hidden in their carriage. Agnes felt certain no one had seen them carry the man inside their house.

They set him down on a bed in the spare room that once belonged to Agnes's daughter Elsa.

'Do you think he's going to be okay?' Thomas asked.

'Have faith,' Agnes replied. 'Why don't you go run a bath?'

'You're going to give him a bath?'

'No. You need to wash that urine smell off yourself, and put your clothes in the basket so I can wash them.'

'Yes mother.'

Thomas left Agnes and went to take a bath, leaving her to deal with the injured man. She fetched a bowl of hot water and a wet rag, and sat down on a stool beside the bed. She began washing the blood off the man's body. He was very muscular, his body firmer than any other man she had ever seen. There were lots of strong men in Oakfield, but none of them had a body like this, a body seemingly designed to withstand pain and judging by the muscles on his arms, inflict pain on others too.

When the awkward moment came and Agnes had to unbuckle the man's pants, his hand grabbed hers, making her jump. He opened his eyes.

'It's okay,' he said, 'I'll be fine.'

'You're covered in blood and cuts,' Agnes said. 'If I don't wash it all off, it could get infected.'

'It won't,' the man replied. 'I'll be fully healed by morning. Just let me rest.'

'But I'm....'

The door behind her burst open and Thomas entered, looking a little panicked. He was about to blurt something out when he saw that the man was awake. He hesitated, but then looked at his mother.

'Mother, there's a man outside on a motorbike.'

'What man?'

'I don't know who he is, but,' he nodded at the wounded man. 'I was thinking maybe he was here looking for someone?'

Agnes tried to pull herself away from the wounded man, but he gripped her hand and wouldn't let go. In spite of his injuries he still had a vice-like grip.

'Don't tell him I'm here,' he said. 'Don't tell anyone.'

He let go of her hand. His head slumped to the side and he lost consciousness again.

'Is he okay?' Thomas asked.

There was a loud, booming knock at the front door.

'Go to your room,' Agnes ordered.

Thomas hesitated. 'What are you going to do? You can't give him up!'

Agnes stood up. 'Leave it to me.'

Telling lies and keeping secrets wasn't something the Amish did much of. It was considered sinful. Dishonesty in particular, had no place in their society. Agnes had to make a decision about what to say to the man at the door. And she didn't have much time to deliberate her options.

There was another louder knock at the front door. Agnes ushered Thomas out of the bedroom and followed him out, closing the door behind her. She walked into the kitchen with Thomas trailing her.

'I told you to go to your room,' she said, keeping her voice down so that whoever was outside wouldn't hear. 'Go, and don't come out. I'll handle this.'

Thomas had already had a rough day, so the last thing Agnes wanted was for him to be involved in any more drama. He was smart enough to know she had his best intentions at heart, so he did as he was told and retired to his bedroom.

Agnes walked across the kitchen and opened the front door. There was a large man standing outside. He was bigger than any man she had ever seen. He was wearing blue jeans and a white waistcoat that showed off the muscles on his arms. His brown hair was held in under a headband. And he also had a very prominent C shaped scar on his forehead just below the headband. She tried not to stare at it.

'Good morning ma'am,' he said. 'My name is Rex. I work for the government. We're currently trying to track down a known murderer who has been seen round these parts. I was wondering, have you seen a strange man around here recently?'

Agnes shook her head. 'No. There's only Amish people round here.'

'Right.' His eyes scoped the kitchen area behind her. 'The man we're looking for is usually unshaven, got kind of a gruff voice, dark hair, and well, basically, he's not Amish. Have you seen any non Amish men at all today?'

'I've seen lots,' she replied, pleased that she was able to tell the truth. 'My son had his first day at high school in Crimson County today, so I've seen more folks than usual.'

The visitor looked closely at her face, studying it, looking for signs that she might be lying. 'Where is your son?' he asked eventually.

'He's having a bath.'

'Has he seen anyone strange today?'

'No.' Agnes was keen to switch the conversation away from Thomas. 'What's this man's name?' she asked. 'The one you're looking for, what's he called?'

'His name is the Bourbon Kid. He's wanted for over a thousand murders, and he kills innocent people for fun. If anyone in this village is foolish enough to offer him shelter, I can assure you, they will end up dead. He's the most dangerous man alive, number one on the FBI's most wanted list.'

Agnes didn't catch everything he said because she had become preoccupied with his clothing. Surely a government agent would be wearing a suit?

He picked up on her disapproving looks, like a mind reader. 'It's okay ma'am,' he said. 'I work undercover, hence the stupid biker clothes.'

'Right. Do you have any identification papers?'

The request didn't go down well. 'No,' he replied. 'Undercover agents don't carry identification papers. That's the kind of mistake that would get me killed.'

'Of course,' said Agnes, feeling rather stupid. 'What did you say your name was again?'

'Rex.'

Another awkward silence followed. It was Rex's turn to take a look at Agnes's appearance. And he spotted some things he didn't like.

'You've got blood on your fingers and some spots down the front of your dress,' he said.

Agnes felt herself burn red with embarrassment. She hadn't thought to wash off any blood before she answered the door. She had specks of the wounded man's blood on her hands and on the collar of her dress. She looked up into the eyes of the giant man in her doorway. She was going to have to tell him the truth.

She opened her mouth to confess, but before she could utter a word, Thomas walked into the kitchen. He had been hiding out of sight and listening to the conversation.

'She was punishing me for not doing my chores,' he said, joining his mother at her side.

Rex looked at Thomas. The boy had a black eye and several cuts on his face. But even so, Rex didn't look convinced that Agnes was responsible for the injuries. Some quick thinking was required. Agnes turned and slapped Thomas across the face.

'I told you to stay back there!' she scolded.

Thomas lowered his head and backed away. 'I'm sorry mother,' he said, sobbing a little, for added effect. Her son was showing some genuine acting potential, at least she hoped he was acting, otherwise it meant she'd really hurt him.

The man at the door looked shocked by what she'd done, confused by the unexpected outburst of domestic violence. But once he'd drunk it all in, he smiled and gave a nod of approval.

'That's good discipline,' he said. 'Don't take any shit from your kids. I admire that. Good parenting.'

'He was asking for it,' said Agnes, playing the part of an abusive mother with a level of proficiency that surprised her.

'Yes, I believe he was.'

'Was there anything else I can do for you?' she asked, pushing the door ever so slightly. 'It's starting to get cold in here.'

'No, but remember, if you do see a strange man around here, don't let him into your house.'

'I won't.'

The man bowed his head slightly. 'Thank you for your time ma'am. Have a good night.'

Just when Agnes thought he was going to turn and leave, he paused and leaned in a bit farther. 'If I don't find this man, I might be back,' he said with a glint in his eye.

Agnes shuddered inside but managed to keep her composure. 'Good luck,' she said, closing the door. 'I hope you catch him.'

Forty Nine

Jasmine followed the spiral staircase down to a sepulchre-like space beneath the church. In total she counted eighty-seven steps down. She shone her torch around to get an idea of her surroundings. She was in a tunnel wide enough for three people to walk side by side. The walls were made of smooth stone, and the floor was littered with small rocks and rubble. A musty, damp smell floated around and made her nose itch.

She shone the light on Diana Jones's journal and flicked through the pages to find the picture of the labyrinth again. The picture did show an entrance at the bottom so she worked on the assumption that she was at the entrance.

She started walking along the tunnel, alternating between shining the torch on the book and the way ahead. She kept her thumb in the page with the labyrinth on it and flicked over to look at what was on the pages that followed. The journal contained lots of pictures of mythical creatures. One of the first to catch her eye was called *The Cyclops*. It looked like the thing she'd seen in the Black Forest. The picture in the book showed it ripping the heads off a group of men with spears. On the next page the Cyclops was surrounded by a tribe of savages holding aloft more severed heads. The picture was called *The Head Shrinkers*.

Eventually the tunnel came to a junction, leaving her with only two options. Go left, or go right. One way looked just the same as the other. This was the kind of place where if she lost her way, it might be difficult to retrace her steps. She wished she could leave a trail of breadcrumbs or something, but she had nothing with her, other than the journal. Yoder probably wouldn't appreciate her tearing the pages out.

She had to do something to mark out her position. She considered making some of the rocks and stones into arrow shapes to point the way back. But, as luck would have it, she saw a rock on the ground, which was shaped like a hand, with four fingers, but no thumb. She picked it up to take a look at it. The hand was impeccably carved from stone, even revealing the lines and contours that one would find on a real hand. She placed it back down on the floor, pointing back the way she had come. She also made a mental note to pick it up on her way back because it would be fun to creep Sanchez out by poking him with it.

She followed the tunnel that went left. The air was very damp, but not to the point where it was uncomfortable. The deathly quiet was more unnerving and made her wish she'd brought a music player and some headphones, instead of the book. She continued flicking through the pages of it, hoping to find some more clues or riddles that needed solving. After a bunch of pictures of men and women having their heads ripped off by the Cyclops and the Headshrinkers, she turned back to check her position on the map of the labyrinth. If she had come from the entrance at the bottom of the picture then she was pretty sure she knew where she was. She looked at the riddle beneath it again.

Those who look for the dagger will see only their demise.
For in the land of the dark, the blind man is King.

This wasn't such an easy riddle to figure out. It seemed to suggest she should close her eyes and walk blindly through the tunnels. But surely that was just a way to guarantee getting lost? She carried on walking while she tried to work out what it meant. But because she had the torchlight shone on the book, she didn't see a large rock on the ground at her feet. She stumbled on it and almost turned her ankle over. She shone the light down on it and saw that it was another body part. This time it was a head. She knelt down and shone the torch over it. Much of the top half of the head was broken off. What remained was the face of a man, with no nose, gawping like he had seen a ghost.

Further down the tunnel something made a noise. It sounded like a trickle of running water. Jasmine stood up slowly to avoid making any noise. She pointed the torch down the corridor. There was nothing to see other than another wall up ahead, with turnings on both sides. She carried on towards it and took a right turn at the end. The next tunnel was even colder. This place was seriously creepy.

She walked along the tunnel for almost a hundred metres before she saw something up ahead, standing at the side of the tunnel. It looked like a woman, or maybe even a statue of a woman, wearing a tatty blue dress. It had its back to her, so Jasmine called out to it.

'Hello?'

It didn't move, so she carried on edging towards it, keeping her torchlight on it. As she got closer she saw that the woman was wearing a long turquoise dress and had thick dreadlocked hair, like the alien in the movie Predator. She decided it was probably best not to shoot it just yet, because it might be an actor. But even so, she didn't want to take any chances. She tucked the journal into her belt and let her free hand hang down by the gun holstered on her thigh. The dreadlocked hair on the person up ahead looked like it was moving gently as if caught in a breeze.

As she edged closer still, a low hissing sound wormed its way into her head. She focussed the light from the torch onto the head of the woman in the dress. As she closed in on it, she realised the horrible truth about the dreadlocks. These weren't dreadlocks at all. They were snakes.

Jasmine recoiled, and took a step back, but it was already too late. The woman with the snakes for hair, turned around, her face contorted in an angry snarl. Her teeth were gnarly and jagged, her eyes, green and sparkly. Jasmine only made eye contact with her for a fleeting moment. But that was all it took. The skin or her arms and legs stiffened. She stopped, frozen to the spot, her right hand touching the handle of her gun.

Before she even had a chance to scream, her entire body turned to stone.

Fifty

Bishop Yoder grew tired of waiting for Jasmine to reappear from the Labyrinth. And when her companion Sanchez fell asleep on the church floor and started snoring, he decided to return to his private chambers, so he could carry on reading his favourite monthly magazine about Choir Boys. He read the magazine from cover to cover over the course of an hour, with the only distraction being Sanchez's occasional snoring filtering in from the church hall.

Eventually, just before midnight, he decided to retire to bed. He returned to the church hall to check on Sanchez and found him sleeping on the floor. He was wearing a pair of sunglasses and his mouth was fluttering open and shut as he snored.

Yoder crept past him and checked the staircase in the floor that led down to goodness-knows-what. It was still open and a cold draft was filtering up from the ground below, but there was no sign of Jasmine.

He walked over to the word DECEMBER that was painted on the wall. The letter D had returned to its normal position, so Yoder pressed it hard with two fingers. It pushed back quite easily and the sound of grating gears echoed around the room as the secret staircase rolled itself back up. The noise woke Sanchez and he sat up.

'How long have I been asleep?' he asked, peering over his sunglasses.

'A couple of hours.'

Sanchez looked down at the floor. 'Where's Jasmine?'

'She hasn't returned.'

'Then why have you shut the secret passage?'

'I just pressed the letter D to see what happened.'

'Well you'd better reopen it.'

'Of course.'

Sanchez stood up and stretched his arms. 'You got somewhere I can take a dump?' he asked.

Yoder pressed the letter D on the wall again. As the gears started grinding, someone banged on the front door of the church, demanding to be let in. One of the trials of being the local Bishop in a small village was dealing with locals who felt the church was a twenty-four hour convenience store.

'I'll get it,' said Sanchez. 'It might be my buddy, Rex. He's supposed to be meeting us here.'

He walked down the aisle to the church doors. For the sake of security he climbed onto a table beside the doors and peeked out of a window to check the identity of the person outside. It was Rodeo Rex.

But not the Rex that Sanchez was expecting. It was the one with the human hand, the C shaped scar on his forehead, and the white waistcoat.

SHIT!

Sanchez climbed down off the table and ran back down the aisle to Yoder.

'It's him!' he cried.

'Who?'

'Fuckin' Cain!'

'Fuckin' Cain? Who's Fuckin' Cain?'

'He's the fella that looks like my buddy Rex, but isn't really him. Quick! You've got to hide me.'

Yoder was tired and in no mood for stupid games. 'What on earth are you talking about?'

'There's no time to explain. Just don't let him know I'm here. Get rid of him.'

Yoder pointed at the secret staircase. 'All right, hide down there. When I've gotten rid of him, I'll come back and let you out.'

'You'd better. Otherwise I'll get Jasmine to kick the shit out of you.'

Sanchez scurried over to the secret staircase and vanished down it. When Yoder was sure he had reached the bottom, he closed the entrance back up again.

The person banging on the front doors was becoming impatient. The knocks were getting louder, and were accompanied by a man's voice yelling things like *'Open up!'* and *'I know you're in there!'*

Yoder hotfooted it over to the front doors and quickly unbolted them. He pulled one door open and peered out. There was a large man with long brown hair outside, wearing denim jeans and a white waistcoat.

'Good evening,' said Yoder. 'I'm afraid the church is closed for the night. Could you come back in the morning?'

The man barged the door open and stormed past him. 'Where are they?' he asked, looking around.

'Uh, who are you?' asked Yoder, acting confused.

'You can call me Cain.'

'Cain?'

'Yes, Cain. Now where the fuck are they?'

'I'm sorry, where's who?'

'The people who parked the motorbike and sidecar at the side of your church.'

'Oh that,' said Yoder. 'The people who rode in on that contraption have gone up to the forest. They won't be back for ages. If you leave now, you might catch up with them.'

Cain grabbed Yoder by the throat and lifted him off his feet. 'Don't fucking lie to me,' he snarled. 'Tell me where they are. And the Bourbon Kid too. You hired them to do a job. Where are they?'

'I'm telling you I don't know,' said Yoder, struggling to get the words out. He wiggled his feet to try and touch the floor but Cain had lifted him up a good six inches. 'This is a church. I don't shelter mass murderers here.'

Cain hurled Yoder down onto the floor. He landed on his back and slid along the aisle before coming to a stop with his nightgown over his head again. By the time he'd wrestled with it and covered his dignity, Cain was looming over him once more. This time he had a sawn off shotgun aimed at Yoder's head.

'Have you heard of the Bourbon Kid?' Cain asked, his tone becoming increasingly menacing.

'No.'

Cain released the safety on the gun. 'You're on thin ice, Bishop. I know you hired The Dead Hunters to kill something in that forest. So if you want to stay alive, tell me where they are.'

'Okay, okay,' said Yoder, holding up his hands as if that would somehow help matters. 'I do know who the Bourbon Kid is, but I've not seen him. He hasn't been here. The others have.'

'And where are they now?'

'The Red Mohawk and Baby, they came here, but they went into the forest and never came back.'

Cain peered over his shotgun at the stricken preacher. 'I killed Baby,' he said. 'And if you don't tell me where the others are, you're next.'

Yoder wanted to be brave. He really did. But he was lying on his back with a gun in his face. Bravery would cost him his life. Cowardice probably would too, but there was a slim chance that if he was cowardly and gave up Sanchez and Jasmine, he might survive. He had his flock to think of. The needs of the many were worth more than the needs of the few. It was worth the calculated risk.

'They found a secret entrance to a labyrinth beneath the church. They went down there to find the Brutus Dagger.'

Cain didn't look like he approved of what he was hearing. 'You're telling me they solved the riddle of the Roman that followed Jason?'

'Yes, Jasmine did. She's quite gifted.'

Cain's mood darkened further. 'Did they get past the Medusa?'

'What Medusa?'

'Don't play dumb with me you sack of shit!'

'I swear to God I don't know anything about a Medusa. Is that what's in the labyrinth?'

'In the land of the dark, the blind man is King,' said Cain, quoting a line from Diana Jones's journal. 'Anyone who looks into the eyes of the Medusa is turned to stone. No one bar me ever made it past her.'

'You've seen the dagger?'

'Seen it yes. But then there's a wall of flames that protect it. No one can get past that.'

Yoder recalled another passage from the journal that he knew by heart –

Only the living can pass the test,
The flames of God will burn the rest,
It takes a man of flesh and bone,
To wield the dagger from the stone.

'You couldn't get past the flames of God?' he asked tentatively, staring into the barrel of the gun.

'I told you, no one can,' Cain retorted. 'How long have they been down there?'

'A long time. I would guess the Medusa you spoke of has turned them both to stone.'

'Does anyone else know about the secret entrance?'

'No,' Yoder promised. 'I only discovered it a few hours ago when Jasmine solved the riddle.'

'So no one can reopen it to let them out, apart from you? Is that right?'

Yoder nodded. 'That is correct.'

Cain lifted his sawn off shotgun away from Yoder's face. 'I believe you,' he said.

Yoder breathed a sigh of relief. 'Thank you.'

'Here, let me help you up,' Cain said, offering Yoder his hand.

Yoder took his hand and Cain hauled him up off the floor. But when Yoder was back on his feet, Cain slammed the barrel of the shotgun into the soft skin underneath his chin.

BOOM!

Yoder's head splattered all over the church.

Fifty One

Zitrone wandered through the barren desert wasteland through the night until he finally arrived at the first sign of civilisation. "Debbie's All Night Diner" was the only place within seventy miles of the crossroads. The parking lot at the side of the diner was filled with trucks of all sizes. As Zitrone walked up to the entrance he could see at least four truck drivers inside sitting at the counter eating breakfast.

A bell chimed above the door to announce his arrival. He stopped just inside the door and looked around. There were a number of booths along the window side, most of which were empty. In an open area at the back, a group of overweight men and women were drinking beer and playing pool. A waitress with blonde curly hair was standing behind the counter smoking a cigarette while she refilled a customer's coffee. This was to be Zitrone's first ever experience of a truck stop diner. He was looking forward to it.

The waitress was in her fifties and her face was plastered in bright make-up. She saw Zitrone and smiled at him, revealing a set of teeth covered in lipstick.

'Hey sweetie,' she said, staring at his yellow tunic. 'Still celebratin' Halloween huh?'

Zitrone got the feeling she was mocking him. He walked up to the counter and stopped next to an old man in a green shirt. Zitrone didn't care much for the man's body odour, so he decided to kill him first. He placed his hand on the man's bald head. The touch of death rippled through the man's skin, into his blood and bones. He started choking and wrapped his hands around his throat as he tried to suck in some air. Zitrone counted to three and released him, then stepped back and watched the man stagger from his stool and collapse onto the floor. He writhed around for a short time until his body turned limp and his heart stopped.

The waitress tried to scream, but the only thing to leave her lips was her cigarette, which fell into a mug of coffee on the counter.

A big portly gentleman in a blue shirt got up from the next stool along. He stared down at the dead man and then glowered at Zitrone.

'What the hell did you do to him, you jerk?' he asked, squaring up to Zitrone, with an angry snarl on his face.

'I did this.' Zitrone grabbed the man's face and squeezed his cheeks. The life drained out of the man's face, and by the time Zitrone released him, his skin had turned a shade of red as his blood boiled and cooked him from inside. His knees buckled and he crumpled to the floor.

Zitrone looked around the diner. A number of other overweight people were approaching him, looking like they intended to confront him. Good. They were easy to defeat. Soft and flabby and oh so gloriously big, this would be fun.

'Do any of you have a phone I could use?' he asked. 'I promise not to kill the person who gives me a phone.'

A man with a pool cue, who wasn't as unhealthy as the others, stepped through the crowd of confused onlookers. This man was definitely more of a challenge. He was only two or three stone overweight, he had a good head of hair and he was wielding the pool cue with the intention of hitting Zitrone with it.

'That does not look like a phone,' Zitrone observed.

The man was clutching the pool cue with both hands, his fingers turning white because he was squeezing it so hard. 'Get the fuck out of here, freak,' he said. 'Or I'm gonna bash your fuckin' brains in.'

'Do it,' said Zitrone, standing with his arms by his side.

The man stepped forward and swung the pool cue at Zitrone's head. It connected, but broke in half, while Zitrone didn't even flinch. The vibrations from the impact shot up the man's arms and he winced in pain. Zitrone moved in and grabbed him around the throat. He too, burned up on the inside until Zitrone threw him back into the crowd of fatties behind him.

'So who wants to give me their phone?' Zitrone repeated.

Every person inside the diner scrambled to find their phone. The waitress was first.

'Here, take mine,' she said, sliding a cellphone across the counter.

Zitrone looked down at the phone. It didn't look anything like the cellphone Cain had provided him with. He pushed it back towards the waitress.

'What is your name?' he asked her.

'Debbie, I own this place.'

'Okay Debbie, I want you to make a call for me.'

Debbie picked up her phone. 'What's the number?'

Zitrone's photographic memory made it easy to remember the eleven-digit number for Cain's cellphone. While he was reciting it to Debbie, he undertook the task of killing all of the other customers in her diner.

Everyone was dead by the time Debbie slid the phone back across the counter to him. 'It's ringing,' she said, trembling.

'Thank you.' Zitrone picked up the phone. 'Why don't you take the rest of the day off? It's kinda dead around here.'

Debbie backed away and disappeared into a back room. Zitrone put the phone against his ear just in time to hear a man's voice answer.

'Hello?'

The problem with speaking to Cain on the phone was that it was impossible to know if it was him or not, because his voice always sounded like the person who's body he was inhabiting.

'Cain, is that you?'

'Zitrone?'

'Yes. How are you?'

'I'm great. But I was beginning to think you were dead.'

'Well I'm not.'

'Have you spoken to Yesil and Blanco?'

'Not since yesterday. I put them back on the ship and told them to rebuild our ghoul army.'

'Well, they've done that and now they're on their way to Blue Corn Island.'

'What? Why?'

'They're coming to meet me. I've tracked down the Bourbon Kid. He's here on Blue Corn.'

'Forget him,' said Zitrone. 'I have something better. I've found the secret entrance to The Devil's Graveyard.'

Cain let out a cry of joy. 'You absolute rooster! This is delightful news. Are you there now?'

'No, I couldn't get in. But I read the mind of the man who guards the secret entrance. He only grants access to members of The Dead Hunters.'

'Did you kill him?'

'I tried, but he was a ghost. But don't worry about that. You're still in Rodeo Rex's body, yes?'

'I am,' said Cain.

'Good. Come straight over to Debbie's All Night Diner. It's on the highway outside The Devil's Graveyard.' Zitrone looked around at the corpses of the truckers that were lying all around the floor of the diner, then added, 'I'll be waiting here for you with a bunch of big ghouls.'

Fifty Two

It was so dark in the secret underground part of the church that Sanchez couldn't see his hand when he held it up in front of his face. He even peered over his sunglasses to see if that would help, but it made no difference. He whispered Jasmine's name a few times in the hope that she would hear him. If she did, she didn't respond. So while he waited for Bishop Yoder to lower the staircase again, he sat down on the cold stony floor with his back up against the wall and closed his eyes.

He had no idea how long he slept for, but when he woke up, the spiral staircase still hadn't come back down. It crossed his mind that Bishop Yoder might have left him there to rot, the weaselly bastard. Sanchez was hungry too. His only chance of getting out was Jasmine, so he had to try and find her.

He stood up and took a step forward, stretching his arms out to see if he could feel anything. He found the wall with his left hand and decided to feel his way along it. The wall was damp and sticky so he just kept one finger pressed against it to keep his bearings as he made his way along the tunnel. The floor was covered in rubble and every few steps he took he inevitably kicked some bits of rock and stone around, which made a lot of noise.

He'd been walking for over a minute and was on the verge of turning back, when his finger slid off the end of the wall. He had reached a corner. He followed it around and after a few more tentative steps he heard something. Keeping a mental note of where he was, and trailing his finger along the wall, he headed towards the noise, which sounded like a low hiss. He hoped it would either be Jasmine or some running water.

After a few more turns and a brief stop to take a piss up against the wall, he bumped into a large object in the middle of the tunnel. It was made of stone, but it was an odd shape. He ran his hands over it, trying to fathom out what it was. It didn't take long to work out it was a statue of a person. He'd seen enough Indiana Jones movies to know that there might be a lever or secret button on the statue so he ran his hands up and down the legs and arms as if he was frisking the statue for drugs or weapons. The only thing he established from frisking it was that it was a female statue, on account of its bumpy chest and lack of male parts between its legs.

He eventually gave up on the statue and squeezed around it to carry on along the tunnel. His foot kicked something on the ground, and this time it wasn't a rock. He crouched down and fumbled around on the floor until he found what it was. A torch.

He picked it up and switched it on. At first nothing happened, but then he realised that it had come loose at the top. He tightened it up and the light automatically came on.

He turned around and shone it at the statue to get a better look at it. It was the most bizarre sight. A grey statue made of stone that looked exactly like Jasmine. He waved the torch up and down her. Tucked inside her belt was a book made of stone. It looked like the journal Bishop Yoder had given her. That confirmed it. This *was* Jasmine, but something had turned her into a statue.

And then he heard a scratching sound approaching from behind him. He spun around. The light from his torch shone on a pair of women's feet, walking towards him, taking tiny but very fast baby steps. He reached out for the wall, hoping to hurry back the way he had come. But the wall felt different to before, and he quickly realised that in his haste and panic, he had actually grabbed one of Jasmine's rock boobs. He tried to fumble his way around her, but "Statue Jasmine" was doing an outstanding job of blocking the way.

The delay cost him dear. The woman pursuing him caught up with him and grabbed his shoulder. She was strong because she yanked him back and spun him around in one swift move. All Sanchez could think to do was to try and dazzle her with the light from the torch. But when the light shone on her face he nearly shit his pants. The woman was hideously ugly. But even worse than that, her hair was a mess. *A mess of bloody snakes.* And Sanchez hated snakes, the sly bastards. Ever since he'd heard about toilet-snakes that crawl up people's asses when they sit on the toilet in the dark, he'd had it in for snakes. And there had to be at least thirty or forty of them on this bitch's head, all poking their tongues out and hissing at him. Sanchez had heard of the Medusa, and even seen it in a few dodgy old films, but he'd never believed it actually existed. But here it was. Right in front of him.

The Medusa bared her teeth and stuck her face up against his, growling like a drunk cat. Sanchez staggered back and steadied himself by grabbing Jasmine's chest again. He prodded the torch in the direction of the Medusa to try and frighten her away. But then a strange thing happened.

Sanchez could have sworn he heard the Medusa call him a *cunt*. And then she went quiet, as if the insult got stuck in her throat. The snakes on her head stopped hissing and went quiet too. They all froze, each of them in a ridiculous (and somewhat offensive) pose, poking their tongues out at Sanchez. The Medusa's whole body stiffened and turned to stone, its face permanently frozen in the snarl of someone who just said the word *cunt*.

At about the same time, Sanchez noticed that the handful of rock in his left hand turned soft. He turned the torch back on the statue of Jasmine. She was no longer made of stone. She had transformed back into her real human self again.

'You broke the curse of the Medusa!' she said, breathing a sigh of relief.

'I did?'

'Yes. You brought me back from the dead. I thought I was done for.'

'I did?'

'Yes. Is there any reason why you're still squeezing my tit?'

Sanchez retracted his hand and tried to make sense of what had just happened. 'So you were a statue just a minute ago, but now you're not. How does that work?'

'Because you turned the Medusa into stone when she looked into your mirrored sunglasses! You're a genius, Sanchez.'

What Jasmine said actually made sense. Sanchez shrugged as if it wasn't a big deal. 'Well, I wore them because you never know when you're going to bump into a Medusa. It seems like common sense to me. I'm surprised you didn't think of it.'

Jasmine snatched the torch away from him. 'Yes, but I don't go around groping statues either.'

'Hey! It was dark, I didn't know what I was grabbing.'

'You know, I've met some creepy guys in my time, with some strange fetishes, but I never met a man who fingered statues.' She shone the torch in his face and shook her head.

'I told you *it was dark.*'

'Yeah right, whatever, *pervert.* Step aside while I finish off this Medusa.'

Sanchez backed out of Jasmine's way. She lifted her leg above waist height and karate kicked the stone statue. It fell backwards and crashed onto the floor, making an almighty racket that reverberated around the tunnel. Its head snapped off and rolled away from the rest of its body. Jasmine shone her torch onto its torso.

'We haven't got much time,' she said. 'So if you want to have a quick grope of that Medusa, you'd better do it now.'

'There's no need to be crude.'

Jasmine shone the torch down the tunnel. 'Let's go find this dagger. It must be somewhere near.'

Fifty Three

The Bourbon Kid woke up in a room he was unfamiliar with. Images from the previous day flashed through his mind at a rate he could not keep up with at first. But as his senses came back to him, the images slowed down and began to make more sense. He remembered that he was in an Amish house, with a woman and her son. Most important of all, he was still alive. It had been a close call, several close calls actually.

He looked at his hands. The holes in his palms were gone, healed up overnight. He pressed his hand against his chest, ran it up over his neck and face. He checked his arms and legs. It was good news. He was back in full working order. Holy blood certainly had its benefits.

The only pains he had were hunger pains because he hadn't eaten in a long time. He could smell warm bread. He wondered if the smell was responsible for waking him. The Amish woman had been good to him. He recognised that if it hadn't been for her, he might not have made it. She and her son had kept him alive when they could have given him up. They had put their own lives at risk to save his. He would have to find a way to repay them at some point. But there were other things to do too. Like find out what happened to Baby. And kill everyone and everything responsible for his near death experience.

The bedroom he was in was small and very basic, consisting only of a bed and a closet. He checked his face one more time for swelling or soreness. Without a mirror it was hard to know how he looked. His stubble had grown longer than he would normally allow, resulting in a short beard.

He stood up and looked down at his pants. They were torn and tattered and what was left of them was sticking to his legs like glue. Fortunately the Amish lady had hung some men's clothes on the door, and they looked like they might fit. He undressed and put on the clothes that had been left for him. Shit clothes. Terrible Amish gear. Black pants, a blue shirt and braces to keep the pants up, this was not a good look.

He left the bedroom and walked along a hall into the kitchen. The Amish woman and her son were sitting at the breakfast table. They both stood up as he walked in.

'I'll make you eggs on toast,' said the woman. 'I hope that's okay.'

'It's fine, erm….' He gestured towards her.

'Agnes,' she said. 'And this is my son, Thomas.'

'Right. Thank you both for your kindness. I'm very grateful.'

'You're completely healed,' said Thomas, staring at him with wide eyed innocence.

The Bourbon Kid pulled out a chair at the table opposite the boy and sat down. Thomas sat down too, while Agnes went to the stove to cook some eggs.

'What should we call you?' she asked, without looking at him.

Before he could answer, Thomas started spouting words out like vomit. 'I spent all afternoon praying that you would come,' he said, looking like he was about to cry tears of joy. 'I'm so glad that God finally answered all of our prayers. We were beginning to think you weren't coming. My mom even sent me to a new school.....'

'Thomas!' Agnes snapped at him.

'I'm sorry mother, it's just that I can't believe he's here. I mean I do believe, of course. You are Jesus aren't you? Or are you one of his brothers?' He looked at the Bourbon Kid's hands. 'Oh my God, even the holes in your hands have healed. It's truly a miracle. Mother look!'

The Bourbon Kid tried to comprehend what the boy was babbling about. More memories from the day before came flooding back. When they had found him by the roadside, Thomas had asked him who he was. In reply, he'd merely cursed his bad luck at being found by Amish people. He'd muttered the words, *"Oh Christ"*. Was it really possible that these Amish folk were so dumb they interpreted that to mean he was Jesus? He glanced at his hands again. The holes through his palms would have added to the confusion. And now that the holes were healed, as well as all of his other injuries, their crackpot theory probably seemed even more believable to them. It was still stupid though. And what the fuck was the deal with the boy's face?

'Did someone beat you up?' he asked Thomas, conveniently changing the subject at the same time.

'He was bullied at school,' said Agnes. 'I enrolled him in the school in Crimson County because I was having doubts about my faith. Does that make me a sinner? I'm so sorry.'

Now it was Agnes who looked like she was on the verge of tears. These Amish folk were mental. But seeing as how they had helped him, the Bourbon Kid chose to show a degree of tolerance that was not part of his usual make up.

'You're not a sinner,' he said. 'You're a good mother and a good Samaritan.'

Agnes breathed a huge sigh of relief and welled up. It looked like she might run over and give him a hug. Thankfully she restrained herself.

On the other side of the table, Thomas was gazing at the Bourbon Kid like a love-struck teenager. The Amish boy had more questions too. 'So what *should* we call you?' he asked.

'For the sake of discretion call me JD.'

'JD?'

'Yeah, see if you can work out what it's short for.'

'Can I ask you something?' Agnes requested.

'Yep.'

'Why have you come to Oakfield now? Why not last year, or the year before? And why were you at the roadside when we found you? Who attacked you?'

She certainly asked a lot of questions. It was hard to know what sort of answers she wanted. But because JD wanted the breakfast so bad, he decided to keep up the facade that he might be some kind of saviour. The best way to do that was to avoid answering any direct questions.

'I owe you two a favour,' he said. 'What can I do for you?'

Thomas answered immediately. 'Can you teach the O'Banyan twins to stop bullying people?'

'Are they the ones who beat you up?'

'Yes. But I can't report them because their dad is the Chief of Police in Crimson County.'

Another memory flooded back into JD's mind. He had a flashback to a moment when he'd been nailed to the cart at the edge of the Black Forest. One of the masked men had made a phone call to someone called Chief O'Banyan. He was the man who oversaw the attempted sacrifice. The man who sent the cart into the Black Forest.

'Their dad is Chief O'Banyan?'

'That's right,' said Agnes. 'He's a horrible man. We've reported crimes to him in the past and he doesn't care. He never even lifted a finger when my husband and my daughter went missing in the Black Forest.'

'They went missing? Did they come back?'

Agnes looked down at her feet. 'My girl, Elsa went missing this time last year. The police said she'd been seen running into the forest. But my Elsa would never go into that forest. After two days we were desperate. My husband went into the forest looking for her. That was the last we saw of him too.' She looked up at JD. 'You were in the forest weren't you?'

'I was.'

'You're the only person to ever go in there during the Fall and come out alive. What's in there? What took my husband and my little girl?'

JD didn't want to tell her what he'd seen in the forest. It would upset her too much. But he saw an opportunity to pay back Agnes and Thomas for what they had done for him.

'I tell you what,' he said. 'When I've had breakfast, I'll take Thomas to the school. He can point out these O'Banyan boys to me, so I can cure them of their evil ways. And when I'm done with that, I'll get you justice for what happened to your husband and your daughter.'

Fifty Four

Jasmine was feeling a little queasy due to the recent experiences of being turned to stone by the Medusa, and then groped by Sanchez. It was hard to know which was the creepier incident. She tried to put it all to the back of her mind as she and Sanchez ventured deeper into the labyrinth.

It took about an hour for them to find what they were looking for, an opening in the Labyrinth which was big enough to be called a room. Directly opposite the entrance to the room was another much smaller room. Inside it was a concrete podium and embedded into the top of it was a golden dagger.

'I'll get it!' Jasmine said, barging Sanchez out of the way.

'Wait!' Sanchez called after her. 'It could be booby trapped.'

Jasmine walked up to the opening of the small room and checked the floor for any trap doors. 'It looks okay,' she said.

'Check the walls. There could be holes that fire spears at you.'

'Spears?'

'Or darts.'

It looked perfectly safe, but Jasmine took a cautious step through the opening anyway, just in case something jumped out at her. The toe of her boot passed through some kind of invisible sensor because without warning a wall of flames burst up from the ground. She jumped back and narrowly avoided being burned or having her boot melted.

'Shit! Fuck! That's really hot!'

'It's okay,' said Sanchez pointing at the alcove. 'Look, the fire's gone out now.'

The flames had vanished, so Jasmine approached it again and tentatively stuck her other foot through the opening. But, as soon as it crossed the invisible trigger line, the flames burst out once more. She leapt back and fell on her backside, this time with smoke pouring from the heel of her boot.

'You okay?' Sanchez asked, pulling her up by her hand.

'Yeah, my sex boots are ruined though.' She looked across at the room with the dagger and saw that the wall of flames had vanished again. 'Oh look. It's okay now,' she said.

'No it's not,' said Sanchez. 'There's some kind of invisible trigger there. When you pass through it, it ignites the fire.'

'How are we supposed to get it out then?'

Sanchez shone his torch on Diana Jones's journal and flicked through it. 'Here you go,' he said. 'There's a picture in here called *The Eternal Flame*. It shows a man walking through fire. And there's a poem at the bottom.'

'Let me see.'

Sanchez turned the book around so she could see it. There was a badly drawn picture on the page of a man walking through fire. Beneath it was the poem. She read it aloud.

Only the living can pass the test,
The flames of God will burn the rest,
It takes a man of flesh and bone,
To wield the dagger from the stone.

'Sounds like a rip off of King Arthur, doesn't it?' said Sanchez.

Jasmine ignored him. 'It says that only the living can pass the test. I think my boots got burned because they're not alive. And look, the man in the picture who's passing through the fire, he isn't wearing any clothes. See, *"it takes a man of flesh and bone to wield the dagger from the stone."*

'What are you saying?'

'I think you have to be naked to pass through the flames.'

'All right,' said Sanchez. 'Try that then.'

'It says "a man" though,' said Jasmine. 'And look, the picture is of a man. You'll have to do it.'

'I'll do no such thing!'

Jasmine grabbed Sanchez by the ear, which made him squeal in pain. 'Don't be such a bitch,' she said, twisting his ear. 'I've had a go. Now you try.'

She stopped twisting his ear and gave him a kick up the backside with her hot boot. Sanchez stumbled forward.

'This is never going to work,' he moaned.

'Just stick your fucking hand in and see what happens.'

Sanchez took off his sunglasses and tucked them into his jacket pocket. Then he stretched out his hand tentatively towards the opening. His fingers got to within six inches of it before he pulled his hand back.

'Nah, it's not going to work,' he said. 'I could feel the burning already.'

Jasmine stepped up behind him and gave him another, much harder kick up the backside. Sanchez staggered forward and his face crossed the invisible trigger line at the edge of the alcove. Just like before, a wall of flames burst up from the floor and down from the ceiling. The fire engulfed his head and the tops of his shoulders. Sanchez yanked his head back out and staggered back. The shoulders of his jacket were on fire.

'Fuck! Fuck!' he screamed. 'Get it off me!'

Jasmine duly obliged and grabbed the lapels of his jacket. She yanked it off, hauling his arms back behind him. A bunch of ketchup sachets fell out of the side pockets onto the floor, and Sanchez danced around, slapping himself on the shoulders to make sure the flames were all gone. Jasmine tossed the burning jacket onto the ground and stamped out the flames until they turned to dark puffs of smoke.

Sanchez stopped hopping around and put his hands on his hips. 'What the fuck did you do that for?' he complained. 'You've ruined my jacket!'

Jasmine pointed at his face. 'Your hair didn't set alight though, and your face isn't burnt at all. See, *only the living can pass the test, the flames of God will burn the rest.* Your jacket isn't a living thing, that's why it burned, but your skin and hair didn't.'

Sanchez felt the top of his head. His hair hadn't burned at all. 'That's just lucky,' he said.

'It's ingenious really,' Jasmine went on, 'because it means no vampires or zombies can get the dagger, because technically they're not living creatures. Go on, try it again.'

'Fuck off. *You* try it again.'

Jasmine grabbed his left arm and rolled the sleeve of his sweatshirt up as far as it would go, which wasn't far because he had flabby arms.

'Just stick your arm in,' she said.

With great reluctance Sanchez approached the small room again. He stood back a few feet and reached out towards it. Jasmine's patience snapped. She grabbed him by the elbow and pushed his arm through the opening. As expected, the flames reappeared and engulfed Sanchez's hand and wrist. He tried to pull away but Jasmine held his arm steady. After a short bout of yelling obscenities, he calmed down.

'That's weird,' he said. 'It doesn't burn.'

Jasmine released her grip and let him pull his hand back from the fire. There wasn't a single burn mark on him. His hand wasn't even red, or hot.

'Brilliant,' she said, inspecting his hand. 'You can walk through the flames and grab the dagger.'

Sanchez shook his head. 'I can't,' he scoffed. 'My clothes will all get burnt. Look at what happened to my jacket.'

'So take your clothes off, dummy! Like I said, you have to be naked to pass through it.'

Sanchez's cheeks turned red. 'But, but....... WHAT?'

'Don't be such a baby, get your clothes off.'

'Can't you try it first? Your catsuit will come off much quicker. It takes me ages to get my socks off.'

'In the book it says a man has to do it.'

'Yes but that's just the way its phrased. *Man* is just a generic term for human.'

'Look fucknuts, the whole fucking world is going to end if we don't retrieve that dagger. So get your clothes off and go get it. If you're not naked in five seconds, I'll undress you myself.'

Sanchez looked mortified. But he was smart enough to know that Jasmine wasn't messing around. And he hadn't forgotten what she did to the last guy whose pants she pulled down.

'All right, turn around,' he said.

Jasmine shook her head. 'No way, you felt me up when I was turned to stone. This is payback, so get on with it.'

Sanchez muttered something under his breath about Jasmine being a psycho but then got on with the business of undressing. He took his sweatshirt off and handed it to Jasmine so that it didn't get dirty on the floor.

After unbuckling his jeans, he turned his back on her and pulled them down. He was wearing a pair of white underpants with suspicious brown streaks on the back that made Jasmine feel ever-so-slightly nauseous. He came close to tripping himself up as he pulled the jeans over his feet. When he eventually got them off he threw them at Jasmine's face and then yanked his underpants down while her view was momentarily obscured. She folded his jeans over her arm and looked up just in time to see the horrendous underpants hit her in the face. She peeled them off and added them to the pile of clothes on her arm.

When she looked back up, Sanchez had covered his genitals with one hand to protect them from the flames. She had a front row view of his ass though and in spite of her claim that this was payback, she decided it would be best to look away, for the sake of her sanity.

Sanchez approached the alcove and poked his big toe across the invisible line. Fire rapidly engulfed his foot but caused him no pain. He took a deep breath and then jumped through the flames.

'I'm through! I didn't get burned,' he shouted back.

Jasmine walked closer to the fire. She could just about make out the outline of Sanchez behind the wall of flames.

'Did you get the dagger yet?' she asked.

'I'm pulling it,' Sanchez yelled back. 'I think it's stuck!'

Jasmine sighed. 'Okay, give me a minute to get my clothes off, then I'll come through and give it a tug for you.'

'I beg your pardon?'

Before Jasmine had a chance to strip off, the wall of flames suddenly vanished and she saw Sanchez standing with his back to her.

'I've got it!' he cried.

He staggered back away from the stone and turned to face her, holding the dagger aloft triumphantly.

'Look at that!' he said.

'Oh my God. MY EYES!'

Jasmine dropped his clothes onto the ground and covered her eyes. 'Hurry up and get dressed,' she said, shuddering.

'Don't you want to see it?' said Sanchez. 'It's very smooth.'

'I'm not opening my eyes until you're dressed. Now hurry up. And let's never speak of this again.'

Fifty Five

Thomas had a strange feeling in his gut. His second day of school was going to be so much better than the first. He couldn't explain it, he just sensed that something huge, something life-changing was about to happen. This could be the day he had waited his whole life for. He'd always felt deep down that there was a reason he had been put on earth, that somehow, in spite of his ordinariness, he was destined to be part of something great.

He savoured the journey to school, unlike the day before when he'd been filled with anxiety and "first-day-of-school" nerves.

JD rode the horse drawn carriage from Oakfield to Crimson County, with Agnes next to him and Thomas behind them in the back seat. There was a chill in the air and a thin fog had settled over the sea. It was a peaceful start to a day that would live long in the memory.

When they arrived at school, JD stopped the horse drawn carriage opposite the school.

'You should wait here,' he said to Agnes.

'Really?'

'You've already got the words *Amish Scum* sprayed on this carriage. Let's not give the vandals an excuse to do anything else to it.'

'That's a good point,' Agnes agreed. 'They painted my Fanny yesterday too.'

JD looked confused.

'Fanny's the horse,' said Thomas.

'Right.'

JD and Thomas left Agnes with the horse and carriage, and headed into the school.

The school corridors were as chaotic as ever. Quite a few of the other students stopped and stared, bemused by the sight of an Amish man and boy walking the corridors together. Thomas had received similar stares the day before. Today was much less intimidating though, because he wasn't alone. He had his own guardian angel in JD. It gave him the confidence to walk with his head held high, making eye contact with anyone who looked his way. What he was really looking for were the O'Banyan brothers. He couldn't wait to look them in the eye after what they had done to him the day before.

'So where are they?' JD asked. 'Can you point them out?'

'I can't see them.'

They walked the corridors for a couple of minutes with no sign of the O'Banyan's. They should have been easy to spot because they were fully grown men, two years older than the next oldest senior.

Thomas caught sight of Mister Romanowski, the Science teacher walking towards them through a crowd of students. He was a short but slim fellow in his mid-thirties, with a wiry moustache. He was wearing an ugly tweed jacket and clutching a stack of text books in his hands. He spotted JD and Thomas and shook his head in disapproval.

'Adults aren't allowed in the school corridors,' he said, addressing JD.

'We're looking for the O'Banyan brothers,' JD replied.

Romanowski rolled his eyes. 'You're going to have to report to the school secretary,' he said. 'You can't just roam the school looking for people, not without a hall pass.'

'Not the answer I'm looking for.'

'I beg your pardon?'

JD slapped his hand down on the stack of books Romanowski was holding, knocking them to the floor. It made a loud clatter and suddenly everyone in the corridor went quiet and stopped what they were doing to see what was going on.

'What in God's name is wrong with you?' said Romanowski, staring at the scattered books in bewilderment.

'I asked you a question. Where do I find the O'Banyan brothers?'

'They're not here.'

JD grabbed the science teacher by the throat and lifted him off his feet with one hand. He pulled him in close until they were nose to nose. Then he spoke in a gravelly voice that Thomas hadn't heard before.

'Tell me where they are,' he said.

Romanowski pointed back the way they had come. 'They're over the road in the Community centre. It's on the other side of the village green. The football team is doing drills in there.'

JD put Romanowski down and let go of his throat. The teacher started sucking in air like a goldfish, while bending over with his hands on his hips, as if that somehow helped him breathe. There were giggles from some of the students who had witnessed his public humiliation, so in order to re-establish his air of authority, he shouted after JD and Thomas as they made their way back down the corridor.

'I'm going to call the police!'

Thomas felt a surge of excitement run right through him. His mind was awash with different emotions, exhilaration, nervousness, trepidation, anxiety and an odd feeling of dread that had come from nowhere. He hadn't expected JD to threaten Mister Romanowski the way he did. He had been anticipating some kind of peaceful intervention by way of reasoning and calmness, not one that involved intimidation and threats.

They left the school and crossed the village green to the Community centre on the other side. The Community centre was used mostly for Bingo nights and kids Judo classes.

JD barged through the front doors without any hesitation. Thomas followed him in, hanging back a few steps. Now that they were close to resolving the bullying issue, he was having second thoughts. They marched through a reception area into the Bingo hall where the football team were training.

Seeing the O'Banyan twins brought back the memories of the day before. And this time, it wasn't just the O'Banyans. There were at least twenty of their team mates with them, all dressed in white shorts and red game shirts with numbers on the front and back. They were lined up in four rows of five, doing star jumps to the count of the sports coach Mr Millwood, who was standing at the front, wearing a green tracksuit and a red baseball cap.

Millwood was the first person to notice the uninvited guests. He stopped counting the star jumps out loud. The players carried on doing the jumps, until a few of them spotted the reason why he had stopped counting. Before long the whole team were staring at JD and Thomas. None of them looked happy to see two Amish folk interrupting their routine.

JD slapped Thomas on the arm. 'Point them out,' he said.

Thomas whispered the answer so that only JD could hear. 'Number sixteen and number fifty four.'

Before JD had a chance to go and speak with them, Coach Millwood took off his cap and threw it on the floor.

'Goddammit!' he snapped. He approached JD, wagging his finger at him. 'You can't be in here!'

It happened in a blur. JD moved towards Coach Millwood and did something that Thomas didn't get a good view of. But whatever it was, it knocked the Coach off his feet and he landed flat on his back on the wooden floor. It made a sound that reminded Thomas of a time when he was ten years old and he'd belly-flopped into a swimming pool, only this looked infinitely more painful. It shook Millwood to the core and he lay there on his back, dazed and blinking, staring up at the ceiling.

The football team were a tight-knit bunch and seeing their coach taken out by a stranger didn't go down well. The first player to confront JD was number sixteen, Dick O'Banyan. A few of his teammates hung at his shoulder, showing solidarity in numbers and eyeballing JD. Dick glared at Thomas.

'Little bitch brought his daddy to stick up for him, huh?'

'I'm not his dad,' JD replied.

Dick looked over his shoulder at his buddies. 'Hey guys, we got ourselves a couple of Amish fags!'

A chorus of laughter broke out all around. Dick turned back to JD to continue goading him. But what happened next was something Thomas would replay over and over in his mind for the rest of his life. Dick moved to shove JD in the chest. It didn't work out as he hoped though. Not at all. He wasn't even halfway through the move when JD snapped into action. He caught Dick's wrist and held it firm, then he lunged forward and threw an uppercut that clocked Dick on the chin. The sound it made as Dick's teeth shattered against each other was worse than someone scraping their fingernails down a chalkboard. Dick's eyes became lifeless and his shoulders slouched, all in the space of half a second. He had lost consciousness from the punch, but JD wasn't finished with him yet. While still holding him up by his wrist, he stamped on Dick's right knee, shattering it and snapping his leg in two. The crunch sounded like a wooden table leg breaking in half.

Dick's demise happened so fast that no one else even moved before it was over. But when Dick landed on the floor, it was the cue for total chaos. Another one of the football players lunged at JD. But this guy was an amateur. He took a punch to the gut that knocked the wind out of him and doubled him over. After that it got worse. JD seemed to get a real taste for the violence. Thomas watched on with a mix of horror and awe as JD took down the football team one at a time, sometimes two at a time.

At least twelve of them were unconscious on the floor by the time Archie O'Banyan joined the fight. He started yelling and charged towards JD like an angry bull. A kung-fu kick to the chest stopped him in his tracks. It dazed him and he struggled to take a breath. JD grabbed him by his hair and yanked his head down, swinging his knee up towards Archie's face at the same time. The two body parts collided with a sickening *clunk* as Archie's nose broke. JD dropped him to the floor and stamped on the back of his head. His skull obliterated, blood and brains squelching across the floor. The force of the stamp made his head look softer than a peach.

That stopped everything. Not one of the remaining footballers made a move after that. When they started fleeing the scene, JD turned to Thomas. He had specks of blood all over his face.

'You should probably go now,' he said.

Thomas stood gobsmacked at the sight before him, absorbing it and trying to make sense of what had happened. JD was standing in the middle of the community hall, surrounded by a pile of unconscious, if not dead, football players, with a few more fleeing through the fire exit.

'I… I thought you were just going to stop them from picking on me?' Thomas said, his voice trembling.

'I did. Now go home because the police are coming. Things are about to get real.'

Fifty Six

'This is a crock of shit,' Elvis complained. 'I've been telling you for years you need to get a phone network installed in this place.'

He was sitting on a cushioned bench in Purgatory, watching Scratch and Annabel at a nearby table. Annabel was poring over her crystal ball, gesturing at it and talking to it, occasionally providing some commentary about what she thought Sanchez and Jasmine were up to.

Scratch looked over at Elvis. 'What good would a phone network do?' he asked dismissively.

It barely made sense why Scratch was staring into Annabel's crystal ball, because she was the only one that ever saw anything in it anyway. And there were certainly many occasions where Elvis suspected she saw nothing and made up a load of bullshit instead.

'If we could make external calls, I could phone Sanchez and ask him what's going on,' Elvis explained.

'He's fifty feet underground, beneath a church in an Amish village. He won't get a signal down there,' said Scratch. 'And besides, I've told you before, we *can't* get a signal in this place, even if I wanted to, which I don't.'

'But you've got satellite TV!'

'Yes I have. But thanks to you and Jasmine, my favourite series has been cancelled.'

'Hey, don't blame me,' said Elvis, wagging his finger at Scratch. 'Jasmine thought they were real apes. I had nothing to do with it.'

'I binge watched six fucking series of that show. And now I'll never know how it ends.'

'You could phone the show's producers and ask them,' Elvis suggested. 'Oh no, wait you can't, BECAUSE THERE'S NO FUCKING PHONE SIGNAL HERE!'

'If we had a phone signal here,' Scratch replied calmly, 'someone would smuggle phones into the cells downstairs and the next thing you know, women everywhere would be getting nuisance calls from Hitler.'

'Hitler is downstairs?'

'Where else would he be?'

Annabel butted in. 'Would you two idiots shut up?'

'I beg your pardon?' said Scratch.

'I'm trying to concentrate here.'

'Have you seen anything?'

Elvis looked around the room. As well as Annabel and Scratch, he also had Beth and Flake for company. Flake appeared to be recovering well from the stab wound in her neck and was healthy enough to sit up, although she hadn't yet spoken to anyone. Beth had stayed with her, the two of them keeping their distance and staying at the back of the bar, where they could avoid Scratch, who had a tendency for flamboyant psychotic rants every once in while.

'They're stuck,' said Annabel.

'Did they get the dagger?' Scratch asked.

'Yes, but they're still under the church. And the secret stairway has been closed up. They have no way out unless someone in the church reopens the secret entrance.'

Scratch chewed on his fist. 'Fuck it!' he grumbled. 'We're going to have to send someone to the church to get them out.'

'I'll go,' said Elvis. He hobbled to his feet, winced in pain and then sat back down again, all in one swift movement.

'You're no use,' said Scratch. 'This has been one massive cock up ever since I got carried away and sent that idiot Sanchez. He's to blame for this.'

Flake finally spoke. Actually she shouted. At Scratch. 'Hey fuck you! I'll go and get them!' She immediately burst into a coughing fit as she tried to hurl some more abuse at Scratch. It was clear she was in no better condition than Elvis.

Beth covered Flake's mouth with her hand and silenced her before she could say anything else that might get her killed. Elvis felt fairly certain that Scratch wouldn't take too kindly to Flake's outburst, so he used a bit of diplomacy and spoke up in her defence.

'Nobody understands her,' he said. 'And she's been stabbed so she's probably in shock.'

Scratch took a moment to think, like he so often did. When he did speak, he surprised Elvis. 'Actually, I like her,' he said. 'Although she is a foul-mouthed little tart.'

Elvis was trying to figure out where Scratch had picked up the term "tart" when suddenly, out of nowhere, another voice shouted out. *'I'll go!'*

It was Beth. She stood up, ready for action. Elvis could see in her eyes that she was serious about going. And what other choice did they have? Annabel was fucking old and really unreliable. Scratch couldn't go because of some unwritten law that meant he couldn't directly interfere in matters of life and death. Elvis himself had a broken leg, and Flake, who was known to be quite a badass, had her neck bandaged up and held together by a medical plug. And she had lost a lot of blood, which left Beth as the only healthy person available.

Scratch scoffed at her. *'You?* What are *you* going to do?'

Beth shrugged. 'Just tell me what you want me to do.'

'She's all we've got,' Elvis pointed out.

'I can do it,' said Beth.

Scratch pondered the idea for a while. 'This is a bad idea,' he muttered.

'It could work,' said Annabel, looking into her crystal ball again. 'All she has to do is get into the church and press the letter D in the wall to open up the secret entrance. Jasmine and Sanchez have the Brutus Dagger already, so once they're out, the three of them can head straight back here with it.'

'We don't want them to bring the dagger back here,' said Scratch. 'We need them to kill Cain with it.'

'Yes, I know that,' said Annabel. 'But I'm getting visions of Cain and one of the Horsemen heading this way already.'

'What?'

'The blond one, Zitrone, he's seen the secret highway from the crossroads. He knows how to get in here and he's coming back with Cain.'

Scratch kicked his chair across the room and cursed in a language that Elvis had never heard before. He watched Scratch pace around like a huge, pent-up jungle cat before he walked over to Beth and stared at her for what seemed like forever.

'Are you sure you're up to this?' Scratch asked her.

'I can do it. Like Annabel said, all I have to do is press the letter D in the wall and free Sanchez and Jasmine. That's not hard. I can do it.'

'All right then.' Scratch pointed at the Men's toilets. 'You know the drill. Head through there. On the other side you'll find yourself in the washroom in the church of St Susan.'

For a brief moment it looked like Beth was having second thoughts. 'What if there's someone in the toilet when I go through the door?' she asked.

Scratch rolled his eyes, but then Annabel offered Beth a crumb of advice.

'Beth,' she croaked. 'When you get to Oakfield, if you encounter any Amish folk, be sure to be liberal with the truth. They're good people, and they're God-fearing. If they ask where you came from, don't tell them *he* sent you.' She pointed at Scratch. 'Tell them that you were sent by the Lord. They will respond to that because their prophecy has predicted it.'

Beth looked like she was psyching herself up. She grabbed her black leather jacket from the floor and slipped her arms into the sleeves.

'Thanks Annabel,' she said. 'I appreciate the advice, but once I've got Sanchez and Jasmine out of the labyrinth, we can just come back through that door, can't we?'

Scratch laughed loud and heartily for an inappropriately long time before replying. 'This isn't Star Trek you know, dear. I can't just *beam you back up!* The gateway out of here works only one way. To get back, you'll have to drive all the way from Blue Corn Island, so when you get there, do yourself a favour and find a fast car.'

'Jasmine will know what to do,' said Elvis. 'You'll be fine.'

As Beth headed over to the Men's toilets, Annabel shouted one final piece of advice across the room. 'Beth, whatever you do, don't go into the Black Forest.'

Scratch turned on Annabel. 'She's not going anywhere near the Black Forest, you fool!'

'I hope that's true,' said Annabel. 'Because my crystal ball is telling me that a woman is going to die in that forest tonight.'

Fifty Seven

The sound of police car sirens racing across town wasn't entirely unusual in Crimson County, but to hear six or seven squad cars with their sirens blaring at the same time was very rare. There was a commonly held belief that sirens were only heard during the afternoon rush hour period, when the cops were trying to beat the traffic to get home for their dinner. But on this occasion, the Crimson County Police department were in a hurry to get to the local Community centre after reports of multiple homicides.

Captain Andrew Lynch and his partner Officer Donald Dickerson were first on the scene. Lynch had waited his whole career for a chance to catch a murderer. Sixteen years he'd been on the force since joining as a fresh-faced twenty-one-year-old and he'd never hunted down a killer in all that time. In all the excitement he drove so fast that he overshot the entrance to the Community centre. And before he'd had a chance to stop, his partner, the slightly older and much chubbier, Donald Dickerson, opened the passenger door and jumped out. He produced a forward roll worthy of a TV cop and ended up on the sidewalk in an action pose, with his gun pointed at the centre's entrance. Lynch was so distracted by the forward roll he took his eyes off the road for a second and crashed the squad car into a pair of metal dustbins on the sidewalk.

A large crowd of local townspeople had gathered together on the village green opposite the Community centre. Roger Dunbar, the janitor at the centre ran across the street and greeted Lynch as he climbed out of the car.

'Andrew, I saw the whole thing.'

Lynch unholstered his gun. 'Is he still in there?'

'He hasn't come out the front,' said Dunbar. 'One of the kids who escaped said the killer is waiting in the Bingo hall for you guys to come and arrest him. He's killed Chief O'Banyan's boys, and a bunch of the others are in a bad way.'

'And it's definitely an Amish guy?'

'Yeah. He was with a young boy, but the boy left with a woman in a getaway stagecoach.'

'A getaway stagecoach?'

Lynch had heard of getaway cars, bikes and trucks, even planes and boats, but a getaway stagecoach? What the fuck? He didn't have time to argue over the details with Dunbar though, because Dickerson was waiting at the front of the Community centre for him.

'Come on Cap,' Dickerson yelled at him. 'We're the first ones here. Let's get this asshole!'

There were other cars screeching around corners on the way to the crime scene so Dickerson had a point. If they were to become local heroes they had to be the ones to catch the killer.

The two cops raced into the building amid a chorus of cheers from the crowd assembled on the village green. This was exactly what Lynch had signed up for. Some serious *Lethal Weapon* style action. They had never had a mass murder in town and even though it was distressing, and really sad that some young men were dead and *all that shit,* Lynch was fucking buzzing, loving it, flying high on adrenaline.

Dickerson was clearly in the mood too. The pair of them stalked the reception area of the centre, mimicking every cop show cliché they had ever seen. Lynch put in a few decent forward rolls, while Dickerson, who was pretty fucked up from his forward roll in the street, edged his way up to the opening for the Bingo hall. The killer was in there waiting for them just like Roger Dunbar had predicted, but finally getting to do all that shit for real was awesome. Lynch had never felt more like a cop.

The scene that greeted them in the hall was more horrific than either of them was prepared for. Lynch forgot all about shouting "Freeze asshole" like he'd been planning ever since they took the call. The Amish man who had done the killing was on his knees in the middle of the hall, surrounded by a pile of bodies. He had his hands up behind his head already, which deprived Lynch of the opportunity to tell him to put them there, which was annoying.

'Freeze asshole!' yelled Dickerson.

'Fuck,' Lynch cursed under his breath. 'I was gonna say that.'

'Put your goddamn hands behind your head!' Dickerson roared.

'He's got his hands behind his head. Just keep your gun on him. I'm gonna put the cuffs on him.'

Lynch took a pair of handcuffs off his belt and edged his way over to the killer. As he got closer, he saw that the man's face was covered in blood. Not just random specks or even splashes. This was different. It didn't take a genius to see that the killer had covered himself in the blood of his victims. He had even used blood to slick his hair back. His shirt was blood red, barely a speck of the original colour showing. Even through all the blood, Lynch recognised the man. It was the stranger from out of town that they had nailed to a cart and rolled into the Black Forest.

He looked back at Dickerson. 'I'm thinking maybe you should shoot this guy,' he said, widening his eyes and nodding at the suspect in a way that was meant to say, "Look, it's *that* guy again!".

It took Dickerson a few seconds to realise what Lynch was getting at. But then he released the safety on his pistol.

Before he fired a shot, the suspect finally spoke, in a gravelly voice. 'Take me in alive and there's a ten million dollar reward.'

Lynch held up his hand to stop his partner from shooting. 'What did you just say?'

'Ten million reward,' the suspect replied. 'Look me up on the FBI Most Wanted list. I'm number one.'

'Bullshit. Who are you?'

'I'm the Bourbon Kid. And I'm your ticket to ten million dollars.'

'The Bourbon Kid?' Lynch had heard the name, but never imagined in a million years the Kid would show up in Crimson County. 'Okay asshole, you stay right there. I'm putting these cuffs on you. Try anything stupid and my buddy will shoot you dead. Understand?'

Dickerson was sneaking glances around the hall at the victims. 'Andrew, that's half the football team!' he yelled.

Lynch didn't dare take his eyes off the Bourbon Kid, but through his peripheral vision he could see all of the victims were wearing football shirts. He couldn't tell how many there were, or even if they were all dead. Some of them might have just been unconscious. It was hard to tell.

He shouted at the Bourbon Kid. 'Lay down on the fucking floor!'

The Kid complied without any sudden movements. He laid down on his front, keeping his hands on the back of his head.

'Dickerson, keep that gun on him,' Lynch ordered as he prepared to put the cuffs on his new prisoner.

He moved around behind the Kid and cuffed his wrists together behind his head.

'You got him?' Dickerson asked.

Lynch glanced over at his buddy and grinned. 'Say hello to ten million dollars!'

Fifty Eight

Beth opened the door to the Men's toilets and walked through it, just like Sanchez and Jasmine had done earlier in the day. On the other side of the door was the public washroom in the church of St Susan.

The church hall was deathly quiet. Beth looked around and saw no one else was present, so she darted across to the main aisle and headed for the altar. As soon as she set foot in the aisle she saw the dead preacher. Bishop Yoder was spread-eagled on the floor halfway down the aisle. His face was a bloodied mess and looked like it had been turned inside out. Beth winced and looked away. There was blood sprayed across the floor around him. She tiptoed past the body, trying her best to avoid coming into contact with any of the surrounding blood.

It didn't take long to find the word DECEMBER underneath the Nativity painting. She pushed the letter D into the wall and immediately heard a set of gears grinding beneath the floor as the secret staircase unravelled at her feet. As soon as it touched down in the underground labyrinth, Beth heard Sanchez's voice float up the staircase.

'Me first! I've got the torch.'

Jasmine's voice followed. 'No way. I'm going first!'

'Too slow!'

'You little shit!'

'Ow! Bitch.'

'Loser.'

Beth shouted down the stairs. 'Hello!'

She heard footsteps running up the stairs. Sanchez appeared first, rounding the last bend on the stairs. Jasmine was right behind him and for the next thirty seconds or so, Beth had to watch them take turns tripping each other up in a childish duel to get to the top first. It ended with Jasmine diving forward and reaching out to touch the floor above the stairs, followed by Sanchez climbing over her back using her head as the final step to the top.

'I win!' he yelled, punching the air.

'Bullshit. I touched the top first!' said Jasmine, climbing to her feet.

Beth cleared her throat to get their attention. They stopped bickering and both stared at her.

'How did you get here?' Sanchez asked.

'Scratch sent me to free you from the underground.'

Jasmine looked around for Bishop Yoder and quickly spotted him. 'Holy fuck, what happened to the Bishop? Is he dead?'

Beth nodded. 'Annabel saw what happened in her crystal ball. She says Cain was here and he killed Yoder so that you'd be stuck down in the labyrinth. He knows you were looking for the Brutus Dagger.'

Sanchez took a step back and ducked behind Jasmine, looking around nervously. 'Is he still here?'

'No, he's gone.'

'Lucky for him.'

Sanchez puffed his chest out and walked over to take a look at Yoder's corpse. He shook his head and tutted. 'Terrible isn't it? Someone bashing the Bishop in church.'

Beth ignored Sanchez and relayed the mission details to Jasmine, who seemed like the slightly more sensible of the two, although it was debatable. 'Annabel says Cain is headed to The Devil's Graveyard. One of the Horsemen has found the secret entrance. So you need to go after him right now. Who's got the dagger?'

'Sanchez has got it,' said Jasmine.

'I walked through fire to get it,' Sanchez added, beaming with pride.

Beth was familiar with Sanchez boasting about his acts of bravery but she suspected the truth was somewhat different.

'He's joking, right?' she asked Jasmine.

'Unfortunately not,' Jasmine replied.

'But if he walked through fire, then how come he didn't burn?'

There was a brief, uncomfortable silence before Jasmine answered. 'It was some kind of test set by God. The only way to do it was by taking all of his clothes off.'

'What?' Beth was confused. '*All* of his clothes?'

'Yes.'

Beth briefly visualised the incident in her mind, which made her shudder. She reached out and touched Jasmine's arm. 'Are you okay?'

'Do you mind!' said Sanchez. 'I also saved her from a Medusa. She got turned to stone.'

It was Jasmine's turn to shudder. 'Did you know he's got a thing for touching up statues?'

Beth didn't want to hear any more of the adventures of Sanchez and Jasmine. 'You know what?' she said. 'You should keep these stories to yourself. Whatever you do, don't tell Flake.'

At the mention of Flake, Sanchez perked up. 'How is she? Is she okay?' he asked.

'Yeah, she's doing good. She's almost made a full recovery.'

Sanchez spotted some cobwebs on his arm and used the Brutus Dagger to flick them off. 'I knew she would be all right. She's as tough as they come.'

'Well if you want to see her again, you'd better get a move on,' Beth warned. 'There isn't much time.'

Jasmine started walking down the aisle. 'Come on then. Let's get moving.'

Sanchez followed on behind her, but Beth hung back. She had no intention of returning to Purgatory with them.

'Aren't you coming with us?' Sanchez asked.

'I'm going to wait here.'

'How come?'

'JD is on this island somewhere. I'm not leaving without him. So if you see him before I do, tell him I'm here.'

Jasmine turned back and pleaded with Beth. 'You'll be safer with us.'

Sanchez disagreed. 'There's no room for her in that bloody sidecar. And I'm not having her on my lap.'

'Seriously,' said Beth. 'Go. Every second counts. Don't worry about me.'

'Are you sure?' said Jasmine.

'Yes, go.'

'Okay,' Jasmine said reluctantly. 'Take care of yourself. Come on Sanchez, we've got to get moving.'

Beth followed them out and waved them off. After an initial delay, while Sanchez had to be wedged into the sidecar, Jasmine started up the motorbike and they sped off up the hill towards Crimson County. Before Beth had a chance to decide her next move, an Amish couple with two young daughters walked up to the church entrance.

The man, who was in his late twenties and had a thick bushy beard, took off his hat as he approached. 'Good day to you, ma'am' he said. 'How have you come to be in Oakfield?'

'Hi, my name's Beth. I'm looking for a friend of mine.'

The man turned to his wife. 'Ruth, why don't you and the girls go on in,' he said.

'Okay dear.'

While the rest of his family entered the church, the man introduced himself to Beth.

'I am Abram Wittmer,' he said, sticking his hat back on his head. 'How can I help you to find your friend?'

'His name is JD. He's about six feet tall and he's usually unshaven,' Beth replied.

'Unshaven eh?' said Abram, scratching his beard.

'ABRAM! COME QUICK. BISHOP YODER IS DEAD!'

Beth felt a cold shiver wash over her entire body. Abram's wife and daughters had discovered the dead Bishop in the church. One of the young girls ran out of the church screaming. She ran straight into Beth and quickly backed away, pointing at her.

'She's killed Bishop Yoder!' she cried.

'Oh no,' said Beth. 'It wasn't me.'

Abram grabbed Beth's arm. 'You've got some explaining to do young lady.'

Fifty Nine

Dickerson and Lynch had played the "Good cop, Bad cop" routine many times before. But on all of the previous occasions the suspect they were interrogating had been a drunk driver, or a shoplifter. Never in all their years had they had the chance to do the routine on a world famous killer. Lynch couldn't even recall ever having a murderer in the police station before. But they had one now, sitting at a table in the interrogation room.

Dickerson leaned against the table they used for interrogation. He kept his body language facing slightly offside of the psycho who had killed the O'Banyan boys. It was his "open and understanding" stance, which worked a treat when playing the good cop.

Lynch had struck gold though because it was his turn to be the bad cop. He got to work straight away, trying out all his favourite routines. He circled the Bourbon Kid, stopping behind him occasionally and whispering threats in his ear. He even stopped in front of him at one point, and leaned across the desk, snarling into his face. None of it worked. The Bourbon Kid didn't flinch, didn't react, didn't show any emotion. It left Lynch with one option, the final intimidation, used as a last resort when a suspect wouldn't co-operate. He did what he liked to call his "Harvey Keitel" routine. It was a nugget he'd picked up from the movie *Thelma and Louise.*

He nodded at Dickerson. 'Donald, would you leave me alone with this guy for a minute?'

'Sure thing, boss.'

His partner patted the Bourbon Kid on the shoulder. 'Sorry buddy, looks like you're on your own. I'm going to get a coffee. Good luck.'

Unfortunately, just as Dickerson opened the door to leave, Chief O'Banyan showed up. The Chief looked furious and tried to storm his way in to get his hands on the Bourbon Kid.

'YOU FUCKING SONOFABITCH!' he raged.

Dickerson wrestled him out into the corridor and slammed the door shut behind him. It left Lynch alone with the Bourbon Kid. Lynch stayed silent for a while, allowing his prisoner to hear the very loud and angry exchange between Dickerson and O'Banyan that was filtering in from the corridor. Lynch used it to his benefit.

'Maybe I should let the Chief in here?' he smirked.

Once more the Kid didn't respond. So Lynch moved to stage two of his Harvey Keitel routine. He perched himself on the edge of the table and leaned forward slightly. This killer was going to know that he meant business.

'Looks like it's just you and me now, buddy,' he said.

The Bourbon Kid ignored him again, staring straight ahead with his hands under the table. Lynch felt an incredible sense of power. Here was this world famous serial killer sitting in front of him, handcuffed, and probably crapping his pants.

'You know, I'm renowned as a bit of a renegade cop,' Lynch continued. 'I'm often in trouble with the Chief because I don't play by the rules. But I think he'll allow me a little leeway with you.'

Still no response.

Lynch took his police badge out of a pocket on his brown leather jacket and placed it on the table in front of the Bourbon Kid.

'I won't be needing this right now,' he said. 'Because for the next few minutes, I'm not a cop.' He took his jacket off and walked over to the corner of the room. He hung the jacket over a CCTV camera that was filming everything. It felt awesome. This was real detective work.

He turned around and rolled his shoulders back to loosen up, knowing it would intimidate his suspect even more. He walked back to the desk, rolling up the sleeves on his shirt, ready to dish out some justice.

The Bourbon Kid was still staring ahead. But something was different. On the table next to Lynch's police badge there was a set of handcuffs that hadn't been there before.

Sixty

'LET ME IN THERE, I'M GONNA FUCKING KILL HIM!'

'Chief, calm down!'

Dickerson slammed the Chief up against the wall outside the interrogation room. He felt bad. O'Banyan had just lost his two sons and now he was being shoved into a wall. It was for his own good though.

O'Banyan was breathing erratically and whispering the phrase *'I'll kill him!'* over and over.

'Chief, everybody knows you're hurting,' said Dickerson, 'but if we're gonna do this arrest right, you need to be away from here. One mistake and this guy could walk. And remember, he's worth ten million dollars to us.'

'Fuck the money!'

'Just think for a minute. This is the guy we sacrificed to the Gods the other night, so it's complicated.'

'We shoulda fuckin' killed him when we had the chance.'

'I agree, but the fact remains that we did what we did. What we need to find out now, is if he knows it was us.'

'Of course he knows it was us. Why do you think he killed my boys!'

'Chief, you're not thinking clearly. This guy never saw our faces, so he can't prove anything. If you go in there all emotional and say the wrong thing, then he could tell the FBI what we did, then we're all fucked. This whole town is fucked.'

It looked like he'd finally struck a chord. O'Banyan calmed down and loosened up a little.

'What are you gonna do?' O'Banyan asked.

'First we're gonna find out what he knows. And we're gonna be rough on him, I promise. So while we're doing that, why don't you go and make the call to the Feds? Don't forget to tell them it was me and Lynch that caught him. I'm thinking we should split the ten million three ways, y'know?'

'Three ways? Have your twin sons been murdered too?'

'No, but come on, we caught the guy.'

O'Banyan tugged at his collar. 'How did you catch him? I thought this guy was supposed to be a badass?'

Dickerson snorted a laugh. 'When he saw me and Lynch he shit himself and surrendered without a fight.'

O'Banyan sneered. 'Fuckin' pussy.'

Dickerson was keen to get rid of the Chief. 'Look, why don't you go upstairs and make the call? While you're doing that, me and Lynch will make it look like this asshole tried to resist arrest. We'll beat him to within an inch of his life for you, I promise.'

O'Banyan stilled, seemingly thinking through everything Dickerson had said. After a few seconds, he gave a short, sharp nod, straightened his tie and wiped some sweat from his forehead. 'When I'm done with the FBI I'm coming back down.'

'Sure thing.'

O'Banyan left the interrogation area and headed back to his office on the second floor. Dickerson breathed a sigh of relief and made his way down the corridor to the staff room to get a coffee. Two other cops in standard blue uniforms were sitting at a table in the middle of the room watching the Country Music channel on a shitty old television on the sideboard.

Dickerson walked up to the coffee vending machine and selected a white coffee with sugar. The sound of the machine gurgling finally alerted the other officers to his presence.

'How's it going in there with the asshole?' one of them asked.

'Lynch is doing the bloody bad cop role again,' Dickerson replied. 'It was my fucking turn too.'

'Is the guy talking?'

'Nah, he's trying to act all tough. We'd have broken him by now if it was me doing the Bad Cop.'

'Yeah, right.'

Dickerson took his plastic cup of filth from the machine and sniffed it. It smelt as rough as it looked. 'I gotta get back,' he said. 'I think this one's gonna require *two* bad cops.'

'If you need a third and fourth, come get us,' said one of the cops, without looking away from the television.

Dickerson left them to it and headed back to the interrogation room. He stopped outside and listened through the door. It had gone quiet inside, which suggested the Kid still hadn't talked, so some violence would be called for. He turned the door handle and kicked the door open with his shoe, spilling some lukewarm coffee over his hand as he did it.

'Fuckssake!'

He licked the coffee off his hand as he walked in. When he looked up things had changed dramatically in the interrogation room. Lynch was slumped on the floor in the corner of the room. His neck had been broken, his tongue was hanging out of his mouth and it looked like he'd pissed himself. Worst of all, the gun holster on his belt was empty.

Dickerson dropped his coffee and reached for his own gun, suddenly aware of a shadow that had been hovering in his peripheral vision. It moved towards him and grabbed his hand before he could unholster his gun.

The cold steel of a gun barrel pressed against the fat skin beneath his chin. Dickerson didn't hear the bullet that burned its way through his mouth, into his brain and out through his skull. He didn't hear the many gunshots that followed either. He was one of the lucky ones who died quick.

Sixty One

O'Banyan

By the time Jebediah O'Banyan got back to his office on the second floor, his shirt was drenched in sweat. The tears he had cried earlier in the day had dried against his cheeks.

He sat at his desk and looked down at the sheet of paper on top of his computer keyboard. The picture of the Bourbon Kid stared back out at him. And beneath it in bold lettering was the one and only good piece of news he'd had all day.

$10,000,000 REWARD IF CAPTURED ALIVE

He picked up the phone and dialled the FBI number that was printed on the page. The phone rang three times before a woman answered it.

'Hello, this is General Alexis Calhoon.'

'Hello General, this is Chief Jebediah O'Banyan from the Crimson County Police Department. I got your number from the FBI most wanted list.'

'How can I help you Chief?'

'We've got a guy in custody here who happens to be number one on your most wanted list. Calls himself the Bourbon Kid.'

'You have him in custody?' She sounded surprised.

'Yes ma'am.'

'Are you sure it's actually him and not an impostor?'

O'Banyan didn't appreciate the patronising questions. 'Look lady, if this guy is an impostor he's a fucking good one because he's murdered half the bloody town this morning, including both of my sons, so you can count yourself lucky he's still alive, because if I had my way--'

'Evacuate the building!'

O'Banyan was annoyed that she had interrupted him because he was about to go into a "full on" rant. And she hadn't even said she was sorry to hear about the death of his sons. Fucking FBI people, ignorant fuckers. Evacuate the building? The words finally sank in.

'What?'

'If you're one hundred percent sure that the man you captured is the Bourbon Kid then evacuate the building right now!'

'Hey, look, it's definitely him all right. We've verified it on your database.'

'Then you should get out of the building now.'

'Are you even listening to me? This is the police department, not the fucking day-care centre. We've got him in handcuffs. We know what we're doing here. Right now this guy is downstairs in an interrogation room with two of my best men. He's not going anywhere.'

He heard Calhoon let out a deep sigh on the other end of the phone. 'Chief O'Banyan,' she said, speaking slowly and clearly, as if talking to a child. 'Those two men, *your best men*, they're probably dead already. So if you have a fire alarm in your building, or any other kind of alarm, you need to set it off *right now*, or the Crimson County Police Department will be a thing of the past.'

This was infuriating. This General Calhoon woman obviously thought the Crimson County Police Department was some kind of inept redneck outfit. 'Like I just told you ma'am, the guy is in handcuffs. We *caught him.*'

'Listen,' said Calhoon calmly. 'If the Bourbon Kid really is in your police station, then he's there by choice, which means he's there to kill you. So do yourself a favour and get out now or you're all going to die.'

O'Banyan was about to lose his shit with Calhoon, but just as he opened his mouth to call her a patronising cunt, the door to his office flew open and Officer Humphrey Tucker burst in. Tucker was in charge of security and had a bank of monitors in his office that gave him a view of what went on, in and around the police station, including the interrogation rooms.

'Chief, we gotta problem,' he said, his face paler than usual.

O'Banyan covered the phone and snapped back at him. 'What's happened now?'

'Lynch hung his coat over the camera in the interrogation room again.'

'So what?'

'So I called him to tell him to remove it.'

'And?'

'And the suspect answered the call.'

BANG!

A gunshot rang out downstairs.

O'Banyan's blood turned cold. He took his hand off the mouthpiece on his phone to speak with General Calhoon again. He wasn't sure what to say, so Calhoon said it for him.

'Goodbye Chief O'Banyan.'

Sixty Two

When Rodeo Rex arrived in Crimson County he was shattered from riding his Harley Davidson across the country. His bike was in need of a rest too, and more importantly some gas.

He liked the look of Crimson County though, recognising that it was probably a nice place to retire. There were lots of small diners, hair salons, grocery and hardware stores, and a few bars. It was the kind of place that hadn't been invaded by the corporate giants and major fast food chains. He cruised along the main road through town, keeping an eye out for a gas station, and admiring how inviting the storefronts looked.

He was running on fumes when he eventually found a gas station in the centre of town. He pulled up next to one of the pumps and filled up his bike. It wasn't cheap, but he had no other choice. When the tank was full he headed into the store to pay with cash.

There was a person behind the counter wearing a red baseball cap and blue dungarees. There were some tufts of blond hair poking out from the sides of the cap, but even so, Rex couldn't tell if it was a man or a woman. The man-lady had three chins and a big warty nose. There were tits too, but whether they were classed as boobs or moobs was anyone's guess.

'Hello there,' said Rex, approaching the counter.

'Back so soon?' said the attendant. The voice was gruff, but not deep enough to be a man's voice, or soft enough to be a woman's.

'How d'ya mean?' said Rex, counting out fifty dollars to cover the cost of the gas.

'You were in here this morning, remember?'

Rex studied the attendant's face. What the fuck was this lady-man talking about? He'd only just arrived on the island. He was about to correct the attendant on their mistake when it occurred to him that his clone, possessed by Cain, must have dropped by for gas earlier.

'You're sure it was me that came in here for gas this morning?' he asked.

'Well yeah.'

'Did I say where I was going?'

The attendant looked confused and stared at Rex like he was being stupid. 'What?'

'What's your name?' Rex demanded, losing patience.

'Jessie.' The mystery continued.

'Okay, Jessie. I've got a twin brother. If he was in here earlier, I need to know where he was going.'

Jessie pointed down the street, 'He was heading back the way you came. Leaving the island, I guess.'

'Did he say anything about where he was headed?'

'No.'

Rex's cellphone rang, which was probably a good thing because he was close to dragging Jessie over the counter, and at this point it was still possible that Jessie was a woman. He pulled his phone out of the breast pocket on his denim waistcoat. The incoming call was from Alexis Calhoon. He hadn't spoken to her for a long time, but he knew that if she was calling him it was going to be important, so he took the call.

'Hello General.'

'Rex, are you anywhere near a town called Crimson County on Blue Corn Island?'

'As a matter of fact I am. Are you calling about my doppelganger?'

'Your what?'

'I've been cloned. Is that what you're calling about?'

'Errrr, no, I'm calling because I just got a call from the Chief of the Crimson County Police Department.'

'What about? Was it about Baby?'

Calhoon's tone changed at the mention of Baby. 'No, why? What's happened to Baby?'

'She's dead. And so is Joey. They were killed on this island. That's why I'm here.'

There was a momentary silence as Calhoon took on board the information about the deaths of Joey and Baby. She had been close to both of them, and cared deeply about Baby in particular. When she finally spoke again, her response wasn't what Rex was expecting.

'That explains it then,' she said.

'Explains what?'

'Chief O'Banyan of the Crimson County Police just told me he had the Bourbon Kid in custody.'

The words hit Rex like a bucket of cold water. He closed his eyes. 'Oh no, is it bad?' he asked.

'Yeah, it's bad. Apparently the Kid killed the Chief's twin boys.'

'He killed his kids? How old were they?'

'I have no idea. And before you ask, I don't know what they did to deserve it either.'

'Probably nothing,' said Rex.

'Can you just get to the police station before the Kid kills the whole town?'

'Hang on a sec.' Rex covered the phone and looked at Jessie. 'Hey, freak, where's the police station round here?'

'Over there.'

Jessie pointed across the forecourt. Rex turned his head to see for himself. There was a building fifty yards down the street, set back from the road. It had four or five police cars parked in bays out front. Was it possible that the Bourbon Kid was in there?

That question was answered almost immediately. One of the windows on the second floor of the Police Station shattered and the body of a man, engulfed in flames and screaming in agony, came flying through it. Rex watched him land with an almighty bang on the roof of one of the police cars. The impact of the landing put an end to the screaming, but not the burning.

Rex smiled at Jessie. 'Have a nice day buddy.'

He left the gas station and continued his call with Calhoon. 'I can see the police station, but I think I might already be too late.'

'How bad is it?'

A handful of gunshots echoed out from the station, accompanied by some terrified screams. The smell of burning flesh from the dead cop on the roof of the car wafted down the road to the gas station too. All in all, it didn't look good.

'Yeah, I'd say it was pretty bad,' said Rex. 'A guy just got thrown out of a window.'

'Is he dead?'

'He's on fire.'

'Oh.'

'Hang on..... Yep...... there goes another one.'

A second police officer, engulfed in flames and screaming, flew head first out of the same window. This one wasn't so lucky. He or she landed on a stretch of concrete behind the squad car. Rex was grateful for not seeing the impact, although the sound it made was unpleasant enough.

'Oh, shit,' Calhoon groaned. 'Listen Rex, I've held off as long as I can. But I have to send a special forces unit down that way. How long before you can get off the island?'

'How long have I got?'

'At best I'd say you've got an hour. Then you're gonna see helicopters and armoured trucks all over the place. And seeing as I'm responsible for them, it would be good if you were gone when they arrive because, *y'know*, most of them have got families and stuff.'

'Understood, General. I'll do what I can.'

'Thanks, Rex.'

Sixty Three

By the time Cain arrived at *Debbie's All Night Diner* he was low on gas again. He cruised up to the front of the diner and parked his bike, expecting to see Zitrone inside.

The diner was empty and when he walked up to the front door there was a CLOSED sign in the window. He pushed the door and it opened easily, a bell chiming loudly to announce his arrival. He stepped inside and the door creaked behind him as it closed.

'Hello?' he called out.

The place was deathly quiet and neither his shout of *'Hello'*, or the creaking door had alerted anyone to his presence.

'Zitrone? Are you here?'

Still nothing.

He walked over to the counter and leaned over it. There was a mess on the floor, but nothing to get too worked up about. He was about to shout out Zitrone's name again when his cellphone rang. He took it out of his pocket and saw that the call was from Zitrone. He answered it quickly.

'Where are you?'

'Behind you.'

Cain spun around. Zitrone was nowhere to be seen.

'Where? I can't see you.'

'Look closer. I'm outside.'

Cain walked over to the windows at the front of the diner. The parking lot was filled with motorcycles, juggernauts and a solitary red transit van. He looked closer at the van and saw some movement in the front seat. Zitrone was waving at him from the driver's side. Fucking weirdo.

Cain snapped the phone shut, ending the call, and headed back out to the parking lot. Zitrone jumped out of the van to greet him.

'What the fuck are you playing at?' Cain complained.

'Look at this,' said Zitrone, as he led Cain around to the back of the van and opened the back doors. There was a group of overweight ghouls inside, perched on benches and squished against each other and the sides of the van. The males all had beards and crap T-shirts; the females were much the same apart from one dressed in pink with curly hair that looked like she was a waitress.

'Great,' said Cain sarcastically. 'You've got some out-of-shape henchmen. Well done.'

'I've also got a van.'

'Yes, I can see that.'

Zitrone tossed Cain a set of keys. 'You're driving it,' he said. 'When you get to the crossroads there's a man called Jacko who controls who gets through the secret entrance. He'll let you in, because he thinks you're Rodeo Rex. I'll hide in the back with the ghouls. If he sees us, he won't let you through, so keep conversation with him to a minimum.'

Cain hated to admit it, but it looked like Zitrone had everything planned out. 'Where do we go once we're through the crossroads?'

'Just keep driving straight until you reach Purgatory. Don't worry, it's just a bar at the roadside. Once we're there, the gateway to Hell is hidden behind the door to the Disabled toilets.'

'How do you know all this?'

'I read Jacko's mind.'

'Aaah, you're a fucking genius.'

'Yes I am,' Zitrone agreed. 'Now let's get moving. I'll ride in the passenger side until we get close to the crossroads, then I'll hide in the back with the smellies.'

Cain saw sense in the plan so he climbed into the van and started up the engine. Zitrone hopped into the passenger side and switched on the car radio. The song *Tilted* by Christine and the Queens was playing. Cain started up the engine and steered the van out onto the highway. In the rear view mirror all he could see was the miserable faces of the ghouls in the back.

'Have you got enough of those ghouls?' he asked Zitrone. 'Because they look a bit, you know, out of shape.'

'They're just fodder,' Zitrone replied. 'I figure when we get where we're going, we'll send them in first, in case Scratch has any traps set for us.'

It seemed like Zitrone had thought of everything.

'Have you spoken to Blanco and Yesil?' Cain asked. 'Because the last I heard they were still sailing to Blue Corn Island. But that was this morning. I've tried calling them this afternoon and I can't get hold of them.'

Zitrone turned up the volume on the radio and started doing some weird dance moves with his arms. 'It's okay,' he said. 'It's all arranged. I spoke to Yesil about ten minutes ago. They've just arrived on the Amish side of the island.'

'Have they still got their hearts set on killing the Bourbon Kid?'

'They have, but I told them not to worry about him for now. Seeing as we're about to unleash Hell on earth, I told them to take over Blue Corn Island and turn everyone on it into ghouls. Then they can start conquering the mainland. The Apocalypse starts now!'

Sixty Four

Walking through the Crimson County Police Station, Rex was confronted by a sight he had seen many times before. Too many times. The bodies of dozens of dead police officers were lying on the floor, and in some cases, hanging from things. Most of them had been shot, but there were a few notable exceptions. One plain-clothes cop had the handle of a knife poking out of the top of his head, its blade hidden deep inside his skull.

Rex headed up a set of stairs to the second floor. Halfway up the stairs he came across another officer whose head had been caved in. He stepped around the blood and mulch and carried on up to the top where he found another dead cop, lying next to a bright red fire extinguisher. The hose was wedged into his mouth and there was a cloud of foam around his head, much of which seemed to have seeped out of his nose and ears.

Rex stepped over the body and tried to avoid getting any foam on his boots. He pushed open a set of double doors that led into the main corridor on the second floor.

BANG!

It was lucky that Rex had good reactions. A bullet aimed at his head, deviated at the last moment, sucked in by the powerful magnet in his metal hand. The gunman who had fired at him was standing at the opposite end of the corridor. It took Rex a second to figure out who he was. He was expecting the Bourbon Kid, dressed in a long black coat with the hood pulled up. What he saw was a man in Amish clothes, his face and hair covered in blood. But it was the Bourbon Kid. That was unmistakeable. The number of dead cops piled up along the corridor was confirmation of it.

Rex held his hand up and dropped the bullet. 'Hey, it's me!' he yelled.

'I know.'

'Then why did you shoot?'

'Because it's you.'

'Yeah, but it actually is me, not my clone.'

'Clone?'

'Would you just put the gun down a minute?'

The Bourbon Kid lowered his gun. Rex took a breath and looked around. As well as the bodies piled up in the corridor, there was a broken window in one of the offices. A heavy wind was blowing through it, sending stray sheets of paper all over the corridor. Rex had seen two people thrown from the window and assumed they'd done something pretty bad, like try to stop the Kid from killing innocent people. But there was still one more cop who hadn't been killed. He was nailed to a wall behind the Bourbon Kid. He was in his late forties or early fifties. It was hard to tell because his face was so fucked up. His shirt was covered in blood too, mostly his own. If the Kid was true to form, this guy was going to get it worse than the others. The last guy always did. There was usually a reason for it, not always a good reason, but a reason nonetheless.

'Did this guy piss you off, or something?' Rex asked, approaching tentatively.

'What do you want?'

'I came here to tell you I've been cloned.'

'What the fuck are you talking about?'

'A body exactly like mine was created from my DNA. It was supposed to be for my new hand. But a demon called Cain took over the body. He used it to kill Baby. He nearly killed Jasmine and Elvis too.'

It was hard to know if the Bourbon Kid was even listening. While Rex was explaining things, the Kid picked a pack of cigarettes from the pocket of a dead cop at his feet. He took one out, stuck it between his teeth and it lit up automatically when he inhaled.

'Are you even listening to me?' Rex moaned.

The only response to that question came from the cop nailed to the wall. He looked at Rex with pleading eyes as the Bourbon Kid smoked his cigarette. He was sobbing and mumbling something that Rex couldn't make out because he was too far away.

'Is that Chief O'Banyan?' Rex asked.

The Kid took his cigarette from his mouth and blew out a smoke ring. 'Yeah. You know him?'

'No, I don't, but I just spoke with Alexis Calhoon. She said he called her office earlier.' Rex picked up a strong scent of gasoline. 'Is that gas?'

The Kid said nothing, but he turned to face Chief O'Banyan, who was mumbling something to him. The police chief was pleading for his life, but his face was so fucked up, nothing he said came out clearly.

'You don't have to kill him, you know!' Rex pleaded on O'Banyan's behalf.

The Kid either didn't hear him or didn't care. He flicked his cigarette up in the air and walked clear of the pool of gasoline at O'Banyan's feet. Rex watched as the cigarette dropped towards the accelerant. Eventually it landed and the puddle burst into flames. The fire whooshed upwards and engulfed Chief O'Banyan who began screaming hysterically as his clothes and skin caught fire and peeled away.

'Was that really necessary?' Rex groaned as the Kid walked up to him.

The Bourbon Kid lit up another cigarette and nodded over Rex's shoulder.

'Jasmine's here.'

Rex turned around and saw Jasmine in her purple catsuit, pointing a gun at him. 'Get away from him. He's been cloned!' she yelled.

'It's okay,' said Rex, raising his hands in the air. 'It's me, look!' He pointed at the glove on his right hand.

'Take it off. I wanna see your creepy metal hand.'

Rex reached across with his other hand and peeled his leather glove off, revealing his metal hand to prove he wasn't the clone.

Jasmine stared at the hand and winced. 'Ooh, creepy,' she said, lowering her gun. 'I can't believe you jerk off with that thing.'

Rex put his hands down and was about to tell her to fuck off, when Sanchez appeared alongside her. Climbing the stairs had left him exhausted, so he leaned on Jasmine's shoulder and tried to catch his breath. He was wearing a ridiculous pair of mirrored sunglasses and a pair of jeans with a black sweatshirt and jacket.

'What's going on?' said Rex. 'How did you know we were here?'

'The burning corpses outside was our first clue,' said Sanchez.

'No, dumbass,' said Rex. 'I mean, why were you even outside? I thought you were waiting at the church for me?'

Jasmine stared right past him. Chief O'Banyan's cries were becoming fainter and intermittent, but he was still cooking away back there. 'Why is that guy on fire?' she asked. Before Rex could explain to her what had happened she moved onto another question, this time aimed at the Bourbon Kid. 'Is that a new product in your hair?'

The Bourbon Kid thumbed over his shoulder at the burning man. 'It's the blood of that guy's family.'

Rex was growing impatient. 'We need to get moving,' he said. 'There's Special Forces people on their way here right now.'

'Fuck the Special Forces people,' Jasmine said dismissively. 'We've got to get back to Purgatory, because that's where Cain is headed. One of the Horsemen has found the secret entrance at the crossroads.'

'Damn, I'm way out of touch,' Rex admitted. 'Did you find that Brutus Dagger? Because if you didn't--'

'I've got it,' said Sanchez. He reached inside his jacket and pulled out a shiny golden dagger, which he held up for Rex to see.

Rex was gobsmacked. 'Holy shit! How did you find it? People have been searching for that for centuries.'

'We'll tell you later,' said Jasmine shuddering. 'Right now we need to get moving.'

The wall behind Rex was now completely engulfed in flames. What was left of Chief O'Banyan was shrivelling and turning black.

Rex beckoned Sanchez towards him. 'You'd better give me that dagger before you stab yourself with it. If someone's gonna use it to kill Cain, I want it to be me.'

Sanchez held out the dagger for him, but before Rex had a chance to take it, his cellphone rang again. It was another call from Alexis Calhoon.

'Hang on a sec,' he said, waving Sanchez away again. He took the call from Calhoon. 'Hey General, we're on our way out of Crimson County now.'

'That's not what I'm calling about,' said Calhoon. 'I've just heard that there's an old fashioned wooden pirate ship docking on the Oakfield side of Blue Corn Island at the moment. Is that anything to do with you?'

'A pirate ship? Why the fuck would an old pirate ship have anything to do with us?'

'I have no idea. But we've had reports of a pirate ship hijacking boats all along the coast. I just thought it might be something you would know about, seeing as how it's sailed to the island you're on.'

The sound of the ceiling beginning to collapse caught Rex's attention. 'General, we've got bigger problems right now. Proper end of the world stuff. Plus a fire.'

'A fire? What the hell is going—'

Rex talked over her. 'So I suggest you get your special forces people to check it out when they get here.'

He hung up the phone. 'We really need to get out of here, guys. This place is burning up faster than Michael Jackson's hair.'

Rex turned to leave, assuming the others would follow. But The Bourbon Kid tapped him on the shoulder. 'What was that about a pirate ship?'

'Calhoon says there's one just docked on the Amish side of the island. Now come on, let's get moving.'

Jasmine's eyes lit up suddenly. 'Oh shit, I just remembered something!' She turned to the Bourbon Kid. 'I was meant to tell you, your friend Beth is at the church in Oakfield. She's waiting there for you.'

'What the fuck is she doing there?'

'Me and Sanchez were trapped underground. Scratch sent her to get us out. She seems really nice.'

The Kid headed straight for the stairs, so Rex grabbed him. 'I'm all for us getting out of here right now. But you can't go after her. You've gotta come with us.'

The Kid pulled a gun from the back of his pants and pointed it at Rex's face.

Rex backed off. 'Scratch will go fucking crazy if you don't come with us.'

'Fuck Scratch.'

'We're talking about the end of the world here,' Rex reminded him. He looked up at the ceiling beams now groaning and cracking. 'And the end of us, if we don't get the fuck out of here. Now.'

The Kid tucked his gun back into his pants. 'I don't care, I'm going to Oakfield.'

Rex watched the Kid turn away and leave. There was no reasoning with him when his mind was made up about something, but at least he was leaving. Which is what the rest of them needed to do as well.

Jasmine called after the Kid. 'Good luck!'

'Scratch is gonna kill him,' Rex grumbled.

'He's gonna kill us too if we don't get moving,' Jasmine pointed out.

'You're absolutely right. Let's get outta here.'

Jasmine looked around. Her face was a mask of confusion, which was nothing unusual. 'Rex,' she said.

'Yeah.'

'Where did Sanchez go?'

Sixty Five

The Holy Church of St Susan filled up very quickly. The entire Amish community arrived for their afternoon mass, only for each of them to be confronted by the news that Bishop Yoder was dead and that Beth had killed him. To Beth's great annoyance, every time she attempted to explain what had really happened, another family would arrive and someone, usually Abram Wittmer, would inform them that Beth had murdered the Bishop. Everyone seemed to want to take a look at the Bishop's corpse too, and they all took their kids to see it as well, which seemed a little weird. Beth was starting to think that Sanchez might have been right. Maybe Amish people were assholes.

Practically the last person to show up for afternoon mass was the village doctor, Elmer Miller. After attempting to resuscitate the Bishop using every known method, he eventually stood up and declared that Yoder was dead, which was fucking obvious anyway, but the entire Amish community let out a gasp of shock when he announced it.

So Beth ended up sitting on a chair, surrounded by the entire population of the Amish village, all of whom were convinced she was the killer, simply because they'd heard it from someone else when they arrived. Rumour and speculation had rapidly become trial by gossip.

With the Bishop dead, Dr Miller had by default become the most respected person in the village, and was therefore expected to pass judgement on Beth. The doctor was a bald man in his fifties with the longest grey beard in the village and a pair of round spectacles with thin wiry frames. The other villagers gathered behind him, peering over each other's shoulders to get a better look at the woman they believed to be Yoder's killer.

'Okay, young lady,' said Dr Miller, looming over her. 'Why don't you tell us all why you killed him?'

Beth tried to remain calm and keep a lid on her frustration. 'Like I tried to tell everyone before,' she said, 'he was killed by a man called Cain.'

'A man called Cain,' Dr Miller scoffed. 'And where is this *Cain?*' he said, using his fingers to put the word *Cain* in air quotes.

'This might sound a little crazy,' said Beth. 'But, he's not really a man, he's a demon in a man's body.'

There were more gasps from the Amish people followed by a lot of muttering. Dr Miller waited for it all to quiet down and then continued his patronising interrogation of Beth.

'Who exactly are you *Miss?*' he asked, putting the word *Miss* into air quotes this time, which was annoying because it was stupid and he clearly didn't know how to use the air quotes properly. Not that anyone should ever use them, in Beth's opinion.

'My name is Beth,' she replied, keeping calm.

'And how did you come to be in our church?'

'I was sent here.'

'By whom?'

That was a tough question to answer. Beth didn't like telling lies but if she told them she'd been sent by the Devil, it would probably confuse matters even further. She remembered Annabel's advice to her before she left Purgatory.

'I was sent by God,' she said, expecting an abundance of gasps from the Amish people. To her surprise no one batted an eyelid.

'And how did *God* send you here?' Dr Miller asked, with the obligatory use of air quotes. 'Or did you in fact come here with the *other woman* and the *fat man* on the motorbike?'

Beth was desperate to berate him for the air quote abuse, but now really wasn't the time. 'Well, yes I was with them,' she admitted, 'but I came looking for a friend of mine named JD. He's here on the island somewhere, I think.'

'You'll excuse me if I find your story a little hard to believe,' said Dr Miller. 'I think this is a case for the police in Crimson County.'

A lot of nodding and murmurs of approval came from the crowd. But then before anyone could carry out a citizen's arrest on Beth, another Amish woman ran into the church. She was clearly distressed.

'Where's Bishop Yoder?' she screamed.

Everyone pointed at Beth and Dr Miller delivered the verdict.

'This woman killed him,' he said. 'We're going to take her to the police in Crimson County.'

'Oh God no, don't do that!' the woman pleaded. Something had her really spooked. 'Something terrible has happened in Crimson County!'

'Worse than the Bishop's murder?' said Dr Miller, his voice filled with disdain.

'Yes, much worse.'

A woman from within the crowd spoke up. 'What's happened Agnes?'

Agnes looked around, addressing the entire congregation. 'Yesterday, my son Thomas and I, we found a man by the roadside. He was almost dead, but being good Samaritans we took him in and gave him a bed for the night. He had holes in the palms of his hands.'

Her revelation didn't generate any kind of reaction from her audience, other than confused looks.

'*Holes?*' Dr Miller jeered, using his air quotes for the first time in a while. 'What do you mean *holes?*'

'Holes, you know? Holes, like he'd been crucified. And when we asked him who he was, he said he was Christ!'

That particular update brought about the biggest gasp of shock so far. So many people gasped in unison, that they nearly sucked the air out of the church.

It was the sort of news Beth was looking for. Even though the odd description didn't exactly match JD, the fact that Agnes was talking about a stranger meant it could be him.

'What did he look like?' Beth asked.

Agnes threw a quizzical look at Beth. 'Who is this?'

'She killed Bishop Yoder,' said Dr Miller.

'I did not!' said Beth. She looked at Agnes with pleading eyes. 'My name is Beth and I'm looking for a man named JD. This man you found, was his name JD?'

Agnes looked surprised. 'Yes, he asked us to call him JD. Do you know what it means?'

Beth nodded. 'I do. He's a friend of mine.'

To Beth's surprise Agnes started backing away from her, wagging a finger at her like a crazy woman. 'She's with him,' Agnes shrieked. 'She's the Devil!'

'AHA!' said Dr Miller, gleefully. 'So you *did* kill the Bishop!'

'What? No.'

Agnes grabbed Dr Miller by his arm and continued wagging her finger at Beth. 'This man, JD, *her friend*, he's just murdered Chief O'Banyan's boys! He killed them in cold blood. The folks over there are going crazy. They think he's one of us. They're coming here now, for retribution!'

The Amish folk began muttering among themselves again. The mood turned very dark and people began to panic. It took a loud shout from Dr Miller to shut them all up.

'Everybody calm down!' he said. 'When the Crimson Police get here, we can hand this *woman* over to them. She's not one of us. They'll understand that we're not to blame.'

Beth finally snapped. 'WOULD YOU ALL SHUT UP AND LISTEN FOR GOD'S SAKE? I DIDN'T KILL ANYONE!'

'She's a liar too!' Dr Miller proclaimed.

That set the Amish folk into a frenzy. A lot of them started shouting names at Beth like "*Blasphemer, Harlot, Murderer and Schijtluis*". Beth had no idea what a Schijtluis was, but it didn't sound like a compliment.

'LISTEN A MINUTE!' she yelled over the din.

To her surprise the place went quiet very quickly with the exception of one woman who shouted out *"Whore!"* just after everyone else had shut up.

Beth directed her questioning at Agnes. 'You said that JD was practically dead when you found him?'

'Yes.'

'But I'll bet, overnight, all his injuries healed, yes?'

'Yes, that's right, they did.'

'Right. That's because he has the blood of God in his veins. He travels the world fighting evil. He's come here to help your village.'

The Amish people looked at each other. Something Beth had said seemed to resonate with them. But then typically, just when it looked like she was getting through to them, a teenage boy burst into the church. He was panting heavily and struggling for breath.

'EVERYBODY COME QUICK!' he shouted. 'SOMETHING'S HAPPENING!'

Agnes rebuked him. 'Thomas, where are your manners? We're in the middle of something.'

'But mother, a ship has docked by the shore below the cliff. Hundreds of strange looking men are heading this way. Some of them have got swords and knives.'

Beth knew what that meant. 'Was it a wooden galley ship?' she asked.

Thomas made his way through the crowd of villagers to find the person who had asked the question. When he saw Beth he looked around at the others. 'Who's she?' he asked.

Thomas was then inundated with people telling him that Beth was the person who had killed Bishop Yoder, and that she was also a blasphemer, a harlot and a schijtluis too.

But when Beth stood up, everyone went quiet. Quite a few people backed away too. Her new reputation as a killer had made them afraid of her. She leaned down to Thomas's eye level.

'Tell me about these men with the swords and knives. Were they a strange green colour?'

'Yes!'

Beth raised her voice so that everyone could hear. 'Okay, everybody listen to me. These things coming off the ship, they're not human, they're ghouls. They've come here to kill us all!'

Sixty Six

Elvis had dozed off to sleep on one of the sofas at the back of the bar room in Purgatory. His sleep had been punctuated by the occasional bickering between Scratch and the Mystic Lady. Annabel was using her crystal ball to try and see what everyone was up to, and what the future held. But she was annoying Scratch by shouting things like *"I see something"* only to then follow it up with *"oh no, wait, it's nothing"*. In return he was calling her all sorts of names, in all sorts of languages.

So all the bickering, coupled with having a broken leg, meant that Elvis didn't get much in the way of sleep. And he was woken up entirely when someone sat down next to him and started rubbing his ankle. He opened his eyes and saw the culprit was Flake. She still had the blood-stained bandage around her neck but she looked surprisingly healthy, considering what she'd been through.

'Don't make any sudden movements,' she said.

'Why? What are you doing?'

'Fixing up your leg.'

Flake had a green First Aid box on her lap, and a bottle of vodka. There was also a wooden crutch on the floor beside her. She put the vodka and the First Aid kit on a small round table next to the sofa.

'Where did you find all this stuff?' Elvis asked.

'It was in Sanchez's ambulance. He keeps a lot of medical stuff in there in case the cops pull him over. It backs up his claim that he's a private ambulance service.'

Elvis knew exactly what medication he needed. 'I don't know about all the other stuff,' he said. 'But I'll take some of that vodka for the pain.'

Flake opened the first aid kit and pulled out a bottle of ointment and a roll of bandage. The only other thing inside the box was a gun.

'You're not planning on shooting my foot off, are you?' Elvis quipped.

Flake picked the gun out of the box and handed it to him. 'Don't be a dick. Just take it.'

Elvis recognised the gun. 'This is the Bourbon Kid's.'

'Yeah, he left it in the ambulance. Okay this might hurt.'

She yanked Elvis's shoe off.

'OWWWW! FUUUUCK!'

He was tempted to point the gun at her and warn her not to do shit like that, but he recognised that it might be a slight overreaction, so he gritted his teeth and let her get on with it, while he familiarised himself with the Bourbon Kid's gun. He'd seen the Kid use it many times, but he'd never actually held it himself. It was twice as heavy as his own Desert Eagle pistol, which was lost somewhere on the set of the recently axed *Planet of the Apes* TV show.

Flake pulled his sock off and started rubbing ointment onto the swollen part of his ankle and foot.

'I haven't had a chance to wash my feet this week,' Elvis said apologetically.

'Yeah, no shit.'

He was enjoying the foot massage more than he'd expected. 'You're good at this,' he remarked.

'I get a lot of practise.'

It wasn't lost on Elvis that Sanchez was a very lucky guy. Flake was a real catch, way out of Sanchez's league. The bloodied bandage around her neck was evidence of how tough she was too. And she was dressed like a cop. Female cops were hot.

'Looks like you lost a lot of blood,' Elvis said.

'Yeah. Thought I was done for.'

'What's that big lump?'

Flake touched the lump on her neck. 'That's what kept me alive.'

'What is it?'

Scratch shouted from the other side of the room. 'It's a medical pressure plug!'

Elvis frowned. 'A what?'

Scratch yelled at him again. 'Elvis get your ass over here, NOW!'

'I've got a broken leg you know!'

'I don't care.'

Flake stepped away so that Elvis was able to roll himself into a sitting position. She handed him the wooden crutch and helped him to his feet. He wedged the crutch under his armpit and hobbled over to join Scratch and Annabel at their table near the entrance. Annabel was peering into her ball, while Scratch was pacing around next to the table.

'What's the matter?' Elvis asked as he approached.

Scratch looked worried, which was a rare sight. 'Annabel has had a vision of the future,' he said. 'She's seen Cain and Zitrone here in Purgatory.'

'Bullshit,' said Elvis. 'Jacko would never let them through the crossroads.'

'That's right,' Scratch agreed. 'But Annabel is certain they've found a way in.'

Elvis tried to play out the scenario in his head. Jacko was smart and would never let any unauthorised parties onto the secret road to Purgatory. Unless…..

Elvis prodded Scratch with the toe of his crutch. 'Hang on a minute. You have *told* Jacko not to let Cain in, haven't you?'

'What?'

'You know what I mean. You've told Jacko that there's an evil clone of Rex trying to get into Purgatory, haven't you?'

Scratch's eyes shifted one way, then the other as if he was watching a game of invisible tennis. Eventually he stopped and stared up at Elvis, his eyes filled with horror.

'I thought you and Jasmine told him when you came through earlier!'

'Well we didn't.'

Scratch turned his rage on Annabel. 'This is your fucking fault! Where was your bloody sixth sense on this one, eh?'

'How is it my fault?' Annabel complained, folding her arms.

'BECAUSE IT CAN'T BE MY FAULT!'

Elvis clicked his fingers at Annabel. 'Have we got time to warn Jacko?'

She shook her head.

Elvis prodded Scratch with his wooden crutch again. 'I told you we needed a phone network here. All we'd have to do is phone Jacko. Then the whole problem would be....'

'SHUT UP!'

When Scratch lost his temper, it wasn't a pretty sight. His face turned red and contorted. Elvis knew it was time to back off. Unlike Annabel who seemed to enjoy getting on the boss's nerves.

'You know you brought this on yourself?' she said.

'I KNOWWWWWWW!'

Scratch was ready to explode, and it didn't help matters when from the far end of the bar, someone whistled loudly. It stopped the bickering, and they all turned around to see Flake leaning against a window, staring out into the desert.

Scratch roared at her. 'WHAT THE FUCK ARE YOU WHISTLING AT?'

Flake turned away from the window and addressed the room. 'Would you lot just shut up for a minute,' she said. 'This is a time for a cool head. And none of you has one.'

Scratch looked like he was going to charge at her, so Elvis stuck his crutch out in front of him, blocking off his attack route.

'Hey, just listen to what she's gotta say,' Elvis suggested.

'Go on then,' said Scratch. 'But make it quick, because in about ten minutes time, the whole fucking world is going to end!'

'Calm down,' said Flake, in a manner Elvis feared might get her killed. 'Now listen, I've lived my whole life in Santa Mondega, the city that for years was the home of the undead. And I work in The Tapioca, the roughest, shittiest bar in the world. If you wanna know how we're gonna survive this, then you should be listening to me. I'm overqualified for this kind of shit.'

Scratch was burning up red again. Elvis could feel the heat coming off him.

'Quit bragging and just tell us your plan, *you dumb bitch!*' Scratch seethed.

Flake ignored the insults and spoke to the Mystic Lady instead. 'Annabel, is Sanchez still at the Police Station with Rex and Jasmine?'

Annabel nodded. 'He was a minute ago. But they're about to leave. They're heading back here.'

'Okay, good.' She pointed at Scratch. '*You*, can you make the Men's toilets connect through to the toilets at the Crimson County Police Station?'

Scratch answered abruptly. 'I can.'

'Great, then we can open the door and bring Sanchez and the others back through it.'

Scratch snatched Elvis's crutch away from him and threw it across the room at Flake. It missed her by a matter of inches, but she didn't even flinch, which probably annoyed him even more than missing her with the crutch.

'You imbecile!' he hissed. 'That won't work because as soon as you step through the door, the portal closes up. It's a security measure to make sure no random members of the public come wandering in here. If you go through it, all that will happen is you'll be stuck in Crimson County with the others.'

'What if I don't walk through it?' Flake suggested. 'I could stay on this side of the door and hold it open for Sanchez.'

Scratch looked like he was going to pass out. 'MORON!' he yelled. 'Sanchez would have to be using the toilet at the exact time you open the portal!'

'Well if we hurry, we'll catch him,' Flake replied.

She looked very confident about what she was saying. And after giving it a little thought, Elvis agreed with her.

'She's right,' he said. 'If they're about to leave the police station to drive back here with the dagger, it'll take them at least four hours.'

'Exactly,' said Flake, winking at Elvis. 'And Sanchez cannot go four hours without taking a piss.'

'Or a dump,' said Annabel.

'That's right.' Flake walked over to the Men's toilets. 'I know Sanchez better than anyone, and I'm telling you there's no way he's going on a road trip without taking a piss first.'

Scratch still wasn't entirely convinced. He snapped at Annabel. 'Is she right? Is he in the toilets? And don't guess. If you lie to me, I'll know.'

Annabel waved her hands over the crystal ball and stared into it. After a few seconds she winced and recoiled as if she'd seen something horrible. Then she looked up and made eye contact with Scratch.

'He's in the toilet right now. You'd better hurry.'

Sixty Seven

Not everyone in the Amish community was convinced by Beth's claim that the green creatures heading their way were ghouls. There was a great deal of panic in the church, with lots of raised voices but very little action. It was incredibly frustrating, knowing what was about to happen but being ignored while everyone else debated what to do. While the arguments raged, Beth was left completely on her own. She could have slipped out and no one would have noticed. But that would mean that the villagers would be left at the mercy of the ghouls. Her concern for them overrode her fears for herself.

The one person she felt she could reason with was the young boy who had seen the ghouls. When no one was looking she grabbed him by the arm.

'What's your name again?' she asked him.

'Thomas. I'm Thomas.'

'Okay, Thomas, at the far end of the church, just past the altar is a secret staircase that leads down to a safe place.'

'Really?'

'Yes, I opened it just now. So, you need to help me convince everyone to go down there and hide.'

Thomas looked like he doubted what she was saying. 'There's no staircase over there,' he said.

'God sent me here to open it for you, so that the village could hide down there when the ghouls came. Please help me guide everyone to safety.'

Thomas turned away from her and stared at the altar. 'Can you show me this staircase?' he asked.

'Yes, come on.'

Beth took his hand and led him down the aisle towards the secret staircase. The villagers paid no attention, but it didn't go unnoticed by Thomas's mother, Agnes.

'Hey, where are you going?' she called after them.

'Mother, come quick!' Thomas shouted.

Agnes dashed after them. By the time she caught up with them, the staircase was close enough for Beth to point it out.

'Look!' Beth cried, pointing at the floor. 'There's a secret staircase. You can all hide down there until the ghouls are gone.'

Agnes stared down the staircase. 'Where did this come from?' she asked.

'I opened it,' Beth replied. 'God sent me here to save you from the ghouls. You must hide down there, or at the very least, send the children down there. I've seen these ghouls before, they're vicious and they eat people.'

'But you said you were with JD?'

'I am. He's a good man, I promise.'

Agnes didn't look convinced. 'Then why did he kill the O'Banyan boys? All they did was bully my son. I didn't want them dead.'

There was no easy way to answer that question, and more importantly, there wasn't time, so Beth did what any priest would do in the same circumstances. She offered a conciliatory smile and said, 'The Lord works in mysterious ways.'

A man's voice from the entrance to the church shouted. 'IT'S TRUE! THEY'RE COMING THIS WAY! THEY'RE NOT HUMAN!'

That was followed by several other people shouting things like, 'RUN FOR YOUR LIVES!' and, 'GOD HELP US!'

And then Agnes shouted, 'THIS WAY, THE LORD HAS SHOWN US A WAY OUT!'

To begin with only a handful of people ran over to see what Agnes was shouting about. But when they saw the staircase and Agnes assured them God had put it there for them, people started piling down it and calling others to join them. Beth and Agnes stood on either side of the staircase waving people down it. And the Amish were well organised. The women and children headed down the stairs while the men set about piling items of furniture up against the front doors.

Everything was going well until a young girl aged no more than six or seven years old stopped at the top of the stairs and refused to go down. She cried hysterically because she couldn't find her parents. Beth felt great sympathy for her, but at the same time the girl was holding everyone up. Eventually, Agnes grabbed the girl and carried her down the stairs. Not for the first time that day, Beth thought of Sanchez and how useful he could be in a scenario like this. He would have had no qualms about pushing the little girl down the stairs to speed things up.

Beth shouted down to Agnes. 'Once everyone is down there I'll close the entrance up until the ghouls have gone.'

Agnes shouted something back but Beth didn't hear it. The sound of the ghouls arriving at the front entrance drowned out everything else. And the panic levels in the church went up tenfold.

A swarm of bloodthirsty green faces appeared at the windows at the front of the church, looking for ways in. Others banged on the front doors trying to break them open. With every bang against the doors, it became evident that there were more and more ghouls arriving. The hinges of the doors creaked under the strain. At least fifty Amish men stood together in a group behind the front doors, ready to fight whatever came through. And one thing was certain, those ghouls were coming through, sooner rather than later.

The last of the women rushed past Beth and headed down the stairs. It left Beth with the responsibility of closing up the secret entrance. So despite being terrified herself, she pressed the D in the wall and closed up the staircase.

CRASH!

A large window next to the front doors shattered into a million tiny pieces. A huge black horse leapt through the window and landed in the middle of a group of the Amish men. The rider of the horse was a man with bright white hair, wearing a white tunic, with a sword hanging at his side.

The shock took the Amish men completely by surprise. While they were shielding themselves from the flying shards of glass, the Horseman drew his sword and cut the head off the nearest man. And that was just the beginning. Ghouls swarmed in through the broken window and clambered over one another in their eagerness to start biting chunks out of the Amish men.

Beth had to think fast and find a place to hide. She dashed over to the wooden pulpit that the Bishop read his sermons from, and ducked down behind it. She knew it wouldn't keep her hidden for long. The ghouls were storming through the church and it was only a matter of time before they spotted her.

Sixty Eight

Flake pushed open the door of the Men's toilets in Purgatory. She wedged her foot against it and looked around, hoping to see Sanchez. On the other side of the door was a large washroom. Along the left wall was a row of washbasins. Further back at the far end was a door next to a row of four urinals, but there was no sign of Sanchez. However, there was an ungodly aroma coming from a row of stalls on the right. It wafted through the open door into Purgatory and made its way around the bar.

Scratch was standing behind Flake, looking over her shoulder. 'Holy crap!' he groaned, covering his mouth and nose with his hand. 'What is that smell?'

'Are you sure this is the right place?' Flake asked.

'Yes, this is definitely it,' said Scratch. 'But where's Sanchez? You said he'd be in here. So where the fuck is he?'

There were a number of groans and grumbles coming from within the bar. Elvis and the Mystic Lady were watching from stools at the bar, and both of them had caught a waft of the stench coming through the portal. But Flake was familiar with this particular foul smell. The bathroom above The Tapioca smelt like it every morning at around eight o'clock.

'I think we're too late,' she said. 'It smells like he's been and gone.'

'It smells like he's died,' Elvis quipped.

But just when it looked like all hope was lost, someone flushed a toilet in one of the stalls. It was like music to Flake's ears. Sanchez walked out of the third stall. Unaware that he had an audience, he sniffed his fingers and paused for a moment, before nodding like he was pleased about something.

Flake called out to him. 'Sanchez!'

The sound of her voice startled him and he looked in every possible direction before he eventually spotted her standing in the opening from Purgatory.

'Come here, quick!' said Flake, beckoning him towards her.

'Are you dead?' Sanchez asked.

'No. I'm in Purgatory. Quick we need the Brutus Dagger. Have you got it?'

Sanchez patted himself down and looked around on the floor, before finally taking a deep breath and remembering where it was.

'I left it in the shitter,' he said. 'Took my jacket off and hung it on the door.'

Scratch leaned around Flake and yelled at him. 'So go and get it you moron!'

Flake elbowed Scratch in the ribs and he stepped back, muttering to himself. Sanchez returned to the stall and came back out with his jacket. He pulled a shiny golden dagger out from the inside pocket.

'Here it is,' he said.

'Wash your hands,' said Flake. 'Then bring it over here.'

Sanchez put the dagger down and started washing his hands. 'You look a lot better,' he said to Flake. 'How are you feeling?'

'Not bad, my clothes still smell of piss though.'

Scratch lost patience and shoved Flake aside again, almost knocking her through the door into the washroom. 'FOR FUCKSSAKE!' he yelled. 'The fucking world is gonna end in a minute. Get your stupid ass in here now!'

Sanchez turned off the tap and shook his hands dry over the sink. 'There's no need to be snippy,' he said. 'I just have to dry my hands.'

Scratch responded by hurling some extreme insults and vile death threats at Sanchez. The insults were drowned out by the roar of a hand-dryer as Sanchez dried his hands, all the while looking over at Scratch with one eyebrow raised.

Flake elbowed Scratch in the ribs again. 'I told you to let me handle this,' she said. 'Now look what you've done!'

'Me?'

'Yes, you.'

Scratch turned and walked away, cursing under his breath. When the hand dryer finally stopped, Sanchez rubbed his hands together one more time and walked over to Flake.

Flake spoke softly so that Scratch wouldn't be able to hear. 'You've left the dagger by the sink.'

'I heard that!' yelled Scratch.

Before Sanchez could retrieve the dagger, the door in the wall behind him flew open and Jasmine walked into the washroom looking for him. She immediately covered her mouth and nose with her hands.

'What the fuck is that!' she cried.

Rex walked in behind her and recoiled in disgust. 'Who's done this to us!' he demanded.

'Quick,' Flake yelled at them. 'Over here! Come through the portal. And somebody bring that fucking dagger!'

Sixty Nine

What have I done?

The question repeated itself over and over in Beth's head. From her hiding place behind the pulpit she watched the Amish men fight in vain against both the swarm of ghouls streaming into the church and the white-haired Horseman cutting down any man he could reach with his sword.

What do I do now?

Where do I go?

'This way! Follow me!'

It was exactly the answer she was hoping for. She looked over to where the voice had come from. Thomas, the young Amish boy was poking his head around a door at the side of the altar.

He waved her over. 'Come on. In here.'

Beth had no other alternatives. She leapt to her feet and darted over to the door. Thomas pulled it open for her and then slammed it shut as soon as she was inside. He stood with his back against the door, his face pale and panicked.

'This is Yoder's private quarters,' he said. 'We can hide upstairs.'

The room they were in was a small office with walls made up of bookshelves. There was an open door in the corner of the room with a staircase behind it leading up to what Beth assumed was the Bishop's home. Beth needed a weapon, but the only thing in Yoder's office was a desk and two functional wooden chairs. The desk was devoid of anything useful. Other than a stack of magazines about choirboys, a few file folders and some books, there wasn't a weapon in sight.

'Can you see any keys?' Thomas asked.

Beth ran over to the desk and started rifling through the drawers looking for any keys to lock the door. While she searched she had some questions for Thomas. 'Why are you here?' she asked him. 'Why didn't you go down with the others?'

Thomas opened his mouth to respond but before he could speak, a ghoul forced open the door behind him. Thomas leaned back against it with all his might, but the ghoul was pushing hard, and growling like a wild animal.

Beth ran over to help him. She slammed her shoulder against the door. Between them, they forced it shut again. Beth was in an unusual position, in that for once she was the responsible adult who had to make life-saving decisions. She looked around the room and her eyes settled on one of the wooden chairs that could be used as a doorstop. More ghouls were pounding on the other side of the door, so she stuck out a leg and hooked the chair towards her. She grabbed the back of it and stuck it underneath the door handle, with the chair at an angle.

There had to be at least three ghouls pounding on the other side of the door, rattling the handle and trying to get through.

Beth pushed Thomas towards the staircase in the corner of the room. 'Go, upstairs. Go!' she shouted.

Thomas dashed across the room and sprinted up the stairs. Beth raced up behind him. She was halfway up the stairs when she heard the chair she'd used as a doorstop snap in half. A group of ghouls burst into Yoder's office and headed for the stairs.

When Beth reached the top she glanced back down and saw three ghouls at the bottom, fighting with each other to get onto the stairs.

'In here!' Thomas yelled.

They both scurried through a door on the landing that led into the Bishop's bedroom. It was a decent sized room with one window overlooking the fields that led up to the Black Forest. Beneath the window was a chest of drawers. There was a single bed up against the far wall. Beth pushed Thomas towards the bed.

'Hide under the bed!' she cried. 'I'll hold the door shut.'

She closed the door and sat on the floor, pressing her back up against it. To her surprise, Thomas slid across the shaggy blue carpet and joined her by her side, pressing his back against the door too.

THUD!

The door shook from the impact of a ghoul slamming into the other side. It shook again as another ghoul joined in. A third shudder was more than Beth and Thomas could withstand. The door came open just a little bit, and even though they pushed back harder than ever, it continued edging open.

A green hand reached around the door and grasped at Beth's arm. She looked despairingly at Thomas.

'Go, hide!' she said. 'I'll fight them off.'

She pushed him away towards the bed and twisted herself around into a crouching position, facing the clawed hand that was reaching around the door. As soon as Thomas rolled underneath the bed, the door flew open and Beth staggered back into the centre of the room. Three ghouls fell into the room and scrambled to their feet, all with the aim of sinking their teeth into Beth.

The only thing available to use as a weapon was a beard comb on the Bishop's chest of drawers. Beth grabbed it and held it out in front of her, hoping that maybe she could poke an eye out with it.

Two of the ghouls charged at her. The third spotted Thomas underneath the bed and dived down to try to get to him.

Beth swung the beard comb at the nearest ghoul. The ghoul was a heavy set male that was more than a match for her. It swatted the comb out of her hand and pounced on her, knocking her back against the chest of drawers. Beth wrestled with the ghoul, but it was too strong. It pinned her against the drawers and pushed its face into hers. It opened its mouth wide, revealing a set of grotesque yellow teeth. Beth leaned as far back from it as she could.

But then the ghoul froze. It let go of Beth and stepped back. The other two turned tail and ran out of the room, bounding down the stairs. The ghoul that had been so close to biting a chunk out of Beth's face took one last look at her, then it too raced out of the room.

Thomas poked his head out from under the bed. 'What's that noise?' he asked.

Beth hadn't noticed it, what with her life flashing before her eyes and all that. But there was a loud horn blowing somewhere outside. The ghouls, as if hypnotised by it, were fleeing the church in their droves, heading towards the source of the noise.

Beth checked her neck and looked down at her arms and legs. There wasn't a scratch on her. Thomas crawled out from under the bed and started doing the same thing.

Beth ran over to the door and closed it. She took some deep breaths to compose herself. What was happening? Why had the ghouls fled? And who was blowing the horn?

Thomas rushed over to the window and looked out. 'It's a bugle,' he said.

Beth recognised the sound of the horn. It was the same sound she had heard coming from the ship filled with ghouls that had docked in Santa Mondega. One of the Four Horsemen blew on the horn to instruct the ghouls.

'Look, they're leaving,' said Thomas, pointing out of the window.

Beth joined him at the window to watch. All of the ghouls were streaming out of the front of the church and sprinting up the hill towards the Black Forest. Blanco, the white-haired Horseman was riding through the middle of them.

The source of the blowing horn was further up the hill. Yesil the green-haired Horseman was sitting on a black horse, blowing hard into a bugle. Blanco and the ghouls were rushing towards the low-pitched sound, drawn to it like moths to a flame. At least, that's how it looked at first. But when the first group of ghouls reached the green-haired Horseman they ran straight past and carried on up the hill. That was when Beth spotted the third horse.

A grey horse was galloping up the hill towards the forest. The rider was a man wearing Amish clothes.

'Look!' said Thomas. 'It's JD. He's leading them away!'

Beth grabbed Thomas's shoulders and squeezed them tight as she watched JD ride the grey horse up the hill. He had a good head start over the ghouls. But they were gaining fast.

When all of the ghouls were out of the church, Yesil stopped blowing into the bugle. Blanco caught up and then the two of them rode up the hill together. They were accomplished riders and they galloped up the hill at twice the speed of JD's grey horse. A hundred or more ghouls sprinted after them, baying for blood

Beth felt her knees go weak. She steadied herself by squeezing Thomas's shoulders even harder.

'They're catching him!' said Thomas.

He was right. But when they were less than three horse-lengths behind him, JD rode into The Black Forest and vanished from view. The two Horsemen charged in behind him with the army of ghouls following close behind.

Seventy

'The crossroads is right ahead. Keep quiet back there. Don't make a fucking sound.'

Cain trusted Zitrone not to make a noise but the tubby gang of ghouls was another matter. Throughout the journey from *Debbie's All Night Diner* to the crossroads they had been making all manner of growling and gurgling noises, as well as a ridiculous amount of banging because the dozy fuckers couldn't keep still for more than thirty seconds. They were like a group of hyperactive kids, and Cain hated kids. Little bastards.

Fortunately, from the moment the crossroads came into view and Zitrone re-joined the ghouls in the back, they kept quiet. So quiet in fact, that Cain wondered if Zitrone had killed them. The blond Horseman had pulled a black curtain across behind the front seats, so Cain couldn't see what was going on in the back. And more importantly, Jacko the bluesman wouldn't see anything either.

Jacko was sitting on in a rocking chair at the roadside, playing his harmonica. His brown pin-striped suit and fedora hat looked weathered as if they hadn't been cleaned in years.

Cain slowed up the van as he approached, and wound down the window. He heard Zitrone whisper one last piece of unnecessary advice.

'Remember, *be casual.*'

Cain wanted to shout back and remind Zitrone that he'd been pretending to be Rex for so long, he was a master at it. He certainly didn't need any fucking acting advice from a chuffing Horseman who'd been imprisoned for thousands of years. But Jacko was close enough to hear anything that was said, so he bit his tongue.

He stopped the van and poked his head out of the window. 'Hey Jacko, how's it going?'

Jacko stopped playing his harmonica and took a look at the red van. 'Evenin' Rex,' he said. 'What's with the van?'

'Some fucker stole my chopper.'

'Tough break.'

'Yeah. See ya later.'

Cain touched on the accelerator and turned the steering wheel to the right, taking the van towards the invisible road, hoping and praying that it would appear. Zitrone had assured him that it would because he'd seen Jasmine and Elvis drive onto it before.

As soon as the van drove onto the gravel where the road was supposed to be, the gravel vanished, replaced by a smooth asphalt highway. Cain's heart fluttered as the adrenaline rushed through his entire body. This was it, the moment he'd waited a lifetime for. He was into the secret part of The Devil's Graveyard. He imagined it was how the rebels felt in every single fucking Star Wars movie when they made it through the invisible shield that led to the Death Star.

He drove on for a hundred metres before he shared the news with Zitrone. 'That's it, Zitrone, *we're in!'*

The blond Horseman called out from the back. 'Yeah, I can see that. There are windows in the back doors you know.'

'All right, you don't have to be a cunt about it.'

At least the ghouls in the back seemed to appreciate Cain's achievement. They started being all rowdy again, but it no longer agitated Cain. They were on the way to Purgatory, for real.

It took another twenty minutes of driving before he saw the bright red letters spelling out Purgatory looming large over the roadside. The place was nowhere near as impressive as Cain was expecting. It just looked like a brothel he'd been to once. The building was made of red brick and had a pair of wooden saloon doors at the front and a big chimney in the roof, which was blowing out thick black smoke.

'Here it is,' he called back to Zitrone. 'To be honest, it's a bit of a shithole.'

Zitrone pulled the curtain aside and took a look for himself. 'What were you expecting?' he asked.

'I dunno. I just thought it might be heavily guarded or something.'

'It probably is, *inside.* Let's not kid ourselves. They're expecting us. Remember that.'

Cain steered the van off the road and parked it up on the gravel outside the building. He killed the engine and looked at Zitrone in his rear view mirror. 'Can your stupid ghoul friends do what they're told?'

'They know exactly what they're doing. Don't worry about them.'

Cain was surprised by how nervous he felt. It had been thousands of years since he'd been nervous about anything. But he was about to fulfil a lifetime's work. His plan to bring an end to everything created by God was so close he could smell it. In fact, he was so close to Purgatory's entrance, he could smell something else too. It smelt like shit, really stale shit.

'Jeeesus, can you smell that?' he asked, gagging and feeling like he might vomit.

Zitrone shoved Cain in the back. 'Forget the smell. You're not chickening out now. Let's do this.'

Zitrone vanished back behind the curtain and opened the back doors. The ghouls piled out of the back, making an almighty racket and screwing up any hopes Cain had of sneaking in undetected.

'Oh well, here goes nothing,' he whispered to himself.

He opened the van door and climbed out just in time to see the ghouls charge past him on their way to the front entrance of Purgatory. Zitrone walked around and stopped next to Cain.

'Ready?' he said.

'I don't know what we're going to see in there,' said Cain. 'Scratch is a sneaky fucker, so watch your back.'

Zitrone lifted open his tunic and showed Cain a semi-automatic pistol he had hanging in a holster.

'When in the hell did you get that?' Cain asked.

'After the Bourbon Kid cut Ash's head off, I took precautions. If anyone takes a swing at me, I'll blow them away with this first.'

Cain felt a renewed sense of optimism. Zitrone was well prepared. He was the smartest of the Four Horsemen by a distance. And the most cunning fighter too.

As Zitrone started walking after the ghouls, Cain felt the need to double check one important detail. 'You're positive the gateway to Hell is behind the Disabled toilets, right?'

'I saw it when I read Jacko's mind. Stop worrying. If there's a trap set for us, the ghouls will walk into it first.'

The ghouls charged through the saloon doors into Purgatory. It started up a ruckus inside.

'You were right,' said Cain. 'They're expecting us.'

'Of course they are,' said Zitrone. 'So let's go kill them all. Then we can smash up the Disabled toilets.'

Seventy One

Beth had been standing at the window of Bishop Yoder's bedroom, staring at the Black Forest for half an hour. All of the ghouls had followed JD and the two demonic Horsemen into the dense woodland, screaming and baying for his blood. And so far, no one had come back out.

Thomas had long since left her to head back downstairs to the church hall. He reopened the underground stairway and released the women, so that they could tend to the injured men. The first person to venture up the stairs to join Beth was Thomas's mother, Agnes.

'Let me open the window for you,' she said.

Beth moved aside and Agnes unhooked a clip at the top of the window. She pushed it open and a gust of fresh air floated into the stuffy bedroom. A mix of sounds flooded in with the fresh air. Beth heard the men downstairs boarding up the windows and repairing the broken doors. Mixed in with all the hustle and bustle from below were loud screeches and war cries from the forest.

'I brought you a copy of The Bible,' said Agnes, placing a book down on the chest of drawers by the window. 'I thought it might give you strength.'

Beth smiled at her. Agnes had a kind face, but one filled with worry lines, something Beth could relate to. 'Thank you,' she said. 'I'll read it later.'

'I'm sorry for how you were treated before,' said Agnes. 'Thomas told me how you protected him from those ghouls. I'd be lost without him. I can't thank you enough.'

'It's okay, really.'

'We're not normally like that here, but it's been a confusing time. Everyone's faith has been tested these last few weeks.'

Beth wasn't really in the mood for a chat, but it was obvious Agnes was hoping to strike up a friendship, or at the very least, get some things off her chest.

'What's happened to shake your faith?' Beth asked.

'Almost a month ago, three stars fell from the night sky on St Michael's Day, one after the other. There's a prophecy in the gospel of Susan, which predicts that the three falling stars will signify the second coming of Christ. And we've been waiting for that for a long time. I lost my husband and my daughter in that forest, so when JD showed up with holes in his hands, and said he was Christ, I believed he was the one, the second coming. But then he killed some of the young men in the Crimson football team, so I don't know what to believe.'

Agnes stared at Beth, her eyes longing for an answer, something that would make sense of all the crazy things she had seen. It wasn't in Beth's nature to lie, but the Mystic Lady had told her she would have to.

'I'm sorry to hear of your loss,' she said. 'You should know, it's no coincidence that JD came here. I know his actions can seem somewhat extreme, like killing people who you think might not deserve it, but he's carrying out God's will. And I promise you, whatever is in that forest, whatever it was that killed your husband and daughter, he will destroy it.'

Agnes almost smiled. 'I would like that,' she said. 'Is it wrong to admit it? That I want those things in the forest dead?'

'No. It's perfectly normal.'

'So how do you know JD?'

'I met him when I was young. After I'd lost my parents, he came into my life and made everything feel good again, for a time. He always shows up in the times when I need him most. But this time, I was sent here to find him.'

'Sent by whom?'

'By God.'

The worry lines on Agnes's face melted away. Beth felt a little guilty about lying, but she couldn't say she'd been sent by the Devil. So in order to avoid getting any deeper into such matters she changed the direction of the conversation.

'How is the mood downstairs?' she asked.

'Oh, umm, everyone is shaken up, obviously. But there is a feeling of optimism, I think.'

Beth smiled. 'That's good.'

Agnes looked up at the sky. 'I think this could be the day,' she whispered.

'What do you mean?'

'The day the prophecy predicted. It's called *"The day it rains blood"*. It's the day when Christ returns and gives his life to save mankind for the second time.'

Beth didn't like the sound of that at all. 'Is this prophecy written down anywhere?' she asked.

Agnes picked up The Bible and offered it to Beth again. 'It's in here,' she said. 'Chapter forty.'

Beth took the book and flicked through it to find chapter forty. She started reading, looking for some kind of clue about what might happen. She'd barely read two lines when Agnes suddenly became very animated.

'Oh my God, look!' she said, pointing out of the window.

Beth glanced up from the book. When she saw what Agnes was pointing at she closed the book and put it back down on the dresser. The two women stood side by side staring out of the window. A grey horse had galloped out of the forest. It was the same grey horse JD had ridden in on, but now it was riderless. It was covered in blood and its saddle was missing.

'Where's JD?' Beth whispered, staring at the forest, waiting for him to reappear.

The response to her question came in the form of an almighty clap of thunder from above. The church building shook like it was about to crumble. Black clouds converged overhead, appearing from nowhere. The air turned cold and nothing moved, a silence followed the thunder, a perfect silence.

And then the heavens opened and the rain came down. It crashed down onto the village of Oakfield like a tidal wave from above. Flashes of lightning lit up the sky and a huge gust of wind blew the window shut, startling Beth and Agnes.

'This is it,' said Agnes, pointing at the window. 'Look at the rain. It's red. It's what the prophecy says. One day, so much blood will be shed that the skies will fill with it and rain it back down upon us. This is it, *the day it rains blood.*'

Within a matter of seconds it became impossible to see anything through the window. The blood rain hammered against it, obscuring the view of the outside world. The only time Beth or Agnes saw anything through it was whenever a flash of lightning lit up the sky for a moment, offering them a snapshot of what was happening. The trees in the forest swayed back and forth like drunk people dancing.

Occasionally, in between the claps of thunder and the crashing rain, Beth heard terrifying screams coming from within the Black Forest.

Seventy Two

Cain hung back and watched Zitrone follow the ghouls through the saloon doors into Purgatory. As soon as the doors swung shut behind him, gunfire rang out from inside. It was loud enough to make Cain's ears bleed. He waited at the side of the doors and tried to see what was going on inside. It was dark in the bar and the only flickers of light came from the arsenal of guns firing in all directions inside. The gunfight carried on for less than a minute, then thin slivers of smoke began filtering out of the entrance.

'Zitrone?' Cain called out his friend's name.

After a short pause, Zitrone responded. 'Cain, I think the coast is clear!'

With his pistol at the ready, Cain pushed the salon doors open and walked in to the bar. As soon as he entered, the lights came on inside, all at once. The bar area lit up in a glow of bright white. Cain blinked a few times as his eyes grew accustomed to the light. Zitrone was standing in front of him. He had been shot several times, but because of his impeccable healing powers the many injuries on his body were healing back up already. His yellow tunic had at least ten bullet holes in it to show just how vicious the gunfight had been.

There were many other bodies lying around on the floor, but before Cain had a chance to identify any of them, a voice spoke out.

'I've waited a long time for this day.'

Cain swung his pistol at the voice, which came from his left. In the corner of the bar he saw a black man, dressed in a red suit with a matching bowler hat.

'Scratch?'

Scratch raised his hands in the air to show he wasn't armed. 'Congratulations,' he said. His words were aimed more at Zitrone than Cain.

'All of your people are dead,' Zitrone gloated.

On the floor behind Scratch was an old woman in a blue dress and grey cardigan, laid out in a starfish pose. She had been shot through the forehead and blood was trickling from the corner of her mouth.

Cain took a look around the bar at the rest of Zitrone's handiwork. There were corpses everywhere. The six ghouls had all been shot dead, and judging by how close they all were to the entrance, they hadn't lasted long. Their corpses were bunched up within a few feet of each other, with huge puddles of blood seeping from them across the floor. A little further away, Cain recognised Jasmine. The best looking member of The Dead Hunters had been shot through the eye. She was sprawled on the floor with her legs propped up against a round wooden table. There was a patch of blood splattered over her right eye trickling down onto her ear. Not far from her was Rodeo Rex. The giant Hell's Angel was face down on the floor. It looked like he had been shot through the heart because there was a patch of blood on his back. And judging by an unfortunate stain on his backside, he'd shit his pants too, as people often did shortly after dying. Further back, in a corner of the bar area was a dead Elvis impersonator with half of his head missing. There was a smattering of blood and brains on the wall behind him too.

But there was one body on the floor that was still breathing. Sanchez was just behind Rex, lying on his back staring up at the ceiling, blinking and sucking in what looked like his last few breaths. There was blood coming from his ears and his neck, so his final breath would come soon enough.

'Can I get you two fellows a drink?' Scratch offered.

Zitrone responded by unloading his machine gun at Scratch. A five second rat-a-tat of gunfire achieved nothing. The bullets zipped through Scratch as if he wasn't there. Zitrone ran out of bullets before he even realised that shooting Scratch was pointless.

'I'm not here to obstruct you in any way,' Scratch assured them. He made a move to walk to the bar.

Cain cocked his pistol. 'Go easy there Scratch,' he said. 'You just stay where you are.'

'As you wish,' Scratch replied, showing a respect for the situation. 'Would you like to know where the gateway is?'

'I already know,' said Zitrone, tossing his empty gun to the floor. 'It's behind the door to the Disabled toilets.'

BANG!

A bullet hit Zitrone in the back of the head. It zipped through his skull, into his brain and then out through his forehead. Cain panicked and ducked down. He swivelled around on his knees and saw that the person who had shot Zitrone was Flake. She had been hiding behind an overturned table, pretending to be dead.

She yelled at Zitrone. 'DIE YOU FUCK!'

She squeezed the trigger three more times, her gun aimed at Zitrone's heart.

CLICK.

CLICK.

CLICK.

She was out of bullets. Cain enjoyed seeing the fear on her face as she realised she was fucked. Even the bullet that had hit Zitrone in the back of the head achieved nothing. The wound healed up almost immediately. The holes in the back and front of his head vanished, leaving just a trickle of blood as a reminder that he had been shot.

Cain straightened up and turned his gun on Flake. 'Time to die, bitch!'

Zitrone waved him away. 'It's okay,' he said. 'She's mine.'

He stepped over a couple of dead ghouls and headed over to confront Flake. She threw her gun at him in a vain attempt to hurt him. It hit him on the shoulder and bounced away without hindering him at all. To her credit, Flake took up some kind of weird karate stance. But with the speed of a snake, Zitrone grabbed her wrist and yanked her towards him. When she was close enough he pressed his hand down on the top of her head. The life drained from her eyes and her skin turned pale. She choked and wheezed as she tried to suck in a mouthful of air. As with all of the victims of Zitrone's death touch, her body went limp. When her eyes rolled up in her head, he dropped her to the floor. She landed on her back with her arms out in a crucifix pose. Her head lopped to one side and she stopped breathing.

A small ripple of applause marked the occasion. It came from Scratch.

'Zitrone, you truly are the best of the Four Horsemen,' he said. 'And you, Cain, I've been waiting a long time for you to show up. You have my congratulations, and my admiration. Many have tried and failed to do what the two of you have accomplished here.' He pointed across the corpse strewn bar room at the door to the Disabled toilets. 'Take your prize,' he said, removing his hat and bowing before Zitrone.

'Go check it out,' Cain urged Zitrone. 'I'll keep an eye out for any other bitches that aren't dead.'

Zitrone made his way around all the dead bodies, broken tables, shards of glass and other debris on the floor and headed for the Disabled toilets.

'This is for two thousand years of false imprisonment!' he cackled. 'I sincerely hope God is watching!'

Seventy Three

<u>Dante and Kacy's wedding Part 2</u>

Dante leaned over the bar. 'Wanna hear something stupid?' he said.

Sanchez's eyes lit up. 'Yeah, definitely.'

'Do you remember the night we killed that mummy, Rameses Gaius?'

'How could I forget? It was *me* that poisoned him.'

'Right. Well you remember how the Bourbon Kid was there because he wanted to get the Eye of the Moon to save Beth because she'd been bitten by a vampire?'

'Of course I do, it was *me* who took the Eye to her and saved her life.'

Dante was clearly very drunk because he seemed to have forgotten all about Sanchez's heroics from the night *he* saved Santa Mondega and probably the world from an undead takeover.

'Well anyway,' said Dante, 'after the Eye brought Beth back from the brink of death, me and Kacy borrowed it to make ourselves human again, because, y'know, we were vampires an' all that.'

Sanchez rolled his eyes. 'Yeah. I know all this stuff. I was there, remember?'

'You were?'

'For Chrissakes, I thought you said this story was going to be funny?'

'No, I said *stupid.'*

'Well it is stupid.'

Dante rubbed his eyes. It looked like he might fall asleep before getting to the meat of the story. But he hung in there, took a swig from his bottle of Shitting Monkey beer and carried on.

'Do you wanna hear this or not?' he slurred.

'Yes, get on with it!'

'Well, me and Kacy were actually considering keeping the Eye for ourselves, but Kacy thought it was bad luck or something, and she decides she doesn't want it. And I pretend to agree with her, y'know, for the sake of avoiding an argument.'

'Yeah, I know that feeling.'

'But then we're walking along the promenade and we spot Beth standing on the pier, staring out to sea like she does....'

'Because she's mental.'

'What?'

'Nothing, carry on.'

'So, we go over and Kacy gives Beth the Eye of the Moon. Now that fucking stone is worth like, what? A billion dollars?'

'It's pretty valuable,' Sanchez agreed.

'Yeah, well you'll never guess what she goes and does.'

'What?'

'She throws it into the sea, as far as she can throw it. And that's it, it's gone, lost forever. Just like that.'

Sanchez politely agreed that it was stupid. But it didn't really surprise him. After all, Beth was known as Mental Beth for a reason. He would have warned more people about her, but he was forbidden from referring to her as "Mental" by Flake who insisted it was an unflattering description, or rude, or something like that. Dante's story confirmed it though. Beth *was* mental. Only a moron would throw the most valuable stone in the world into the sea. A stone that provided immortality. A stone that had brought Beth back from the edge of death after she'd been bitten by *Jessica* the vampire Queen. Jessica, Sanchez shuddered at the thought of her. What a two-faced cow she had turned out to be.

'Are you okay, man?' said Dante. 'You've kinda gone quiet and you're clenching your fists.'

'Huh, oh yeah. I was just thinking how stupid it is what Beth did.'

Dante picked up his bottle of Shitting Monkey and slid awkwardly off his stool. His feet got tangled in the legs of the stool and he ended up dragging it along the floor until it toppled over. He stopped and looked down at it, confusion all over his face. 'Where did that come from?' he muttered.

'You should probably call it a night,' Sanchez suggested.

Dante nodded. Then he staggered back to the bar and leaned over it so he could speak to Sanchez without anyone else hearing. 'Wanna hear somethin' stupid?' he said.

'Is it about the Eye of the Moon?'

Dante gasped in shock. 'You already know?'

'I have ears everywhere.' He patted Dante on the shoulder. 'I think Kacy wants you over there.'

Dante swivelled around, miraculously staying on his feet. He spotted his bride sitting at a table in the corner of the room and staggered over to her. She was asleep with her mouth open, snoring and grumbling, because she was even drunker than him.

While Sanchez watched Dante's feeble attempts to start up a conversation with Kacy, he thought about what he'd just heard. The Eye of the Moon was apparently lost forever, stuck at the bottom of the sea.

Thrown from the end of the pier.

Impossible to find.

But it *wasn't* impossible to find. It wasn't as if Tom Brady or Peyton Manning had thrown it into the sea. Beth had thrown it, which in Sanchez's mind meant that it was very findable. Beth was weak and couldn't throw for shit, so even if she had hurled it as far as she could, it still wouldn't be more than twenty metres from the end of the pier.

****

The day after Dante and Kacy's wedding, Sanchez travelled into town and bought himself some cheap diving gear. And for the next three nights he trawled around at the bottom of the sea, twenty metres past the end of the pier. On the third night, after an epic fight with an extremely spiteful lobster, Sanchez retrieved the Eye of the Moon from the sea bed.

In the days that followed, Sanchez returned the diving gear to the shop and claimed a refund (apart from the goggles, which he kept behind the bar in the Tapioca, just in case the sprinkler system ever went off). He also the taught the selfish lobster a lesson when he gave it to Flake on her birthday, and she cooked it for dinner.

For a long time after that, Sanchez managed to keep the Eye of the Moon without Flake or anyone else ever seeing it. At night, he slept with it under his pillow, but most of the time he kept it in one of his pockets, or in his underpants.

And for the next year or so, Sanchez never got sick. And no one found out that he had the Eye in his possession. Not until the awful moment in the ambulance, when a ghoul stabbed Flake in the neck.

Although most of the time, Sanchez concentrated solely on looking out for himself, there was no denying that he loved Flake. Every day without fail she made his breakfast, his lunch, his dinner, and did everything around the Tapioca that he didn't want to do (which was pretty much everything). And on top of all that, she was also the most beautiful person in the world, and no one apart from Sanchez could see it. So when he saw the life draining from her after she was stabbed, there was only one thing he could do. He pulled the Eye of the Moon out of his underpants, took some dressing tape from a medical box in the back of the ambulance and pressed the stone against the bleeding wound on Flake's neck. He wrapped the bandage tightly around it, strapping the Eye up against the wound. Flake cried out in pain, which Sanchez took as an early indication that she had enough life left in her to hang in there while the Eye worked its magic. Unfortunately the scream alerted Beth who was supposed to be driving the ambulance. She climbed into the back with them and tried to interfere. Because she's mental.

'Is she gonna be okay?' Beth asked.

'I don't know.'

Sanchez kept putting pressure on the wound, while ensuring the Eye of the Moon didn't come loose. It soon became apparent that Beth didn't trust him to deal with the situation though.

'Oh God, what the hell is that swelling?' she asked, gawping at the lump underneath the bandage. 'You should have let me do this. That doesn't look right.'

'It's okay,' Sanchez replied, thinking on his feet. 'I've put a medical pressure plug over the wound. It helps to stem the bleeding.'

'What the hell is a pressure plug?'

'It's a medical thing,' he lied, 'I only found out about it when I bought the ambulance. There was one in the back with the defibrillators.'

The sparkle slowly crept back into Flake's eyes. Sanchez knew if he could keep the ghouls away from her she would make a full recovery thanks to the miraculous healing powers of the Eye of the Moon. As Sanchez knew only too well, a healthy Flake was a badass and good to have around in a crisis.

Seventy Four

Cain watched with great anticipation as Zitrone opened the door to the Disabled toilets.

'Is it there?' he shouted across the room to the blond Horseman.

To his great annoyance, Zitrone ignored him and walked through the door, blocking off Cain's view of what was behind it. Then the door swung shut behind him.

Cain called out to him again. 'Is it there!'

BOOM!

That wasn't the reply he was looking for. But it definitely came from the Disabled toilets.

'Zitrone?'

No reply.

Cain clicked his fingers at Scratch. 'Hey you, what was that noise?'

Scratch shrugged.

Cain edged across the bar area towards the Disabled toilets. He sensed a trap of some kind, and maybe Zitrone had walked into it. There was still a lot of gun smoke floating around at ankle height. But that wasn't the only thing moving. Sanchez, who was laid out on his back was still breathing. His eyes were closed and he had blood around his throat, but his stomach was still moving up and down. Cain stepped over a dead ghoul and pointed his gun at Sanchez's head. He fired off one shot.

BANG!

One shot to the head should have been enough to kill Sanchez, but nothing happened. No blood spurted out of his head. It was as if Cain's gun was firing blanks. He took aim at Sanchez's chest this time, a much easier target.

BANG!

Sanchez's belly carried on moving up and down. His nostrils were still sucking in air and breathing it out again. Cain checked the weight of his gun. It was definitely loaded, but when he fired it, he wasn't hitting anything. Something wasn't right. While he was trying to work out what it was, out of the corner of his eye he saw one of the dead bodies roll over. He spun around and pointed his gun at the moving corpse.

But it was no corpse. It was Cain's identical twin, Rodeo Rex. Rex had rolled into a sitting position. Cain pointed his gun at him and fired two more shots. The effect was much the same as when he'd shot at Sanchez. His gun was completely impotent. *Or was it?* He was tempted to shoot himself in the foot to see if it hurt, but if it worked, he wouldn't be able to live with the irony of it.

'What the fuck is going on?' he snapped at Rex.

Rex stood up and opened his gloved hand. A fistful of bullets fell out and clattered onto the floor. And then Jasmine sat up too, which was strange because she'd been shot in the eye. Cain turned his gun on her and fired another shot. The bullet didn't reach her either. The moment it left the barrel of his gun it was redirected to Rex's magnetic metal hand.

Cain took a step back and tried to make sense of things. If Rex had been catching all the bullets, then how come everyone was covered in blood? The answer was in Sanchez's jacket. As the tubby bartender sat up, a bunch of empty ketchup sachets fell out of his pocket onto the floor.

'What the fu—'

Cain didn't finish the sentence. A sharp pain ripped through his back. His heart ripped open and a burning sensation coursed through his whole body. Blood surged up through his lungs and over his tongue, dribbling out through his lips. He looked down and saw a golden blade poking out through his chest. It wasn't the first time he'd been stabbed. Over the centuries, swords, bullets, fist punches and many other things, had wounded him but on each of the previous occasions he'd felt no pain. But this was different, *very different*. The blade on the dagger was no normal blade. Cain had seen it before when he'd been in possession of the body of Julius Caesar. It was the Brutus Dagger. He'd avoided it that time by exiting the body before the blade pierced his skin. But this time he'd been caught off guard. It became hard to breathe. In the past, he had always had the power to exit a body at will, now he found he was trapped inside the dying body of a Rodeo Rex clone.

As he weakened, his gun slipped from his grasp. The muscles in his legs lost all their power and his knees buckled. He toppled over, smacking his head against an upturned chair leg as he went down. As he lay on the floor, his life ebbing away, he finally saw who had knifed him in the back. It was Flake.

'How?' he whispered, with all the strength he could muster.

The door to the Disabled toilets burst open and Zitrone staggered out. Cain's friend, the blond Horseman, was no longer blond. His head had vanished, replaced by a fountain of blood gushing out from between his shoulders. The headless body staggered around for a while, clattering into things as the former blond Horseman's life ebbed away. Eventually it tumbled over, crashing through a table.

As Cain's vision began to blur he saw Elvis stagger out of the Disabled toilets. He was walking with a wooden crutch and in his right hand he was holding a large handgun that had smoke floating out of the barrel.

The reality of the situation hit home. Cain, the son of Adam and Eve, inventor of murder, one of humanity's greatest conquerors, had been outwitted by Flake, Sanchez and a bunch of ketchup sachets. The last thing he saw as he took his final breath and vanished from existence was the face of Sanchez, smiling cheerily at him.

Seventy Five

Beth stayed at the window of Bishop Yoder's bedroom throughout the night watching the storm. The blood rain pounded relentlessly against the window and the thunder boomed every minute or so. The only thing louder than the thunder and rain were the occasional ear-piercing screams from the Black Forest.

Agnes and Thomas were curled up asleep together on the Bishop's bed. The trauma of the day had caught up with them. There was no other possible reason why anyone would be able to sleep during the storm. The rest of the Amish community stayed down in the church hall, praying and thanking God for saving them from the ghouls.

At just before five o'clock in the morning the first glimmer of sunlight appeared on the horizon beyond the Black Forest. Something about that first sliver of light triggered something deep inside of Beth. An aching, a longing to be with JD that had been gnawing at her since she was a teenager. Where he was, she wanted to be, even if it was the Black Forest. Leaving the sanctity of the church was an illogical thing to do, but Beth's relationship with JD had never been based on logic or reason. She remembered the Mystic Lady's warning to her -

"Beth, whatever you do, don't go into the Black Forest because my crystal ball is telling me that a woman is going to die in that forest tonight."

When Beth saw that first glimmer of light on the horizon, she took it as a sign that the night was almost over, so she left the Bishop's bedroom and headed downstairs.

Bishop Yoder's office was being used as a storage room for the dead bodies of the men slain by Blanco and the ghouls. Blankets covered the corpses. A woman and her daughter were asleep next to one of the dead men. Beth took care not to wake them when she passed through.

The church hall wasn't much better. Quite a lot of the Amish people were asleep on the floor, or trying to sleep. Some of the women were awake, busily tending to the injuries of the men, or calming the sobbing children. Even though many of them saw Beth walking among them on her way to the front doors, none of them bothered with her. Beth's presence was nothing more than an irrelevance to them now.

Abram was standing guard by the front doors. His shirt was soaked in blood and his left arm was in a sling. When he saw Beth approach, he took off his black hat and nodded at her.

'I'm sorry about before,' he said. 'I misjudged you. It was wrong of me.'

'It's okay,' Beth whispered.

'It's still raining blood out there, you know.'

Beth nodded.

Abram frowned. 'Are you looking to leave?'

'It's time for me to go.'

It looked like he understood. He offered her a sympathetic smile and put his hat back on. With his good arm he unbolted one of the doors and pulled it open just wide enough for Beth to squeeze through.

'May God be with you,' he whispered.

Beth thanked him by way of a smile and then stepped out into the pouring blood rain. Within seconds of stepping outside she was soaked through, her clothes drenched in it. Her boots sank into a thick stream of blood that was flowing down from the hill, weaving its way through the grass. Beth needed to know what was causing it. How many people had to die before blood rained down from the sky? It had to be a lot.

It was a hard slog fighting against the wind and rain as she trudged up the hill towards the forest. But the feel of the blood pounding against her face made her feel more alive than at any time she could remember. In spite of the lack of sleep she'd had in the last couple of days, she felt wide-awake, and at one with the world. She knew from previous experience that the closer she came to death, the more alive she felt.

When she finally made it to the top of the hill she was faced with the ominous tall trees that lined the edge of the forest. Her face was covered in blood and she could taste its bitterness on her lips. She took a moment to catch her breath, not out of any trepidation or fear of what lay in wait in the forest, but in readiness for what might be the last thing she ever did. All she needed was ten seconds to get her breath back for a sprint into the unknown. She counted it down in her head. When she reached the end of the count, she didn't hesitate. She sprinted into the forest, past the first row of trees and into the darkness.

Seventy Six

Rex took a look at the mess all around Purgatory and allowed himself a wry smile. It felt good to be back among friends. He'd learned to live with the fact that no one ever thanked him for his contributions. On top of that, they repeatedly took the mickey out of his metal hand, but even so, they were true friends.

On one side of him, he had Jasmine dry-humping Elvis, who could barely stand. On the other, Flake was all over Sanchez, who was complaining that she was hurting his back. With the exception of Flake, all of them would be dead had it not been for Rex's magnetic metal hand. The only casualty was Nigel Powell who had been dragged up from downstairs and dressed up to look like Elvis. Rex hadn't been able to catch the bullet that blew a hole in Nigel's head. Sad though it was to lose him, there was only one Elvis impersonator Rex cared about, and that was the guy with his hands all over Jasmine's ass. The lucky sonofabitch.

After all the initial hugging and celebrating, there was a quiet moment of reflection as each person drank in the scene, realising how close they had come to the end of the world.

'Wait a minute,' said Elvis, looking around. 'Where's Annabel?'

There was an upturned table in the corner by the entrance. A thousand tiny pieces of glass were scattered around the table, signifying the demise of Annabel's crystal ball. As for the old Mystic Lady herself, she was laid out on the floor close to where Scratch was standing. She wasn't moving.

'Is she dead?' Rex asked.

Scratch shook his head. 'No, she's just unconscious. She's been feeling faint ever since that stink from the toilets wafted in here. She'll be up and about in a few minutes I expect.'

Rex sniffed the air. In spite of all the gunfire and dead bodies, the aroma that had followed them in from the toilets in the Crimson County police station was still the most overpowering scent in the room.

'That is quite a stink,' Rex commented.

Jasmine suddenly let out a squeal of horror. 'Ewww Rex, you've shit yourself!'

'What?'

Rex was pretty damn certain he had done no such thing.

'Look,' said Jasmine. 'There's brown skids on the back of your jeans!'

Rex reached back and touched his butt. His fingers came upon something sticky. He looked at his fingertips and saw a brown substance on them. Jasmine was right. He sniffed his fingers and realised straight away what it was.

'It's brown sauce,' he grumbled.

'What's it doing on your ass?' asked Jasmine.

The guilty party wasn't hard to spot. Sanchez was nudging Flake and smirking.

'Did you do this?' Rex bellowed at him.

'Added authenticity,' said Sanchez. 'I had one sachet of brown sauce, so I thought I ought to make it look like someone had soiled themselves. You were the only person lying on your front, so I did it just after Scratch turned the lights out.'

'You idiot!' Rex hissed. 'You could have fucked everything up. It's bad enough that you were breathing heavily the whole time you were supposed to be playing dead.'

'I wasn't breathing,' Sanchez protested.

'WOULD YOU ALL SHUT UP!' Scratch roared. As usual the constant childish bickering was getting on his nerves. 'We're not in the clear yet. There are still two Horsemen somewhere. And I want to know where the Bourbon Kid is!'

'Wake Annabel up,' said Rex. 'She'll know.'

Scratch pointed at the shattered remains of Annabel's crystal ball. 'We've got no way of knowing anything,' he said. 'At least not until Annabel regains consciousness and we find her a new crystal ball.'

'Screw that,' said Rex. 'Just send us back through the portal. We'll find him.'

'I can't,' said Scratch. 'Look.' He pointed at the door to the Men's toilets. It had been peppered with bullets and was hanging off its hinges. While Rex had caught all of the bullets that came near the group, he hadn't been able to stop the ones that had been aimed over at the corner where the Men's toilets were.

'Damn,' Rex cursed. 'We'll have to drive there.'

'Uh uh,' said Scratch, wagging his finger. 'No way.'

'Why not?'

'I need all you guys here. Didn't you hear what I just said? There are still two more Horsemen out there. For all we know, they could be on their way here right now. Until Annabel's crystal ball is fixed, everybody stays here.'

Elvis agreed with Rex. 'But the Kid's one of us.'

'I know that,' said Scratch. 'But you all work for me, and I'm telling you this place cannot be left unguarded. I need all of you here.' He pointed at Sanchez. 'Even him.'

Seventy Seven

The air in the Black Forest was thick and damp. A dense fog wreathed the trees and covered the ground, limiting Beth's visibility. The tree cover was so dense it held most of the blood rain at bay, but still, little smatters of red danced in the thick, white fog.

She was at least a quarter of a mile into the forest when she stumbled on something underfoot. She stopped and looked down. She pushed the thick fog away with her hands and saw the corpse of a black-skinned creature, its head separated from its torso. Beth backed away from it and covered her mouth with her hand to stop herself from screaming. But she stepped back onto something else that crunched beneath her boot, startling her again. She darted to the side, only to be met with another snap of charred flesh and bone. Everywhere she stepped, she heard a sickening crunch. She realised she had walked into an area of the forest where a slaughter had taken place. All around her on the floor were the rotting and dismembered corpses of ghouls and more of the black creatures. Rather than be scared, she felt reassured. With this much death and destruction, JD had to be close and had to still be alive.

She heard a few faint screams in the distance and decided to head towards them, using the trees as cover.

'Jack,' she whispered. 'JD, it's Beth.'

She recognised how foolish she had been to enter the forest, but if history had taught her anything it was that if JD was nearby he would come to her rescue if anything attacked her.

She called out for him again, much louder this time. 'JD, are you there? It's Beth.'

Something heard her cry out. A set of very loud footsteps pounded on the ground, heading towards her. She ducked behind a tree and braced herself for whatever was coming. But as the pounding of feet came closer it was suddenly accompanied by the sound of horse's hooves coming from another direction.

Beth backed away and looked for a better place to hide. If two creatures were about to converge on her position, it would be better if they found each other first. Then hopefully one of them would eliminate the other. The heel of her boot crunched down on another dead creature, giving away her position again. Through the fog she saw the outline of the first creature to respond to her call. It was a beast that stood over eight feet tall. At first it was nothing more than a black outline in the midst of the fog. But as it came closer Beth saw its face. It had scaly brown skin and one giant yellow eye with a black pupil in its centre. The eye was looking for the source of the voice that had called out. Beth hid behind another tree and stayed as still as a statue, watching the creature lumber through the forest looking for her. As it came closer still she saw it was holding a severed head in its right hand.

The Cyclops stopped between two trees and sniffed the air. It soon picked up Beth's scent and its giant eye zeroed in on her behind the tree. It roared like a lion and charged towards her, its movements lumbering and uncoordinated. Beth turned and ran. The Cyclops bounded after her, gaining ground on her with every huge stride it took.

Beth hurdled over corpses of ghouls and other creatures as she raced through the forest. The sound of the Cyclops bearing down on her got closer and closer, but so too did the sound of a horse's hooves bearing down on them both. It was hard to know which would get to her first.

And then suddenly she heard a loud swishing sound behind her, followed by a piercing scream. Something crashed to the ground nearby. The ground shook beneath her feet causing a dead ghoul's torso to bounce up in front of her. In trying to avoid it she tripped on something else and fell forward, face-planting into a bed of rotting corpses.

Before she could get back up, the giant head of the Cyclops bounced past her, dipping in and out of the fog. It came to a stop nearby, its ugly lifeless eye staring at her. Almost immediately, another head rolled past her and landed alongside the Cyclops's. This one was only half the size and was badly disfigured.

The horse that had come to her rescue trotted up behind her and someone dismounted. Beth rolled over into a sitting position and looked up at the figure that had climbed down from the horse. It was holding a long sword in its right hand. As it walked towards her its face was masked by the shadows from the trees.

Beth wiped some blood away from her face and smiled. 'I knew you'd come,' she said.

The person stopped and pointed its sword at her. A sliver of light through the trees lit up its face. This was not JD. The person standing before her had shiny green hair and a pale face, speckled in blood.

Beth felt the life drain from her. Her will to stay alive deserted her too. She laid back, her head resting on the bodies of the dead beneath her. She turned her head to the side and looked at the head of the Cyclops. A smaller head was in front of it, staring back at her. It was the head the Cyclops had been carrying around with it. Beth stared into its vacant eyes, and they gawped back at her.

A shadow loomed over Beth as the green-haired Horseman approached. Beth closed her eyes. She felt at peace, accepting what was to come.

A brief silence followed. And then one more decapitated head rolled across the ground.

Seventy Eight

Flake missed home. And clean clothes. Purgatory was a pretty dull place to hang out, even with great friends. Scratch had forbidden anyone from leaving. It was only when a news channel reported that the FBI had cordoned off the bridge to Blue Corn Island that he allowed someone to leave. That someone was Rex, who was sent to buy pizza and also to find out what was going on in Blue Corn. The rest of the gang had to hang out in the bar and survive on alcohol and bar snacks. And unfortunately, Sanchez had eaten all the bar snacks before anyone realised it was all the food they had.

From the minute Rex departed, Scratch had been pacing back and forth, cussing and fussing, and generally dampening the mood in the place. Flake liked to keep busy so she was working behind the bar, which seemed like a good way to keep in Scratch's good books.

Elvis and Jasmine were sitting on stools at the bar, drinking bottles of Shitting Monkey. Their mood was fairly sombre because they were reflecting on the loss of their friends, Baby and Joey. The Mystic Lady was on her own at a table in the corner, trying to glue her crystal ball back together, which wasn't working out too well.

'Where the hell is Sanchez?' said Scratch, looking around and suddenly waking up to the realisation that Sanchez wasn't there.

'He's in the Ladies toilets,' Flake replied.

'Why?'

'Why do you think?'

Scratch closed his eyes and gritted his teeth. '*Not again*, surely?'

'Yeah, he's been eating all the bar snacks you had behind here,' said Flake. 'I don't think the pork scratchings agreed with him.'

The roar of a car engine outside made Scratch forget all about Sanchez. 'Rex is back!' he yelled.

Everyone stared at the entrance and sure enough, a few moments later Rex sauntered in through the front doors with a shopping bag and a stack of pizza boxes.

'Hey folks, dinner is here,' he said, walking up to the bar. He placed the pizza boxes down on the bar. Flake could smell the aroma of food, which was heavenly.

Scratch slapped his hand down on the pizza boxes to stop anyone from opening them. 'Did you speak to Calhoon?' he asked Rex.

'Yeah.'

'And?'

'She says the FBI and Phantom Ops arrived on Blue Corn Island last night. The FBI is investigating the massacre at the police station in

Crimson. And her Phantom Ops team went to Oakfield this morning and interrogated the Amish people. Every man, woman and child swears that an army of ghouls and two dudes on horses attacked the village.'

'What about the Bourbon Kid?' Scratch inquired eagerly.

'And Beth,' Flake added.

'Calhoon says the Bourbon Kid led the ghouls and Horsemen away from the village. They all followed him into the Black Forest. After that, a storm broke out and apparently it rained blood for the rest of the night.'

Jasmine butted in. 'But is JD okay?'

'Calhoon says her people are dragging bodies out of the forest as we speak. It's been a total fucking massacre in there. So far they've found at least five hundred bodies, but only two of them are human. And because this is a supernatural case, Calhoon can't source any help from other departments, so it's gonna take time to identify all of these bodies.'

'But what about the two human bodies?' Flake asked. 'Can't they be identified?'

Rex took off his Stetson hat and placed it down on the bar. He wiped some sweat off his brow before answering. 'The human remains were for a man and a woman. They found a driving license on the woman. It was Beth's.'

The words chilled Flake to the bone. 'What was Beth doing in the forest?'

'Apparently she was in the church, but in the early hours of the morning she left and ran into the forest. I guess she went looking for JD.'

'We need to go to Blue Corn to see for ourselves,' said Flake.

'We can't,' said Rex. 'Phantom Ops are going to be in that forest for the foreseeable future, taking forensic evidence and bagging up bodies. And the army has set up a perimeter blockade to prevent anyone from going in or out. If we show up, we either get arrested or we kill all of Calhoon's people, which I don't think is advisable.'

Scratch agreed. 'I don't think it's necessary anyway. All I care about is the two Horsemen. There's every chance they're still on the loose. Stay in touch with Calhoon and see if she identifies them among the dead.'

'Sure thing, boss,' said Rex.

The sound of a toilet flushing interrupted proceedings. The door to the Ladies toilets opened and Sanchez walked out, rubbing his stomach.

'I wouldn't go in there for a while,' he said. 'Ooh is that pizza?'

Sanchez bounded over and tried to grab one of the pizza boxes but Scratch slapped his hand away.

'Did you get Annabel a new crystal ball?' Scratch asked Rex.

'I did.'

Rex reached into his shopping bag and lifted out a crystal ball. 'Annabel, I got you this,' he called out to her. He shaped as if he was going to throw it to her, but Scratch stopped him and prised the ball away from him.

'Don't throw it, for *Chrissake!'* he said. 'It'll only end up smashed like the old one.'

Scratch walked over to Annabel and handed it to her. 'See if you can find out what happened to the Bourbon Kid.'

'What's that smell?' said Jasmine, sniffing the air. The door to the Ladies toilets was still open and something unpleasant was wafting out.

Elvis covered his mouth and nose. 'Christ, Sanchez, not again!'

Jasmine jumped up from her stool. 'Oh my God, cover the food!'

'It's those pork scratchings,' said Sanchez. 'They don't agree with me.'

Rex picked up the pizza boxes. 'Let's eat outside,' he muttered.

The whole gang headed outside to the parking lot. While Rex dished out the pizzas, Annabel and Scratch climbed into the back of a red van that was parked outside, so they could study her new crystal ball.

Flake took one bite out of her vegetarian pizza and realised straight away she had no appetite for it. For one thing, the pizzas were all cold because Rex had driven about a hundred miles to get them. And second of all, Flake wanted to know for sure what had happened to Beth and JD. So after one mouthful of cold pizza she joined Scratch and Annabel in the back of the van.

'Is it working?' she asked.

Annabel went through the motions of her usual routine for a while, staring at the ball from various different angles and waving her hands over it. Eventually after almost a minute she became very animated. 'I see the forest,' she said.

'The Black Forest?' queried Scratch.

'Yes, of course it's the Black Forest. What other forest would it be?'

'Don't get snooty. What do you see? Is the Bourbon Kid there?'

Annabel squinted into the ball again. 'Hang on,' she said. 'I see lots of bodies, dead bodies.'

'Can you see Beth,' Flake asked, hopefully.

Annabel peered into the crystal ball and pulled some strange faces that didn't tell Flake anything. 'I see them,' she said eventually.

The other members of the group gathered around at the back of the van to listen in on what Annabel had to say.

'Are they alive?' Flake asked.

Annabel lowered her head and chewed on her lip, but she did not respond.

'Well?' said Scratch, his impatience palpable.

Annabel shook her head. 'No. I'm sorry. They didn't make it. They died at the hands of something terribly evil.'

The mood of the group flat-lined immediately. Everyone apart from Sanchez lost their appetite and headed back inside Purgatory. Sanchez gathered up all the pizza boxes and scurried off with them, leaving Flake with Scratch and Annabel.

Neither Flake nor Scratch was willing to accept Annabel's revelation quite so easily as the others. Scratch grabbed a handful of Annabel's cardigan and pulled her towards him, pressing his face up against hers.

'Are you sure?' he said, eyeballing her.

'I'm positive.'

Scratch continued to stare into her eyes, watching for the slightest twitch or hint that she was fibbing. Eventually after about ten seconds he let go of her cardigan and shoved her away. Then he stormed off and headed back into Purgatory. Flake heard him shout something about *"the fucking smell in here!"*

Flake perched herself on the back of the van and thought about Beth. It was easy to imagine her running into the forest looking for JD. She'd spent most of her life longing to be with him and she'd come so close to fulfilling that dream. Perhaps it was a consolation that she had died with him, or in the same forest as him, at least.

Annabel climbed out of the van and smiled sympathetically at Flake. 'Are you okay?' she asked.

Flake tried to smile, but couldn't. 'Are they really dead?' she asked.

'I'm afraid so.'

Flake looked into Annabel's eyes. The old fortune-teller looked away, avoiding the eye contact and then stared up at the sky.

'Did they suffer?' Flake asked.

Annabel's response was odd to say the least. 'You know they shouldn't really be called the Four Horsemen,' she said, shaking her head.

Flake sighed. 'Why not?'

'Because one of them is a woman.'

Seventy Nine

'There is nowhere you can stand without getting splashed!'

'Yes ma'am.'

A convoy of vehicles had splashed filthy water over Alexis Calhoon as they drove off the bridge. The road out of Blue Corn Island was flooded, so every single time a jeep or truck passed by her, it sprayed a wave of dirty black water over her no matter where she stood. The long white plastic raincoat she had been issued with was doing little to protect her army slacks from the water.

It was early afternoon and the skies were covered in dark clouds, which had been pouring torrential rain down on the island ever since the morning. On the plus side it was water, not blood raining down this time.

Calhoon was trying to have a conversation with Colonel Walt Smith, who was updating her on what had been found in the Black Forest. Like everyone else, he was wearing the standard issue, flimsy white raincoat. The raincoats made everyone look creepy, like ghosts wandering around on the bridge.

'Is that everyone now?' Calhoon asked.

'Yes ma'am. All twenty-two trucks are loaded up and shipping out now. Five hundred and seventeen bodies are headed to Fort Hampton for evaluation.'

'What about the two human bodies? Did you confirm their identities yet?'

'No ma'am, but Jenkins promised me an update within an hour.'

Calhoon stepped around Colonel Smith as another truck splashed past them. The brunt of the spray hit him, shielding her from it.

'Can you contact Jenkins now?' she asked. 'We can't reopen the bridge to the public until we've confirmed that the Bourbon Kid was the deceased male.'

Smith fumbled around inside his coat and pulled out a burner phone. He dialled a number and stuck the phone inside the hood of his coat. A few more trucks passed by, spraying them with rainwater. The noise from the trucks made it impossible for Calhoon to hear Smith's phone conversation.

Eventually he hung up the phone and replaced it in his pocket. It was hard to tell what news he had because he was permanently grimacing from the wind and rain.

'That was Jenkins,' he shouted over the din. 'He says they've still not identified the bodies.'

'I thought you said the female was Beth Lansbury?'

Smith shook his head. 'No, that's what we thought. But it looks like that's what someone wanted us to think. The driver's license was planted on the body.'

'How can you tell?'

'Jenkins questioned some of the Amish people and they all say that Beth Lansbury has dark hair with a red streak in it.'

'So?'

'So the female we pulled out of the forest had bright *green* hair. It's not her. It's just got her driver's license.'

Calhoon cast her mind back to an earlier telephone conversation she'd had with Rodeo Rex. He had told her to look out for two demons on horses, one with green hair and one with white. 'What colour was the male's hair?' she asked.

'The man's hair was bright white. I know that because I saw him myself. Strange looking dude.'

Calhoon watched the last of the trucks roll past her off the bridge. The convoy of army trucks containing corpses from the forest were cruising right past a fleet of press vans and soaking wet journalists who had no idea that the trucks contained the biggest story of their reporting careers. In a way Calhoon was grateful for the terrible weather because it kept all the press helicopters grounded.

'Did the Amish people give you a description of what the Bourbon Kid was wearing?' she asked Smith.

'Ha!'

'What's so funny?'

'They're fucking nuts those Amish,' said Smith scornfully. 'You know they're saying the Bourbon Kid was sent by God to deliver them from evil? They actually believe he came here to save them from the forest monsters. Can you believe that?'

Calhoon smiled. 'Yeah, that's crazy.'

'So what are you thinking, General?'

'About what?'

'Our next move,' said Smith. 'I think we should keep this island as an exclusion zone for another forty-eight hours. My gut is telling me the Bourbon Kid is still here.'

Calhoon took a moment to consider what Smith was saying. She turned away from him and watched the convoy of army trucks that had left the island. They were driving in single file along the coastline of the mainland, on their way to Fort Hampton.

'So what do you wanna do about the Bourbon Kid?' Smith shouted over the rain.

Calhoon continued watching the trucks while she contemplated what to do. The answer came to her when she saw the truck at the back of the convoy peel away from the group. While the others continued driving along the coast, the final truck took a left turn and headed North at high speed.

She turned back to Colonel Smith. 'The Bourbon Kid's not here,' she said. 'Wrap everything up and let's go home.'

Eighty

'Does he have a beard?'

'No.'

Sanchez and Flake were sitting across from each other in the last remaining table in The Tapioca. During their time away from Santa Mondega, the bar had been looted and they had lost just about everything they owned. And because they had no money left, they'd had to cover the broken windows with cellophane, which wasn't much of a deterrent to potential criminals, but at least it kept the wind out.

It was late on a Friday night and the day had been a total washout. With no beer left to serve the clientele, they were on the verge of going out of business. There were lots of bills arriving in the mail and they had no way of paying them. In fact the only thing to arrive in the mail that wasn't a bill, was a blank postcard from Belize. Flake thought she knew who it was from, but wouldn't tell Sanchez unless he could beat her at a game of "Guess Who?".

The "Guess Who?" board game was the only thing that hadn't been stolen. Flake had bought it for Sanchez on his birthday. All of the characters on the cards were people he had met over the years on his adventures. They had only played the game a handful of times though because Flake always won. But Sanchez had a feeling this was going to be his big moment. He knew Flake's card was a woman, and Flake had established that his was a man without a beard, which meant she could only eliminate Bishop Yoder and Santa Claus from her side of the board.

Sanchez studied the faces of the women on the cards he had yet to eliminate. 'Okay, do I find her annoying?' he asked.

'No,' Flake replied.

Sanchez flipped over the cards featuring Nora Bone, Ulrika Price, Annabel de Frugyn, Stephanie the receptionist from the Hotel Pasadena, and Beth. It left him with just three remaining candidates. Nina Forina, Kacy Vittori and Janis Joplin. Victory was so close.

'Is it a monk?' Flake asked.

'Nope.'

Flake turned over two cards, which Sanchez knew would be Kyle and Peto, a pair of dimwit Hubal monks. It left Flake with four possible candidates to choose from, Marcus the Weasel, MC Pedro, Archie Somers and El Santino. The correct answer was El Santino, but there was surely no way Flake would get it before Sanchez correctly guessed what her card was.

He looked at the remaining candidates on his side of the board, and deliberated what question to ask. The picture of Janis Joplin had a speech bubble coming from her mouth, which was filled with expletives.

'Okay, does this person swear a lot?' Sanchez asked.

Flake winced. 'Yes.'

Sanchez could barely contain his excitement. He flipped over the pictures of Kacy and Nina, leaving him with just Janis Joplin. It meant Flake had to guess correctly on her next turn, or Sanchez would win for the first time ever. God bless Janis Joplin and her potty mouth.

Flake took a deep breath. 'Is it Marcus the Weasel?'

'No!' Sanchez jumped up and started gyrating his hips, performing his victory dance for the first time ever.

'Okay then,' said Flake. 'Who do you think mine is?'

'It's Janis Joplin!'

'It's Jasmine.'

Sanchez frowned. 'What? It can't be.'

Flake pointed at the window. 'It is. Look! Jasmine's here.'

A dark blue Mercedes screeched to a halt outside the cellophane window. The passenger door sprung open and Jasmine climbed out. She was wearing a white catsuit that showed off more skin than it actually covered.

Flake jumped up and accidentally knocked the game of "Guess Who?" off the table. It hit the floor and all of the cards flipped up.

'Oh for fucks sake!' Sanchez grumbled.

Flake raced over to the front doors and unbolted them. Sanchez got up and walked over to join her. Jasmine was standing outside in the street. Elvis was sitting in the Mercedes, keeping the engine running. He waved at Flake and Sanchez.

'Hi guys!' said Flake. 'Come on in.'

'We can't stay,' said Jasmine. 'We're on our way to a job. It turns out half of the A list actors in Hollywood are actually aliens.'

'I knew it!' said Sanchez.

'We wondered if you might wanna come with us?' Jasmine asked. 'Since we lost Joey, Baby and the Bourbon Kid, we're short of Dead Hunters. We're looking for some new recruits.'

Flake looked at Sanchez. 'What do you think?'

'I'm not so sure,' he replied. 'I mean we can't just leave the Tapioca, can we?'

'Oh, there's one other thing,' said Jasmine. 'Sanchez is wanted for murder.'

'Murder?' Sanchez was shocked.

'Yeah, remember you killed the bartender in The Fork In Hell? Well there was a hidden camera behind the bar, which recorded everything. The footage is on every porn site in the world.'

Flake looked confused. 'Why would it be on a porn site?'

'Didn't Sanchez tell you?'

'Tell me what?'

'Well, while he was pouring poison into the bartender's asshole, I was doing naked somersaults and kung fu moves. You wouldn't believe how much fan mail I'm getting now.'

Flake shoved Sanchez. 'You never told me this!'

'How could I know she was getting fan mail?'

Flake shoved him again. 'You saw her doing naked somersaults and you didn't tell me about it!'

'I didn't think you'd be interested.'

Flake looked murderous. 'What else haven't you told me?'

'Well anyway,' Jasmine continued. 'If you stay here, you're gonna get arrested and prosecuted for murder. The FBI are on their way here right now. So are you gonna come with us, or what?'

'I don't think so,' said Sanchez.

Jasmine offered him an incentive. 'Did you tell Flake about the time you walked through fire?'

Flake frowned. 'You walked through fire? You never told me that.'

Before Sanchez could think up a reply, a chorus of police sirens rang out in the distance, heading towards The Tapioca.

'All right, I'm in,' said Sanchez. He pushed past Jasmine and headed for the car. 'Come on Flake, what are you waiting for?'

The three of them piled into the Mercedes. Sanchez and Flake squeezed into the back, and Jasmine dived into the passenger seat. Elvis hit the gas and they roared off down the street with a convoy of police cars in hot pursuit.

'Can you go any faster?' Sanchez asked as Elvis swung the car around the first bend.

'It's all right,' Elvis replied. 'They'll never catch us.'

'Are you sure? There's a lot of them.'

Jasmine leaned across the front seats and put her hand between Elvis's legs. She winked at Sanchez. 'Don't worry,' she said. 'Elvis has learned how to multi-task.'

Sanchez whispered in Flake's ear. 'What do you think she means by that?'

'She means buckle up,' Flake replied. 'This is gonna be a bumpy ride.'

THE END (maybe…)

Manufactured by Amazon.ca
Bolton, ON